Alias Hook

LISA JENSEN

snowbooks

Proudly Published by Snowbooks in 2013

Copyright © 2013 Lisa Jensen
Lisa Jensen asserts the moral right to
be identified as the author of this work.
All rights reserved.

Snowbooks Ltd.
email: info@snowbooks.com
www.snowbooks.com

British Library Cataloguing in Publication Data
A catalogue record for this book is available from the British
Library.

ISBN 978-1-907777-87-5

To my own James. We're on this journey together.

Neverland

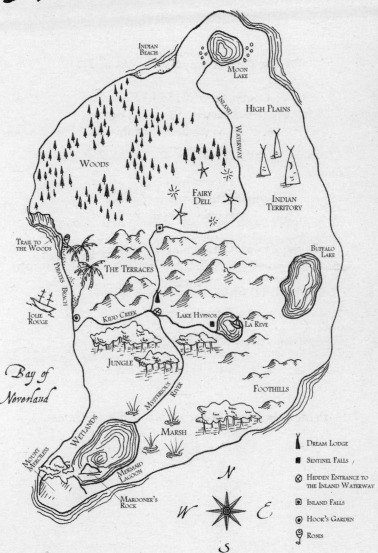

INDIAN BEACH

MOON LAKE

INLAND WATERWAY

HIGH PLAINS

WOODS

FAIRY DELL

INDIAN TERRITORY

TRAIL TO THE WOODS

PIRATES BEACH

THE TERRACES

BUFFALO LAKE

JOLIE ROUGE

KIDD CREEK

LAKE HYPNOS

LA REVE

Bay of Neverland

JUNGLE

FOOTHILLS

MYSTERIOUS RIVER

WETLANDS

MARSH

MOUNT MERCILESS

MERMAID LAGOON

MAROONER'S ROCK

N

W · E

S

Ψ DREAM LODGE

■ SENTINEL FALLS

⊗ HIDDEN ENTRANCE TO THE INLAND WATERWAY

▣ INLAND FALLS

◉ HOOK'S GARDEN

♀ ROSES

"Perhaps everything terrible is something that needs our love."
— RAINER MARIA RILKE

"Childrens' plays are not sports, and should be deemed their most serious actions."
— MICHEL DE MONTAIGNE

"Everything has its beauty, but not everyone sees it."
— CONFUCIUS

"Desperado, why don't you come to your senses?"
— THE EAGLES

PRELUDE
Him Or Me

Every child knows how the story ends. The wicked pirate captain is flung overboard, caught in the jaws of the monster crocodile, which drags him down to a watery grave. Who could guess that below the water, the great beast would spew me out with a belch and a wink of its horned, livid eye? It was not yet my time to die, not then nor any other time. It's my fate to be trapped here forever in a nightmare of childhood fancy with that infernal, eternal boy.

No one knows what came next, the part you never read about in the stories. I clawed through water bloodied by the corpses of my crew driven overboard to make a meal for the sharks, flailed for the hull of my ship before the sharks caught up to me.

I saw it all by moonrise as I hooked my way up the chains to the deck. One of my men lay asprawl on the hatch coaming, dead eyes staring at the moon, curled fingers frozen over his ruptured belly. Another had dragged himself a few paces toward the rail before he expired, leaving a smear of fresh blood on the deck that could never be stained red enough to disguise it. Half a dozen others lay about in shadowy heaps, limbs twisted, faces ghastly, silent as waxworks. Everything stank of blood and decay. One man was draped face down over the foredeck rail, arrows sprouting from his back. The redskins were teaching the boys archery, as if they needed any more advantage over us in battle. None of the dead were boys.

Those who'd gone over the side screamed no more. The ship's bell, rung when the battle commenced, tolled no more. Even the monstrous ticking had subsided. My ship was as silent as the tomb she had become. The boys had gone larking off again, but not in my ship; all of the fairies' black arts could not raise my *Jolie Rouge* out of her moldering berth in the bay. Solemn drumbeats from the island told me the Indians were collecting their dead from our skirmish in the wood, but none were left to mourn my men but me.

I started for the nearest body, to drag it to the ship's boat, but as I passed the deckhouse, something groaned within. The deckhouse. That's where he'd hidden to lure us into his trap.

I shoved open the door, peered into the reeking gloom. Jukes I recognized by the sprawl of his tattoos in the ghostly moonlight. The Italian lay nearby, face frozen in an eternal scream. I crept in across sticky planks toward a soft grumble of pain, a sudden seizure of breath. My fingers touched still-living flesh, and Jukes groaned again. There was a new hieroglyph on his naked chest, thrust in with less art than the rest, and still leaking red. I knelt in the puddle, worked my hook arm round his back and propped him up. Heavy as a corpse already, yet his head lolled back on my arm and his dull eyes opened to look at me.

One. The boy had left me only one.

"Well, Bill." I could scarcely steady my voice.

"Sorry, Cap'n," he lisped through the blood in his mouth. "He come at me in the dark."

"Don't talk," I cautioned, yet I was desperate for the comfort of his voice. We'd sailed together since New Providence; his pictographic skin was a living gallery of our exploits from the Indies to the Gold Coast. He was the closest thing I'd ever had to a friend in the pirate trade. "Save your strength."

But it was already too late. We both knew it. The boy hadn't even done it proper; life was escaping in an agonizing drip, not a clean burst.

Jukes dragged another tortured breath out of his ruined lungs. "Thought you was done for," he wheezed.

"Come, now, you know me better than that." I clenched my teeth in assumed heartiness. "No mere boy is a match for me."

A furtive smile glimmered briefly amid the blue and black dots and calligraphic swirls on his face. I could see what even so slight a movement cost him in misery. There was only one way to help him now, could I but steel myself to do it.

"The women are warm in Hell, eh, Cap'n?" he prompted.

"Save me a place at the Devil's mess," I answered by rote, summoning every ounce of my resolve.

Red bubbled between his teeth. "Aye, aye—"

His eyes bulged for an instant, whites agleam in the shadows, then the lids drooped in relief. "Thank'ee, Cap'n," wafted out on his last breath, as I extracted my knife from between his ribs.

Gone, all of them gone now. Slaughtered one by one, like a game. It's all a game to the boys.

I stretched Jukes out beside the twisted Italian, sat back on my heels, forced my brain to think on practical matters. Two or three trips in the gig it would take to see them all properly consigned to deep water. The eerie, animal keening of the loreleis singing to the moon rose up across the water, cold and tormenting. I was the last human left alive in the Bay of Neverland.

***

The Neverland, they call it, the infant paradise, the puerile Eden where grown-ups dare not tread. They are wise to fear it. But all children visit in their dreams. He finds them by their longing, stray boys for his tribe and girls to tell him stories.

They are not always English children, although he is partial to London. They have erected a statue to him there. Fancy, a public statue of Pan, the boy tyrant in his motley of leaves, like a king or a hero. While Hook is reviled, the evil pirate, the villain. There is no statue to me.

I've heard all the stories. I know the world thinks me not only a simpering fop but a great coward, so affrighted by the crocodile I would empty my bowels at the first sinister tick of its clock. But it's the ticking itself I can't bear, the tolling of the minutes, the very seconds, that I am forced to spend in the Neverland for all eternity. Elsewhere, time is passing in the normal way, but not here. Not for me and the boy.

"It's Hook or me this time," the boy jeered as the massacre began. But it's never him. And it's never me. Since then, he has defeated me innumerable times, but never quite to the death. He wills it so, and his will rules all. How often have I felt my skin pierced, imagined in my wounded delirium that Death has relented and come for me at last? Yet every time, my blood stops leaking, my flesh knits. Sooner or later, my eyes open again to yet another bleak new day, with nothing to show for my pains but another scar on the wreckage of my body.

Is it any wonder I so often tried to kill him? Would not his death break the enchantment of this awful place and release us both? But I can never best him. He flies. He has youth and innocence on his side, and the heartlessness that comes with them. I have only heartlessness, and it is never, ever enough.

8

***

Outside the deckhouse, the night had gone dark. I crept out again, still drenched in Bill Jukes' blood, and saw that the moon itself, so full and white an hour before, had turned red, as if she too were awash in blood. A red eclipse, as mariners say, but never before had I seen the shadow of the old world fall across the Neverland moon. Perhaps it was only a trick of my fevered imagination, or some monstrous reflection from the deck of the *Rouge*, yet it glared down on me like a bloodshot eye, catching me out in all my crimes.

Once, I thought I could never have enough of blood. It was all that could satisfy me, for so long. But it wearies me now, the tyranny of blood-lust, the serpent that feeds on itself. The game that never changes. The game that never ends.

"How long can you stay angry at the world?" she asked me once. Why didn't I listen?

CHAPTER 1

BRISTOLT, 1688: JAMIE

"James Benjamin Hookbridge! What is the meaning of this object?"

My father was a mild man, most often buried happily in his accounting books or off to his warehouse. He did not countenance disobedience, but on this morning, I had no notion I had disobeyed, eager to claim credit for the marvel he held in his hand.

"It's a ship, Father," I crowed, jumping up to greet him, glad to escape my tutor. My father's appearance in the nursery was a rare event to a lad of seven. "I built it!"

For weeks I'd scavenged scrap wood, chips, shavings from the floor of the woodshop down by the stables on our estate. It was a patchwork affair, dark mahogany from the Indies jumbled with native oak and white pine, no larger than a small half-melon, discounting the thin doweling mast and handkerchief sail. But old Turlow himself, the senior carpenter, had shown me how to lap the narrow strips of board for the hull and nail down the deck.

"So I heard." Father did not look pleased. Perhaps my work wasn't fine enough.

"Turlow said it was handsome done," I said hopefully. "He says I'm clever with my hands."

My father gazed down at me, pale blue eyes stern behind his spectacles. "I shall have a word with Turlow. You are not to go to the carpenter's yard anymore."

"But…why?" I stammered, horror-struck. My happiest hours were spent among the joiners and planers in that busy place.

Father bent down with a sigh and laid a hand on my shoulder, and unusual gesture of affection. "You are a gentleman, sir. Only common laborers work with their hands."

My mother always received me with warmth and tenderness when I came to her with my troubles. I recall the armies of tiny pearls worked into her bodice, a halo of fine white dust from her powdered curls, her fragrance of violets and tonic. She was a fragile creature to be cherished and honored, but she had no power to influence my father on my behalf. "You are his only surviving child," she told me gently. "He only wants what's best for you."

But I forgot my disappointments on those grand days when I was permitted to go with Father down to the Bristol docks to his warehouse. How I loved to go racketing round the waterfront, its cobbled streets worn smooth from the horse-drawn sledges that ferried heavy loads to and from the ships. But my father had ambitions for his only son, and shortly after the incident of the toy ship, I was sent off to school to be educated as a gentleman.

***

Master Walters was snoring like an army of kettledrums in the next room by the time we finished the Purcell prelude. It was the hour after midday when no one had any business in the chapel and we were least likely to be disturbed. Carver and his mob of bullies were off shrieking at their games. Master Walters, the organist, was sleeping off his dinner of mutton and port, but his servant knew to let us into the study where he kept a harpsicord for his private compositions.

"Bravissimo!" I cried, as we made our final flourish. Four hands gave the music wings. By then I might have managed a tolerable accounting on my own, but it was always more fun with two of us.

"Nay, sir, we have put our audience to sleep," said Alleyn in mock reproof, with a nod toward the rumbling from the next room.

"Then we have played well," I pointed out, "for I am sure no one can hear us over the din."

Teddy Alleyn was eleven years old, two forms above me, and by his careful instruction alone had I progressed thus far in my illicit studies. He'd been playing since he was big enough to sit on a bench. Our stolen hours playing preludes and airs were my greatest pleasure. He grinned now, and tucked a glossy curl behind his ear with one of his long white fingers. Alleyn's delicate features and soft curls enraged the other boys; they thought him weak and girlish, harried him without mercy. But he was kind to me. He taught me to play. He was my friend.

"You must learn to get on, Jamie," my mother tried to soothe me after my first year away, when I complained of how the bigger boys taunted me. They derided my small size, my fancy clothing, a father in trade. My father's advice was more succinct. "Be a man," he commanded me.

"You're certain no one saw you come in here, Hookbridge?" Alleyn asked me.

"No one pays any attention to me," I reminded him.

Alleyn's mother paid extra fees to continue his musical instruction, which the organist earned chiefly by allowing his pupil access to his instrument whenever he pleased. It was our only refuge, and Alleyn guarded it absolutely, as he guarded the fact of our friendship, to spare me the stain of our association in the eyes of the mob. Alleyn had a way of turning inward when the older boys tripped him up in the commons or called him names. He neither cried, nor fought back, nor defied them with insults, and they could never forgive him for it. I hated to see him so abused, longed for the power to defend him.

12

"When you've attained my great age, sirrah, you will understand what a mercy that is," Alleyn said loftily. And then we both snickered, outcasts together, confederates in exclusion.

"Come, what next?" he went on, paging through the sheets of music on the stand above the twin keyboads. "We've time, I think, for the minuet—"

A babble of voices erupted out in the passage; the study door burst open to disgorge a gang of shouting boys, Carver in the lead, stout, ruddy, sandy-haired, eyes bright with belligerent glee.

"There they are, the little lovebirds!" he cried, and several of the others made smacking noises with their lips.

"I told you!" shrieked another, as a half dozen more tumbled in, above the feeble protests of the servant out in the hall.

Two boys dragged Alleyn away from the bench, held him fast. Carver himself came for me, plucked me from the bench like a flea off a hound, pinned my arms behind me.

"Don't touch him!" shouted Alleyn, setting all the other boys atwitter.

"I won't have to, will I?" Carver smirked down at me, looming, feral and terrifying in the enormity of his power. "He kissed you, didn't he?" His big hands were crushing my arms. "Say it, Hookbridge! The filthy invert kissed you. Say it!"

I shook my head, but the other boys were all crowding around us, chanting, "Say it! Say it!" like a game. Alleyn stood frozen, dark eyes sad and urgent, watching me. His guards were heavy, pitiless boys, baying with the others, itching to strike.

"No!" I yelped in my impotent outrage, only to see Alleyn wince in pain; one of his captors was twisting his fingers.

"Yes," I squeaked.

Such whooping and confusion followed this utterance, I scarcely knew what I was about, but that the racking of my arms out of their sockets ceased, and Alleyn's captors let him go. No such thing had ever occurred between us, of course, but my heroic delusion that my false confession had saved us lasted just until I saw the usher, the headmaster's assistant, in the doorway, pursing his lips in a very worried look.

"You heard him!" Carver crowed over the heads of the throng.

And the chattering boys parted as the usher came to lead Alleyn away. The last look he turned on me was not angry, nor hurt at my betrayal, so much as resigned, as if he had expected no more. It stung worse than if he'd peppered me with invective.

"Well done," Carver said to me. He motioned to one of his toadies, a smaller boy clutching the muddy stick Carver liked to use at games, and nodded for him to give the thing to me. "Carry that for me, Hookbridge. Let's go, men."

Teddy Alleyn was expelled the next day, collected in a carriage and bustled off the grounds. I never saw him again. But I was taken in by Carver and his mob. At first, I consoled myself that I'd worm my way into their good graces in order to wreak a terrible revenge on them all. But as time passed, I was glad enough to have traded a lie for their protection, bartered away my only friend for a pack of allies in petty schoolyard rivalries. They were wild things searching for a target for their malice, and Carver was clever enough to give them one, else they had fallen on each other.

Alleyn's weakness had forced me to perjure myself on his behalf, or so I convinced myself. How else could I bear what I'd done? Affection made a person vulnerable, and so I learned to mask whatever feelings might be seen as weak in myself behind a show of bravado, and advanced among their ranks.

Thus my education began.

CHAPTER 2

LOST MEN

Winds have been fractious all day, heavy weather for the Neverland. The boy prefers blue skies and bright sun. The blow is not so hard it disturbs the slovenly tilt at which my ship, the *Jolie Rouge*, has lain at anchor for two centuries, but there is reefing to be done, and yards to be swung and set so she rides more easily. My crew is eager for activity, but unskilled at the work, lubbers that they are, and I must do most of it myself.

Fractious too are the men, much later in the day, when the breeze has slacked off. I go below to find a brawl in progress in the mess room, onlookers circling in to watch, hooting and braying. "Hey, foul!" yodels a voice above the din, to which another yelps, "Aw shut it, this ain't the bleedin' Marquess of Queensberry rules!"

As I head into the melee, somone blunders into me out of the shadows, and my sword scrapes out on pure instinct, bloodrage erupting in my veins, and it's only by the narrowest glimmer of reason that I prevent myself slicing open one of my own men, the big one they call Nutter. Stooping under the deck beams, face as crimson as his curly red hair, fists knotted beneath the tattered sleeves of his blue and white striped jersey, he's rounding on an assailant who crouches low in the shadows. I whirl about as well as his opponent comes about, the gleam of a blade in his fist, and I recognize another of my crewmen. I leap between them before the small, wiry one we call Dodge can skewer his shipmate.

Both men stumble to a halt on either side of me, Nutter held back by my hook arm, Dodge crouching before me at the business end of my sword. Fingers gripping his clandestine knife, eye purpling from a blow, he's gauging if he might yet warp round me and strike home with his vicious little blade. His name is well earned.

"Think again, Mr. Dodge," I suggest. Did any of them bother to think even once, I'd swoon in ecstasy. "Consider the odds."

Dodge is a gaming man; I've seen him yowling over dice. He takes one step back, defiantly shakes a forelock of dark hair off his battered eye, but his weapon thumps to the deck. Good. I've no wish to be bled by that cunning device, a wicked weapon for its size, with a narrow blade that pops out with the flick of a switch. They are always bringing the damnedest things back with them from their world, my men.

"Well?" I prompt.

These men are not like my original crew, Bill Jukes and the rest of them, gone these two hundred years. This lot scarcely qualify as sailors, should that word imply the act of actually sailing anywhere, yet they are my responsibility still. Now the others fall back, give us room, shift about, eyeing each other for an advocate. My roving gaze picks out Filcher, my current first mate, shrinking into the shadows. Colorless hair straggles out from beneath his red bandana. His long nose, forward teeth, and shiny black eyes give him the look of a startled squirrel, uncomfortable in the spotlight of my glare.

"Well, Cap'n, Dodge 'ere said the Addicks could whip Millwall," Filcher begins, "and Nutter said 'e was full of shit."

Nutter growls at my shoulder, "Millwall could murder 'em!"

"Millwall is a bunch of pussies," Dodge croaks.

"*You're* the blee—"

"Silence!" I bark. "Someone will explain this to me in the King's English, or you'll all tell it to the cat," I add, with a suggestive flourish of my sword. It's been ages since I flogged anyone, but these men don't know that. Men don't last for ages in my crew.

"They're clubs, Captain." It's Jesse who dares to enlighten me. The others set to nodding and murmuring; they know I give him more leeway than most. "Millwall and the Addicks," he elaborates, limping toward me out of the gloom. "Football."

I gape at them all. "Football?" I try again, as if a different inflection might improve the taste. *"Football?"*

This is what comes of idleness. The boy has not been seen much of late, off rounding up new recruits for his tribe, I suppose, but intead of luxuriating in this brief respite of peace, my men spend their wrath on each other. They want a nursemaid, not a captain. Some things never change.

Look at them. Big, florid Nutter panting like a mastiff at my elbow, wiping sweat off his face with one fraying sleeve. Dark, spidery Dodge, at whom I nod to retrieve his weapon, snap it shut and pocket it. Filcher, blinking his rabbity eyes in search of the nearest escape, every inch the Covent Garden pickpocket he was in his last employment, my mate by default, the only one aboard at present with even a nodding acquaintance with a criminal trade. They can scarcely remember their real names when they come here, yet the tribal rivalries of some meaningless sport persist in them still. And none of them, not even Jesse, whom I credit with a modicum of sense, had the wit or inclination to stop this fracas.

It says little for the state of their world that my men grow more foolish with each generation. The boy will have them all writhing in Hell soon enough, yet they're ready to murder each other now over a game. None of them would last five minutes in a fighting crew under sail in my day. They are Lost Boys still, the lot of them.

The urge to send them to bed without their tea is all but overpowering, but the jest would be wasted on them. They already believe me half madman, that is why they obey me, but I mustn't let them think me feeble-minded. Before I can utter a word of dismissal, however, a mighty clang like Hell's judgement trumpets from above. My men and I exchange a look of round-eyed alarm. Bugger me crossways, it's the damned ship's bell, silent for centuries at my command. Who dares to ring it now?

***

Flax, our newest recruit, stands at the belfry above the forward hatch; what's left of the corroding bell rope has come off in his hands. As we all stream up on deck, Gato, my Spanish lookout, stretches out of the crows nest gesturing like a wild man, but a quick scan of the dusky sky reveals no warlike flying wedge of boys.

"*Oye, Capitan!*" Gato cries, cupping his hand to his ear.

Once I raise my hook for silence, I hear it too, a low rumbling of Indian drums, echoing down from the distant High Plains of the island and rolling across the water, such relentless drumming as I have not heard in decades. It's been ages since the tribes went on the warpath, not since the boy made them his pets. What's got them stirred up?

"Wot's it mean, Cap'n?" ventures Filcher, at my elbow.

I'm all but sniffing at the breeze, like a bloodhound. No, not the tattoo of war drums of old. There is something of excitement, almost anticipation in these drums, an *allegretto con brio*, not unpleasant, yet ominous in that it has never been heard before. Do I only imagine a rattling of fairies, a rippling of mermaids, something foreign, dangerous in the air? The boys are enchanted to sleep at night, but the Indians and the diabolical fairies are active at all hours, and we never know from what quarter a new game will be launched. Glancing back, I see all eyes turned to me as the distant, rhythmic pounding goes on and on. This is not the moment to lose my place in the text. Time to bring the clown Hook out of his box and rally these fellows to some purpose. What else am I fit for? Why else am I here?

"It means we must stop and consider who our true enemies are," I tell them smoothy. "Ignore them at your peril. A double watch tonight and a sharp lookout for war canoes, men. Jesse and Burley, for'ard," and Jesse nods and limps for the ladder with my square-rigged bos'un, a fisherman by trade who actually knows something about boats. "Flax, astern with—" I peer back again at Dodge, his eye near swollen shut. "Needles!" I hail the sailmaker I spy lingering in the hatchway. "See if this man requires stitches."

A certain cure for malingering in my day, this has the desired effect, as Dodge mutters his, "Aye, Cap'n," and hurries off to pair with Flax and move astern.

"Nutter, you have the Long Tom." And the big redhead clambers eagerly up the ladder for our swivel gun in the starboard bows.

"It's been long years since the redskins were foolhardy enough to attack this ship," I begin again.

"I say let 'em come!" howls Nutter from his gun, with the absolute ferocity of one who has never had to grapple in the mud and blood and gore for his life.

"But if it's Hell they crave so much, we'll give 'em a taste!" I agree, and the men burst into cheers.

It's all theatre here, illusion and flash-powder, from the moment they first set foot upon this cruel stage until their tawdry exit. Let them think I've engineered this event for their benefit. Anything but let them see I've no idea what the damned drums mean.

***

It begins with a bell. A rustling in the leaves that startles me.

Don't be afraid.

Who speaks thus to the terrible Hook? I can't tell; it's gone dusky in the garden while I tend my irises. A new bloom of heartbreaking loveliness has just opened, its upper bonnet lavendar, its lower petals deep indigo purple. A pale moon is already visible above the island, peering down on the curly cabbage leaves and ferny tops of parsnips and carrots, but the shadows have grown so long, I can't see whose voice it is that speaks to me from the surrounding shrubbery.

May I help?

No one else ever labors willingly in this garden. And I need not say in words there is no other way to help Hook in this place.

The stranger remains hidden from my view, but, as if speaking to my thoughts, the voice draws nearer. *There is always a way.*

It's as if one of my bearded flowers were granted the gift of speech. These are my most constant companions, these bulbs that regenerate themselves year after year after year; they know my thoughts better than anyone. I'm a raving Bedlamite at last, or else it is some trick of the boy's to goad and torment me.

Peter doesn't know everything.

I sit back on my heels, chilled; even stray thoughts about the boy can have dire consequences here, let alone unchecked words.

There is always a way, the voice tells me again, quite nearby now. *We can find it together.*

And I begin to percieve some subtle shift, some change in the very atmosphere, almost as if the attention of

20

the Neverland were slowly turning aside, as if I am in the presence of some greater power. Greater than the boy.

I reach tentatively into the shadows. "Take my hand."

The faintest grazing of skin on skin; another tinkling of a tiny bell; a fleeting impression of warmth and something more. Connection. Alliance. And for an instant, all of my senses respond to a weird lessening of the tension that always oppresses me here, borne off like a storm cloud on a freshening breeze.

And I am no longer kneeling in the earth, but standing on board the deck of a ship. Too trim and responsive for the *Rouge*, no, it's a fleet little craft under such a press of sail she seems to take flight, soaring up into the sky above a dark sea that sparkles like stars, bearing me aloft into the night. And my weary spirit soars as well, toward an uncanny moon gone as red as a sunrise, glowing like an ember in the night sky, lighting the way. Outward bound at last, it must be, deliverance at last, freed at long last from this awful place!

And thus I come awake, aching for the rapture of release that never comes, to find myself still here, sprawled across my bed in my cabin on board the *Rouge*, still trapped in the Neverland, the nightmare that never ends.

Who is it that haunts my dreams in this manner? Which of the hundreds of men I have led and lost in this place over time can it be?

Or is it Death I dream of with such ardor? Who else can it be, this stranger with the power to end my misery? There is nothing else I crave so much.

My stern cabin window tells me it is still dark night. I hear the tread of men on watch above, a mumbling of idle voices, the hollow cloppping of dice in a cup, but the redskins' drumming has slacked off. The sirens' nightly wailing, however, is already at full throttle. I reach for my bottle to moisten my lips, but find it already drained and let it sink to the deck; then I roll over and grope about for a pillow to cover my ears and drown out the mermaids' infernal noise. But in that moment, a renegade draught of air whispers overhead, trailing a mineral scent of sulfur and allspice across my bedthings. And piping along with it, another disembodied voice, feathery light,

    Seize your chance.

What mockery is this? I haul myself up by the nearest bedpost, fumble out a flint at my little side table, strike a spark off my hook to light the lamp, peer about in the gloom. But my cabin is empty, of course. I sigh and rake back my hair, swing my legs over the side. I've had enough of dreaming.

***

The twin keyboards of my harpsichord grin up at me like rows of teeth in the flickering lamplight. The low, rolling pitch of the loreleis' song adds extra menace to the night. I long to drown it out with the contrapuntal clarity of my instrument, voiceless, impotent, yearning for so long. The fingers of my left hand strike the first notes of a bright *arpeggio*. But the urge to sound a richer harmonic on the lower manual clashes iron against the wooden key, and the unpleasant thunk of the jack under my clumsy hook ruins all.

"Play for your life." That's what she said. What mockery. Two centuries and more it's been since the boy chopped off my hand, and my pointless life rattles along unabated, a runaway cart down a long and rutted road. Play meant something different to me once. Now I am only fit for playing games.

I spiral up off the bench and pace round my cabin, lamplight glistening on polished wood, shimmering silks, far more lavish appointments than I ever kept at sea. Comfort matters to me now, a refuge from the world outside. But there's scant comfort in the image I glimpse in my oval glass, even with my gruesome stump buckled out of sight in the leather cuff that holds my hook. Even now, I can scarcely bear to look at the stunted thing my hook conceals. Dead it may be, yet it sends me phantom feelings: the urge to grasp a hilt, or a joint of meat, or strike a chord, which can never be satisfied; a maddening itch where there's nothing left to scratch. The scorching pain where he hacked my hand away tortures me often in the dark of night, beyond all soothing. Sometimes, when wine warms my belly and fouls my wits, I fancy there's another withered stump, a twin to this one, inside my chest, that beats out of habit alone with only phantom feeling.

Still I gaze, like a yokel gawping at a fire or a hanging or some other grim spectacle. Hard to believe I was reckoned quite the blade, once, tall, lithe, muscular, sky-blue eyes to make women swoon. Even now, I'm scarcely an hour older, physically, than the forty-odd years I'd accumulated on the day I sailed away from that blasted island in the Caribbees, when the obeah woman cursed me to this place. It's a matter of sheer, stubborn pride that I carry my tall frame without stooping; he will never see me cowed. The contours of my body have been pared down to hard muscle over time, but my flesh is battle-scarred, my long, dark hair a travesty of the fashionable wig I once wore. The eyes peering back at me from the glass have lost none of their vivid blue, but they have seen too much.

The muddled voices of my men waft down from above, a thin, indignant protest, a low gurgle of laughter, but nothing that sounds as if it might erupt again into violence or any kind of alarm. I sigh and turn away at last. My men.

What is the spell of eternal childhood that they cannot resist? Women, music, theatre, fruitful labor, the lure of the sea, the comforts of home and family, the delights of a garden, are there no such diversions in their world that might have rooted them in that place, where they belong? A dry internal laugh is my only response, from that irritating voice in my head that I can never quell of late.

Might not the same be said of me?

CHAPTER 3

LONDON, 1702: YOUNG BLOOD

A luscious display of womanflesh, ripe for the plucking, greeted us at Mrs. Ralston's that evening. Most of the girls lounged in chemises, straps falling off plump shoulders, hems hiked thighward. One or two wore silken dressing gowns; haughty Marie arranged herself artfully on the divan in a plum-colored velvet overdress with no underdress beneath. In their arms, my friends and I would be received like conquerers, no matter what deficiencies wine had wrought on our prowess after a raucous afternoon at the playhouse in Drury Lane. Not all the finest acting in London was done upon the stage.

Mrs. Ralston glided up to greet us, garbed in rich but sober midnight blue. "Lord Spendler, an honor," she hailed my friend with a demure nod.

Spendler gestured back with impressive grandeur, given that his arms were draped round Dartmouth on one side and Harrow on the other as they struggled to bear him up. The young lord was slender enough, but like to have consumed half his weight again in port wine during the course of the day.

"Young Mr. Hookbridge, always a pleasure," the proprietess smiled at me.

"Kind words indeed, Madam, from such an expert in the field." I swept off my gaudy hat, letting my dark hair spill free under the warm, flattering light, and made a bow that scarcely wobbled at all.

My father was an importer who had made his fortune in the sugar trade out of Bristol. I came often up to London on his business, where I sought out the company of other preening young males like myself to enjoy all the pleasures the city had to offer. Since school, I had journeyed many times to the Indies as supercargo on my father's ships. I learned to sail from his most daring captains and found a life to which I was far better suited than the dreary routine of account books and business affairs, haunting quarterdeck and boatyard alike, far from my father's eyes. Back in town, I fancied myself irresistible in my wine-colored coat and gilded frogs, trim breeches, and bucket-cuff boots. In business, I often affected a wig of fulsome curls in the manner of the late king, merry Charles Stuart, who had restored profit and gaeity to the realm. But I was vain of my own dark curls, which had grown long and luxurious at sea and delighted the ladies.

"Come on, man," grunted Harrow. He and Dartie were already listing off toward the taproom, with Spendler in tow. The young lord was in disgraceful condition, as usual, yet I suppose we were no worse than any other young bloods of twenty or so with coin to spend and sap rising in our veins.

"Will you play for us this evening?" Mrs. Ralston asked me.

"With the most intense delight," I said, and I turned to the others. "Raise a glass to the fair sex, gentlemen, and meet me in the parlor."

"Aye, aye, Hooky!" Spendler agreed, and risked a wave of his hand. "On, on, noblesh Englisss…" he exhorted the others, as the three of them turned again toward the taproom. He was my superior in blood, breeding and fortune, yet he deferred to me. They all did. I was their leader.

Others of our acquaintance were already hailing us from the taproom, calling out jests, greetings, carnal encouragement. We were the envy of every clerk and apprentice in London, and most of their masters. We were dazzling. We were immortal.

***

An excellent Flemish harpsichord occupied the back corner of Mrs. Ralston's parlor. Painted in primrose yellow with an abundance of gilding and floral motifs, it featured an edifying scene of pagan nymphs and satyrs afrolic inside the raised lid. I suited my repertoire to the occasion, beginning with "My Lady Has A Pretty Thing," which delighted what damsels were still downstairs and their prospective gentleman clients.

My father thought music a frivolous pursuit for a man of business and permitted no instruments in his home. Since school, I'd had to take my education where I could find it, most often of late in houses of this nature, where my particular gifts were appreciated. After concluding a spirited account of "A Maid Must Have A Youngman," my hands flying across the twin keyboards, and most of the house warbling along, I stood at the bench and made an exaggerated bow from the waist to the company, knowing full well how scandalized my father would be to see it. Perhaps I hoped the tales would carry back to him, that he might know me at last for who I was, not who he wanted me to be.

After a deal of careful attention, I finally saw my men disposed among the most forgiving of Mrs. Ralston's seraphim. Then it was time at last to address the business of the evening. Some of the younger girls were primping hopefully, but I was in no humor to be flattered and chattered at all night after a tumultuous day out and about in town. We'd had words that had nearly come to blows with Lord Mortimer and his men over a singer in the entr'acte at Old

Drury. She was a drab and timorous little thing, to be sure, but the lady said 'no,' and so we saw our duty to intervene. Although she might just as easily have said 'yes' to much the same effect, for it was ever our purpose to oppose Mortimer and his dogs in all things. There would be hell to pay when my father heard about the altercation, of course, a homecoming I intended to delay as long as possible, and so I made my choice.

Flora did not bestir herself with any particular haste on my account, rising calmly, adjusting the drape of her dressing gown. A veteran of the profession, perhaps ten years older than myself, she knew better than to come at me like a spaniel, all nervous quivering and twitchy tail, and I admired her the more for it. We knew each others' ways, by now.

***

"Ah, Flora, I've had a hellish night," I sighed voluptuously, sinking back into her plump armchair.

"Not surprising, for such a devil," she sauced me back from her perch on the tufted ottoman, as she pulled off my boot. She wore her dark hair pinned up in loose curls on one side, the rest tumbling down her back; it glistened in the soft candlelight of her small, private chamber that smelt of dried rose petals and crushed lavender and the sweat of commerce.

"Hell is not just for devils, you know," I sallied, as she slid off my other boot. "The poet Dante tells us there are circles for even the most ordinary sinners," I went on, showing off the education for which my father had paid so handsomely. In other matters, Flora was the tutor, and myself an apt and eager pupil.

"Aye, and who might those be?" Flora prompted, as she rose. She reached for my hands to pull me up, and I stood before her in my shirtsleeves.

"Oh, traitors and thieves and suchlike are the worst," I said. "Panderers," I added, and peeled off her dressing gown to puddle on the floor at her feet. She obligingly struck a languid pose, displaying her nakedness to alluring effect. "Seducers."

"Ah." She slipped her hands beneath my shirt and stroked me beneath my breeches for a long moment before loosening my laces. I closed my eyes and drew a freighted breath, but I'd not cry quarter so soon.

"The violent," I whispered. Flora grasped the hem of my shirt in both hands and ripped it off over my head with a great show of savagery, then raked her fingertips down my chest, not deep enough to cut; only to make the blood sing beneath my skin. Laughing, I wrestled her onto the bed.

"The gluttonous," I went on, nipping playfully at her naked shoulder. Rolling her over in my arms, I began to feast with more attention on the delicate lobe of her ear, the tender flesh beneath her jaw, the succulent cleft of her throat, running my fingertips all over the delectable landscape of her body until she was murmuring and arching in response. "And last of all, the lusty," I breathed into her ear.

Flora nudged me aside. "If lust is such a sin, why did God make us to feel pleasure?" she demanded reasonably, leaning up on one arm.

"Well, it's only a little sin," I shrugged. "Far closer to God than all the rest. The next circle up is Limbo, for pagans and unbaptized innocents. Then comes Purgatorio, where those who might yet be redeemed serve out their time before their release into Glory."

"And what's the punishment for such a little sin?"

I raised a sardonic eyebrow at her. "An eternal gale of passion where the lustful copulate ceaselessly without gratification."

Flora's expression dimpled into a grin. "There's proof your poet is a man," she exclaimed, pushing me over on my back. "Gentlemen never appreciate how much pleasure might be had on the way to being gratified."

She came to lick the last of the wine off my lips while her reckless hand slid once more beneath my loosened breeches, probing and teasing. *Steady on, my bully*, I cautioned myself, as my blood began to pound; *the night is young and we must make the most of our time.*

"A *gentleman* knows the difference," I said huskily, knotting my fingers gently in her hair, while the fingers of my other hand performed a slow, urgent *glissando* over all the rounded swells of her flesh and down into her secret crevices. "But man in general is a race of warriors," I murmured, "and in love and war, we are schooled to demand satisfaction."

She sprawled back among the pillows, laughing, and braced up her heels. "Oh, hush now, Jamie, and put that clever tongue of yours where it will do some good!"

My father wished me to marry, but time and my father's fortune were mine to waste in those days. It was all a game to me, then. A wife required patience, indulgence, and some pretense to affection, skills I had no need to cultivate so long as there were willing females like Flora to be bought at my pleasure.

Indeed, we had nothing but time, my men and I. Life was ours for the plucking. Were we not immortal?

CHAPTER 4

PURGATORIO

I never even hear the thump, the crash, the final bloody *au revoir* of yet another departing life. Once again, Death has stolen aboard and left without me.

The first I know of it is my steward, Brassy, lantern aloft like Diogenes, breathing the news at me from beside my bed in the dead of night. Dodge, who spent the night dosing himself with extra tots of rum for his injuries in the brawl, missed his footing in the ratlines during the middle watch above and dashed out his brains on the deck. Gone are the days we fought to the death for gold and glory; now my men die for football and stupidity.

"Rouse Filcher to get him cleaned up," I mutter. "Tell the men we'll perform the ceremony at first light."

It would be fearful bad form just to chuck a fellow over the side, or attempt to inter him in the shifting sands of Pirates Beach. There's not sand enough on the whole island to bury all the crews I've lost.

I take the fresh bottle my steward has brought me to sweeten his grim news. I've had the dream again: *Don't be afraid. Take my hand.* An unknown companion I could almost touch. Pale moonlight streams in my stern window. *Seize your chance,* that's what it said, the voice I must have dreamt. It's no surprise my very dreams turn against me here. It's folly to believe in phantom chances whispered on the wind in this kingdom of delusion.

The breeze is fresh but not squally as I go above in the purpling dawn in my sober black coat with the silver figures, and my plumed black hat. My best sword depends from my sash, my French cutlass, lightweight, sturdy, flint-edged and sharpened to a rapier point for both thrusting and cutting. The cultivation of coffee is unheard of here, so I always train my stewards to brew a foul decoction from local bark wood, bitter and bracing enough for whatever the day might bring. I clutch a steaming tankard of the stuff now and pace my quarterdeck.

My ship lies at anchor in the bay like a debauched whore, as she has for centuries, one broadside to the beach, the other to the sea that refuses to carry us out of the Neverland. Her head lolls to the north where the blue terraced hills beyond Pirates Beach rise into the densely forested bluffs of the wood where the beasts and the boys keep their lairs. I gaze astern to the southern end of Pirates Beach, where sprouts the fertile mouth of Kidd Creek, aburst with green ferns and palmettos. The creek snakes inland to join up with the Mysterious River which flows southward into the noxious heart of the jungle around the loreleis' lagoon, the most treacherous place in the Neverland. Even I have never gone so far as that. Out of the jungle at the island's southernmost tip rises the green cone of Mount Merciless, spitting a little funnel of white steam into the sky above its coronet of pink clouds. The volcano is permitted to spit, just as the beasts are permitted their razor claws and my men and the redskins our weapons. The boy delights in real danger, or his mastery over all would not be as sweet.

At the larboard rail, the men haul out the boat and lift in the slack weight of the corpse, tightly bound in hammock netting. All are somber, even Nutter, who'd have happily stove in Dodge's brains himself yesterday. I order Needles, my sailmaker, to throw a length of canvas over the body, then I give the order to lower away.

There comes Jesse across the foredeck, his lopsided gait far less noticeable with a pistol in his hand. Sartorial splendor is no longer the fashion in their world, as it was in mine, judging by the pedestrian dress of my men. But even by their pitiable standards, the plainness of Jesse's rig—dun-colored trousers, shirt, and cloth jacket, clean-shaven, brown hair cropped short—along with his quiet demeanor, bespeak a lifetime of fading into the crowd, escaping notice. That has changed since he came aboard the *Rouge*.

Carpenters called Chippy or Sticks I've had aplenty, stewards called Brassy for the buttons in their care, canvas-stitchers named Needles, galleymen called Cookie, each man named according to his use or temperament. Only I recognize them as remnants of the babyish names they once wore with such pride in Pan's tribe. A fellow in the piratical trade needed an alias back in my day, but the sobriquets adopted among my crew aren't meant to disguise a man's identity, but to give him one.

But this fellow has earned his name. How much more formidable he looks, strapping on his brace of pistols in the molten dawn, than the furtive club-foot he was when he first arrived, before I discovered his singular talent. *Gimpy*, they called him then, until his first weapons drill; I'd loaded a pistol for him, and he put a ball in the center pip of a Three of Spades nailed to a canvas target. *Jesse James*, they call him now, in honor of a gunman famed in their world, as I understand it. Since then, Jesse has devoted himself to learning the secrets of my antique weapons. None of my men has had any notion of handling a flintlock for generations; the boys consider themselves immune to pistol shot. Bravado may make them careless, one day.

And it hits me like a broadside: a weapon the boys no longer fear. Can this be the chance foretold to me? A chance to end the boy's tyranny forever. A chance to win. What else can it mean? Why else am I here yet again with another crew? My sojourn has not been entirely unbroken here. There have been long passages now lost to my memory, stretches between those times when blessed solitude is welcome and the inevitable crushing despair of loneliness. But always, I find myself back on board my ship, providing refuge for another wandering soul, or two, or more, defending them from the boys, back in the teeth of war yet again. I've brooded over a thousand Neverland dawns in this manner, praying for inspiration—the weapon not yet deployed, the advantage not taken, the weakness not yet discovered that might bring me victory over the boy at last and end my bitter tenure here forever. And, there it lopes across the foredeck, within my grasp. Jesse.

I down the last caustic drop of Brassy's potion, struggling to nurture this tiny seed of an idea into a bloom of possibility, as my steward himself bounds up the ladder. A quadroon, perhaps, with his café au lait complexion and a thumbprint-sized birthmark like a dull bruise on his cheek, the fellow has no conversation, but he's quick about his work and knows to tread with better care than most belowdecks. He comes for my empty tankard, fresh from his excavation of the dead man's effects. Their memories of what they were begin to fade like coral bleaching in the sun as soon as they arrive here, but it's unusual not to find some forgotten souvenir from their world squirreled away somewhere.

"Sorry, Captain," Brassy murmurs, and proffers a species of that object he knows I loathe above all others: a watch. I have banned all ticking timepieces from the *Rouge* for the same reason I've forbidden the tolling of the hours on the ship's bell; the eternity I spend here is no fortune to be measured. I take the thing gingerly, inspect the small case of some base metal without fob or chain, strung on a leather band. But the name *Hopkins* is engraved upon the back of the case, which will do for now, and I hand it back to Brassy with instructions to tuck it into Dodge's shroud.

"And what of that fleet little blade of his?" I ask.

This Brassy produces as well, with no further explanation, the blade folded innocently into its black horn handle with metal findings. I do not ask if it came from the dead man's things or his corpse; all my men are scavengers. I examine the mechanism, revolve it in my hand with a care for my fingers, and press the button. The thin stiletto flicks out with a rasp of steel. I shove the blade back in with the curve of my hook, and drop it absently into my own coat pocket, my mind on other things.

***

We are six in the boat, not counting the dead man: Burley, my bo'sun, at the helm beside me in the stern, Nutter and young Flax, with his upswept bristle brush of fair hair, at the oars facing us. Jesse and lean, weathered Swab, my jack of all work, sit at the oars behind them. They are dainty with their feet so as not to tread upon the lifeless thing stowed in the bottom, and I order a north-westerly heading according to the sun.

"Stay clear of the fog bank," I remind them.

There's witchcraft in it, the low fog that encircles the bay and prevents escape. Only Pan knows the way through, and none of the Lost Boys he's guided out of the Neverland ever remembers the way out when they come back to me as men. Of course, none of the Wendys ever come back.

When we are far enough out in the bay, we put a drag over the side and muster the corpse out of the bottom.

"Receive this, our good shipmate, er, Hopkins," I intone. "May he ever find a fair berth, strong drink, welcome companions, and eternal peace in the kingdom beyond."

To whom do I address these remarks? The sea, perhaps? My men have little interest in spiritual matters, but I always

34

mention drink and companions in my makeshift service, things they will understand. Eternal peace I cite for myself. My crews never expect to die here. They are young men still; Burley, who cannot be much above five and thirty, is senior among them at the moment, Flax scarcely twenty. Could I but lop off a score of years from my own vast eternity for each man, perhaps we could grow into a kind of companionship over time, or at least I might content myself with their prolonged company. But their lives here are brief. I teach them to trim the ship and defend her against the boy and his allies, school them in hunting, fishing, swordfighting, curing meat, working the garden we keep at the mouth of Kidd Creek. Such men as prove apt, I drill in artisan skills— gunnery, carpentry, sailmaking—all in hopes of extending their brief lives a fraction longer. But I can't defend them forever, nor send them home again. All I can do is try to see that each man dies well, without suffering, without fear. For Dodge's sake, I pray he hit the deck before his muddled wits could comprehend his fate. Another pointless loss in the game that never ends.

Why do so many come back here? Cast out of the Neverland as boys when they begin to grow up, they find themselves at odds with the other world; the dream of Neverland, however faded, haunts them still. Some dormant part of themselves beyond the grasp of memory must cry out in sleep for the tribal society of a childhood they can't even remember and the comfortable tyranny of a leader. With the willfulness of the children they were, they dream of this place with such ferocity that Pan brings them back; perhaps he senses something familiar in the tremor of their dreaming that he has known before. But they are no longer boys and have forgotten how to fly. Pan soon chases them off to wander the Neverland as homeless outcasts, which leads them to me. Where else can they go? They were half-pirate anyway as boys, with the Pan directing their blades to any target he chose.

Are they sorry to call Pan their enemy? Certainly not. None of them remembers exactly that they were ever his creatures. They've simply been bred to follow a leader, and any leader will do, so long as their thinking is done for them.

We send the shrouded figure over the side, weighted down with a length of chain so no errant swell will keep it afloat, and gaze into the last of the ripples that tell where the corpse has gone. The men are sober but dry-eyed in the face of this finality, certainly untouched by the envy that consumes me. Perhaps one has to grasp at life as lustily as I once did to appreciate the majesty of death. I neither expect nor require a good death for myself; it may be as hideous as he likes so long as it is permanent.

This is what I am, what I've become in this place: handmaiden to the dead. My last, my only desire is to one day be rewarded for my centuries of service, earn my own passage into the Kingdom of Hades, and allowed to rest in peace. But I am aged Charon ferrying the souls of the damned to the Underworld where I can never follow. The obolus has yet to be coined that will purchase my passage out of this neverending Purgatorio.

Until now. Perhaps. I glance again at Jesse. Can I but muster the wit to seize my chance.

***

Last night's drumming has long since ceased, nor do any war canoes blot the pristine blue bay, so I order Burley to make for the island. Our timber supplies are low on board the *Rouge*, and subject to damp and wormrot, but I have in mind to erect some sort of breastwork for Jesse to shelter behind if he's to be effective. I try not to find the silence ominous as we tie up under the rushes in a shallow inlet beyond the northern end of Pirates Beach, a barren expanse of rock, sand, and scrub grass at the base of a bluff. A steep path has been worn into of the face of the bluff over time, a goat trail amid the bristling shrubs and bramble that marks the boys' territory. I've had stakes driven in along the trail so Jesse may climb more easily, and we claw our way up, eager to work off the sobriety of death, emerging at last into the outer reaches of the wood.

Yesterday's winds have wrought some havoc here. A few entire trees are down, those most derelict with age, bark peeling, roots exposed, shrubs and bramble flattened beneath them. Many more branches litter the ground in confusion amid the pines and twisted scrub oaks. Odd to find such damage right here in boy country, but a boon to my plans, to stumble upon so much felled wood ripe for the taking—although it occurs to me now we'll have to go back to the *Rouge* for saws and axes to hew it into lumber. Which thought no sooner crosses my mind than I notice a more than usual squawking of birdlife and rumbling of earthbound beasts from the dark interior. As if the Neverland itself can hear the subversive plan in my head.

"Let's check our traps," I call to the men, a bit too loudly, by way of subterfuge. And I herd them away from the green, grassy, jasmine-scented path that leads into the heart of the wood, where the fairies dwell, and into a neglected thicket on the periphery where we set our game traps, where the Indians, who have the lion's share of the great wood to hunt in as well as their own buffalo plains, rarely bother us. Yet we go in stealthily, clawing aside more fallen limbs, all of us alert to some nameless tension in the air.

"On your guard, Jess," I murmur.

He shuffles up beside me, teeters for a second on his clumsy foot, rights himself with a fleeting grin of apology as my hook arm shoots out to steady him. The maimed and the halt. "The blind leading the blind," I cannot help but mutter.

"Mind the ditch, eh?" he agrees, sliding out his pistol. I gaze at him sidewise, absurdly touched by the small, shared jest.

Shafts of daylight stained piney green glisten between the tree trunks, and as no shaggy predator rustles up out of the shadows, I dispatch the others to fan out ahead for our traps. We leave them yawning open under bushes and nestled between tree roots, small wooden cages, canted and weighted with painstaking precision to spring shut when the bait is taken.

"This one's empty," calls Burley, bending over a patch of reddish bramble. "The door be open, but the bait's gone."

"Same here," reports Flax, at a stand of rocks overgrown with weedy shrubs, some distance in the other direction.

I've never known coney nor quail could unlatch a trap door once it's eaten its fill. Is this some new game of the boy's to starve us out? Hand on hilt, I strain to sense a larger trap, nod at Jesse, his pistol at full cock. A skittering of leaves behind us startles me like cannon shot; I whirl about to see a fat grey hare dart round the base of a thick pine and race off into the undergrowth.

Some formless something quivers up on the other side of the tree trunk, knocking over the now-empty trap in its haste. Too big for a boy, too small for a bear, it crouches there, swathed in some garment as gold and copper and green as the wood itself, something plaid above shapeless trousers. Fingertips stretch out to brace against the gnarled trunk; a white face peers out at us, under short-cropped hair. A human face.

This is how I always find them, plucked from their world by some errant dream to fend for themselves until I take them in. I shrug at Jesse to lower his weapon, and—

"Oi! That was our rabbit!" Nutter howls from behind me and gives chase, animating the others, who come crashing out of the underbrush from all sides, whooping and yelling.

The stranger by the tree goggles, turns and flees in the direction we've just come. I roar at the men to stop, but they are too excited by their game; too eager to release the tension. I can only hope to catch up to the fellow before the others frighten the wits out of him. He's no use to me demented. I pump after him furiously, lungs heaving. If only he wouldn't run. There's nowhere to go.

The fog-edged horizon of Neverland Bay stretches out beyond the bluff as we emerge out of the trees. If he escapes down the trail, 'twill be a devil of a job tracking him all over the damned island. But at the edge of the bluff, his gait falters with indecision. With my men yelping at my heels, I lunge at the fellow, hook the flapping corner of his plaid coat. It jerks the stranger round in his tracks, coat yanked open, upper body twisting toward me. For a frozen instant, his wide eyes fasten upon my hook, as mine gape at a white shirt revealed under the coat, a white shirt stretched over an ominous female bulge.

God's bollocks, a woman in the Neverland?

"What in the bloody hell...!" she cries, and rips her plaid off my hook, stumbles backward, trips on the scrub, and plunges over the bluff with a shriek like a banshee.

CHAPTER 5

THE INFERNAL BOY

Do I expect her to fly? Soar out over the bay on harpy wings? I could not be more astounded if she did. A woman! A fully formed female woman abroad in the Neverland. I'm a raving Bedlamite at last, or something very dire is afoot. Only Indian women who cook the food and heal the sick, who make it possible for the tribes to reproduce themselves, are allowed on this island, and they must keep to their villages, out of the boy's sight. And ours. No other grown woman has ever been seen in the Neverland. Never, ever.

But she does not reappear. Instead, a crunching of shrubs and a cascade of gravel and pebbles rattling down the trail echo back to us, along with her falling cry, abruptly cut off. We descend with far less speed, but more care, down the bluff through a cloud of choking dust to find the creature sprawled on her stomach in the soft sand at its base, unstirring, head turned to one side. I am near enough to spy an arrangement of plain, metallic pins meant to contain her hair, although most has come loose in her tumble down the slope to spill across her cheek. But otherwise, she appears to be not much damaged; no pool of blood, nor twisted limbs.

You'd scarcely know her for a female, garbed in her plaid jacket, a glimpse of white shirt tail peeking out over loose dark trousers. Her feet are scarcely clad in soft, useless satiny things that expose her toes and heels. And she is surely not Indian; her face and hands are pale, her hair brownish and dusty, not long and silky black, much less done up in pearls and powder, as was the fashion in my day. But I am scarcely reassured.

"Where did she come from?" grumbles Nutter, at my elbow.

I stand back, frowning. "Who saw her first?"

"You did, Cap'n."

"Did no one notice any commotion back in the wood?" I ask them all. "Any sign of boys?" The flying boys are not invisible; did they dump her in our path, someone must have seen them, but my men only shake their heads.

"She can't have fallen out of the sky," I begin again, but of course, she might have done just that: this is the Neverland, where no witchery is impossible.

The question is not how, but why?

I gaze down again at the puzzling figure. This is no Wendy.

They are not always called Wendy, the eager girls who are not yet women, his make-believe mothers. There have been many others: Imogen, Clara, Hortensia. Fatima. Genevieve. Wherever they come from, he speaks to them in their own tongue—the language of youth. But that element has flown from the visible part of her face. Care lines bracket her silent mouth in the harsh daylight. Her body has ripened well beyond girlhood, as I saw up on the bluff, a matron of no less than thirty, if I am any judge.

Has the boy got himself a mother, a real mother, after all these years?

I draw a sudden, anxious breath. "Not dead, is she?" I demand of the men.

Nutter visibly draws back, Jesse totters uncertainly on his lame foot, and my gaze falls on young Flax. Peering about resentfully at the others, the fair-haired youth creeps

41

forward, crouches low over the woman, stumbles awkwardly back.

"Dead pissed, more like," he says, wrinkling his nose, staggering again to his feet.

Daring to bend nearer again, I too detect a whiff of stale alcohol. She's begun to snore very softly now, through wet, parted lips. Small wonder she seems so little harmed. The devil protects drunkards and fools.

"Beg pardon, Cap'n," Burley's soft, West Country voice tiptoes out to me from where the others have all regrouped, further down the beach. "Best be out on the tide."

Their unease reinforces my own. Time was, a solitary female might have feared ravishment at the hands of my crew, but those were not these men. Females are what they come back to the Neverland to escape.

But what now? I could leave her here to rot, that would be the sensible thing; this is Pan's domain, let him deal with her. But the boy is not usually so careless with his mothers. Far more likely she is part of some diabolical new game, a spy the boy hopes to plant aboard my ship, possibly to divide my men from each other. True, she scarcely looks like a temptress, dressed like a hoyden in breeches in a threepenny farce, but what else can it possibly mean? A woman in the Neverland! Nothing happens here without Pan's knowledge.

Peter doesn't know everything. Who said that? A voice out of a dream. I frown down again at the insensible creature. If she does not belong to Pan, how the devil has she broken through the sorcery that guards this place to come here? A way to break the enchantment; it's worth any risk to understand if such a thing is possible.

I order the men to make a sling from the loose tarp in the boat with which we covered Dodge. Nutter at one end, Burley at the other, they stretch it on the sand beside the slumbering woman, then back away, as if she might explode in their faces like a Spanish grenado. Let them fret. I will know why she is here. If she proves to be a pawn in some dreadful new game, I must find out what it is before Pan can claim another victory in blood.

***

The men are not happy to have her in the boat, concealed in the tarp in the bottom. They shrink to the ends of their thwarts as they pull out into the bay for the current to carry us back to the *Rouge*. I raise my spyglass and scan again for war canoes from the north, where the high plains of Indian Territory abut the boy's wood.

The Indians are not like me. They have long since made peace with the boy. The Pickaninnys, he calls them, a foolish name that sounds suitably aboriginal to his untested ear. What they call themselves in the oblique syllables of their own ancient tongue, I cannot say. Their battles with the boy are play; when he does not want them, they are free to tend their families, their corn, their buffalo and their ceremonies. To live, age and die. The Neverland is their refuge, not their prison, especially now that so many of the Wendys' stories tell of the destruction and enslavement of the Indian races. To preserve it, they go on the bloody warpath at the boy's pleasure against their common enemy: me.

But no dark canoes pepper the bay today. I twist round to sweep my glass northward one last time, before my view goes black, like a curtain rung down on a play.

"Hook!" bleats a shrill voice I know only too well. "What do you think you're doing out here?"

He's come upon us with the stealth of a fairy, flown up from behind my oarsmen while I was too distracted to sense the chill of his presence. Pan, our nemesis, the demon king of the Neverland, author of all our misery.

How little he's changed over time: a rag-mop of tawny hair, bright, feral grey eyes, still hovering on the youthful side of eleven or so, despite his wicked little baby teeth.

Vines of ivy cinch his middle over the napless pelt of some no longer recognizable animal. More vines twine from hip to shoulder for a bandolier where he stows his badges of office—his pipes, an ancient bear claw, a once proud raptor feather tattered with age and filth. His short sword is thrust through his belt, the knob of a knife handle protrudes from the top of one fur-skin boot as he circles in the air above the men, facing me. He appears to be entirely alone.

"Well, Hook," he cries again, "what game is this?"

Tension thrums among the men, staring up at this impossible vision, a boy riding the air currents overhead with the ease of an albatross. None have ever seen him so close-up before. Beneath the Pan, behind his sight line, I see Jesse's fingers inch off his oar, stretch toward his pistol. Something thrills in my blood, but prudence snuffs it out: no, not here, a misfire now will cost all their lives. I hastily signal him to halt in the act of raising my hand to tilt back my hat.

"No game," I tell Pan. "We are burying one of our shipmates,"

"I don't believe it." He frowns down at the suspicious canvas at our feet, buzzes closer to me. He takes special delight in punishing deceit. "We haven't even had a fight!"

"It was none of your doing," I begin, and instantly regret it as his keen expression clouds over. It's utter folly to suggest anything could happen in the Neverland beyond his command.

"I think you're trying to escape again!" he counters.

"Come, my bully, you know me better than that," I cozen him patiently. "Do you think me a fool?"

"I think you're a liar and a cheat," he sneers at me, with that maddening half-smile that is so often a prelude to death. "I think you're a *man!*"

Should he take it into his head to draw his sword, my men will be at a fearful disadvantage; there's buggering little room to maneuver in a boat, and we are vulnerable on the water. None of them can swim, I venture; for myself, I dread eternal life underwater above all things, forever at the mercy of monsters like the loreleis and the crocodile, eyes bulging, skin spongey, lungs forever bursting for want of air. I shake off the thought.

"You're up to something, Hook," Pan accuses, peering at me with combative intensity. "I can feel it!"

"We are a funeral party, nothing more," I say calmly, banishing all thoughts of the cargo we carry. I've learnt to think nothing, care for nothing, in his presence. But if he planted that woman in our path, why come all the way out here, alone, instead of bringing a formal war party of boys to the ship? That's the way it's always been.

Unless he doesn't know.

"But since you've come all this way, let's have a game," I add quickly, my fingers sliding into my coat pocket in search of one of the many objects I keep about my person to barter with the little magpie. I must turn this moment to my advantage before he can set his own rules. My fingers close round something smooth and hard, which I withdraw. Too late, I recognize the stiletto recently liberated from Dodge. It's folly to arm the boy with another weapon to use against us, but there's no time to find anything else. I stand carefully in the stern, leg braced against Burley's solid bulk, and Pan rises too, giving the men some breathing room.

"This blade says you can't give me true answers to three questions," I challenge Pan, holding the closed knife aloft. He's arrested in mid-air, watches with birdlike curiosity as I press the metal button to snap out the blade. Slowly, he bares his baby teeth and nods. "How many men in this boat?" I begin, hooking the knife closed again.

"Not enough to beat me!" the boy gloats.

True enough. Pan can't count past three, but neither does he lie. "Where are your boys?"

"I sent them to the Indians to learn how to scalp."

No shrieking has been heard on the water that would signal my men are their victims, back aboard the *Rouge*. Surely Pan would not be here, missing all the fun, if they were. In any case, his wild pack of boys will not attack without their leader. But I must gather my wits; an extra question out of turn will forfeit the game. I revolve the prize in my fingers. I'll not to let it go without something of value in return, if I can play one audacious trump without tipping my own hand.

"For what reason would you ever bring a grown-up woman into the Neverland?"

"That's a stupid question!" snorts Pan.

"And that is no answer," I shrug, and begin to lower the weapon.

"I never would! Never, ever!" he shouts indignantly. "No grown-ups allowed in the Neverland, especially no lady! I would never let one come here, and nobody else better, either," he adds with a furious glare. "That's the truth!" And he swoops down to snatch the weapon out of my grasp. "I win again, Hoo—"

But Nutter springs up, all yowling impulse and no strategy at all, his giant fingers closing round one of Pan's mangy boots, and for an instant Pan flails sideways in the air.

"No fair!" the boy shouts. Like all tyrants, he believes he himself always acts with the utmost fairness. Then up he goes in a detonation of fiery sparks, a reek of brimstone, and a shrill cacophony of fairy language, leaving Nutter grasping empty air, and the boat near scuttled beneath us.

"Hey!" Pan cries in irritation from high above us. "Kes!"

Of course his imp is nearby. I throw mysef over Nutter to shield him from the inevitable retaliation, glancing up just as a dazzling flash scorches my eyes. Amid the frenzy of shouting men and harsh fairy noise, hands I cannot see pry me off Nutter and grapple me back to my seat in the reeling boat.

"Nothing happens in the Neverland unless I say so!" Pan's voice shouts from his magical updraft. "Don't you forget it, Hook!"

Then nothing but grumbling men and water lapping against our boat. Whatever the fairy threw in my eyes burns there still, although I presume it will not last; fairy spells, like all their humors, are fleeting. But she'd already bustled the boy out of harm's way, was it necessary to half-blind me into the bargain? The wooden thwart rocks beneath me as the men fight to steady the boat, grunt at their creaking oars. Their acrid man-sweat mingles with the pungency of brine and salt and fish off the water. But the menace I felt in my bones when the boy was about has subsided.

"Gone, Cap'n." It's Flax's voice, directly across from me, clotted with incredulity. It's always a shock, the first time they actually see an aviating boy.

"Sorry, Cap'n, I couldn't get a clear shot," Jesse apologizes.

"Almost had the little wanker," grumbles Nutter.

At least they still have breath to voice their defiance. No more lives were lost today, and all I had to forfeit was my sight. I might almost count it a victory. To say nothing of the information I gleaned from the boy. No grown-up women allowed? He could not have been more vehement on that point.

If Pan didn't bring her here, who did?

CHAPTER 6

PERISH

"It'll have to be up front, Cap'n,' mutters Sticks, my carpenter.

"The foredeck?" I echo, peering at him in the gloom belowdecks. "It's no use to me there. Why not build it where I mean to use it, on the quarterdeck?"

I am deep in the hold in my shirtsleeves as Sticks and I inspect the store of timber we keep on board for building shields. The imp's spiteful charm has worn off over the course of the day, but my vision is still tender in dark places, and for close work, I must resort to a pair of gold-rimmed spectacles I keep about me these days, left behind by a former crewman who needs them no more. Squinting through them now, I frown at what I see. Our shields are primitive wooden devices that offer my men some protection against airborne blades and arrows in hand-to-hand combat, but these staves are short, to be nailed onto a frame and carried. I've something more substantial in mind for this new barricade, a shelter from which to deploy a long-range weapon, wielded by a skilled marksman.

Sticks scratches at the top of his pink pate, where the hairline has begun its retreat, twirls at the stubby yellow pencil behind his ear. "No room t'set up my table and tools," he shrugs at me.

The fellow was certainly in some sort of building trade back in the world. He's learnt he has nothing to fear from me so long as he speaks sense; I am not unfamiliar with the carpentry trade myself, and he knows it. And in this case, I know he is right. I had my quarterdeck severely chopped for faster sailing, back when the *Rouge* could still call herself a sailing vessel; there's scarcely room there now for more than my daily pacing. Then too, action on board the *Rouge* always occurs forward, where Long Tom is stationed, or in the waist. It may indeed be best to erect this new battlement in the bows, should any imps or flying boys come snooping about, to conceal our purpose of launching an attack from the rear.

"We can build 'em in sections," Sticks offers.

"Hinged together," I agree, absently pushing the spectacles up my nose. "Lightweight, for easy transport later. Excellent. Make your preparations."

He stops playing with his pencil, ducks his head slightly. "Aye, Cap'n," he murmurs, and turns away to tot up what he'll need.

Wan daylight seeping in from the hatch provides the only illumination as I slide off my spectacles and fold them into my hand. Heading for the hatchway, I step gingerly through rank bilgewater, round the shadowy shapes of casks, crates, and forgotten ancient plunder that's served as ballast for centuries. I near leap out of my skin when one of the shadows presumes to speak.

"Cap'n? Fink I could 'ave a word?"

"Yes, Filcher?" I command myself to resume breathing. He's scarce more than a wraithlike silhouette in the gloom.

"Well, you always want to know wot's going on below decks, like," my first mate reminds me.

I nod. That is the chief commission of his office, one to which his life of petty crime has made him particularly well suited.

49

He fidgets with a wisp of his limp, straw-colored hair. "Well, it's the lads. They fink we 'adn't oughter 'ave 'er aboard, Cap'n."

"Ah." The men have been restive on this point all day, ever since I had the woman stowed in one of the smaller cabins adjacent to mine, where a great litter of empty bottles, spare cordage, fouled, moldy canvas and the Devil only knows what other disgusting flotsam have been abandoned for centuries. At present, she is still too stuporous to tell me anything, but I can wait. We've nothing but time in the Neverland.

"Fink it's bad luck, like," Filcher goes on, uneasily. "A Jonah."

So it always is in the stories, whenever a Wendy is brought on board as a hostage, else how would these lubbers even know the word? "On what grounds?" I prompt him carefully.

"No women allowed," he reminds me. "We all 'eard the little brat. She opened all our traps. And what about Dodge?"

"Dodge?" I frown at him. "Are they saying—"

"Nobody's saying nuffink, Cap'n," Filcher rejoins quickly. "But Dodge were pretty sharp up in the, um, you know..."

"Yards," I remind him patiently.

"Yeah, and the ropes 'n' all."

"And he were pretty drunk," I point out.

"I'n'it odd, though, that she shows up the very day we lose Dodge?" Filcher persists, with an emphatic nod.

I fail to see this connection, exactly, but I know how idle minds crave a scapegoat for all their ills.

"And them bleedin' drums last night."

This is a point worth taking. Should there be some new game in play, the Indians might well be involved. Was their infernal drumming a warning meant to cow us, or a rehearsal for victory meant to mock us? But there is no one among my

50

crew to whom I might unburden myself of these thoughts. They must be led or they will be twice as vulnerable.

"Mr. Filcher, " and I drop my voice to a low, conspiratorial tone, "do not imagine for one moment that Hook does not have a reason for everything he does. This woman may harbor information we can use against the boys, something that could save our lives. You would oblige me by telling the men that for all our sakes, she's not to be harassed or provoked until I get it out of her."

"Aye, aye, Cap'n," Filcher agrees, perkier now to think he's privy to an important confidence, and he melts back into the shadows.

If this woman is a chit in some hideous new game, I will know it soon enough. But if she is here in spite of Pan's wishes, that too is worth knowing. If the boy's power over all in this place is not absolute, if there is a chink in his glamorous amour, I must be prepared to bend events to my advantage. To seize my chance.

***

The tinkling of a tiny bell.
Don't be afraid.
An unseen companion almost near enough to touch.
There is always a way out. Take my hand.
And there in the darkness, a fleeting smile in a face I still can't see, yet warmth floods into my blood, and I am on board a ship sailing straight into the sky, under a blood-red moon, over a dark sea that sparkles like stars, and I am rising with it, surging toward something wonderful. Yes. Please. Sail me all the way this time...

The dull thud of my hook against the bedpost rattles me awake, as if I were attempting to flap into the air like some deluded albatross, and I sink back into the bedclothes, disoriented, aching. Betrayed, yet again by my infuriating dream. More real than ever tonight, and thrice as terrible, beguiling me with a ghostly smile. A lamp burns on the bedside table, next to another bottle my steward must have brought in whilst I slept. My stomach churns at the very thought. Wine is no proof against dreaming.

Children find the Neverland in their dreams; their longing bores through the barrier between their world and this one, and in they tumble. My men, too, return in this way. For ages I deluded myself it must be possible to dream a way out. But my dreams were coy and would not come at all, or else plagued me with dark and muddled shades of my old world, bitter memories to which I have no desire to return—my heedless youth, the cruel circumstances by which I turned to piracy, the sorcery that brought me here. Or else I dreamt visions of appalling violence, cities in ruins, fire raining down from the sky. These are my dreams: savage nightmare or mocking torment, a phantom ship that never quite bears me away.

I stagger up from my bed, and a length of silk rustles over the side in my wake, a waterfall of peacock, gold and burgundy that glistens in the firelight, puddling at my feet. It's still dark night out my stern windows. I turn to my ancient sea chest at the foot of my bed, the deck cold against me bare feet, my linen shirt sweat-drenched and reeking, throw back the lid of my chest and fall to my knees before it. My shoulder aches inside my harness as I hook aside more shirts and cravats, braided breeches of ancient vintage, my fingers probing the mustiest hidden crevices of the chest for any packet I might once have squirreled away and forgotten.

But my medicines are long gone.

They always bring him medicine, the Wendys, hoping to control him in the way parents have hoped to control their children for centuries. In my day, a pot of gin did for the little whelps, but medicines have grown more subtle since then, more dark and alluring. I have tried them all. They never can control the Pan, of course, and even though the Wendys leave their medicines behind when they leave him, he soon forgets the promises he made them. I suppose one day he comes upon the bottle or packet or cunning little jar gathering dust on his shelf and can't recall what it's for; more often than not, he pitches it over the cliff onto my beach. That is where I find them.

The black drops are the best, lazy in the mind and sweet with forgetfulness. Aches and pains wash away, along with cares, worries, anger, despair. Nothing hurts any more. Nothing matters. My sleep is sound and dreamless. Time is beguiled; for a few hours, I can be content. It was a very great pity to me when the drops fell out of fashion. Later medicines have been foul in the nose, vile on the tongue, and unsettling to the bowels, causing more anxiety than they relieve. More recently I've found hard little pills that spark in me a false brittle cheerfulness and make my head pound, as if there were too much sun and I could not shut my eyes. Others make me dense and sluggardly. Wool fills my brain and the air around me turns to treacle. I care little enough for the pills, but I'd gladly swallow a hogshead of them this minute, could I find any.

I slam shut the lid of my chest and sway up by the bedpost as an idea glimmers, wraith-like, in my brain. The woman. The mother. Perhaps she's brought medicine for the boys. I hook up the lantern by its ring and stagger out into the passage.

It's still as a tomb inside the dark little cabin, and it stinks of the mold of centuries. Lamp hanging from my hook, I halt in the doorway until its jittery light washes over her plaid garment, tossed over the foot of the makeshift bunk. Ignoring the lump in the bedclothes where she lies, I stalk the few steps across that narrow space, flatten my hand over her coat. Some woolen stuff it is, nappy under my fingers as I pat it for hidden recesses. From one square pocket, I withdraw a small circlet of some dark, tarnished metal that might have

53

once been silver, tiny ornaments of a nautical character— a seahorse, a dolphin, a miniscule sailboat, a tiny bell that has lost its clapper, as I notice when I shake it, but none large enough to conceal even a grain of powder, and so I thrust it back in its pocket. I flip the thing over, feel along the satiny lining, but discover no other bulges, no ridges, not so much as a single friendly drop.

"What are you doing?"

Her voice cleaves the shadows and I jerk up my hook to widen the dim pool of light to where she is, propped up on one elbow in the furthest corner of the bunk, wide eyes on me.

"That is no concern of yours," I rumble, releasing her useless coat with an angry flourish.

"I don't have any money," she persists, sitting up by inches, her back pressing into the corner.

"Your money is no use to me," I spit back. How dare she take me for someone like Filcher, a common thief? Yet how must I look to her, shirt askew, hair unbound, my hook in the shadows above the circle of light.

"Who are you?" she asks.

"Who are you, Woman?" I parry. "That is the question."

Her eyes are dark and steady in the dim room, where all else seems to pitch with the swaying light. "I'm called Perish."

The light trembles under my hook, cold shock jolting through my bones. Perish. Has my savior come at last, formed like a woman? Who else can it be? He whose name is Legion: bone-crusher, blood-drinker, life-taker. Reaper. Ravager. Ruin. Perish. Almighty Death, the only god to whom I've prayed in two hundred years.

Is that why I had the dream again tonight? This must be the chance I am meant to seize, could I but find voice to respond.

"Have you come for me?"

CHAPTER 7

MAKE BELIEVE

Have I cursed Death in my drunken belligerence?

"No," she said, "I don't think so," she said, and I heard myself refused again, mocked again, cheated out of my reward yet again. I had no more sense than to reel out of her cabin, damning her for her mockery.

But now, in the bleak, cold light of daybreak, I realize it must have been a test, some formal exchange I was too witless to perceive in my rage. What else can it mean, a woman in the Neverland, but a chance extended to me at last? Now I can only pray it is not too late, that I can yet fulfill whatever is required by this Angel of Death. Perhaps she didn't even know me last night, mistook me for some other ruffian in my crew.

I rouse Brassy, my steward, as the first grey tentacles of dawn slither up over the island. I call for a pot of his vile brew, and a bucket of cold water in which to dunk my head and brace up my wits.

"Has my guest been seen to?" I demand, wringing out my hair.

Brassy pauses at the row of my hats hanging on their pegs beneath the stern window, caught in the act of selecting my pink-feathered tricorne to lay out beside my canary breeches. Did I leave it to my steward, I'd be dressed like a clown at Bartholomew Fair. He eyes me with more than his customary uncertainty.

"Food? Drink?" I elaborate. Death may not consume mortal food, but for form's sake, I must offer hospitality.

"No, Captain. No one told us to feed her."

This is a canto from Spenser, coming from my monosyllabic steward. "Have Cookie stew a decent piece of fish and take it in with a bottle of my best madeira and my compliments," I instruct him, sending him off.

Turning to my wardrobe, I select dark breeches, white hose, a lawn shirt with a waterfall of French lace at the throat. My ceremonial scarlet coat, braided in gold, my grandest bucket-cuff boots, and a black velvet ribbon to tie back my hair. Elegant hats have always been my most shameless indulgence, and I choose my most impressive, indigo, upswept on one side, its wide brim boiling over with fat ribbons of scarlet and gold. I mean to impress. This time, my savior will know me.

***

She's perched on the bunk, one leg tucked up immodestly beneath her, the other outthrust, a bare toe peeping out from the ridiculous slipper beneath her trouser leg, her shirt tails hanging out. She scoots forward as I sweep open the door, but freezes there when I display myself in all my finery, hat cocked at a rakish angle, my fine French cutlass at my side, hand fisted at my hip, hook tilted slightly upward. Her eyes dilate like a cat's in the dark; they seem to fill her entire face.

"Bloody hell," she exclaims.

Eons of practice have taught me to keep a grip on my composure. "Welcome to my ship."

Her dark, wary eyes move to my upraised appendage. Slowly, slowly, she inclines her head.

"Captain Hook."

"At your command," I reply with elaborate politesse, as I decide how best to play her. If I am recognized as the scoundrel who affronted her last night, she does not show it. At the last moment I remember to sweep off my hat and make a leg like a courtier in a Italian comedy. My manners are as rusty as the corroding hull over which I stand, but I've never needed them more. Her eyes remain fixed on me. Only a few token pins still cling to her dark hair; the rest is loose, wavy, bouncing just above her shoulders. "To what do I owe this great honor?" I prompt her delicately.

She remains utterly still but for her keen, roving eyes. Savior or not, I don't care for the impudent way she's staring at me, her gaze traveling up and down my finery, plume to boots and back again, as if I were a dish of flummery. No, I don't care for it at all.

Then her mouth tilts upward. "Oh, I must be dreaming!" she titters, shaking her head. "That's it! You've had dreams before, old girl, but this is a real doozy!"

Death dares to mock me again, his faithful servant for all these years? I am outraged, advance another step into the cabin, and the charge of my anger crackles across to her. In an instant, her expression deflates, her fingers clutch at the bedclothes.

"Good God," she breathes. "You're real. I thought you were...make-believe."

"I am as real as daylight," I assure her, stepping into the sunny rectangle leaking in through the skylight over her bunk.

"But—aren't you supposed to be dead?" she blurts.

Breath catches in my throat as phantom hope races through my blood, and I step closer, all anger forgotten. "By all the laws of justice and reason, yes," I whisper.

She stares at me, lips slightly parted. One hand flutters upward in a small, impulsive gesture. And as my own gaze drops in humility and gratitude for that imminent benediction that will end my suffering forever, I spy an old bailing bucket, warped and wormy, on the deck at the base of the bunk. A pungent stench distinct from all the other odors of decay and neglect in the cabin arranges itself in my nostrils: human waste. And hope curdles within me. Even were Death's minion to partake of a convivial meal for form's sake, why subject herself to the lowly business of voiding it?

Whatever she is, she follows my gaze. "I beg your pardon, Captain," she begins carefully. "I'm...sorry for the mess, I couldn't get outside. I found a bucket over there." Her hand waves vaguely toward the debris still cluttering the far corner of the cabin. "I had to empty it out," the reckless creature babbles on, indicating a little pile of objects heaped on the foot of her bunk. "I didn't know where I was, or what I was sup—"

"Silence. Woman." Shamed that she has seen me so exposed, I ward off further scrutiny with terse words "Your name, Madam."

"Perish."

"Liar!"

She jumps where she sits, fingers braced against the wall. "That's my name. Like a church district, but with two—"

"I can spell," I grimace. Parrish. Wine alone deluded me last night. She is something far less kindly than Death, and more terrible, a grown woman of unknown provenance aboard my ship. I've given too much ground already, come in as an abject supplicant, not the wily gamesman I must be to gain the advantage. "Who are you, Madam Parrish," I begin again. "Where are you from?"

She eyes me cautiosly. "Name, rank, and serial number, eh?" she murmurs. "Well, last thing I knew, I was in London."

Of course, that's where he always goes to round up new confederates, although I should have expected the sun to rise in the west before he would ever ally himself to a grown-up, especially a woman. Noticing the bottle of excellent madeira I sent in to her, of which she has sampled less than would sustain a gnat, I affect a congenial tone. "I fear my hospitality does not agree with you?"

Her gaze follows mine to the bottle. "It's a little early in the day, even for me," she says tartly. "You wouldn't happen to have any strong, black coffee, would you?"

"I might," and I raise my hook to scratch thoughtfully at my beard, "would you consider answering my questions."

She peers at us both, my hook and myself, her expression unreadable. Then her mouth tilts up again. "Oh, all right, then, who are you really? Did Freddie Grange put you up to this? I swear, I'll throttle that—"

"I am Captain Hook. This is my ship. And you are a long, long way from London."

This silences her again, and I press my advantage. "We are not at war with his mothers, Madam. I seek only to know your business in the Neverland."

This last word has an extraordinary effect. At last, she wrenches her gaze away from me, scans all about the cabin as if for the first time, takes in the deck beams above, the junk heap of reeking, salt-corroded nautical gear in the corner, slides tentative fingertips along the ancient, wormy bulwark to which her bunk is fastened, peers out through the skylight, where nothing much can be glimpsed but a bit of spar and sail and boy-blue sky beyond. Avid for every detail, her gaze travels down to the unprepossessing objects she's piled at the foot of the bunk: the remains of a tallow candle stub, a couple of French ecus, a small, tarnished silver bell with a tall handle, the kind a fancy fellow might use to summon his servant, relics perhaps dating all the way back to the original captain of this vessel. The sorts of things some crewman might have taken for valuables and stowed away in a handy bucket generations ago. "It's all real," she whispers, as if to herself. "Oh my God." She turns back eagerly to me. "But where are the children? I thought there would be children."

"Is that why you were in the wood?"

If possible, her eyes go even rounder. "I was in a wood? I thought that was a dream!" She shoves a hand back through her unruly hair, dislodging a few more pins. "God, I must've really tied one on," she murmurs to herself. Then she frowns again at me. "Then what am I doing here?"

"My question exactly," I sigh.

"I mean here, on board your ship," she counters, in some agitation. "I'm supoposed to be out there. In the Neverland."

"For what reason?"

"Because something called me here! Something I couldn't resist."

"The boy?"

"No! No, it wasn't Peter," she says hastily. Peter, she calls him, like one of the doting Wendys. "I know that much." She retreats somewhat from our engagement, eyes shifting about more cautiously. Her fingers pluck up the silver bell at the foot of her bunk, from which she shakes a nervous little peal. "Tinker Bell, perhaps?"

I shrug off this name out of the storybooks; all the wretched imps are one to me. "Then who brought you here?"

She shakes her head. "You tell me. I went to sleep in London, on a perfectly ordinary spring night in 1950, and I woke up here. That's all I know."

"Only the boy knows the way," I point out quietly. "Please consider the matter very carefully before you lie to me again."

She straightens, frowning, alert. Unable to resist a moment of pure theatricality, I add, "You've heard of the plank?" As if any pirate ever bothered with a plank; chucking a fellow overboard was good enough in my day.

But the woman laughs. Laughs! No nervous titter this time, but a sarcastic yip worthy of a dockside harlot. "Oh, surely not, Captain! No pirate has ever walked the plank in the history of the world! It's complete fiction!"

Devil bugger me! Most folk are eager enough to swallow that lie. My new men are always disappointed to find no such object aboard the *Rouge*. "I do not speak of *pirates* walking the plank," I point out icily.

She swallows her hysterical mirth, peers at me again, shakes her head. "I can't believe I'm having this conversation with a fictional character."

"Believe what you like," I begin, "but we are at war—"

"What? I'm not at war with anyone!" she cries.

"All of Neverland is at war, and that is not make-believe either."

"No" she exclaims. "This is a fairyland for children!"

"Confess your business, and perhaps I can ransom you without bloodshed," I press on, pleased to have needled out her weakness at last.

"Oh, God, this is crazy," she wails, shoving back her hair. "Men and their stupid wars! You can't ransom me; nobody cares about me. Peter doesn't even know I'm here. I'll leave, I don't care, but don't hurt him!"

Spare him, Captain. Take me instead. I've heard it a thousand times in the pirate trade, a crescendo of pleading that fouls my dreams still. It's always mercy they want. As if anyone ever showed mercy to me.

" I don't want to make any trouble," Parrish babbles on. "Please, Captain. Send me back."

I can only freeze, breath suspended, for what she might say next, the charm, the sorcery that would make such a thing possible. Back. To London. Out of the Neverland.

" Whatever it is you want of me, Captain, whatever your price, take it, get it over with, and let me get out of here!"

"You think I know the way out?" I bluster. "God's bowels, would I still be here if I did?"

A dropped bucket clunks and rattles above, followed by a collective rumbling of unease, from which I pick out a single word.

"Fairy."

The woman hears it too, stares again at me. "Oh my God—"

"Stay where you are!" I order, glancing again at the skylight. If Pan is searching for his lost mother, I can't have her discovered aboard my ship, and I step out into the companionway, pulling the door shut behind me.

But a tiny fizz of light is already spiraling down the aft hatch, flitting toward me in the gloom of the passage. The faces of my men are crowding into the hatchway to watch, and I step boldly forward to greet the creature, concealing my trepidation. I suppose she's female; the ones in thrall to the boy always are.

"Madam," I hail her, as if I disport with fairies every day. Best not let on to my men what a rarity it is, a fairy on board the *Rouge* to parley with the pirates. We are sworn enemies, her tribe and mine, but nothing is the same in the Neverland today. The light pauses in the air above me. "How may I be of service?" I raise my arms, so she can see I make no move toward my sword. As if our clumsy weapons are any use against the imps.

She darts down at me, and such high, discordant chiming fills my head that my mind closes instinctively against it; I back away, struggling not to cringe from her blistering assault. The imp veers suddenly off toward the shadowy gun deck, an indigo blur trailing light and harsh, tinny noise; she comes about just as swiftly, speeds past me in the direction from which I've just come, but as I pivot about, the passage goes dark and quiet. In the sudden gloom, it takes a moment for my eyes to recognize an outline of pale light as the gap of Parrish's cabin door, lit dimly from within by the skylight.

I shove into the cabin, and the imp bolts straight back from the door until her tiny wings are humming against the skylight. I slam the door shut behind me, revealing Parrish braced against the wall on its other side, staring after the fairy. Stooping between the deck beams, I lunge for the bunk to hook up Parrish's plaid jacket, stretch it like a net between hook and hand, and feint toward the imp, still beating her wings at the skylight. She can only be a spy for Pan; why else has she come? If she gets free to tell him what she's found, my men will pay with their lives. It will be another massacre. My first swipe just misses; I hear alarm in her frantic noise as she skitters sideways. Swooping the garment toward her again, I trip on the feculent bucket and she flies over my head to the other side of the room.

By the door, Parrish stares into the imp's glimmering light, lips forming words, fingers touching the latch. Is she bewitched? Parrish pulls the door open a crack and the fairy light shoots out. I race after it, but there's naught in the dim passage but a trail of sparks and a lingering odor of sulfur and allspice. I scarcely know what I roar in my fury, but someone bleats from above that the fairy is gone.

Hurling the plaid across the room, I glare at the woman. "Are you mad?" I rage, shoving her against the wall with my hand, pinning her there between my hand and my hook.

"Well, what harm could she do you?" she cries. "You're a hundred times her size!"

"Fairy power has nothing to do with size," I retort. "She belongs to the Pan, and Pan is the enemy."

She stares at me. "He's only a boy."

I stare back, my face only inches from hers, my phantom hand itching to strike. "Your precious boy will come looking for you, now his fairy knows you're here. There'll be a fight," I add maliciously.

"You were trying to kill her!" the blasted woman persists.

"I wanted to talk to her."

"She was talking!" Parrish exclaims. "Didn't you hear her?"

"Madam, if your fairy confederate—"

"*My* confederate? What do I look like, Titania, the goddamned fairy queen? She came here to see you!"

My jaw all but unhinges at this delusion. "What?"

"She came because she heard the bell," Parrish elaborates. "She said she had a message for you."

I back away, struggling to lace her insane words into coherent meaning.

"She said, 'This is your last chance,'" Parrish insists. "That's what she wanted me to tell you."

What madness is this? "Meaning what?" I demand.

"I don't know! I just got here."

She must be in league with the boys after all, if the imps speak to her. And then another awful possibility wavers into my brain: that she's telling the truth, that she's only an ignorant intruder who's just allowed the one ceature in the Neverland who might have explained my phantom chance to escape.

"Stupid, stupid woman!" I cry, and storm out of the cabin, locking the door behind me.

I should know by now to expect nothing but treachery from a woman.

CHAPTER 8

LONDON, 1709: CAROLINE

Up in London, great things were expected of me in the marriage trade. I'd have gladly delayed this venture indefinitely, but my father threatened to stop my allowance if I did not take a suitable bride, and I knew I should not long be welcome in the society of my friends could I not pay my own way. So, in short order, I was promised to the daughter of an aristocratic family all too eager to trade away their distinguished name for a share of my father's money. Caroline was small and fair and easy to charm, and I daresay she found my person not entirely disagreeable. I wooed her with music, and flowers, and poesy, and she was easily won, the artless young thing. For my part, I was charmed by the idea of romance. Sweet, timid, pretty, obedient Caroline; surely I could learn to care for her in time.

But as buoyed as I was by my prospects in the word as a gentleman of means with a titled wife, and as eager to discharge my duty to my father, matrimony seemed a dull thing next to the adventures of youth. There was something yet astir in me that a quiet life of ease with the pliable Caroline could not quench, a desire to achieve something worthy on my own account, beyond my father's fortune. We were ever at war with France in those days, over some foolery or other, and I thought brave action against the French might become the ship to the stars I'd sought from boyhood, a means of securing my reputation. So we postponed our nuptials for one year. I told Caroline I was going to manage the sugar estate my father had purchased on the island of Jamaica in the Indies, to better learn the business.

"A kiss to seal our bargain," I begged her on the eve of my departure.

"Oh, sir, I cannot."

"Nay 'sir'; I am your betrothed," I rebuked her gently. She colored prettily. "Jamie, then. But I dare not."

"A kiss, a nothing, a mere trifle," I persisted.

"Then should it not betoken a trifling sort of love?" she dared to riposte. "Our Savior was betrayed by a kiss."

She could not know how her words unnerved me; I claimed my token with more force and less joy than I'd anticipated, and she was too mild to protest. Or too shamed, or perhaps she enjoyed it too immodestly. I would never know. Poor little chit, I believe we might have loved each other in earnest, had I stayed with her. How much misery might have been avoided if only I had. Why didn't she make me stay?

But I was all hot blood and foolish youth in those days, eager to cover myself with glory in the world. And what a grand thing it seemed, to go to war! I fitted out one of my father's ships and got a privateering commission out of Kingston to harass the French. I captured many ships and put aside the profit against such time as I would set up as a gentleman with my bride.

Back in port after one such successful sortie, I learned from my father's agent that my mother was gravely ill back in Bristol, that she had been asking for me. But my crew and I had intelligence of a train of French supply ships heading out within the week, and an expectation of our greatest, most profitable victory yet, so I stifled the pain in my heart over my mother's welfare and made the choice to lead one more cruise of prey. I'd return to her in triumph, I told myself; would that not be the best possible tonic? Surely she would wait for me.

But the supply ships were more heavily guarded than we anticipated, and the battle turned against us. I was taken captive and imprisoned in a crumbling stone fortress on one of the French islands. I've heard that captured military officers are well-treated in enemy prisons if they are gentlemen of noble birth. Their families may pay a sizeable ransom for them, or perhaps their captors expect to encounter them again one day on a diplomatic mission or at the gaming tables when the hostilities are over. But my family was in trade, my commission not strictly military. My captors cared little for my good opinion. And as undermanned as the place was out in that island backwater, they had little enough time or supplies to spare for the decent maintenance of the prisoners.

It was a dark, dank place, damp in all seasons and sweltering hot through most of the year, although sunlight rarely penetrated to the cellar where I was shut up. I was kept separate from the other English prisoners for fear I would rally them to foolish heroics, and the French prisoners were all in use in the war. Some Englishmen too, I believe, were permitted to work off their parole in servitude on French plantations. But not me. I'd made off with too many of their ships, mocked them with too much bravado. I was shut away in the dark, and little more notice was taken of me.

My outrage, my sense of injustice soon enough gave way to the more pressing concern of my starving belly. Rations could not always be spared for the prisoners, and I took to feasting on the straw in my cell, if that were all I could find, or, on one or two grim occasions, whatever burrowed within it. Dining on rats does little for the digestion, much less the disposition, but it kept me alive in that hellish place. That and my dreams of Caroline, a goddess of mercy and devotion grown to Titanic proportions in the desperation of memory. How she would welcome me home, succor me, heal me. I came to regret squandering my youth in empty bluster and braggadocio. I set myself to recalling all the many ways I knew how to please a woman; should I survive, I vowed I would devote the rest of my life to earning my Caroline's love. It was all that kept me sane.

In that condition I was left to fester for an eternity, as I reckoned it then, until a tenuous peace was once more declared, when I was released sans ship, crew or fortune. I was scarcely more than a rat myself by then, hair and beard long, filthy and unkempt, my fine clothing in rags. I worked as a common seaman for my passage back to Jamaica, a grimy hammock slung before the mast a dream of luxury after my long confinement.

***

"But my father owns the place," I tried to explain, yet again, to the carter. He was a surly-looking white fellow, a bookkeeper, perhaps, or assistant overseer off some struggling plantation, no doubt miffed that he had to drive the team all the way into town, like a slave. I could see he took me for a beggar, and who could blame him? Stooped, cramped, and exhausted from the ship, sweltering in the midsummer heat, I'd arrived in Kingston dressed in tatterted seaman's slops, the few meagre coins of my pay jangling forlornly in my shirt. Dusk was falling, and my father's warehouse was shut up for the night. Oddly, there was a sign in the window that said "Murchison," but that was the least of my concerns, at the moment; I couldn't pay for a hired horse, and I doubted my aching legs would bear me all the way to St. Elizabeth Parish on foot.

"Eden Estate, in St. Elizabeth's," I told the carter.

"That's too far away," he grumbled.

"My father will pay you something extra for your trouble," I promised. "I'm James Hoo—"

"Young Mistah James?" A strapping black youth, dressed like a dock worker, had paused in the street, eyeing me. I didn't know him, but there was something familiar about the eyes, even as they rounded to look on me.

"It is you," he exclaimed. "I used to sweep out your daddy's warehouse."

I peered at him, trying to bore through the fog in my brain. "Why...Thomas?" I was rewarded with a smile that revealed a distinctive gap between his front teeth. "Thomas!" I exclaimed. "You're a man grown!" By God's blood, how long had I been away?

"You used to bring me cane," the fellow grinned.

"You remember me?" I cried, relief like the purest spirits pumping through my blood. My trials at an end, at long last. He knew me!

But his expression sobered even as he moved close enough to slide a surreptitious hand under my elbow and steer me ever so slightly away from the suspicious-looking carter. "Let's you an' me take a walk, Mistah James," he whispered.

There were many as would think it an affront to have their person touched by a black man in public, but I craved human contact after my long isolation and was grateful for his support, besides. I let him guide me down the road through lengthening shadows, across a planked walkway and into a sour-smelling grog shop populated by waterfront types like himself: haulers, loaders, porters, along with a few white mariners off the ships in the harbor. He sat me down on a bench deep in the shadows in the back of the room, went off to the counterman, and presently returned with a couple of jacks of spruce beer. The first long draught settled my nerves somewhat and improved my humor immensely.

"Thomas," I began, "I've got to get up to Eden. Can you help—"

But he was shaking his head. "Oh you dasn't go there, Mistah James."

"What? Why not?"

"The island militia post a guard at that place, in case you turn up. They clap you in the guardhouse for true."

I was too astonished to speak. With an apologetic glance, Thomas drew a paper out of his shirt and handed it to me. I squinted at it in the dim light; it was some sort of handbill. Across the top was printed, *Proclamation by Lord Hamilton, Governor of Jamaica. 18 November, 1712*. In the center was a crude engraving of a smug, fatuous-looking popinjay in a fancy hat, sculpted goatee, and a great foaming of neck lace, above the legend: *Reward offered for James. B. Hookbridge, for the Crime of Piracy and High Treason against Her Majesty's Ships, Kingston, Jamaica. Dead or Alive.*

I stared again at Thomas. My tongue had turned to dust.

"I snatch it off the wall when the tapster not looking," Thomas murmured. "But the same one posted in every shop in town."

"But it's not true!" I exclaimed.

"Best keep your voice down," Thomas urged me, glancing quickly about the room, then moving closer. "We heard the charge laid against you up in London, oh, a year ago, it must be now. Some fellows here in Kingston swore against you in the Court House 'round Christmas, and them bills been up ever since."

"What fellows?" I demanded, reaching automatically for a sword long since taken off me. "By God's bollocks, I will know who perjured himself to see me hang!"

"Hssst!" warned Thomas again. "Them no-count fellows of no consequence." He pressed his lips together in an instant of hesitation, sighed, and plunged on. "It was Mistah Ryland laid the charge against you."

"Harry Ryland?" I gaped at him. Thomas nodded. Harry Ryland, an ambitious young master's mate on one of my father's trading ships, eager for adventure. I'd made him my first lieutenant in the privateering trade, my closest confidant, the one I trusted to captain prize ships back to Kingston in my stead. We were friends.

"Where is he?" I asked Thomas. "I need to—"

But Thomas was already shaking his head again. "Gone, Mistah James. Retired to London after we heard you was captured. They say he become a wealthy gentleman."

"On my profit," I muttered, as the awful symmetry of the thing began to occur to me. How much had he put away on his own account over the years? All of it? There must have been plenty to pay others to give false evidence against me. But I was not about to roll over like a whipped dog and let him make off with everything I'd worked for, dreamt of, for so long. "Listen, Thomas, I need to send word to my father. Is there anyone you know up at Eden—"

"Murchison's," he said quietly. "That's what they call it now." Murchison's, the strange name on the sign I'd seen on my father's locked warehouse. "It's not your daddy's place any more."

"Since when?" I bristled.

"Since it fall in the hands of the overseer." Thomas shook his head sadly. "Your daddy's dead, Mistah James."

A chill racketed through my bones worse than any I'd felt in all those years in prison. My father could not be dead! That enormous, infuriating presence that had shadowed my entire life, not dead, not gone. Not yet! I still had so much to prove to him. What was the use of all my grand plans to reform myself, to give up the follies of youth and become a man of worth and substance in the world, if he were not here to see it? My father gone to his grave, never knowing the man I was inside? Now he could never, ever forgive me.

"I'm sorry, Mistah James," Thomas murmured. "You was always good to me. I thought you should know. It happened last winter. We was all let go at the warehouse. I load boats now on the docks."

I nodded mutely. "My mother?" I whispered at last, but Thomas only shook his head again.

I closed my eyes in that shadowy place to collect and focus my wits. An orphan I may have become, but as long as I had breath and life and spirit, I could regain what was rightfully mine. I hadn't a sou to call my own here in Kingston, but I was still my father's heir. I was Caroline's betrothed. That thought heartened me above all others, and I rallied myself. For her sake, I would persevere.

"Thank you, Thomas," I began. "I won't forget your kindness now that I'm back—"

"No, Mistah James, you can't be back," he hissed at me. "You can't tell anybody who you are; it's Gallow's Point if you do…"

Of course, I had no means to prove my innocence; my commission had been taken off me long ago, and there was nothing in my appearance, nor indeed, my reputation, to belie the foul charge against me.

"Well, then, I'll go to London," I counter. "Lots of people know me there." I had friends among the peerage who would help me; no one who had ever really known me would ever believe such calumny of me. Caroline would never believe it! I could work my passage back to England, back to my Caroline—

"Jamie?"

Was it the softness of the unexpected female voice, or the shock of hearing my old pet name after so long a time that so startled me? I turned upon the instant to see a female figure wafting toward me through the gloom of that place. Some gauzy thing covered her head, but her bodice was cinched tight over long, clingy skirts. My heart turned over and I stood up as if in thrall as the apparition approached me. Only inches away, she slid back her veil to reveal the dusky face and shoulders and dark eyes of a dockside mulatta wench who smelt faintly of salt and rum. But her smile was warm as she took my face in both her hands and pressed a long, slow, probing kiss into my mouth that I was too witless or amazed to refuse.

When at last she drew aback, her cunning smile returned.

"Caroline returns your pledge," she murmured. Then she turned and sauntered away, back into the shadows that had spawned her.

I stood there, staring after her like a simpleton, my mind in too much turmoil to respond, until what little daylight was still sifting in through the doorway was blotted out by two island constables blowing their whistles and shouting. It was Thomas grabbed me by the arm and hauled me out through a little door in the back, out past the cook-hose in the yard and into the maze of alleyways behind the main road. By the next corner, Thomas, too, had melted away, and I was alone, completely alone in the world, and fleeing for my life.

***

I escaped the island on a trading ship bound for the Gold Coast of Africa, captained by an incompetent drunkard who took it into his head to raid a few ports on the way. We were captured at Cape Coast and tried for pirates by a Vice-Admiralty court at the castle there. I was new to the crew, and the accusations against me had not traveled with us from Jamaica; I was convicted with the rest but received a lighter sentence, not hanged on the spot, nor transported to Execution Dock in London, as a warning to other young bloods who fancied the rogue's life. No, I was sentenced to hard labor in the gold mines of the Royal Africa Company.

We labored in chains in the belly of the earth by day, shackled together at night in what the Spaniards among us called *barracoons*, the barracks constructed for holding captive slaves for transport to the Indies. We were treated no better than slaves, but at least we were fed, albeit on some foul-tasting mash highly regarded by the flies of that place. Many of my fellows died in that hard service. But on the day I collapsed in my chains, sheer stubborn rage kept me alive. Rage was all I had left, and I nurtured it like a tiny blossom on the withered stalk my life had become.

I came to myself in the choking blackness but did not stir. I knew I'd be unfettered and carried off somewhere; if I were tossed over a cliff into the sea, it could not be any worse than my present situation. Cadavers were subject to dissection in the teaching hospitals of London, and if such were the practice here, some care might be taken to preserve my body intact until the moment came to bolt. The guards who unshackled me from my fellows in the mine hauled me briefly through sweltering daylight into the close gloom of a building, and threw me onto a table in some dim back chamber buzzing with insects. By the stink of medicines, I understood it to be the surgeon's quarters.

The guard's voices and footsteps drifted away. I opened my eyes and found myself alone. I got up and tried to push open the shutters of a little window in the wall above a shelf of equipment and a cupboard of potions. I dared not go out the way the guards had gone, for fear they were still nearby. Two or three of the thin jalousie shutters were missing, which accounted for the agitated flies, but the latch on the frames holding the others in place over the window was crusted shut. I was trying to drive a wedge through it with some small, sharp doctoring tool I found to hand when the surgeon entered from a door in the back.

He was a harried fellow of middle years with a long, lined face and thinning hair, his pink pate unprotected by any wig. He was not expecting his latest corpse to be up and about.

"Well, I'm damned—" he gurgled before I grabbed him by the neck and jabbed the cunning little blade into his throat. It was the first time I'd ever murdered a man in cold blood. It would not be the last.

He sank away with a gesture of impotent protest, blood streaming out of his open mouth. I bolted out the door he'd come in, through his private apartment and outside into the blistering sun for the cover of the tropical wood. When nightfall filled the wood with the racket of chittering things, I made my way down the coast to the next port, where I found work on a slaver back to the Indies.

We made port in Hispaniola, and from there I joined a party of desperate fellows heading to the island of Nassau and the pirate haven of New Providence. That's where I went on the account in earnest. My own account, for I had a score to settle with all the world. I captured a fleet little French brig and fitted her out for a pirate, rechristened the *Jolie Rouge*, in honor of my long and memorable association with the French. I assembled a crew as rash and savage as myself with which to harry the Caribbees, plundering and burning ships and terrorizing outposts. I would make them all pay for what they'd done to me.

The vow I'd made myself in prison now seemed to me the mewlings of a weak, defeated fool. Bravado was all I had left. Power was all that mattered to me now, rage and revenge against the world that had stolen everything from me—family, fortune, fiancee, reputation. I would carve out a new reputation in blood.

Every opponent I bloodied with my sword, every victim I robbed and terrorized was the friend who had betrayed me, the woman who abandoned me, the father who hadn't believed in me, the world that spun placidly round and allowed such injustice to go on. I learnt from an old shipmate that Harry Ryland had gone back to England to woo my betrothed, after seeing to it that I would never return. Or if I did, a well-paid network of spies was in place to make sure I knew my connection to Caroline was severed in the most intimate, devastating way.

My former shipmate also told me that my father died damning me for a pirate. All the follies of my youth argued in favor of the slanders against me, in his ears.

It would be better for all if I died too. Indeed, James Benjamin Hookbridge did die in that squalid surgery on the African coast, forgotten and unlamented. But Hook was born.

CHAPTER 9

SUITE: THE FAIRY REVELS

1

It's taken all morning for our expedition into the wood, to re-set our game traps and hew suitable lengths of timber from the fallen trees. But not even hours of sawing in the fierce Neverland sun has entirely burnt off the heat of my anger, so I bid the men row the gig down to the opposite end of Pirates Beach, near the mouth of Kidd Creek, that we may labor another fruitful hour or more in our garden. The men don't care for it much, but no one disobeys Hook.

I've little fear that the boy will launch an unprovoked attack on the skeleton crew I leave behind on board the *Rouge*; that wouldn't be fair. But a reckoning is coming, and soon, now that Pan's fairy knows the woman is here. All women are half-witch, as I know to my cost, and who knows what improvements have been made in the Black Arts since my day? But whatever she is, this Parrish woman, confidante of fairies, neither she nor the boy will get the better of me.

Burley I sent out again in the gig with his lines and tackle to catch our supper while the rest of the men and I raked and culled. And now, as we head back for the *Rouge* in the late afternoon, laden with fragrant lumber, ripening fish, and a pile of cabbages and potatoes, I feel something useful has been accomplished. We are well supplied against any siege, and the building of our new barricade may begin directly. I'm prepared to work through the night while the boys sleep to gain ground.

Once we gain the *Rouge*, I am the first up the chains and on deck. Waving off Brassy with his proffered bottle, and some yammering from Filcher, I turn to supervise the others hauling in the gig and offloading her cargo, the victuals to Cookie in the galley, the timber into the charge of Sticks at his work station on the fo'c'sle deck. With this business noisily underway, I plunge down the ladder for her cabin; now she sees I am in earnest, I'll give the Parrish woman one more chance to speak the truth to me if she means to forestall a bloody battle with the boys.

But no sooner do I thrust the key into the lock than the door gives way. Pushing it open and peering about, I see her cabin is empty. She's not there.

I scarce set foot across the threshhold when my boot crunches something against the deck. Stepping aside, I stare down at one of her black metal hairpins, bent straight; I see now how she used it to prise open the lock in the cabin door from the inside. She does not want for cunning, this female. Would any of my men have had the wit to do it?

Storming above again, I find the men fastening the dripping gig boat. But this time, I notice the chocks for the skiff, our smaller boat, stand empty.

"It's like I tried to tell, you, Cap'n," Filcher says bleakly, "Nutter 'n' them forgot to 'aul it in last night. Left it in the water."

I race up to my quarterdeck, peep astern, but I already know what I'll find.

"Gone," Filcher confirms. "She took it."

Well, at least she wasn't magicked away by the fairies. "Did it not occur to anyone to stop her?" I ask conversationally. This is what happens when I leave the ship to Filcher and a few idlers.

"Never saw her, Cap'n," Needles blinks behind his round black spectacles.

"Gato didn't even see her until she was already out in the bay," chimes in Sticks, which my lookout confirms with a guilty shrug from the crows nest. "And we couldn't chase her," Sticks adds. "You had the other boat."

Astonishing, how little pointing out the obvious improves my humor. I pluck off my hat, shove back my hair.

"What do we need 'er for, anyway?" Filcher grumbles, *sotto voce.*

A fair enough question. Despite what Pan said, she must be his creature; where else could she be off to so late in the day, with such impunity? The redskins watch over the bay and the fairies are always in the wind. Only an ally of the boy would risk it. Clearly, her mission to me has failed, whatever it was, and now she's obliged to report back to him. And when she does, when she enters the boy's wood and beats a merry path straight to his secret lair, if I have the wit God gave a turnip, I'll be right behind her.

"No one defies Hook!" I declare in ringing tones. "'Vast hauling there, men! Put the boat back in the water," I translate, clamping my hat back on. "I'm going ashore!"

***

We spied the empty skiff lolling under the rushes in a shallow inlet beyond the northern end of Pirates Beach, near the bluff where we climb to the wood. I've changed into my black coat with the silver figures, all the better for stealth, but damnably hot as I claw my way up by the stakes for the second time today, with the sun slanting to westward behind me. The men didn't like to leave me, but I told them I could always come back in the skiff, should my venture come to naught, and they were eager enough to return to the *Rouge* before nightfall.

Gaining the crown of the bluff, I creep into the outer reaches of the wood. Bypassing the neglected thicket where we keep our traps, I stay to the main grassy path, which soon becomes a verdant tunnel into a towering greenwood of firs, pine, and scrub oak, reeking of sweet jasmine, the boy's favorite, that twines blithely round every trunk. On I press, deeper into the wood where the trees grow more thickly together, their loftiest branches forming a kind of canopy that blots out the last of the daylight. Peering about in the gathering gloom, pierced now by only the most heroic rays of the sun, I spy an unnatural tremor in the green and brown shadows up ahead, as if a shrubbery had uprooted itself to stagger off on its own. That is her plaid. I fall into step some way behind, watching. She doesn't appear to be in any haste, or perhaps her insubstantial slippers impede her in this unfriendly terrain of rocks and twigs and bristlecones. But she stops often to examine the grasses and flora growing among the trees, some of which she plucks and stuffs in her jacket pockets.

A chill begins rustling through the trees. The gloom in the wood is total. No more gilded shafts of light pierce the darkness. Drawing my black coat closer, I strain to discern the woman's form before me, crunching dead leaves and bracken underfoot, yet the black shapes of the nearest trees grow more visble in the gloom, trunks twisting like gibbeted outlaws, limbs curling like predator claws.

Through an archway of trees, Parrish emerges into a clearing of overwhelming green, as if it were raining emeralds and diamonds. Unnatural light, insane music, and an undertow of pulsing menace assaults all my senses at once, but it's too late to turn back. The archway of trees has closed behind us, the path disappeared.

It's not the boy who calls Parrish so doggedly. It's the fairies.

The full moon shines faintly green tonight above the Fairy Dell. All round the clearing, trees thrust up like spikes and jagged teeth, indigo-violet against a tarnished pewter sky, but the center glows green and silver, where the fairies hold their revels. At first glimpse, it's like a bright silver coin in the distant grass. But it grows larger as I come nearer, until it seems high as a bonfire on May Eve, framing the woman's dark silhouette before me as she emerges from the shadows into a wall of silver flame that draws us both forward. Every particle of my being hums with dread. But for two hundred years, the fairy world has been closed to me, and now it opens like a chest of riches before Parrish. I must know what power she wields among them, so I shut away the warnings of my creeping flesh and press on.

The surrounding trees are enormous, scraping the dark sky, while the revels spread out before my eyes, a vast green ocean of brazen activity. The fairies themselves, never any bigger than dragonflies before, are grown to grotesque, obscenely human proportions. I don't feel shrunken, as if my body were compressed down to imp size; it seems my perception alone has altered, and I'm all the dizzier for it, reeling and disoriented.

It's like a scene out of Dante. The screeching of dozens of fairy fiddles pitched higher than human hearing erupts like grapeshot inside my nerves; I feel raw and fragile, licentious and despairing, all at once. Vocalists hover above the fiddlers like hummingbirds, carried aloft on the updraft of their pagan songs, some plaintive in tone, others mocking. A corps of fairies dance raggedly in a wide circle, three steps this way, three steps that, red-faced with drink, laughing and reeling, shiny with sweat to the very tips of their dripping wings. They go by in a haze of color, sparkling, evanescent clothing, skin stained in vegetable hues—saffron yellow, pea green, the violet of beets; some have scored their bodies with tribal designs Bill Jukes would envy. Others stumble off into the shadows, hoisting buttercup wineskins, too besotted to join in. Small wonder the boys are compelled to sleep so deeply at night, lest their precious innocence be defiled.

My gaze follows one plump and forlorn fellow, his wings doused and dragging behind him, as he passes a hollow between two tree roots. Inside, a sloe-eyed female bares her rump for a grizzled artisan; by rushlight, he etches a lewd design in her skin with a blackberry thorn. In the surrounding shadows, other revels are in progress. Pale, languid bodies, too close together to tell which limbs are whose, sprawl in the grass beneath a drooping poppy blossom, passing the dripping end of its style from mouth to mouth. A randy crone groans in the weeds, faded wings flattened beneath her, the head of an industrious young male busy between her legs. A pair of young bucks frisk by; one has dyed a garish, berry-red mouth in the fur round his pendulous prick. Other tangled bodies in confounding combinations fornicate merrily wherever they fall. Harsh, bubbling mirth, husky moans and raucous cries chime in counterpoint to the manic fiddling, a crescendo of abandon.

My legs wobble beneath me, the urge to dance overpowering, as is the urge to tear off my clothes and wallow like a beast in mud and moonlight and fairy glamour, the urge to plunge my sex into any warm, yielding thing, the urge to throw myself off a cliff, all are one: wholesale madness without limits, a frenzy of nameless desire.

A tawny minx spangled in gold like tattered cobwebs flutters by me in the close dark, brushing my cheek suggestively with her downy wing. I'm ripping the lace from my throat, eager for more of her caress, when I spy ahead a singular shadow against the dazzling palace of light the glowing sphere has become. Another human, not a creature of gossamer and moondust, but an unmistakably earthy figure approaches the palace steps unobstructed. She's going into the fairy palace, the citadel of power in the Neverland, the very heart of enemy country. I grasp hold of my few remaining wits, shove past the lusty fairy, glimpse a flash of indignant golden eyes, and blunder toward the light, caring not where I tread, nor whom nor what I interrupt. But by the time I maneuver round the ring of flailing dancers, elude a pair of chattery young females in heat and the tumescent intentions of a predatory male, I've lost sight of the Parrish woman. Yet the fairy palace suddenly shudders up into being before me. The palace steps shimmer and shift like a false vision of water in the desert, yet they support my weight, and I mount them.

I scarcely climb at all, finding myself suddenly inside, or at least surrounded on all sides by a brilliance of light with no visible source. There are no torches, no lanterns, not so much as a firefly, yet all is aglow with a light of staggering volatility. The damp, dark, shadow world of the forest seems very far away. Never have I beheld such light before; there are layers of light like shadows, gold, silver, green, violet, concealing gauzy depths within, and I flounder about dazed, certain of nothing but solid ground, slick and shiny as marble beneath my feet. When I glimpse a movement of something more solid than light, I follow it. Parrish. She must know the way.

Yet around a fold of purplish mist, a different figure emerges, a graceful young woman, small and willowy, golden hair dressed in pearls, one long roll of it hanging down her back. Recognition stabs me to the core. No. It's not possible. Not Caroline. Not here.

She halts, grasps up her ice blue skirts in both her little hands, whirls about. Her eyes, as pale and unclouded as the fabric of her gown, peer out beneath her smooth, white forehead. Her face and bosom and arms are powdered moonlight white, deadening the effect of her dewy youth, in the fashion of the day. My day. My Caroline. Rooted to the spot, I'm unable to speak, nor do I believe my worthless eyes. She looks back at me intently, yet her gaze passes over me, as if I were a phantom, and her features droop in anxiety.

"Where have you gone, Jamie?" she cries.

A ragged breath catches in my throat; I scarcely remember to breathe at all. "Caroline," I gurgle, "I'm right here."

"They say such horrid things about you," she goes on. "How can it be true? We are in love, I tell them. He would never, he could not ever—"

I choke on my next attempt at speech, cannot force the words out. Had she truly been in love, how could she betray me so completely? How could she be so easily persuaded? How could she believe it of me? And familiar anger courses through me as it always has, blotting out whatever desire for Caroline I harbored in my foolish youth. I'd have done my duty by her had she waited for me. Had she only believed in me. Vixen, who is she to come here moping about when it was she who betrayed me?

"Why did you never come back to me?" Her pretty little voice wavers plaintively.

"Why didn't you wait?" I spit back. How could I have ever cared for this duplicitous little chit, with her airs and her grand family name, and her black, faithless heart? Even as I stare at her, daring her to answer me, her image fades like a distant ship lost in a blinding sun. All that's left is a pitiable voice, soft and sad.

"I waited all my life."

It's too hot, too bright. Throwing my arm across my eyes, I stagger with hand outstretched for some retreat. My fingers touch bark, and I know I must have stumbled outside again. A salty breeze ruffles my hair, bearing a whiff of thyme and jasmine. Peeking out, I find myself in blessed shadow again, in some underpopulated part of the forest with sand, not grass, underfoot. A giant green lizard lumbers across my path and scrabbles halfway up a bare tree trunk, where it pauses to glare at me. I back off, round another trunk, and a more substantial figure, slow and sensual, rises up out of the shadows. God's cursed life, I know that languid shape. Proserpina, her body bursting out of its colorful rags, her dark eyes as narrow and pitiless as the reptile's.

"Why are you here?" I gape at her.

"Why are you still here, *Capitaine,*" she murmurs back. The timbre of her voice alone, so well-remembered, so undiminished by time, is enough to rouse every part of me capable of standing, a helpless tide rising to her moon. I so crave her touch, I might fling myself at her like a drowning man upon a spar, until I see the insolence in her black eyes, hear the amusement in her throaty purr.

"Because you sent me here, Witch," I seethe, a release hotter and more gratifying than desire surging through my body.

Her bare, shiny brown shoulders rise in a careless shrug, her black eyes glittery. "La, la, *Capitaine,*" she croons at me. "As quick as ever to give in to the fire of your rage. You should have chosen more wisely."

"I had no choice!"

"There is always a choice," she coos. "I offered you peace, but you chose war. I offered you love, but you chose hate."

I shut my eyes against the memory of the man I was then, abused by life, commander of a crew of murderers who cared for nothing by blood and revenge against the world. Why didn't I choose her when I had the chance?

"You said you loved me," I whisper.

"You will never know how much. That is your tragedy, *Capitaine.*"

"Enough to curse me to this place because I would not stay with you," I say bitterly.

She rounds her eyes at me like a stage ingenue. "You believe I punish you for my poor broken heart? La, la, no wonder you never came back."

"Back?" The single syllable, musty with impotence, all but chokes me.

"I waited for you so long," she murmurs, toying idly with the strings of coral, turquoise, and ebony beads that decorate her breast. "How could I know it would take you so long?"

To do what? I can scarcely grasp the notion before she stretches out one brown hand to me. And for all my rage, for all the suffering she has caused me, the dead stump in my chest shudders for an instant and I see my own hand reach for hers. Yet I feel no warmth, no weight, no solid flesh; my fingers clutch at nothing but air, and I stumble in the sand as her teeth shine in a cruel smile.

"It is too late to choose *me*," and she waves me away like a meddlesome fly. "I am dead."

Of course she's dead; they are all dead these two hundred years and more. Dead, the only choice that can never be mine. This is how she loves me. "How long will you torment me?" I demand.

"Wrong question, *Capitaine,*" she sighs. "Perhaps you are still not ready. I may regret I gave you this chance."

"What chance?" I cry. But Proserpina is evaporating into the shadows, leaving nothing behind but a last, insinuating purr. "Play well."

Jezebel, to torture me with phantom hopes and riddles. I will never play again, and she knows it. And as I whirl round and round in the shadows, desperate for escape, the trees and the sand and the night all vanish with Proserpina and I am once again in the midst of blazing light with a solid surface under my feet. I cringe, narrowing my eyes against the sudden brilliance, until the lights mute themselves to a softer glow. Somehow, I've strayed into a vast hall. Elegant alabaster columns support an arched ceiling too distant to be seen, mountains of fragrant flowers—lilies, jasmine, narcissus— on huge piles of greenery erupt out of urns and pots and tubs and baskets in every direction, and the surrounding walls shine like glass, mirroring the light. I turn round and round in my dazzlement and terror. The Great Hall of the Fairy Queen.

***

She enters by nothing so prosaic as a door. Rather, a shifting in the quality of light, as indistinct as the edge of a rainbow, and a rustling among the flowers announces her presence. In any direction I look, there she is, advancing upon me, the dark intruder in her proud domain of light.

She's draped in some gauzy stuff, ephemeral as morning mist, all flowing, glittering train with no substance. Her body is entirely visible within, skin so smooth and rounded she gleams in the light, nipples sparkling on creamy breasts, like fine confections tipped in silver dust. Arcane symbols painted in royal purple decorate one exposed shoulder and trail down to swirl suggestively round one breast. Her pale hair is not blonde but bright, waves of it shimmering all around her in a spectrum of colors too brilliant to register on mortal eyes. Her own vivid eyes are shifting echoes of the moonlight, circled in violet and shadowed in green. She's like an effigy of spun sugar and ice, fragile as breath, but for the primordial power of her presence.

She needs no throne, no pedestal, to loom before me, nor does she disturb the silken, translucent wings that arch so high above her head and trail their filigree appendages upon the floor. She merely glimmers there, an imposing figure of more than my own height, less than an armspan away, radiating unnatural heat, and a dangerous earthiness born of an underworld mortal men are wise to fear. And yet, every part of my traitor's body, my palm, my sex, my withered ghost of a heart throbs in unison just to behold her, do I will it or not.

"Welcome to our revels, Captain." She addresses me not so much in language as in sensation I am powerless to resist, not discordant like the common fairies, but slow, beguiling; her meaning flows inside my head, a shivering of distant chimes on a warm breeze. "To what do we owe this… pleasure?"

Too late I remember who I am and what business has brought me here. "My Lady—" I stammer.

"I am Queen BellaAeola, sovereign of this place."

"Majesty," I amend, remembering at last to make a leg and bow. "I mean no harm," I lie. I can't confess I've come to her forest to ferret out the boys. "I seek…a friend."

The fairy monarch flutters closer, her expression lively. "You have found one."

My flesh crawls even as my blood boils from her nearness. Her purple tattoos dance about on her skin like living things; lacy patterns twist and unfurl round the fullness of her breast, tongues of liquid flame stretch lewdly toward her swollen silver nipple.

"Ask of me what you will, " she murmurs with drowsy intimacy. "This is not a night for refusals."

I open my mouth, but no sound emerges. My wit has flown with the queen's arrival, leaving only hungry flesh and gnawing desire, defenseless and exposed. How can she not know me for what I am? She is the queen of all witchery.

Her fluting merriment sounds again, echoing all round the iridescent walls. I sense her pressing closer, although she does not appear to move, her rich, musky scent, her simmering laughter, the sheer voluptuous power of her person cocooning me, shutting out all else. "I know what you seek, Captain," she chimes.

I am not fit to reply.

"Release," she hisses softly.

"Yes," I whisper.

"Comfort," she murmurs, her inflection slow and musical. "Rest. Peace."

"Please," I groan, closing my eyes. Respite, release, indeed, such pleasure as I have not known in centuries, all could be mine, if only I would surrender. She can do it, I know it, I can feel it. My bully self, my pride, my wit, my rage, all are dissolving, along with my will. I have no will. I have no self. Her glamour oozes over me like aspic, trapping me in helpless thrall. Yes. Please.

The round, precise notes of her voice are a rippling *arpeggio* of unparalleled beauty. "What will you give me, Captain?"

"My life," I rasp.

"You do not value your life," the enchantress replies carelessly.

My eyes startle open, a tremor of fear shivers through me. She watches me avidly, tilting her head from side to side like a curious sparrow.

"My...my soul," I babble, and receive only another volley of brittle laughter worthy of Proserpina for my reply. "Majesty," I plead, like the most creeping, cringing, vilest sot, "whatever I have, it's yours—"

What might I not promise away next, in my humiliation? But the fairy queen is already disengaging me from her spell, the trembling promise of peace, respite, comfort, hope ebbing away, leaving me shipwrecked and stranded on cold, unfriendly shoals.

"Talk, talk, talk," she flutes in her sing-songy manner. "Foolish man. You have changed nothing."

With a single massive swoop of her wings, she rises up into the limitlesss vault of the hall above me.

"Majesty, wait!" I'm all but sobbing, falling to my knees on the hard stone floor.

"You value nothing, Captain. You are of no use to me."

"But—"

"Twice before, the Red Moon has risen, and you have done nothing," her waterfall voice pipes down to me. "This is your last chance. You will not get another. Seize it soon, or your cause is lost." And she sweeps herself up out of the light, and all is suddenly darkness and stillness and despair in her wake. The hall, the mirrors, the bountiful flowers, all vanish, and I'm on my knees in the forest, the wet of trampled grass seeping into my stockings. The laughing moon is slinking to westward, the forest is black and still and unpopulated to my eyes so recently bedazzled by the light. A mournful breeze stirs in the trees, bringing with it the acrid scent of crushed nectar and the occasional fleeting sigh or snuffle of an unseen sleeper in the dark, but the revels of Faery are concluded, or else I can no longer see them.

I'd have wagered anything that my deliverance was at hand at last, but nothing is won here without the forfeit of something else. Not until I shiver with more than the night chill at how close I've come to losing my grip on all that I am do I begin to recover my senses.

By what unbalanced delusion could I even imagine the imp queen would help me? This is the Neverland. No one will help me here. I'm no more than a game to Queen BellaAeola, as I am to her ally, the boy. Fairy seduction is only another victory to win over me, and I exposed my back to the cat like the most witless gull, begging and sniveling for the favor of her rejection. As if my encounters with Caroline and Proserpina were not cruel enough; by God's black heart, how could they still wound me so completely after all this time? This chance they all taunt me with, surely no more than another means to unbalance and humiliate me. What cause is not lost here? We are all lost. We are all damned.

I've not risen from the grass, as immobilized by despair as I was in BellaAeola's erotic web. In the damp silence, I begin to notice a low, quiet, miserable sound. It's not the distant sirens this time, nor the moaning of fairies, but something more wretched. A human voice.

Shifting to my feet, I follow it in the dark, picking my way across tangled roots and pine needles to an ancient tree stump, half as high as a man, covered over with moss and bramble. Something shelters there, on the ground between two roots. By the last of the moonlight, I recognize the Parrish woman on her knees in the lee of the stump, her pale face bent over something cradled in her arms. She reacts not at all to my approach, only kneels there, keening mournfully. Too weary to maintain the game of cat-and-mouse, I steady my hook in the old bark and lower myself to crouch beside her, peering at what she holds. What I take at first for a moldering bouquet proves to be an armload of dead, dry grasses, reeds and rushes. A dark shape lies within them, and I peep closer over her shoulder to see what it is. A brown sparrow, stiff and cold, stares up at me out of its dead, glassy eye.

Parrish turns her white face up to me, her dark eyes glazed with sorrow. "My baby," she rasps. "I've lost my baby."

I should flee for my sanity, had I an ounce of strength left, but I can only cling to the stump as she gazes up at me from the depths of her unvarnished wretchedness.

"Madam." My shaking voice betrays me, and I stop.

"I tried to hold on to him," she murmurs. "I held him in my arms, they let me hold him." She lifts up her ghastly burden a little, and I struggle not to recoil. "He lived. He looked at me. He knew me, I'm sure."

She turns back to the bundle in her arms. "We knew each other, didn't we?" she croons softly. "You and I. My baby. You were so much stronger than me, so much wiser, such an ancient soul, oh, God—" Her voice catches; she clutches the dead bird closer, and my blood chills. She begins to rock her upper body, back and forth, back and forth, cradling the thing to her breast.

"I was the failure," she whispers to it. She looks back up at me, a white face so beyond tragedy it seems inanimate. "I couldn't keep him alive. I lost them both. I failed them both."

"Madam," I try again, shaken to gentleness by our fearful encounters, desperate to break through this last grim enchantment. "This is not your child."

She blinks at me. "I know," she agrees sadly. "My baby's dead. I killed him."

3

Chilled by more than the pre-dawn cold, it takes me a few moments to command my wits to action. At last, I inch my hand toward her bundle, and her gaze slides down to watch.

"Let me." I can scarcely breathe the words.

Parrish nods slowly, and when my hand is near enough, she sighs and shifts her little burden to me.

"Don't hurt him," she whispers.

I lower the creature in its bed of brown grass as carefully as I might into the shelter of the next root, steady the makeshift nest with my hook to see the little corpse does not tip out. She watches in stoic silence.

"Thank you, Captain," she murmurs at last.

"You know me?" I almost groan with relief; she's not yet a madwoman, and I am still a creature of flesh and blood and sanity.

Her gaze turns to me, and I see some faint trace of life and purpose returning to her eyes. They have a greenish tint here in the wood, or perhaps it's the moonlight. She regards me in silence for another moment.

"You are Captain Hook," she says, at last, "and I am a long way from London."

"Welcome to the Neverland," I say drily.

She shivers a little inside her jacket, darts a wistful glance at the dead bird in its nest. "I thought it might have been him," she adds softly. "I thought maybe he was the one who called me here."

"This is scarcely Paradise. The dead do not come here to seek their reward."

"I saw him just now," she says to her empty lap.

As I saw Caroline and Proserpina, nearly forfeiting my wits for the fairies' idle amusement. A part of me longs to fly like wingéd Hermes back to the protection of my ship, my cabin, and my pots of rum, to obliterate the memory of all I've seen in the Dell. Yet I crave the presence of another mortal in this desolate place, for if Parrish were truly one of their witchy tribe, why would the fairies discard her so cruelly?

"You saw phantoms only," I tell her. "The imps will find out your weakness and use it against you. They will turn your dreams to ash, destroy even the memory of whatever might have once been good in your life—"

I have her full attention now. I stop talking, embarrassed by her scrutiny.

"Come away, Parrish," I begin again. "We mustn't stay here. This is an evil place."

I grasp the tree stump to steady myself, offer my hook arm to help her up, and she takes it. Her grasp is strong, substantial, alive, and I am grateful for it. We are not out of this wood yet.

***

Some primordial thing as out of time as myself flaps by overhead on leathery wings with a raucous shriek that startles us both out of our separate reveries. The forest answers with a volley of restless snarling and trumpeting; shrubs rustle, twigs crack, a covey of starlings spooked up out of one roost, circle in a fractious black cloud, and alight in another. Night in the wood belongs to the imps, but dawn belongs to the beasts.

It's not yet daybreak as I herd Parrish along an old hunter's trail, but a rising tide of birdsong greets the promise of dawn. If we lose our turning, I listen for the boom of surf and sniff the air for salt to keep us heading for the bluff above the bay. But she can't be hurried, shuffling along in her useless slippers, now sodden and filthy, lost in her own thoughts.

"I'm sorry I took your boat," she offers, after a while. "I didn't mean to keep it. But I didn't want anyone fighting over me. I thought I could prevent it if I left your ship."

"You meant to warn the boy," I suggest evenly.

"Well, I suppose if I'd found him, I'd have tried to talk him out of it, yes," she agrees. "But I was trying to find out what called me here."

"Your child?"

"He's not here," she sighs. "I know that now."

"Then your other loss?" I prod carefully, eyeing her. "You spoke of 'both.'"

Her gaze drops. "My husband."

Husbands do not typically venture to the Neverland and then call for their wives. It could never have been one of my own men; they are all unloved and unlamented when they arrive here.

"Why search for them in the wood?"

"I know about the forest, where the fairies live," she says at once. "I've seen it in my dreams." She shakes her head. "I thought the fairies could help me."

94

And the Dell opened readily to her eyes so they could have the pleasure of humiliating her. Dead leaves skitter across our path in the dawning breeze like empty fairy promises.

At last, we come to the edge of the bluff, where the path winds down for the beach. I hope I haven't idled away another hundred years among the imps, for fairy time obeys no laws but its own. But the dark smudge of my ship is still visible out in the bay. The skiff bobs in the scrubby grass at the foot of the bluff, neither covered over in barnacles nor sunk to the bottom with age.

Parrish is all but hobbling in her useless slippers; I must give her my arm all the way down the trail, clawing brush and bramble aside with my hook. At last we plough into powdery sand at the foot of the cliff. Off to our left, Pirates Beach stretches away southward, under its treeline of palms, ghostly in the moonlight. I glance again out at my ship, and begin to long for the quiet and comfort of my bed.

I look at Parrish, who gazes stoically back at me, trying not to let me see how she's favoring one foot.

"Let's rest a moment," I suggest. "It won't be light for a while yet."

She nods gratefully, and I draw her back round a curve in the bluff, protected from the shore breeze. She slumps down in the sand and starts rubbing at one battered foot. I sit beside her, sweep off my hat, set it down on the sand.

"Peter doesn't even want me here, you know," she sighs. "I'm old and silly, he told me."

"He spoke to you?" I peer at her. "When?"

"In the nursery. Back in London." She reads the confusion in my face and begins again. "My dreams of Neverland gave me no peace. I was so sure I was meant to be here, that someone needed me. I did everything I was supposed to, got a situation as a governess near Kensington

Gardens, left the nursery window open every night, just like in the stories, and sat up waiting for him."

She must be a madwoman after all. "And he came for you."

"I think so." Something sardonic lurks in her sideways glance. "He might've been a hallucination. He might've been make-believe. The fact is I was drunk, Captain. I'd become that worst of clichés, the tippling governess."

I nod. In truth, we are all as drunk as bishops most of the time here, thanks to our never-ending liquor supplies. Pan prefers his enemies pickled in bravado.

"But he didn't want me," Parrish sighs. "He refused to take me with him. Said he'd have no silly ladies about the place, bothering him. He swirled his cloak of fairy glamour about him and stalked off, as it were, if such a thing can be imagined three floors up and in mid-air. 'Grownups can't fly!' he taunted me, and off he went. I was devastated. I wanted it as passionately as any child, the Neverland, more than anything I've ever wanted before."

"But...why?" I blurt.

"The grown-ups have made an awful bloody mess of the world," she says tartly. "I couldn't stand it any more. I wanted out."

This, at least, makes a kind of sense to me. I watch covertly as she shakes out her dark hair, turns back to her blistered foot. She never went to the boys tonight, nor was she welcomed with anything like affection by the savage fairies. Can it be she is not Pan's creature at all, but the victim of some powerful sorcery? If this woman killed her child, might she have been sent to this vile place for punishment, as I was? I sign her death warrant do I leave her here alone, for there is nothing Pan so despises as a grown woman, the destiny of all the Wendys he can never forgive for growing up and leaving him. I've seen it hundreds of times. He sends the Wendys off with a great show of indifference, but he cannot purge them completely from his memory; that miracle is reserved only for those enemies he kills in battle. The pain of so many losses accrues over time, as I know too well, and Pan is more than capable of making this woman pay for them all.

Of course, it is no concern of mine what the little whelp chooses to do in his kingdom of witchery. But who knows better than I what it is to be friendless and alone in this place? And in one instant of resolve, however foolhardy, I set my course, for good or ill.

Pale dawn is already creeping up over the island, chasing off the moon. "Daylight is coming," I tell Parrish. "Perhaps you ought to come back to my ship."

She looks at me warily. "As your hostage?"

"As my guest."

She draws a breath, gazes down the beach, gives her head another little shake. "I don't want to cause any trouble. Surely there must be some...cave, or something, that—"

"Madam, I have lived here for two hundred years," I tell her plainly. "There is no other safe place."

She's still looking at me uncertainly as I stand up and slap the sand from my breeches. "If what you say is true, you cannot imagine the danger you are in," I warn her. "Let me help you." I offer her my hand.

At last she nods, and takes it. "Thank you, Captain," she says as I help her to her feet.

I turn back to sweep up my black hat and notice some tiny red thing poking out of the sandy dirt beneath it. Some species of sand crab, I think at first, or cocooning insect, but for the speed with which it's thrusting itself up out of the ground, the length of a finger already, now two.

No, it's not a sentient creature at all, but tiny red leaves at the tip of a sturdy green stalk. Up it comes, winding out of the sand as I stand frozen in the act of shaking off my hat.

Green leaves, fully formed, begin unfurling from the stalk, whilst the small, shiny red leaves at the tip belly into a fecund round bud. Other buds on other stalks are sprouting out of the earth as well, all within the little crater in the sand and scrub where we were just sitting, green stalks stretching up toward the dawn, splitting into branches spiked with thorns, shaking out their leaves, buds popping open like ripe figs.

Roses, by God's blood! A little thicket of them growing into being before my dazzled eyes: knee-high, now waist high, aburst with heavy blooms—blood crimson, violet, sunset pink, yellow blossoms as vivid as the sun.

I turn to see Parrish frozen in astonishment behind me, all agog, staring at this impossible spectacle.

"How did you do that?" she demands of me.

For once, no glib retort rises to my lips.

"Well, don't look at me!" she exclaims. "I couldn't grow moss in a swamp!"

It's some witchery, of course, some fairy spell. Clamping on my hat, I reach out to the nearest bush to touch one of the scarlet blooms. The petals are velvety soft against my skin; its heady fragrance lingers on my fingertips. They are as real as they are beautiful. And sinister, for Pan despises roses, as well as climbing bougainvillea and all species of citrus, any devious plant whose fragrant fruit or lovely blossoms conceal thorns to prick him. Briars and bramble he adores; his wood is carpeted in sharp, bristling things to be beaten back and mastered, but he's outraged by the perfidy of beautiful things that tempt him only to wound him, and he will not have them on his island. He favors the jasmine that runs riot in the wood, honey-sweet, uncomplicated. All through this island, where anything grows at his command, Pan has banished roses. Why do these disobey him now?

This is some new sorcery unknown even to me. And I thought I had seen them all.

CHAPTER 10

SAINT-DOMINGUE, 1724: PROSERPINA

They called her Proserpina. Tall and straight, she was, with mahogany skin, and lustrous eyes as deep and rich as Spanish chocolate. We'd run afoul of a frigate off Saint-Dómingue; laden with plunder, we'd barely limped away with our lives. One of my men was native to the place and knew of a hidden bay where we could shelter and careen the ship. I'd taken a wound in the thigh that would not heal, dripping pus and bringing on bouts of fever, so they took me to Proserpina.

It was whispered that she knew voudon, that she consorted with spirits of the dead, jumbies and demons, a queen of the underworld indeed. But it made little difference to me. For days I scarce knew where I was, beyond a straw pallet covered in some indigo stuff where I lay writhing. In more lucid moments, I perceived a shadowy chamber of earth and straw, low mud walls open to the breezes under a high roof of thatch. My pallet lay in one corner, near a table littered with baskets and hollowed-out gourds filled with powders, buds and seeds, small clay pots sealed with moss, bunches of dried grasses and herbs strung upside down across the open space, all of it reeking of spice and ferment, the sweet-sour perfume of dying things.

In the opposite corner, Proserpina kept her private altar of piled stones, a shallow basin on the bottom, little niches above for candles, festooned with flowers and beads, a gourd rattle, feathers, small bleached bones. Once or twice, woken in the night by a tang of smoke in the little hut, I heard the witch chuckling at her altar, conversing softly in her motley island patois with unseen visitors whose formless voices rasped like the dust of centuries. One night, the sweet scent of jasmine crept into my dreams. "*Bienvenu,* Mama Zwonde," I heard the witch murmur. "Your daughter greets you from the living time."

***

My fever had broken at last, but my thigh was yet too tender to bear me up. I awoke one sun-glazed afternoon to see some yellowish thing moving across the shadows above my pallet. Peering closer, I saw it was a spider, fair the size and color of a gold doubloon, creeping along an invisible line. I lashed out with a cry and a wave of my hand, but the thing scuttled up out of my reach.

"No, no, no, *Capitaine,*" Proserpina scolded me softly from where she stood at her table, fiddling with her pots and balms. Turning my head to look at her, I noticed a large spider's web glowing faintly gold in the sunlight in the opening above her table, between the edge of the roof thatch and the top of the wall. With a small coaxing sound, Proserpina raised a hand above her head.

"Come, Sister," she murmured, tugging gently with one finger on a thread I could not see. The spider hastened along it over my head, all the way back to where the witch was waiting, and crawled onto her hand with long, probing, tiger-striped legs. My own flesh prickled with dread, but Proserpina turned to gently place the creature on a broken upper spoke of its web, where it set at once to spinning and weaving.

"Your pet," I said gruffly, to cover my unease.

The witch smiled faintly, returning to her pots. "We have an understanding. She gives me what I need."

I glanced again at the shimmering halo of web behind her.

"It spins gold," I whispered.

With a low chuckle, Proserpina turned again to the web. At an outer edge of its intricate pattern, some distance below where the spinner squatted now at its own task, Proserpina's deft fingers pulled loose several strands and eased them out, scarcely disturbing the rest of the orb. She brought the oozy stuff and one of her pots, and a little clamshell dish over to me, and sat on the floor beside my pallet. With a practiced hand, she shifted aside the hem of my shirt and spread something warm and fragrant from her little pot over my wound. After working the sticky bit of webbing with her fingertips, this too she began to stretch across the gash in my leg, where it clung of its own accord without bandage or splint, as light as down against my skin. A small contented groan escaped me. I had no need for pretense with the witch; she had seen me raving with fever, weeping in shame. I could be myself with her as I never dared among my men.

"Gold," Proserpina clucked. "This far more useful. It will knit you up like a second skin, *Capitaine*. So many come to me with stings, scrapes, cutting wounds. My sister, she is very busy."

Again, I peered up under the palm-thatch roof, where the yellow creature the witch called her sister plied her web. "Surely there are other spiders."

"Not like this one. She is the best. She came to us so long ago, in the sail of a broke-up ship our wrackers find out in the shoals. The only one of her kind ever seen on this island." Proserpina paused in her work to gaze up at the industrious thing. "I was not even born then," she murmured. "This was my grandmere's house."

I swallowed a grin that this native woman, for all her skills, could be so credulous. "It cannot be the *same* spider," I pointed out.

She shifted her gaze back to me, her expression amused and indulgent. "Of course she is. I see to it. Like my mother before me."

Eerie cold gripped my spine over a fugitive memory, fearful villagers mumbling among themselves. The living dead. "Zombie?" I whispered.

"*La, Capitaine*, she is alive as you and me," Proserpina chuckled. "The *loas* agree not bear her away to the time beyond until her work here in the living time is done." The witch gestured upward with one expressive hand. "They lift her out of the current of time for as long as she is useful to me."

The *loas,* shadowy beings who interceded in the world between the living and the dead on the witch's behalf, so the villagers said. I had thought them myth, superstition. But by then I had cause to appreciate Proserpina's powers, had heard dry, ghostly voices rasping gibberish in that very hut in the dead of night. I glanced again at the superannuated spider busily tending her web. "But—is it not monstrous?" I could not help but ask.

Proserpina gave a careless shrug. "She breathes, she feeds, she spins in the normal way. One day, she will return to the current of time. By this service, her spirit will find honor and peace in the time beyond."

The witch returned to coaxing her websilk appliance along the length of my wound, her fingertips soft and tender against my skin. Only a bit of the gash was still visible when she lowered her head and pressed warm, full lips to my thigh. All but scuppered in an answering wave of desire, I could only stare as she lifted her head and spit into the clamshell dish, stippling its pale surface with my blood.

"The *loas* must have something in return," she said, when she saw my face. "Is a delicate thing, the balance between their world and ours."

I was not overfond of the notion of my blood in possession of her spirit familiars, if indeed such things were not a fantasy of my own delirium. But Proserpina healed my injury so completely that I didn't complain. It had been years since anyone had touched me with tenderness for any reason, and the respite I found in that fragrant, ramshackle hut was worth an army of immortal spiders and muttering ghosts.

As I grew stronger, and her ministrations turned more frankly erotic, I was less and less inclined to discourage any of her whims and fancies. She was on intimate terms with my body by then, and she undertook to rouse and pleasure me with the same skill. It was sweet and easy at first. She wanted nothing, and I had nothing to prove to her. Her body and her mercy, even more than her potions and balms, began to heal the misery that had driven my life for so long. Often on those languid island nights, after we had sated each other, I boasted I would compose a rhapsody in her honor, or at least play her something to make her weep with joy.

But my men had had their fill at last of gluttony and drink and idleness, and voted to resume our voyage of terror. Proserpina offered me the protection of her hidden village and the sanctuary of her bed would I but stay with her.

"Give up your roving, *Capitaine*," she crooned. "Let me be your world."

I laughed her off, perhaps too harshly. By now, the men suspected me of weakness for the time I'd spent with her. I had to act boldly to restore myself as leader in their eyes. I knew all too well what mob rule was like, and I dared not let the men see how tempted I was by Proserpina's invitation, lest they turn on me, on us both. "You deserve better, Pina," I amended, more gently.

In truth, recovered health and more time spent among the men as they made the *Rouge* seaworthy once more had rekindled my old bloodlust for revenge against the world.

Believing I'd had my fill of tenderness, I reminded myself there were still those at liberty who had not yet tasted my blade nor yielded to my power. I would not be satisfied until the name of Hook was regarded with the same terror as Blackbeard and Morgan along the length and breadth of all the world's oceans.

I was forty-three years old, and that was all the more life meant to me.

She came to the beach with a basket of fruits for our voyage. When they rowed her aboard, she asked me to play. The men were already testy and sniggering to have her there, waiting to see how much power she yet wielded over me. She seated herself on the bunk in my cabin, the men craning to watch from the doorway, Bill Jukes squatting in the forefront, eyes narrow and appraising in his decorated face. I made a great show of seating myself at my harpsichord, stretching my fingers. I ran up the scales in a lively *arpeggio*, paused for effect, then commenced, with salacious gusto,

"A ship must have a buntline to haul up her bunt
And a maid must have a youngman to tickle her—"

The men hooted and cheered, but Proserpina stalked off in silence. No word was spoken between us all the way back in the boat, nor any leave taken when she stormed up the beach, back into her jungle.

"You insult me. You insult yourself," she rebuked me when I went to see her later and collect the rest of my things. "This is not you. You are better than this."

"I am no better than I should be," I barked. Could she not see I was trying to protect her?

"How much gold will satisfy you?"

"Gold!" I laughed bitterly. I had seen enough in the mines of Cape Coast to last a lifetime.

"How much blood?" she countered. "How many more must die? How long can you stay angry at the world?"

"The world made me, and now it must reckon with me," I exclaimed. Bloodrage alone could purge the cruel memories of all I had lost, revenge on the world that had taken it all from me. It was all I had left to believe in.

"You better reckon with yourself! Do you want to be a child all your life?"

Stung in earnest, I barely stopped myself striking her. "It's my life to live as I damn well please," I spat back.

"You destroy who you are under the angry scar of what you become," she said.

I was fair shaking with rage. Who was she to hound me with her tedious expectations? But in fact, I could not bear to see myself as she saw me, a diminished echo of the man I ought to be.

"I see into your future," she hissed at me, "a violent end without remorse or pity, unloved, unmourned. Dying brings you no peace, your spirit forced to wander without refuge in misery for all that might have been."

I recoiled in horror that she would curse me so cruelly, she who professed to love me. Gone were all the pretty phrases with which I'd meant to extricate myself; now I longed only to retaliate in kind. My rage needed someone to blame. It was easier than facing the truth about myself. "I can't expect an ignorant, barefoot female to understand," I shouted.

"I understand you must go where you belong." Her voice was low and terse, unmuddied by the emotion in mine, her dark eyes unnerving now in their resolve. "I will give you time. All the time you need. Play well, and think of me."

But I lurched aside with the bundle of my things, tossed it over her doorsill to the sand below, and clambered down after it.

"*Capitaine,*" she called after me. "Play for your life."

Outside, where my men were waiting, I glanced back to see Proserpina in her doorway. "Your spells don't work on me any more, Witch!" I cried.

Or so I thought.

***

We sailed with the tide that very evening. At first only small things plagued us—a leaky water cask, a runaway boom, a freak wind that gusted up out of nowhere and carried off a spar. Our lookout sighted warships, devil ships, that seemed to bear down on us out of the mists, then disappeared on the next roll of the sea. We tried to put into trading ports, but found them burnt out by raiders or stinking with pestilence. We captured no more prizes, and our supplies ran low. We could not eat the rich plunder stowed in our hold, nor trade it away for supplies at any port. There might have been a mutiny had anyone wanted to captain so unfortunate a ship in my stead. No, that they left to me, and I drove them the harder for it. If the Caribbees were so inhospitable, I vowed, there was plenty of plunder in Africa, and there we would change our luck.

But once we made the Atlantic, we hit a freakish squall. It raged with the fury of a hurricane, blowing us far off course and out to sea. When it finally spat us out, crippled and disoriented, we found ourselves in a dense fog. We could take no bearings. Our lead showed that we were in very deep water, our compass reeled about like a drunken man. We saw neither sun nor stars to steer by, nor the lights of any other vessel or coastal settlement. Nothing penetrated that damn fog. We drifted for days, thirsting, ravenous, hopeless. My men were dying of sickness, or their wounds, or murdering each other over nothing at all. They were the lucky ones.

Then one morning the fog lifted, and a current carried us toward an island of unparalleled beauty. A wide strip of soft, white sandy beach welcomed us, in the natural shelter of a deep bay. The beach was shaded by green foliage, palm groves and ferns and fruit trees, with blue, terraced hills rising majestically behind. At one end of the beach, sheer cliffs rose away to a densely forested plateau that promised game and tinder. Far in the distance at the other end of the island, an elegant green volcanic cone rose into a coronet of pink clouds, above lush tropical jungle. And nowhere was there any sign of habitation—no battery, no warehouse, no ships in the bay. The place was ours alone. We made for the mouth of a pretty little creek protected by windswept arching palms and dropped anchor at long last, certain our torment was finally over.

Of course, it had only just begun.

CHAPTER 11

ROSES

One chance, Proserpina's shade had taunted me in the Fairy Dell. A buggering sort of chance it must be to lie fallow for two centuries before it can be taken. The imp queen too chided me about a last chance; the very wind breathes it at me. And why should I believe any of them in this place, where every other word is cozenage and moonshine? The fairy queen spoke too of a red moon, a Blood Moon, twice risen. Once when I did for old Bill Jukes, centuries ago. When was the other time? Only in my dreams.

But something is afoot in the Neverland, something the boy can't control, and if some way exists to end his tyranny, by God I will seize my chance.

***

We call it Long Tom, our murdering piece, the swivel gun mounted on the rail in the starboard bows, trained on the northwest quarter of the island, from which the boys usually launch their attacks. We've a moldering armory of useless cannon on the gun deck below, but the swivel is our principal means of long-range defense, the only gun that can be aimed high enough for flying boys and low enough for war canoes. The agile boys can dance above the half-pound shot it was built to fire, but a peppering of grapeshot will sometimes chase them off, or at least buy my men time to get their shields up.

On the fo'c'sle deck nearby, Sticks is progressing on the first of the barricades we designed, the scent of spicy cut wood rising on the tangy salt air. The triangular side frames are already built, and he's begun nailing the long timbers across the front, canted sightly backward to conceal a man standing behind from airborne boys and their arrows. Shorter timbers used in the middle will provide an aiming port, and the side frames are hinged so we might transport the entire contraption flat, when the time comes to move it aft to the quarterdeck.

The men were so relieved to have me back, they made up a hunting party into the wood to harvest our traps without complaint, while I saw Parrish fed and stowed in her cabin below. I sent Gato aloft with the others to try the standing rigging—there is always climbing involved in a fight with flying boys—while I stole an hour of sleep below, for once untroubled by either nightmare or the mockery of my phantom ship dream. Filcher reports that all was calm in my absence last night, but whatever is upsetting Pan, he will take it out on us soon enough. Now, as I prod about Long Tom's hinges and carriage, I see that Nutter has proven equal to the daunting task of maintaining it in this damp and salty clime. I was right to give him charge of the gun; he's no marksman, but his raving is an ornament to any battle, even if he never fires a shot. And an excellent decoy.

***

"They tell me you felled a duck today, Jesse."

I find him oiling and cleaning the brace of pistols I gave him in a quiet corner of the gun deck, his swabbing tools laid out neatly beside him on a cloth. A boyish flush of exertion stains his pale neck under his short brown hair as he bends over his work under the skylight, but by the sobriety of his concentration suggests he is nearer thirty than twenty.

He glances up at me. "The lads startled him out of the bushes. He was probably hurt already," he adds modestly, extracting a little brush from the bore of one pistol to inspect its blackened contents.

"Nonetheless." I nod my approval. A moving target, if not yet a flying one.

With a self-effacing shrug, Jesse returns to his weapon. I watch him covertly, lean against one of our useless cannon, edge the tip of my hook into the thick patina of grime and rust that fouls the muzzle, gaze out the gun port at the distant strip of Pirates Beach.

"Were you ever a soldier, Jesse?"

"Not me, Cap'n," he chuckles, but I notice he surreptitiously slides his deformed foot further into the shadows, out of long habit. "The Army wasn't that desperate, not even for the war."

I nod at the pistol in his hands. "I just thought, your training—"

He bends to his work again, applying cloth to muzzle for a long, thoughtful interval. "Me dad it was taught me to shoot," he says at last, as if the idea surprises him. He lays aside his cloth, his brown eyes intent at the effort to draw out the furtive memory. "He was a gamekeeper. At the Trundell place. When the Depression hit, he was let go. We had to move to town." He frowns, lifts the pistol, sights down the barrel. "It wasn't reckoned much good among the other lads, shooting. Nobody there had guns."

How his life must have changed in town, a country lad with a club-foot, who couldn't run with the other boys. But I'll wager he could fly as well as any of them when he dreamt himself into Pan's tribe. No wonder the buried memory of this place called him back.

"I reckon it very highly indeed," I tell him.

He glances at me briefly, and I glimpse in his eyes the pleasure of a man not accustomed to praise. These men do not expect intimacies; they want only commands from me, the more horrible the better, but I would inspire his confidence.

"Julius Caesar was an epileptic, you know," I observe. "Given to fits. One of the greatest generals who ever lived."

"Yeah?" Jesse eyes me again. "Fancy that."

"I'm shifting your battle station to the quarterdeck," I tell him, nodding at his pistols. "You've earned it."

"Aye, aye, Cap'n," he grins.

***

"Hey, lads, look at me, I'm an Indian!" Flax cries, holding up a fistful of black and blue-green duck feathers behind his blond head.

Sticks lent them a makeshift worktable of spare planks set up amidships, near the deckhouse, and the men are happily plucking and skinning their two coneys and Jesse's fat duck in the open air, where the stench of flesh and blood is not so burdensome.

"I'm a bunny rabbit!" guffaws Nutter, grabbing the skin of the hare he's pummeling and waving the ears over his head.

"You're a horse's arse, is wot you are!" jeers Filcher gaily, swatting Nutter across the face with his own coney hide. They are all bellowing with laughter now, as more fur flies than in an alley full of cats. They are grown in size when they come back here, but scarcely mature, by even the most lenient definition. It cannot be possible that any of these fellows ever attempted matrimony with a female.

"I'll tell you what I know, Captain." Parrish greets me. "It's not much."

She's put the basin of water I sent in to good use. Her hair is clean, the color of cinnamon, falling in loose, bouncy waves nearly to her shoulders. Her skin is pink with scrubbing, pale and fragile next to her grimy outfit. It's more breathable in here since I had Brassy dump out her shit bucket, and she perches on her bunk holding a tankard of dark, steaming liquid in both hands. She's hardier than she looks if she can stomach Brassy's evil brew in the middle of the day. I ask her how she finds it.

"Absolutely vile, thank you," she replies, fine, cobwebby lines crinkling up round her dark eyes. "But addicting in a loathsome sort of way."

It's the first time in ages anything has made me laugh in the Neverland.

One corner of her mouth tilts hopefully up. "Somebody's busy out there," she adds conversationally; now the hunters have ceased their foolery, I notice how Sticks' hammering echoes across the ship, even down in here.

"The men like to be occupied," I say, spying an old barrel amid the debris in the corner. "Casks, and the like." The less said about the true nature of my carpenter's labors, the better, and I roll out the barrel, seat myself opposite her, and invite her to continue.

"Well, Peter turned me down, back in the nursery, as I told you," she begins. "No amount of whining on my part could move him, and off he went. I was devastated. I just collapsed, weeping, and I cried myself to sleep, or passed out, or something. That's all I remember until I woke up here, on your ship."

I shake my head. "What is the fascination for Pan in your world?"

"He is youth and joy and innocence, all the things my word now craves," she rhapsodizes.

"He is sorrow, guile, death," say I. "You venerate a phantom."

She peers at me quizzically. "No," she insists, "an ideal."

I frown. "And you remember nothing else, after the nursery?"

"Nothing that makes any sense," she sighs. "Dreams, I suppose. Have you ever had a flying dream, Captain?"

"Never!" I snort.

"Well I must have had one. But it was all jumbled up, lights, color, a roar like the ocean." She's pursing her mouth, trying to think. "I rather remember trees, a forest. Animals in cages?"

This last is a question, and I nod.

"They looked so sad, I thought it was cruel," she says. Then she frowns at me. "Were there men? Somebody had a gun."

"We found you in the wood," I remind her.

"Oh, yes. So you said." She's chewing her lower lip thoughtfully. "I don't remember anything else. Except the noise. A kind of pounding, like a drum, or something. It went on forever."

I keep my expression composed. Was she already in the wood the night of the redskins' infernal drumming? Did they drive her off for the same reason the imps thwarted her last night—because she was coming too close to the boys?

"And you still believe something called you here?"

She nods, her expression more intent. "It must be a boy needing a mother, don't you think? Maybe not Peter, but one of them. Perhaps some other lonely boy regrets his decision to run off to this place."

It must be a powerful need to draw her here in the teeth of so many obstacles. Unless it is all part of her diabolical punishment for committing some crime against a child.

"And you left your charges behind in the nursery?" I prod carefully.

"I'm not the most conscientious governess, I suppose," she agrees, with a wry little smile. "But they do have a proper nanny to see to them. I was just an affectation of their parents, a governess after the war, when few families could afford such things. Very Jane Eyre," she adds with an arch of her brow. I know not how to respond to this cryptic remark. She sits back, watching me. "Have you really been here two hundred years?"

"At the very least," I sigh. "I may have misplaced a few decades here or there."

"How is that possible?"

"How do boys fly?" I grumble. "How do fairies exist?"

"Magic!" she gushes.

"Dementia!" I counter. "Mass delusion. Folie à deux, as the French say, multiplied to an infinite degree."

She grins. "Well... you're remarkably well preserved."

"I am positively pickled."

"Um...you're not a ghost, are you?"

"If I'm not make-believe, I must be spirit?" I raise my hand before her, the one with which I shoved her against the wall of this cabin, the one with which I helped her up from the floor of the Fairy Dell, and she looks a little abashed.

"Sorry, Captain. There's a lot to take in."

"You don't believe in me?" I fold my arms in pretended injury. "I fear you'll be disappointed if you expect me to vanish in a cloud of vapor. That's not how it's done here."

She takes another draught of Brassy's barkwood poison, studying me, trying to decide what to believe. "Well, but, in the stories, they say you served with Blackbeard."

A cackle of laughter escapes me. "Served? I knew Teach, but I was never so great a fool as to join his crew."

Her fingertips rise to her mouth, her dark eyes ready to pop. "You knew Blackbeard? Oh, this is too much! Either I'm completely mad, or I'm having the best dream ever! Well, what was he like?"

"He was a maniac. Drank black powder in his rum and lit candles in his own beard when he boarded a prize, to impress upon his victims exactly what sort of a lunatic they had to deal with. He slew whatever got in his way, friend or foe, drank himself into severe states of delusion, and took out his rage on his own men, whom he mistook for demons. Bugger me for a Bedlamite was I ever witless enough to sail with Teach!" She looks utterly thrilled. "Do you mean to say they still speak of Teach in your world?"

"The most ferocious pirate of them all," she nods vigorously. "He's considered rather romantic."

"I can think of no less likely a figure of romance," I reply drily. "Except the Pan."

***

"How come she's still here, is all I'm saying," rumbles Nutter through his beard, fingers worrying the edge of a card, his curly red hair a halo of flame in the light from the lamp on the table.

The others round the table grunt in assent over their cards and rum. I edge closer behind one of the derelict guns, listening from the shadows. I've just come from totting up our supplies in the galley, when I heard their covert muttering round their mess table, those men not on watch above. It's less stifling below in the dark of night.

"What good is she?" Nutter demands.

"Maybe she can teach Cookie not to poison us," Jesse suggests, folding his cards.

"She'd 'ave to be a bleedin' miracle worker, Jess," snorts Filcher, rolling a couple of coins into the little pile on the table between them all. Those men who lack coins or notes have staked other objects procured from some forgotten corner or other: I spy the glint of a gold ring, the sheen of an ancient rope of pearls. Objects of no practical value to them in their present circumstances, but venerated out of habit for the presumption of status they confer. That little silver bell I saw in Parrish's cabin, polished to a fine sheen I recognize as Brassy's handiwork, has already joined their pot, although my steward is no longer in the game.

"Females be better off in the kitchen or the salting house than on the boat," comes Burley's soft Cornish brogue, as he slides a note into the pot.

"Or in the bedroom," young Flax chimes in.

"How would you know?" Nutter guffaws, closing giant fingers round his cards and making to cuff Flax about the head.

"I know!" the youth protests, elbowing off Nutter's blow. "And then they want the earth, and you're trapped. Then all you hear is 'Do this, do that. Grow up.'"

"Women are trouble," agrees Filcher, who likes to portray himself as a fellow of some dash when I am not about. "Cap'n oughter give 'er a good poke, like any other piece of tail, and 'ave done with 'er."

Tail, trull, cunny, twat, snatch, tart, slattern, cunt, slut. I have heard them all, every rude name for the female sex furtively bandied about in this messroom for centuries, although the braver the talk, the less acquainted with experience it tends to be among my men. They have little enough use for women, these fellows; the only females ever seen here are the little Wendys.

Nutter's outstretched paws devour the pot as I retreat into the shadows. Of course, now and again one of the Wendys takes it into her head to reform me. The boldest among them seek to practice their infant wiles on me in retaliation for the boy's indifference, for soon enough they learn they are mere gamepieces to Pan, and children love revenge above all things, even girls. Especially girls. So they think to make a trophy of me, a black and sinister plume in their pert little caps. But they are infants to me, scarcely out of their christening gowns, however hard they strain at the bit of childhood. There's naught to do but laugh at them. They are not even any use to me as hostages; over long time I came to realize the challenge of a rescue only goads Pan to more inspired savagery against my men.

One menacing slash of my hook is enough to send the little chits screaming off home to their own mothers. Or I let them glimpse my horrible handless stump, gruesome enough to defile their dreams all the rest of their lives. No one gazes upon my deformed stump, not my men, nor the Pan, nor anyone in the Neverland, but by my design, and only when I want to see them pale in revulsion and horror. That is how to deal with a Wendy.

It strikes me so suddenly, I nearly trip over the nearest gun carriage. My men were all Lost Boys once. What if Parrish was a Wendy? I should never remember myself, they all look alike to me, but suppose it was the Neverland itself that called to her, as it calls to my men? She would not remember; they never do, once they return to the world and grow up. But that may be why her instinct to mother the wretched boys is so strong. Did she once live in the wood at the boys' secret lair, might she not carry within her some vestigial memory of how to find it again?

***

"I'm sorry, Captain," Parrish sighs, grasping the last stake and skittering down the bottom of the trail to hop to the sand below. "I've wasted your time."

She readjusts the bill of the sailor's watchcap over her pinned-up hair against the angle of the sun, dusts off her checked smocked shirt, both items culled from our slops chest to give her the look of any other anonymous pirate. Although we needn't have bothered. A fruitless hour in the wood brought us nowhere near any boy, let alone any phantom voice calling out to her.

"No harm done," I grunt, stepping down into the sand behind her. I sweep off my black hat, wipe the sleeve of my hook arm across my forehead, set my hat back on. From under the brim, I peer again at the stand of roses a few paces away, still blooming brilliantly in the noonday sun.

"Still, it was kind of you to bring me back here," she says.

I make a noncommittal nod. She fair leapt at my offer to escort her back in the daytime, when the malevolent fairy presence is not so keen, and the boys' childish minds are awake and active. It was a risk, but Hook and a single pirate seeing to their traps are unlikely to cause arouse much suspicion, or interest, or so I hoped. And the reward should have been incalculable had the connection she sought reeled her in to the boys' hidden lair. But she was unable to pick up the trail of her dreams.

"It's so odd," she goes on, as I usher her past the roses and down the strip of beach to where the skiff is once again tied up amid a great sprouting of weedy vegetation. "The feeling was so strong when I was in London, I dreamt of nothing else, but now that I'm really here..." she shakes her head. "I don't hear it any more."

"We'll flush 'em out next time," I sigh, moving ahead to claw aside a patch of scrubby weeds above the boat. But when I turn back, Parish has come to a halt in mid-beach, staring at me.

"You're using me to find the boys!" she exclaims. "That's why you were so eager to come back here!"

"Madam—"

"You bastard! You thought I'd 'flush 'em out' for you! Oh, my God, I'm such an idiot! I can't believe I fell for it—"

But before I can even think of a plausible lie to defend myself, a faint, rapid glittering of light against the stony blue-grey of the cliff above the roses behind her draws my attention. And rising over the cliff top, comes that most dreaded silhouette. Parish turns in mid-cry and sees him too, falls silent, standing as if mummified, staring up at that ominous shadow.

"Peter," she whispers.

I'd not be surprised did she bolt away, run up the beach, seek his protection, but she stays rooted in place, staring. Without thinking, I lunge to grasp her arm and drag her down into the shelter of the weeds and scrub that shield the boat.

The greenish fairy light comes bouncing down above the rose bushes as Pan circles down for a closer look. Scowling, he flies all round the bushes and their rainbow blooms. He does not land, as if afraid to be contaminated by the renegade sand that spawned them. The fairy light throws out a little shower of saucy sparks, rusty gold and green.

"See, Kes?" Pan cries to his imp. "Knobby was right! But where did they come from? Who dares to plant them here?"

The imp shrills something indecipherable.

"But they're not supposed to be here," the boy rounds on her. "I said so!" With another menacing look all about, he adds, "Something is very wrong…"

And I'm on my feet before my impulse can confer with my brain, striding up the beach, intent on herding them away from Parrish; his imp never leaves him unprotected if I'm about. The fairy swooshes to Pan's side, shimmering with menace, and I pause some little distance away.

"Hook! What are you doing here?" Pan growls at me.

"Merely strolling along my beach," I say innocently.

"*My* beach," the boy insists, quite as agitated as his fairy.

I respond with the slightest shrug of indifference. "Then they must be *your* roses," I observe. "Charming!"

He flutters higher in a fury of paddling limbs. "This better not be your doing, Hook!" he shouts.

"You are master here," I remind him smoothly. "It's *your* beach, after all."

Playacting composure is my habit with the Pan, but beneath it I'm fascinated. I've never seen him so thwarted over so little, a nothing, an innocuous patch of flowers. I've never seen him thwarted at all.

He glares at me stormily, his imp glimmering in the air between us, ready to charge in either direction. Then the boy glides up a little higher and makes a sweeping gesture toward the roses.

"Here's what I think of your charming roses," he cries. He swirls his hand in the air, and I wait for the roses to disappear in a burst of fairy light. Pan is not a sorcerer, as far as I know, yet all things in the Neverland bend to his will. But instead the rose petals begin to fade to the colors of sand and rock, curl up like parchment, fall to the ground. Green leaves yellow and shrink into themselves, disintegrating like ashes. Rose hips droop on their naked stalks and wither into dry husks until the weight of each one snaps off the twig supporting it. And when all that remains is a bramble of blackened stems and naked thorns, the boy nods his head, and the entire stand of withered sticks crumbles to dust before my eyes. Dust. He doesn't command them to vanish; he commands them to die, while he watches with venomous pleasure. His keen gaze shifts to me to see the effect of his will, although I'm careful to keep my expression impassive.

"I win!" he cries, but his words are more hollow than usual. He was too piqued to call a game, so I owe him no forfeit; perhaps he hopes I'll crumble in despair like the cursed roses. His imp seems eager to herd him away, and he flutters up to go, but at the last moment turns again to me.

"Whoever did this will be very sorry!" he shouts crossly. "I better not find out it was you!" And off they soar over the cliff.

The mocking sun shines more boldly now as I gaze at the pile of ash and dust that was such magnificent beauty only moments before. When I no longer feel the malevolent chill of his presence in my bones, I plod back down the sand to where Parrish still shelters behind the weeds.

"You wanted a word with the boy, I believe?"

She wrenches her gaze away from the cliff and stares up at me. "What's the matter with him?"

"He has banned roses from the Neverland," I tell her. "These disobeyed him. That is how he deals with defiance."

She clambers slowly to her feet. "This is not how I imagined it."

"You supposed the land of eternal childhood would be a happy, carefree place, full of gamboling elves and unicorns," I suggest drily. "A bed of roses."

We both glance again at the pile of ash, smoking in the pitiless sun. It's a ghastly thing to see, such wanton destruction. He didn't smash them in a petulant temper; he reduced them to ash with the force of his hatred.

At last, Parrish shifts her gaze back to me, her expression bleak. "Now what am I supposed to do? Off to see the wizard?"

The fairies and the boys are proven inhospitable. The woman is running short of options, and I believe at last she realizes it.

"There are dark, dire forces at work here you know nothing about," I tell her plainly. "Whatever brought you here is more powerful even than Pan. I seek only to understand what it is. The lives of my men may depend on it. Your life may depend on it."

She frowns at me. "I won't be part of your stupid war," she says.

"Perhaps you are here to end it," I improvise.

The effect of these words is immediate. I see her eyes widen hopefully at this possibility. "Come back to my ship," I urge her, pressing my advantage. " We want the same thing, you and I: to understand your purpose here. Dine with me tonight, and I may be able to help you."

She is watching me very carefully. "And what do you want in return?"

"I would appreciate your honesty."

She sends a last, baleful glance at the smoking ruin where the roses had been, peers again at me. "I hope I can expect the same from you, Captain." And she turns and climbs into the boat.

It may be true that she's told me all she believes she knows. But memory is a coquette that wants coaxing, and I must plumb the depth of hers soon, before the Neverland can erode it entirely, as happens so often with my men. The most interesting things slip out unbidden when people are divorced from their wits. Shameful secrets. Hidden desires. Buried memories. And Parrish is fond of drink.

CHAPTER 12

HAMMER AND TONGS

Still, it's not without a great deal of deliberation that I permit her into my cabin, my sanctum sanctorum. All the relics of my long, weary life are here to be discovered, possibly mocked by her, yet I determine to hazard all. I clear the little cherrywood table, set silken pillows on the chairs, unearth a gilded candelabra from a forgotten corner of my wardrobe. I have more plunder than even I remember stowed away in the shadows. I lost my taste for fine things during my long years in that French island prison, but I regained it with a vengeance when they came at the expense of other, more fortunate men.

I'm once again in ceremonial scarlet and gold lace, my beard trimmed to shadow. The inverted bells of two polished crystal goblets sparkle in the candlelight. Parrish arrives in her own vagabond shirt and trousers, agog at my finery.

"I'm sorry, Captain," she murmurs. "I didn't realize this was a formal occasion."

"Not at all," I assure her. "I have so few guests, I'm afraid I no longer know what fashion is."

She darts another of her speculative glances at me, as I withdraw a chair for her. I see she has taken some trouble with her toilette; her hair is pinned back from her face in a few strategic places, while the rest falls loose and wavy to just above her shoulders. As I seat myself opposite her, one corner of her mouth quirks slightly upwards. "You look very dashing," she flatters me.

"Ah!" I say, in relief, as Brassy scuttles in with a decanter of port, and just as quickly out again, his eyes averted to the deck.

"Your men don't like having me about," she observes as I fill her glass.

"I am captain here," I shrug, filling my own.

We salute each other, sip.

"Ooh, this is excellent!" The wine coaxes a genuine smile out of her, then she leans forward. "But can't they overrule you? Your men?"

"Mutiny?" I scowl. "You take liberties, Madam…"

"No! Democracy. I've read that pirate captains only command at the pleasure of their men. They can vote you out, or challenge you to trial by combat."

I bark a derisive laugh. "Nobody wants my command, I promise you." I knock back another bracing gulp. "Democracy, Blackbeard. Where do you get such notions?"

"I studied history at university," she sniffs, but already her attention is wandering as she gazes wide-eyed all round my cabin. Thinking to disarm her further, I give her leave to satisfy her curiosity. Was she ever a Wendy, she might have been aboard this ship once, in this very cabin. Something might stir her memory, although it must have been longer than this woman has been alive since I realized how pointless it is to take hostages. She rises and begins to rove about, drinking everything in with her eyes, slides a finger along the sleek wood of one of my carved bedposts, takes note of their pineapple-shaped finials, a device recalled from the Indies. Coming to my old sea chest, she studies its arched lid branded in frilly script with the legend "Jas. Hook Esq." A relic from my peacock days. Her fingertip follows the

124

elaborate course of the "J" up and down and around, and up again. She glances back at me.

"Jacobus," I tell her loftily.

Her mouth tilts up again. "Oh, I see," she smiles. "James."

How odd and empty that name sounds, as distant from me as my severed hand, so long gone.

I watch her fingertips trail along the lavish scrollwork of the stern window frame, above the curly pegs from which my hats depend, caress the carved wooden cabinet mounted above my writing table. I am mesmerised by the way her fingers glide over everything, as if the act of touching feeds her more information than her eyes can take in on their own. My phantom fingers stretch longingly, but my hook does not stir.

"You have a skilled carpenter aboard, Captain," she tells me.

"It's been an age since any of my men had the skill of a rhubarb," I reply. "I find that whittling helps to pass the time."

She glances back at me. "This is your work? It's very fine."

She has no idea how long I've had to perfect my craft, how little there has ever been to distract me. Indeed, a rhubarb might have produced such work had it had such an infinity of time. "You mean, in spite of this," I suggest, tilting up my hook to save her the bother of pretending not to look at it.

She gazes briefly at us both, my hook and myself. "Quantity of hands must not matter so much as the skill with which they're used," she says with an easy shrug.

"There are few pieces of scrap wood so worn out and damaged they can't be put to some use," I mumble, and I swallow another deep draught so she might not see how her praise discomposes me. "Even by so poor a craftsman as the terrible Hook."

"Oh, that's just an alias," she replies, with a brazen smile. "This is the work of a maestro."

She comes at last, as I knew she must, to my harpsichord, so long silent, its polished mahogany shining bravely in the candlelight. Unlike the *Rouge,* I can't bear to let it fall into disrepair, but tune and polish it as attentively as any fatuous lover.

"Do you play, Captain?"

"I did once."

"Surely there are one-handed compositions?" she persists.

"Perhaps you would care to play me one," I ooze.

Her laugh is light, not mocking. "Not me, Captain, I haven't the gift. Females no longer learn music and needlepoint and drawing in the nursery any more, you know. It's an altogether different world."

"What do you do, then, in your world?" I prompt her. "Besides misinterpret history?"

Impudence fades from her expression, and she gazes down at the keyboard. Her fingertip depresses one key so gently the note does not strike.

"I used to write books," she murmurs. "Romances."

"Like masques in Shakespeare? Magic, fantastical journeys, exotic scenery, whimsical Fate?"

Her eyes crinkle up. "Your education is showing, Captain."

"The education of the playhouse," I shrug. Not at all the sort of schooling one was meant to boast of in my day. "I am not unacquainted with Shakespeare, as well as the modern scribblers. Congreve, Farquhar, and the like." I find I am boasting after all.

This amuses her, for some reason, then she shakes her head. "My books were trifles in which a man and a woman defeat obstacles through love. I gave them up when I realized what lies they were," she adds wistfully. "I lost the heart for it."

I pick up the glass she left on the table and carry it to her. "Heartlessness is a quality we all share in the Neverland," I point out. "Is that what brought you here?"

"For that I might've stayed where I was, thank you very much," she scoffs, and downs another sip. "I dreamt this would be a happy place. Childhood reborn."

Dreams or memories? "You dreamt often of this place as a girl, I suppose?"

She looks surprised. "I don't know. I don't remember."

"Perhaps to escape some childish sadness," I try again, raising my own glass. It's my impression that the children who dream their way here in fact, as opposed to those who only visit during their dreams, are at odds with the other world somehow, dreaming their way here out of desperation.

"Not me, Captain. I had the most boringly happy childhood," she grins. "My parents were still alive. We had our house in Devon, and summers I spent with my aunt and uncle in Scilly; I had beaches for my playground, and the whole of the ocean to dream on!"

So that's how she knows her way around a boat.

"It wasn't until after the war, a year or so ago, that the Neverland started really haunting me," she goes on thoughtfully. "When I found the book."

"Book?" I nearly choke on my wine. Is she an enchantress after all, mistress of some volume of arcane lore?

"*Peter and Wendy,*" she replies. "My aunt gave it to me when I was very small. It was autographed. Lovely, ornate old thing, dark green binding, Peter and the mermaids on the cover, I believe, done in gilt." I marvel over her recollection of such details, not at all like my men. "I only just found that book again, it was put away for years. And inside, beside his name, I found that he'd written one word. 'Believe.' And that's when the Neverland started coming alive in my dreams."

"Do you say the Scotch boy sent you here?"

Now it is her turn to stare at me.

"The one who went home and wrote down the stories of Pan for the first time," I explain.

Her eyes widen. "You knew him? He was here?"

"Oh, aye, Inky or Blinky, or some such as they called him, nearsighted little fellow, always scribbling things down," I mutter, and take another satisfying draught. "Previous to him, they were just stories whispered by children to each other. I should scarcely recollect him now, but for the way the stories have altered since he laid siege to 'em." Parrish is still staring, enrapt, so I go on. "He got it all wrong, of course, wrote about Pan as if he were a product of his own era, newly run off to the Neverland, although this place is eternal and Pan has been here so much longer than that. Always trumpeting about that he would never grow up, the Scotch boy, that he would never forget."

"And he never did," Parrish murmurs.

"A pixilated distortion of the facts, at best, and happy enough he was to invent the rest," I correct her. "I suppose he's still spewing the same bilge back in your world."

She gazes at me for so long a moment that I nip again into my wine glass to escape her scrutiny. "Mr. Barrie is long dead," she tells me at last. "Why are you still here, Captain?"

Her question so surprises me, my tongue fails to produce a sound, like the jack on my harpsichord. "Spite," I mutter at last. "I should have died a thousand times by now, if I could. But Death will not have me. The boy wills it."

She regards me in silence.

"You alone defy him," I add, peering back at her.

She draws a breath, shakes her head in apology. "I guess I must have slipped in under his radar," she says.

"What?"

"Sorry, Captain, I keep forgetting. In the world I left there are ships that fly in the air—"

I gape at her. "By witchcraft?"

"By engineering," she explains. "They carry passengers."

"A world where people fly. In ships," I marvel, trying to regain my *savoir-faire*. Flight, the thing so much sought after in my day, but never more than a dream, like the Philosopher's Stone of the ancients. "Extraordinary," I murmur.

"Very useful in warfare," she says tartly. "Imagine cannon shot out of the sky, but much, much more powerful." A vague shudder of recognition stirs within me. Ships that fly in the air, raining fiery destruction. I've seen them in my dreams. I drain my glass and move back to the table and the decanter.

She joins me. "The world has not aged at all well since you were in it," she says, thrusting out her own glass. "Hatred and greed run riot. Wars are global. It's a fucking nightmare. Oh, pardon me, Captain," she adds hastily.

"I am a pirate, Madam," I remind her.

"Yes, but I suppose ladies in your day were more genteel in their speech." Her grin slips out again. "In the stories, you know, when Captain Hook swears, it's always," and she affects a *basso profundo* comic opera voice, "'Brimstone and gall! Hammer and tongs!'"

"May harpies rip out my liver did I ever utter such nonsense," I reply and nod her back to her seat. "They are entirely fabrications of the Scotch boy. In real life I am no stranger to oaths," I promise her.

"Such as?" Her eyes dance wickedly. "Oh, come, Captain, you've seen what a guttersnipe I am. Indulge the historian in me."

I sit back in my chair. "Well, in my day it was considered quite reckless to refer to God's hooks or God's wounds,"

"Gadzooks!" she titters. "'Zounds!"

My mouth twitches. "Aye, it loses a little something with age," I agree. "To actually name the deity or any part of his anatomy was a terrible blasphemy, and the more intimate, the better."

"God's gallstones!" she chirps.

"By God's putrid bile," I counter.

"God's cods and tackles!" she cries.

We're both chuckling now; I can't stop myself. "Have they no more cause to curse in your world?" I prompt.

"More than ever, but it's all so boring!" she exclaims. "'God damn it', fucking this or that, 'Bloody Hell,' so prosaic! Nobody swears with any imagination any more. It's not the art form it was in your day."

I laugh at her backward compliment, down another drink. "Men no longer dare the Almighty to smite them down?"

"Blasphemy doesn't seem like much of a sin any more," she says, with another sip. "It's been upstaged by all the others."

"If you're already in Hell, there's little more to fear from divine retribution," I observe.

"Absobloodylutely," she agrees, and clinks her glass to mine.

***

A shaved silver coin of moon, no longer completely round, has risen over the island; her ghostly light floods down the hatchway as I creep along the passage after escorting Parrish back to her cabin.

I go up the hatch for a breath of air, peer out at the bright confetti of Neverland stars. I have sailed all the world's oceans and never seen their like, for the fixed pattern of Neverland stars shine in this place alone and no other. Were any of them the stars I once knew—the Dog the Bear, the Southern Cross—I'd have some notion of where the Neverland stands in the world. It's a lonely feeling, a million stars ablaze in the night and none to ever guide me home.

The candles gutter as I enter my cabin, filling it with jittery shadows, ominous, wraithlike things who give me no peace. They're not Parrish's memories I've uncorked tonight, but my own.

CHAPTER 13

THE NEVERLAND, 1724: HOOK

For a while we found respite in the Neverland, although we did not know to call it by that name. It was our Eden. After the storms and fog, we craved peace above all things, careened the ship without urgency, in part because we'd lost so many men, but also because we were none of us anxious to sail off again. There was wild game in the forest, and fish in the sea. We continued to think the place uninhabited, a paradise provided solely for our pleasure. If there were never any ships on the horizon for us to plunder, neither were there any warships to hunt us down. We grew indolent and stupid.

The redskins found us first. A party of my men encountered a hunting party of theirs in the wood. My men had known Africans in the islands, mulattoes of native blood, and fierce runaway maroons, but they had never known warriors of such swift and ferocious skill. Only two of my men returned that day to tell the gruesome tale. We set about final repairs to the ship in earnest, making her seaworthy again, protected by our Long Tom and the stern-chasers on deck as we worked. But the tide that had brought us to the mouth of Kidd Creek would never carry us far enough out to sea to escape. Always, we found ourselves becalmed in the fog. Always, the current brought us back to the Neverland.

We dropped anchor further out in the bay, a more defensible position than the shallows by the creek. We kept to our ship, and the warriors kept to their villages, but still there were skirmishes. A raiding party I led to cut out a few ripe females for our pleasure was a miserable failure; all but myself were butchered. They lost many braves canoeing out to our ship in the dead of night, repelled by our pikes and pistols. Time and again we tried and failed to chart a course through the fog back into familiar waters, until a party of drunken men murdered the navigator they blamed for failing to get us out of there. But the powerful forces that ruled in that place were far beyond the control of any one puny man.

And never were we more certain of it than the first time we saw them swarming toward us, a cloud of children dressed in leaves and animal skins laughing and shrieking in mid-air above our ship. The latest tribe of Lost Boys with the Pan in the lead.

I shall never forget my first sight of him, soaring overhead as I stood my ground amidships, my moonstruck men cowering in disbelief. He was not a very little boy, perhaps eleven or twelve years of age, and yet in possession of a full set of tiny baby teeth, which made his expression eerie. That and the keen light in his grey eyes peering out from under his dirty, tawny hair. Green leafy vines wound over his shoulder and round his middle, over a pelt of ragged fur. He went bare-legged above boots of furry skins, with a short sword at his side and a knife stuck in his boot. In one hand he grasped the musical Pan pipes which gave him his name. He hovered in the air above me, a light like a firefly buzzing about his shoulders, and whooped with delight.

"Pirates!" he cried, and all the other little boys in skins began to cheer. A dozen perhaps, of all races, gabbling in all tongues, and all as befouled by filth and grime as the blackest Moor among them. "And what is your business in the Neverland?" he demanded of me.

I gazed up at him coolly, not to be undone by a mere flying boy. A whelp was a whelp to me. "My only business is to leave this place," I replied. I closed my hand round the hilt of my sword but did not draw it. "You will oblige me by showing me the way."

Derisive laughter greeted this remark as he peered at me with unvarnished disdain. "Oh, *will* I? And who might *you* be to order me about, dark and sinister man?"

I made my eyes glinting slits of menace. "I might be the devil."

"Or you might be a codfish!" he cawed, not the least daunted, and all the boys took up the chant. "Codfish! Codfish!"

I had seen too much of Hell to mind the taunting of little boys, but this one had witchy powers I intended to possess. While they were all still bouncing about, I slid my sword out and upward in one swift movement, catching not flesh but a length of vine girdling the boy's middle. His weight pressed against my sword and I dragged him down through the air so his startled face was opposite mine.

"They call me Hook," I seethed at him. "And you are my prisoner. Boy."

Even as I spoke, I saw excitement kindling in his grey eyes. He bared his little teeth and strained upward as the air between us began to pulse with uncanny glittering, like a hail of diamonds in a shaft of brilliant sunlight. The firefly light was dancing about us too. The boy began to rise, and my blade rose with him, and even as I gripped with all my strength, my sword was sucked up out of my grasp like a loose spar in a hurricane. With a shout of triumph, he grasped the hilt, slithered the blade out from under the vine he wore, and hurled my fine French cutlass to the deck with disdain.

"I'm called Pan!" he crowed, as all the other little boys cheered. "And no man is a match for me!" He swooped down toward me. "Next time, Hook, you better fight fair!"

He blew a shrill bleat on his pipes, peeled off higher into the air and led the flying boys away past the shrouds and off over the creek in a cloud of chattering laughter.

My men thought they were bewitched or dreaming. But it's children all over creation who dream the Neverland into existence because they crave it so much. Such was the powerful force we could not name, the unconscious, uncensored desire of children.

***

Much has been made of my obsession with the Pan, how I ignored the wise council of my shipmates to leave that place in search of more hospitable waters and fatter prizes elsewhere. How sheer childish obstinacy kept me in the Neverland, determined to have my revenge on the clever boy who'd got the better of me. But there was never any hope of escape from the Neverland. I was under a curse, and what few of my men who'd not had wit enough to die or desert me beforehand were bound to share it with me. We made every attempt we could, yet however far we sailed, neither the pattern of the stars nor the shape of the coastline ever altered. Every current, every breeze, brought us back to the Neverland, where the braves and the beasts and the boys were always waiting.

It was foolishness, grown men fighting little boys. My men never took it seriously until one of their fellows had his bowels stove in by a blade wielded with boyish delight. After that, they took better care defending themselves, but it was never an even match; the boys were fleet and ferocious as mosquitoes in the air, doling out death on a whim. Between battles, my men were glad enough to give themselves over to drink, for the Pan called on the enchantment of that place to see our rum casks ever replenished. Drink made them even more likely to get themselves killed in battle or do some fatal injury to themselves. Or risk my wrath, which grew hotter with every tedious new day.

I would have given the boy anything, done anything he asked to purchase our escape. But our presence was all he wanted, a party of bloodthirsty pirates to make his fantasy complete. Along with my eternal humiliation, which he came to crave above all things. My crew diminished, along with our memories of the world we'd left behind, our wits as befouled by rum and torpor as the stinking hull of the *Jolie Rouge*, rotting so long at anchor in the bay.

Silver strands glinted in my dark hair and beard when I looked in my glass. The aches and pains from a lifetime at sea, so long ignored in violent action, began to make themselves felt. I was as twitchy from inactivity as I'd been in the French prison, or during my time chained in the filthy *barracoons* of Cape Coast. So I hit upon a proposition I believed Pan could never resist: I would invite him to join my company of brigands. I hadn't any notion of holding to the bargain for long. But once taken into my crew, I was certain he would long to sail off in search of real ships to plunder, and that would take us out of the Neverland at last.

He came aboard alone, without the usual company of boys in his wake. He had a lot of cheek to come unarmed, although we both knew he could fly away at any moment.

"Well, Hook," he hailed me saucily, "have you more favors to beg of me?"

"Indeed no, I've one to grant you," I sallied back.

He cackled like a little crow. "What do you have that I'd want?"

I told him, gratified to see the greed for adventure in his eyes. But he shuttered his greed and peered at me with suspicion.

"Why?" he demanded. "Why me?"

"You have proven yourself a worthy adversary, Pan," I responded silkily. I had treated with the likes of Edward Low and Black Bart Roberts in my day; I knew how to coo and flatter. "You would be an ornament to our enterprise. Surely you've heard the stories of pirate captains granting their most valiant opponents a place in their crew?"

"Only when the pirates win the battle," he piped up. "You have to beat me first!"

"No need for another battle if we are on the same side," I reasoned. "Besides, I have had plenty of opportunity to judge your …skill and cleverness." I fair choked on the words.

That mollified him for the moment, long enough for me to produce a rolled up parchment from my coat pocket. I had labored all day to limn the word "Articles" across the top, with all due flourishes, and to write out some nonsense about ship's rules and the reckoning of plunder against the most gruesome injuries I could imagine, the sort of stuff that would appeal to a boy. In truth, I'd rarely bothered with such niceties; my men were bound to me by fear and greed and malice for as long as there was profit in it. But such things were much in fashion in other crews, and the stories always made a fuss over the fabled pirate articles. So I spread out the parchment on a barrelhead for his perusal. I'd had my men scrawl their names or their marks in a column with an empty space at the bottom. All very official looking.

"It's a great and solemn honor to be sworn in," I went on, raising my right hand. Pan was fond of ceremony. "But first you must sign the Articles, my bully, and we shall be in business."

He leaned his elbows on the barrel, squinting down the paper, then up at me. "Do I get to sign in blood?" he asked eagerly.

I inclined my head, swallowing a smile. "If you like." I produced a sharpened quill from my other pocket, gingerly testing its point against my forefinger. He returned his gaze to the paper, scowling in perplexity. And it occurred to me that my calligraphic efforts had been wasted; the boy could not read. Small wonder he needed the Wendys to tell him stories. "There," I added helpfully, placing the nib of the quill upon the empty space.

"Is that where it says Captain Pan?"

"Captain Pan?" I gaped at him.

His gaze darted up to me. "I get to be the captain," he barked. "I'm the one who always wins."

"But my boy," I struggled to recompose myself, "there is a world of ships to plunder out there. You may captain any one you—"

"Out there?" he cried, eyes widening at me. "You mean to trick me, Hook! You want to go out there! You want to run away! It's a foul trick!" he bellowed, and a cloud of Lost Boys swarmed up over the wales and flew to us, brandishing their weapons. My men had been sent below so as not to alarm the boy, and that is how I came to be surrounded by angry swords and buck knives with only a quill clutched in my sword hand.

There must have been a dozen of them, devilling and poking at me. I swatted at them like insects, but they were much bigger and heavier, and they were armed. Half of them fell on my flailing arm as I roared for my men. Pan had a grip on my other hand; he'd shaken out the quill and was waving my hand like a prize.

"By this hand you would have sworn falsely to me!" he cried. "You would have tricked me out there, made me grow big, made me grow up! But I will never live in the grown-up world." He drew a raspy breath, and I saw more malice in his glittering eyes than I'd ever seen in any pirate. "And neither will you! Never ever! And this is so you won't forget!"

Three of the little beggars pinned my hand to the barrelhead, while another who'd been flitting all over the deck brought something back to the Pan. I couldn't see what it was, for all the boys shrieking in my ears and cuffing me about the face as I tried to duck and bob. It wasn't until he brandished it over his head that I recognized one of our boarding axes.

It took both his hands to manage it. I saw the downward course of the heavy blade and I struggled desperately, lunging and writhing, but my limbs were sandbagged with squirming bodies, and I could not twist away.

The pain was exquisite, a perfection of white-hot agony so consuming, I couldn't hear my own shriek for the thundering in my head. The children were all shrieking too, giddy in their triumph and whooping as the ax came down again. Of course, he couldn't do it all at once. Flesh and bone are more resistant than you think; the blade was old, and he was not experienced. It took several good whacks to break down the skin and pulp and sever the bone within.

There was no need to restrain me after that. I've heard of Blackbeard fighting on and on with blades and pistol balls twisting in his vitals, but it was not like that for me. I sank to my knees, stupid with pain, clinging to the barrel for support, watching red blood spurting out of my pulpy wrist like wine out of a spigot, as the boys jeered gaily all round me. My fingers were still clutching wildly, I could feel them, but the hand to which they were attached was already gone. Pan flew to the side with it, dripping blood across the deck, and held it aloft like a trophy. At the rail, he paused and whistled. I shall never forget it. He whistled, and the crocodile came splashing up under the hull for its treat.

Pan lighted upon the rail, still grasping his grisly prize, and turned back to me. "I win again, Hook!" he cried. "I'm the true captain of the Neverland!" He dropped my bloody hand over the side, and the boys all cheered, yet for all their din, I heard the greedy snap of reptilian jaws.

It was like an afterword in a tedious book by the time my men mustered themselves on deck to chase off the boys with Long Tom. I don't remember much about it. I was slumped against a pile of cordage, my arm cradled in my lap, watching blood soak through my breeches and into the deck, until blessed oblivion gaped open before me like a great black welcoming sea.

The shock of it was not so much that I had been overmatched by little boys. I have seen green youths scarcely older than the Pan battle ferociously for their lives on the bloody deck of a prize ship. No, it was the glee with which they did it, the jeering, jabbering Lost Boys. We were not in a battle. No lives were at stake. They mutilated me for the sport of it. For the fun.

That is what it is to be a boy.

CHAPTER 14

THE FALLEN

I awake to daylight, stiff-jointed and sore where I've slumped in sleep over my voiceless harpsichord. A sullen drumbeat in my temples reminds me of my last fruitless interview with Parrish. Even if she were once a Wendy, she has no memory of it. Would that *I* were so fortunate; my memories have come back with alarming clarity, and I go above, eager to purge their bitter taste from my mind.

It was foolish to believe that Parrish would ever lead me to the boys, even if she knew the way. She is not so easily maneuvered as my men, and I dare not lose her confidence again: whatever called her here in defiance of the boy's wishes is a power to be reckoned with. Surely it is well within my best interests to keep her under my protection, until whatever it is that wants her can claim her.

Yesterday's high foolery has given way to a more apprehensive atmosphere on deck. The men must have heard Parrish and myself cackling away in our cups last night. I set them to scrubbing away the gore from yesterday's skinning and plucking session, and cheer them up with the order to sand all the decks for action. Up on the fo'c'sle deck, I find that some of the timber we cut from those dead trees in the wood has proven too dry and brittle in the intensity of the Neverland sun, cracking round the nails and splitting from the barricade frames. Sticks had to rip out several useless pieces yesterday and replace them, and today he's got Flax helping him to nail crosspieces across the vertical timbers to better hold the contrivance in place before it can be removed to the quarterdeck.

After a fortifying tankard of my steward's black death, I plunge into the bowels of the hold with Nutter and Jesse to see sufficient quantities of grapeshot and powder tamped into breeches to be ready for Long Tom. Peering about in the gloom for other useful occupations to put them to, I spy in the deepest shadows an ancient, cobwebby trunk taken from a lady passenger of quality on one of our last voyages back in the world. It strikes me this might amuse Parrish, and I order Filcher to have taken in to her cabin. I expect the effects of last night's conviviality will keep her below this morning, but it's best to keep her occupied and out of the way today, while I decide what use can be made of her.

***

But there she reclines on her bunk in her usual shirt and trousers when I look in on her at midday, poring over a small, leather-bound volume.

"Captain," she smiles, sitting up. "Thank you for last night. It was lovely—I think." she makes a wry mouth. "I hope I didn't embarrass myself too badly."

"Not that I should have noticed," I remind her, and her mouth tilts up again. Her hair is unpinned this morning, her feet bare under rolled-up trouser cuffs. "Did you not receive the gift I sent you?" I go on, as if the old trunk were not standing open on a crate at the foot of her bunk.

"I did indeed, Captain," she says eagerly. "Such beautiful antiques! How thoughtful of you to show them to me! The historian in me thanks you."

"But not the woman?" Her bright smile wavers. "Damnation, Parrish, I never thought I'd have to explain to a woman what clothing is for."

"Stella," she laughs.

142

"What?"

"My name. I was only 'Parrish' in service. My name is Stella."

I gaze at her. "A fallen star."

Her mouth tilts up again. "You remember your Latin, Captain."

"I ought to, it was pummeled into me soundly enough."

"But they are much too fine for me to wear," she goes on, nodding toward the trunk. "Besides, gowns of that fashion require, ah, certain undergarments and a battalion of ladies' maids to get into them."

"Well, do what you will with them," I say airily, "they are of no use to me." I nod at the book she's put aside, gilded letters etched upon a wine-dark cover: *Paradise Lost*. "That is not one of mine."

"I found it in there," she replies, nodding again to the trunk.

"No doubt it was thought an improving tract for a young lady on the voyage home," I observe.

"It would certainly improve me," Parrish laughs. "This book would be worth a fortune in my world, among the antiquarians."

"I regret my hospitality is so poor you must resort to Milton."

"Oh, no, I'm enjoying it!" she grins again. "I haven't read it since school. It's quite the heroic ballad."

I frown. "Unless I misrecall, the topic is the Fall of Mankind."

"Well, yes. But, he's made Satan a rather a dashing figure, witty and resourceful. In my world we'd call him a hero with a tragic flaw."

"Well, he *is* Satan," I point out.

"He was an angel once," Parrish rejoins stoutly.

"But that was long ago, before his fall. Now his only choices are infinite wrath and infinite despair. 'Which way I fly is Hell. My self am Hell,'" I recite from the musty bowels of memory.

"His problem isn't his badness, it's his ego," says Parrish. "Repentance and remorse are weaknesses to him. He doesn't know how to seek forgiveness. He's stuck."

I stand agape at her subversive notions.

"He only embraces Evil because he believes Goodness is denied him," she persists. "'Farewell hope, and with hope, farewell fear.'"

"Believes?" I echo. "He is the chiefest villain in Christendom."

"He made a foolish choice once," she counters. "Who hasn't? He could change his mind if he wanted to, but he thinks his time's run out."

I stare at her, but it's Proserpina's face that suddenly swims before me, the witch's voice that thrums in my head. *I will give you all the time you need.* That's what she told me on the day I left her, ages ago. By God's thorns, for centuries, I've blamed Pan for the eternity of my life here. But suppose it was never him at all, but Proserpina keeping me alive all this time, like her spider confederate? But why? For malice alone, or is there some other reason? I thought she was speaking in riddles that day; I didn't listen. Time for what? What was I meant to do here?

From whom would I beg forgiveness, if I could? There are so many I have wronged, all who ever bled on my sword in the pirate trade, the thousands more I have led and lost in futile battles here. *How many more must die?* Proserpina asked me once. Suppose each death, however good or brave, only lengthens the chain of my crimes. Could I but halt this march of death, somehow, would my exile end at last? Is that the chance they all speak of? Is that what Proserpina meant by going back?

Death is the only release I've dreamt of for centuries. Can there be another?

A thundering like a broadside erupts on deck; footfalls pounding, weapons clattering, men shouting. Brassy races into the passage.

"Captain, quick," he pants. "Boys!"

By God's bile, not now! If Proserpina, not Pan, prolongs my life here, she must have had a reason, a key, a plan, but there's no time for pretty theories with the boys on the attack. "Battle stations!" I roar. "Shields up! To your weapons…"

Halfway out the door, I see Parrish on her feet behind me. "Stay out of sight," I warn her.

"But—"

"I beg you! My men will pay with their lives if you are seen."

She pales, retreats, and I charge down the passage and up the ladder.

They are just now racing above the treeline over Pirates Beach, a cloud of racketing boys in their furs and foliage, Pan blowing a shrill fanfare on his pipes. My mind is racing too: I must think of some game to turn Pan away from bloodshed. Nutter and Swab have shoved aside the half-built barricade to position Long Tom; Filcher is passing out arms. Jesse, confident and resolute, is readying his flintlocks up on the quarterdeck, where I ordered him to be.

"Stand by there, Nutter!" I shout as the boys veer into range. Chase them back into the sky for another blessed moment; give me time to think! Turning for the ladder, I see Parrish crouched in the hatchway behind me, staring out at the swarm of boys.

"Bugger me!" I sputter, throwing myself across the opening to block her passage.

"Captain! They're children!" she cries indignantly.

"I know what they are," I hiss.

"Fire!" Nutter shrieks, and I spin round to see all the little boys beating higher up into the air to dodge a peppering of grape fired one second too soon, while I was distracted. Laughing and jeering, they swoop in over the starboard bows, above our now harmless cannon. Nutter and Swab fall back into the waist as the boys hover above us, out of range of our hand weapons.

"Where's that codfish you call a captain?" Pan cries, lighting on a spar on the mainmast, stowing his pipes in his belt of vines. "Show yourself, Hook!"

I stride out amidships, and the men on deck fall in behind me, clutching their swords, axes, pikes. "Well, Pan," I hail him, "just the fellow I want to see." Out of desperation, I reach for the brim of my black hat with its fine white plume. "I'll wager this feather—"

"I make the rules here!" he brays at me. "Whatever's going on in the Neverland, you know you can never beat me, and I'm here to prove it! You get three chances to try." He motions down toward our spent Long Tom. "That was one."

Damnation, I wasn't quick enough; the game has already begun. I circle beneath him, my sword still sheathed. So long as we are engaged in a parley, he'll not unleash his boys, but can I hope to win this challenge with words alone? "But surely nothing ever goes wrong in the Neverland," I parry. "Who would dare defy the great Captain Pan?"

"No one!" He cries down at me. "And noth—"

A crack of shot; iron whistles overhead, but Jesse's ball only comes close enough to make the boy jump on his spar.

"No, no, no!" I yelp, beside myself, as three or four outraged flying boys shear off toward the quarterdeck, shrieking, brandishing their weapons.

Pan's feral grin is showing. "No fair!" he trumpets at me.

"A misfire," I counter desperately. "My weapons are old and unreliable—" But Jesse's second pistol is already drawn, his intent unmistakable. He raises it, and fairy glitter explodes in his face.

"Liar!" Pan yodels, as his whelps close in on Jesse.

I scarcely know what I cry, feinting back toward the starboard ladder as Filcher and Nutter race up the larboard side. Miraculously, the arc of the poleaxe Nutter whirls over his head with such ferocity checks the advance of the first two flying boys, lunging in with swords drawn. They're forced to veer aside while Jesse, even blinded, holds his ground, squeezes off a second shot. But Pan has leapt out of range, and as Nutter and Filcher slash at the first two boys, a third darts round them straight for Jesse. Unarmed, I think, until I see what's clasped in his grubby hand, a weapon that doubles in length before my horrified eyes, a deadly stiletto rasping out of a black case.

"Jess!" I bellow.

Jesse raises his shield arm to ward off a flying assassin he can't see, and the boy dives in with his wicked blade. He rams it up to the hilt between Jesse's upper ribs, viciously yanks it out, sparkling gaudy red in the sun, and shoves it in again. All the boys erupt in cheers.

Even I am stunned by the savagery of it, howling impotently at the foot of the ladder until my men finally drive the boys back into the air with their longer blades. Jesse stumbles blindly about, hands outstretched, his twisted foot buckling under him, his expression perplexed. A dark stain begins to spread across his shirt. He staggers toward the rail, misses it, and crumples to the deck, felled by the blade I stupidly put in Pan's hand.

"That's two," Pan smirks at me.

Outrage boils up in my vitals. I turn on the little murderer, drawing my sword. "Come down and face me like a man!" I roar.

He leaps eagerly down to the deck while I wave back my men to make a clearing. The boys will not attack them again unless they try to interfere; Pan likes things fair, after all. We round on each other, weapons drawn, as anguish and wrath consume me. "How soon before your boys learn there's something in the Neverland you fear?" I goad him.

"I'm not afraid of anything!" He swings his blade angrily at me.

"Then why are you here?"

"To teach you a lesson!" He scuttles sideways, out of my reach, rounds on me fiercely. "How many of your men will it take before you learn it?"

I crash my blade into his, give myself up to bloodrage, slashing and driving. When he loses ground, he rises into the air. I flail after him, stretch to my full height, greedy to injure him, cost him his buoyancy so he might fight me on even terms just this once. But he shoots up out of range, defiance, and exhilaration shining in his eyes, baby teeth bared in a chilling smile. My hook curls round a line, and I claw up the shrouds after him. We battle on, rising above the deck, blades singing, my feet on the ratlines, my hook anchoring me in the shrouds. He darts under the lee of the shrouds, and I lurch round with a vicious slash.

But I thrust at empty air, my body twists out above the deck, and I jerk to the force of his pointed blade through my shirt.

"That's three!" he crows, as deck planks rush up to meet me, and all is black.

CHAPTER 15

SUITE: RESURRECTION

1

It's not so hot in Hell as I imagined, and it stinks of wet wood and brine. A smudge of dim light moves from side to side beyond my closed eyelids, as with the motion of a ship, and my sluggish wits surrender their last tiny hope. Not Hell. Not yet.

My eyes open on the all-too-familiar appointments of my cabin aboard the *Jolie Rouge*. I'm flat on my back on my bed as murky shadows dance below the swaying lantern hung from a peg in the deck beam above me. I wince at its brightness. My phantom fingers twitch, but the dead weight of my hook is still fixed to my arm. I can force naught but a dry wheeze past my thickened tongue.

Something rustles up out of the shadows beside my bed, a black silhouette in the dim light.

Stella Parrish gasps, staring down at me. "You live!"

"I always live," I croak. I should know by now the Neverland is my eternal Hell. I taste stale blood; pain thrums in the small of my back, and when I try to shift, it flares up my spine like a thousand stinging hornets. I can't stifle a groan, which effort awakens acute throbbing in a network of muscle beneath my collar bone. I shudder and lie still again.

"But…it's not possible! I saw you die!" Her gaze draws mine to the rusty red staining my shirt. "I saw the blood."

"I can bleed," I rasp at her. The ravaged hulk of my body can absorb an infinity of scars and holes and mutilations. "I can fall out of the rigging like an imbecile." Animation is returning slowly to my tongue. "Only Death eludes me."

She must shrink from me now, unnatural monster that I am. Yet there she stands, the light moving across her ashen face, a glistening in her dark eyes. She snorts in a most ungenteel fashion and wipes a hand under her nose.

"What are you blubbering about?" I bark. The effort produces a sputtering cough like grapeshot rattling through my lungs.

"It's the usual response when someone dies," she snaps back, pawing at her tears with the back of her hand before gliding away into the shadows.

But it's not usual at all, not for me. No one has ever cried for me before, not the Wendys, nor generations of Lost Boys, nor any of the children to whom the story is so often told. They always cheer when Hook dies.

She reappears above me, holding something that catches the light, one of my fluted wine goblets, clear liquid aswirl inside, and my dry mouth convulses with longing. She pours from the glass into her cupped hand; stray drops fall into my beard. The heel of her hand presses gently against my lip, leaking its cargo of blessed water into my mouth, until I've drunk my fill.

"Easy, Captain, easy," she murmurs.

A fresh tattoo of pain rattles through my shoulder; I bite back another groan as each reawakening muscle adds its own unique voice to the symphony of torment.

"Does it hurt?" she asks.

"Hellishly, thank you," I mutter again, closing my eyes. When I open them, she's wrestling something out of a pocket in her trousers, some piece of dried vegetation.

"Here," she says, "chew on this. For the pain." She slips the dubious thing between my lips. It tastes bitter, but not rancid. "I'll be right back." And then she's gone.

How I crave sleep; there is no part of me that's not stiff or aching or drumming with pain. But I can't stop thinking. She mourned me.

***

Woodsmoke, as sweet as one of Burley's pipes, but more intense. Fire, I think, forcing open my eyes against its sting, but there is no inferno, no alarm, only a haze of smoke and a distant, flickering light. Top notes of smoke give way to other scents: hewn pine, cured hides, sweat. Anticipation.

Bodies move all round me in shadowy half-light, not men at work, but men, women, even children, in a kind of dance. Their slow, swaying motion answers the rhythm of a hollow drumbeat, to which the shadow people respond by chanting syllables foreign to me, silhouetted against the wavering light of a small fire contained in the middle of their circle. Its silver smoke curls up into cavernous shadows overhead, and out a hole in the roof, a roof of thick notched logs, like the walls supporting it. My hand connects to solid ground and dried grass, where I sit in the outer shadows.

This is not the *Rouge*.

Long plaited hair and leather fringe drip from the figures around me; I hear the *clack-clack* of shell adornments clattering together with their movements. The ominous drumming continues. Redskins, for certain, yet none is taking any notice of me.

The drums and the chanting cease. I blink through the gloom, see an elder of the tribe rise up beside the fire in the center of the circle. So frail does the creature appear, so small and wiry, with such long silver braids, I can't tell if it's male or female, a face as wrinkled as a raisin beneath a towering headdress of buffalo horns. Swathed in robes, with strings of corn kernels, shells, dried berries, animal bones depending from its neck, the creature rises on a staff sprouting feathers and beads. The people shush each other.

"Grandfather Buffalo speaks," someone whispers nearby.

151

"For suns and moons beyond counting, the story has been told," the old man begins in a light musical piccolo of a voice. A tiny, bell-like tinkling of adornments accompanies his every move. "One sign from the earth, one out of the sea, one in the sky, so say the ancestors. Three signs."

"Three signs," the crowd chants back. "One from the earth, one from the sea, one from the sky."

"Now hear Running Fox," the old man says, with a gesture of invitation. A seasoned brave, hawk-beaked and sinewy, steps out of the pack, long plaits shiny black beneath his beaded headband.

"I was in my canoe in the bay, at first morning light near the end of Pirates Beach," the fellow tells the others. "The empty place of rock and waste where nothing green can live. But I saw them!" His dark gaze flits all round the crowd. "Under the bluff. Growing out of hard rock and sand. The forbidden flowers. As many colors as a bird has feathers."

"So our Earth Mother creates beauty out of waste," the shaman intones. "One sign from the earth. The great dream quest begins."

"For which warrior?" one of the men asks eagerly.

The old shaman shakes his horned head with a rattle of his heathen adornments. "For the one who is brave enough to follow the dreampath."

A note of anxiety seems to pulse through the crowd.

"Are the people in danger?" a woman's voice asks.

"The Great Spirits who cradle the Dreaming Place in their hands will protect the people," the shaman reassures them. "The one who follows the dreampath must dare to go another way." He raises his feathered staff. "It is a perilous quest. The risks are great. So too is the reward."

As the people fall to muttering again among themselves, the old man's quavering voice rises once more. "If the dream quest is not fulfilled when all three signs are seen, the time will never come again to follow it. Never, ever."

And the crowd chants back, "Never, ever."

"Welcome back, Captain."

I force open sluggish eyes to see Stella Parrish dipping her hands in a water basin on my little cherrywood table, drawn up beside my bed aboard the *Rouge*. Her shirtsleeves are rolled up, her bouncy hair drawn back with a length of twine, and some voluminous scrap of sailcloth tied at the waist covers her clothing. Pale purple dawn streaks through my stern windows; the last of the loreleis' discordant yowling is just ebbing away. I glance down to see my shirt sliced open and peeled away from some kind of poultice of crushed greenery and paste and other witchery tied over my latest wound. But one reflexive twitch assures me my hook is still buckled in place, the straps criss-crossing my uninjured shoulder.

At the table, she stirs something into a tankard and brings it to me. "Drink this," she says. "You'll feel better."

I struggle up on my good elbow, although she still has to hold the vessel. How helpless I must appear to her. The thought makes me irritable, and I sniff at the tankard. "What is it?"

"I found some useful plants in the wood, near where the fairies dwell," she shrugs.

"Toadstool?" I suggest. "Nightshade?"

She peers at me coolly. "What would you care if it was?"

"Excellent point," I agree, and drink some down. She'll not get to the windward of me. Whatever she put in it, I taste only rum, and savor it, watered down as it is, and lay back again. They are never mortal wounds, which never stops them hurting most damnably. But at this moment, my breast no longer throbs, nor does my back complain, and a calming warmth seems to ease my other scrapes and sores and aches as well. I'm almost lulled to contentment, but for a sudden jolting vision worse than any nightmare.

"Jesse," I rasp at the woman. "My marksman. He's the one you ought to be patching up."

She frowns at me, shakes her head. "There was nothing I could do for him."

I grimace at the memory. Jesse, his modesty, his easy grin, his quiet competence, his courage, all dispersed like particles of dust. All because I duped him into thinking he could ever prevail against the boy. Another soul across the Styx without me. Another pointless death. Another loss. "Then what use are all your black arts?"

"Not much," she replies wearily. "I'm a nurse, not a witch. I can't raise the dead. Usually," she amends, with another tentative glance at me.

"And the others?" I groan. "The rest of the butcher's bill?"

"There were no others. When the two of you…died… he flew off with his boys."

I nod grimly. "He prefers to slaughter them in front of me. I took the fun out of it for him, dying first."

She peers down at me. "Then you saved their lives."

"Stupidity is not twin to nobility," I mutter. She turns away with the tankard, as if to move off, but I stretch out my arm, trap her wrist in the curve of my hook. She halts, gazes down at my hook, and then again at me. "All this fuss," I say coolly. "What do you mean to gain by it?"

She looks at me in silence for another moment. "You offer me protection, at no small cost to yourself," she says quietly. "I mean to deserve it."

I release her, and she goes back to her table, littered with fragrant little piles of mint, jasmine, bay laurel. "I'd have sworn you'd lost a lung, but it turns out the wound didn't go very deep, it only creased the muscle," she goes on, as she wipes the base of the tankard with her apron and sets it back on the table. "And something must have broken your fall, although I can't imagine what; you didn't hit with near the force you should have, just enough to knock you out."

"As usual." I peep again at the reeking plaster over my breast. "I suppose you studied doctoring at university."

"Oh, I'm scarcely a doctor," she smiles wanly, tying up a bunch of her weeds. "I learned herbalism from my aunt, and I've had some nurse's training. I won't poison you or cut open a vein. At least not by mistake," she adds, with a sidelong glance.

The creases round her eyes, her mouth, are more defined by the cold morning light, her eyes vaguely shadowed. "Surely, you haven't been about it all night, Parrish?" I say gruffly.

"It wasn't so bad," she shrugs. "Someone sings so beautifully here at night." She straightens, shoves back a wisp of loose hair with the back of her hand. "After they brought you down here, they took that other fellow off in the boat. I thought you were next."

"I am never, ever to be buried at sea!" I exclaim.

Her eyes round in surprise, but she nods slowly. "The thing is, you never stopped breathing. Not like…" and she darts another guilty glance above. "I did try, Captain."

I frown. "My men didn't stop you, I hope?"

She shakes her head. "No, they all wanted to help. That Cornish fellow, he was pretty good at it. We tried everything I could think of, mouth-to-mouth, chest compression, but it was too late. Your Jesse was already gone."

I recall Filcher nattering on about a Jonah. "They didn't blame you, did they?"

"They blamed the boys," she says quietly. "In very expressive terms. Your Mr. Burley sent me back down here. Your steward has been in to see how you are." She gives a little shrug. "They seem to have got the idea that I saved your life. You won't blow my cover, will you?"

"You're welcome to take all the blame."

She toys thoughtfully with the stem of one of her plants. "Where do they come from, your men?"

"The dregs of society, I imagine. They were all Lost Boys once, banished for the crime of growing up. They dream themselves here out of sheer perversity. Like you," I add.

"Ah," she murmurs, wiping her hands on her makeshift apron. "And how do they get back?"

"Back?" I stare at her. "They never go back."

She frowns at me. "No? Well, why are they here?"

"I scarcely inquire into their biographies," I snap.

"Why not?"

"Because they are going to die!" I exclaim, hauling myself up on my good arm again. "Every one of them! They are dead men already. They will all go the way of Jesse before long; I've seen it a thousand times." She peers at me as if she too could see the vision I choose to spare her: bodies heaped in blood, rotting in the sun and wet for me to find whenever I crawl out of whatever dank hole I've found in which to lick my wounds. All of it waiting for me to begin the entire wretched business again. "Grow up or die; those are the only ways back from the Neverland."

She nods, her face sober. "How many crews have you lost?"

"Countless. The Bay of Neverland is littered with their bones."

She is quite still by her table, watching me. "How often has he...killed you?"

To this I can make no accurate response, only shake my head.

"And, who takes care of you, after?" she persists.

"Obviously, no one with your skill," I mutter, twitching a loose flap of shirt across my middle, over the protruding tip of one of my angrier old scars. I dislike all these questions.

Her pitiless gaze is unwavering. Then she sighs. "I may have misjudged you, Captain," she murmurs. "I've misjudged everything."

I ease myself back on my bed. "You are not the first."

She pretends to return to her business, neatening up one of her little piles. "What are the three signs?" she asks. "You spoke of them in your sleep."

"Nothing. Some nonsense in a dream."

"Dream?" she echoes. "You had a dream? Just now? Tell me!" She comes nearer, absently wringing her hands in her apron. "Dreams are important!"

"Not mine," I sigh.

"Dreaming brought me here," she insists. "I just don't know why. Maybe another dream will explain what's going on around here."

Something odd is going on, that's true enough. Even Pan senses it. It also occurs to me Parrish might have gone off with the boy when she had the chance, claimed herself my hostage and been rescued. Yet here she is. Whatever she might have been to the Pan before, she's made herself his enemy now, caring for me. And so I tell her my foolish dream.

"A quest, that's what he called it?" Her green-glinting eyes widen again when I describe the elderly shaman in his buffalo headdress.

"I've seen him too!" she exclaims. "In the Fairy Queen's hall of mirrors. He's the one who gave me those buds, like the one I gave you yesterday, or at least he directed me where to pick them in the wood. I thought it would just be a mild soporific, you know, to help you sleep. He called them Dream Flowers."

"So the Indians are opium-eaters."

"Not exactly," she replies. "The shaman told me Dream Flowers are supposed to have...certain properties. It's said they tell the dreamer what he needs to know."

"Why should I need to know about redskin humbuggery?" I protest.

"I don't know, Captain, but someone is on a quest. And this is the last chance to take it."

***

The sun shines triumphantly in a bright blue sky. Whatever was troubling the boy before, the salubrious act of killing a pirate and another sound trouncing of me has restored his humor. In another few days, I am fit to go above and show myself to the men. All witnessed the grisly fate of Dodge when he landed on this very deck. Now they view me with awe, as if it were some talent I've perfected, this cheating of Death, not a wretched curse worthy of their derision. They are quick to snap to my commands, all but salaaming like Turks as I parade by. No one dares question the presence of the Parrish woman, still in her doctoring apron, on the quarterdeck, watching covertly to see her poultice stays in place.

Burley has been out fishing, and the men are making ready to haul in the gig boat. It sobers me anew to recollect her previous grim mission, and when I cross the dark stain on the quarterdeck where Jesse fell, I hasten down the ladder to join them.

"Who spoke the words over Jesse?" I ask Burley.

"I did," he replies, as they sway the dripping boat in over the wales, and make her fast on her blocks. "And, Cap'n," he goes on, wiping a sleeve across his sweating forehead. "The lads wanted to put one of his guns—yours, I mean—in with him. Didn't seem right t'send him off without it. I told Filcher I'd take the blame."

He peers at me resolutely through pale, seawashed eyes, ready for his punishment. Stout fellow, Burley.

"You did right," I assure him, then turn away before he can see the fresh anguish that washes over me. However bravely Jesse met his death, there was nothing good about it. Another life wasted. Thanks to me.

Our skiff is in the water as well; someone must have gone off to the garden. The tackle sways out again, and Flax climbs astride the rail and reaches for the line to carry it down to the second boat.

"Oi!" he yells suddenly, grasping the line, staring down over the side. "Sod off, you!"

A mighty splash reverberates up from the water. Crocodile, I think, my blood chilling, as I rush to the side with the others, hooking Flax inboard by the elbow before he tumbles himself into the bay. Choppy water rocks the little boat, then something long and gleaming unfurls from its greeny depths, a massive fishtail, too sinuous for a shark, and far too pert in the saucy flick of its long, gelatinous fin. A low wailing sullies the air before the thing dips beneath the surface again, leaving a wake of burbling, clamorous laughter, such as a drowning man may hear as the last of life is sucked out of him.

Lorelei.

3

No familiar commands leap to my tongue. I have no words for this emergency; no lorelei has ever come this far out into the Bay of Neverland before. They may be snaking up the chains even now. Do I order battle stations, or have Burley throw out his nets?

"Bows," I yelp, "stern!"

"It's gone, Cap'n," Burley says at my elbow.

"How many was there, Flaxy?" Nutter cries from the tackle, straining to see over the side.

"Just the one," says Flax. "She put something in the boat and swam away."

I dispatch men fore and aft anyway, while the others haul in the skiff, but no more sirens are found. The object left in our boat is so indistinguishable from all the other flotsam in that neglected bottom, it takes a moment to find it, knotted inside a kelp leaf in the stern. It appears to be the rubbery corpse of some expired marine creature, stinging tentacles cut away and sides sewn together to form a little pocket. A slim, hollow reed protrudes from the seam. It resembles nothing so much as a slimy bagpipe for some amphibious fairy, but otherwise appears neither harmful nor useful.

"Wot's it do?" asks Filcher.

"It's meant to confound us," I tell them, as if arcane lorelei intentions are as clear to me as daylight on the beach. "But we'll not be gulled," and I drop it scornfully back into the boat.

The men begin to disperse, but Stella Parrish has come down to the rail by the skiff, watching us all. Her avid eyes shift to me.

"It's for the journey," she says.

***

"What journey?" I've hustled Parrish round the far side of the deckhouse; from the expressions of the men, they expect her to sprout a fishtail next and disappear cackling into the deep. I half expect it myself.

"I don't know, do I? That's just what the mermaid said."

"How is it they all speak to you, the fairies, the loreleis?" I mutter.

"Why doesn't anyone else listen?"

"Have you no more sense than to let the fey creatures of this place beguile you with their lies?"

"It's their world, not mine," she exclaims. "How else am I to know how to get on?"

"And where did it get you last time? The damned Fairy Dell," I remind her.

"Where I discovered all that," and she nods to the bandaged poultice beneath my shirt. "It's come in rather handy since then, don't you think?"

I'm in no position to deny this; my wound scarcely throbs at all. Clearly, I've never felt so well so soon before.

"Well, since you are privy to their speech, what else do they say?" I whisper.

"But I've told you. The fairy who came on board that day said this was your last chance. And she told me to ring a bell to call a fairy—"

"Hey, lend a hand there!" Burley calls from the boat tackle.

I glance up just in time to see Nutter chugging past the deckhouse, huffing, "Okay, okay, hold your horses…" Then I nod at Parrish to follow me below.

"You're the yarn-spinner," I begin, when we are in my cabin again, dropping into the chair by my writing desk. "Journeys, quests, dreams, the whole lot of it. What do you make of it all?"

She's pleased to be asked, seating herself beside her table of herbs. "Well, in the old fairy tales, things happen in threes. Magical tools. Portents and signs," and she eyes me meaningfully.

"One from the earth, one from the sea, one from the sky," I recite the shaman's words.

"And there's usually a task to be accomplished," she goes on.

"A victory?"

She frowns. "Maybe. Or a heroic journey completed."

"A 'heroic journey' can have bugger all to do with me," I point out.

"Not necessarily." Her mouth tilts up. "The old tales are full of disguised heroes—frog princes, animal bridegrooms."

"You are whimsical, Parrish."

"Can it be one of your men on a journey?" she suggests.

"They come here to follow a leader, not strike out on their own."

"And you're the one who had the dream vision," she agrees. "Besides, the fairy said it was *your* last chance."

Mockery, nothing more. I think of the imp queen's sinister riddles and repress a shudder. "Surely you are the one on a journey," I suggest.

"Oh, the heroines of the stories are never like me," Stella laughs. "They are beautiful young virgins of irreproachable character."

"Fairies, roses, Dream Flowers, all of it began with your arrival," I remind her. "Please Parrish, you've seen the dangers facing my men here. Is there nothing more you can tell me that might help me save their lives?"

***

"His name was David Islington. A big, bluff fellow, full of fun. We met at university." Her mouth tilts up impishly. "He was reading history, and I started taking some of the same courses, you know, to throw myself in his way."

"Minx," I observe, and her smile broadens with tenderness; few enough women have ever smiled that way for me.

"Oh, I was completely shameless," she agrees. "It's a good thing too; subtlety was entirely lost on David. He preferred his life painted in very bold strokes." Her grin fades. "When the war came, there was no holding him back. A world war, they called it. Everyone was involved, Europe, Russia, Asia, America—"

"That colonial backwater?"

"It's a very powerful nation. They all are. Oceans of ships, armies of men, weapons you can't even imagine…"

"Flying ships," I inject. "Raining hell."

She nods. "He was teaching history, by then, to boys who'd be off fighting in another year. History was happening all around him, and he wanted to be part of it." Parrish shakes her head, eyes downcast, as if one of her plants were arguing with her. "I had his pay, and I'd published one or two silly books by then. The war was winding down. Then…he was killed in the liberation of France."

162

I pretend to fuss with my shirt cuff. "And your child?"

She shakes her head again. "I never told him. David. I'd miscarried before. I was going to surprise him when he came home for good. But…when I got the news…I went into labor early." Her expression is dreadfully composed. "He did not survive the hour of his birth. He died in my arms. Our son."

A more gallant fellow might offer her a manly shoulder, however damaged, on which to weep. But she is far from weeping.

"I hated them all so much," she says. "The world of men who made the war. I could never, ever forgive them."

"So you came here."

"At first I only wanted to die. But I was too cowardly," she sighs. "Besides, I thought, what if it was my duty to survive?"

"Duty?" I echo. "To whom?"

"To my son. To David. To myself. What right had I to toss away what had been so cruelly stolen from them? So I sold our flat in town and went to live with my aunt in the Scilly Islands, a widow herself by then, my last living relation. I'd spent summers there as a girl, a rugged, wild place at the end of the world."

"I know the Isles."

"But they were all in such a great hurry to cheer me up, my aunt and her friends. Accused me of living too much in the past." She makes a wry mouth. "The last place I wanted to be! I couldn't even write any more. Every word was a complaint, or an outcry, or some mawkish ode dragging me back into the damned past. So I took myself back to London, found work in a military hospital. They were always in need of nurses, experienced or otherwise."

"A strange choice of professions, did you mean to escape the spectre of war," I observe.

"I so wanted to be of use to somebody. But I was surrounded every day by sickness, hopelessness, dying.

London was a burnt-out wreck. When my aunt became gravely ill, I went back to Scilly; it rallied me out of myself for a while, tending her." She sighs. "It was a blessing when she went; her life had become so diminished. But it was another ending. That's when my dreams turned beyond rational time and place, beyond war and its never-ending aftermath. Beyond the world the grown-ups made."

"The Neverland," I murmur.

"My dreams were unrelenting. That's when I found that old book again, the one signed by Mr. Barrie, in a box of things my aunt was storing for me. *Believe*, he wrote. I began to dream of the Neverland as a real, physical place—this bay, the beach, the wood, the laughter of children, they were all so real! A haven of childhood innocence, a place undefiled by war and poverty and hatred, where children might need a mother, where I might finally do somebody some good. Then my dreams became more abstract, as if some force were calling me."

I peer at her. "You never saw who? Did someone speak to you?"

But she shakes her head. "It was never a conversation. It was more like a sense of exhilaration, like a flying dream. It was irresistible! I just knew I'd find something wonderful here. I got that situation in Kensington Gardens, worked for nothing, even used my maiden name, to start completely over. I had to find some place untouched by the war, to recover from my losses. I needed to come back to life."

"You might have married again," I suggest. "There was always a brisk trade in widows in my day."

"But how could I confess what I'd done?" she beseeches her plants.

"Done?" I echo.

She glances up, startled that her words were spoken aloud. "I let him go," she falters. "David. That's what his mother said. I wasn't...enough for him, not enough to keep him at home."

"That is the spitefulness of females, Parrish."

She shakes her head sadly. "She was grieving too. Anyway, I couldn't reveal myself to strangers, could I? I was still too raw."

"You've revealed a great deal to me," I point out.

Her mouth tilts briefly up. "I take liberties, I know." She slides a stray wisp of hair behind her ear. "But…it's different with you."

"Because I'm only make-believe?"

She does not smile, but studies me frankly. "Because you're the first person in ages who seems to have any idea what I'm talking about. Men in my world don't speak of such things. They hold it all in. With what they went through in the war, who can blame them?"

"I've had two hundred years to keep silent," I mutter. "They'd not care for it so much had they no other choice."

She peers at me for another long interval. "Whatever are you doing here, Captain?"

And I begin to tell her some of my own history, my sordid piratical career, as much of my dealings with Proserpina as I can recall. I spare her nothing of the Pan's wiles, so she might grasp exactly where her reckless dreaming has got her. My words, halting at first, begin to flow irresistibly; it's an enormous relief to have them out at last. Thus we while away the afternoon, exposing our darkest sorrows to the pitiless Neverland sun.

CHAPTER 16

THE PIRATES ARE AFRAID

We are like motley dancers in an opera ballet. I pirouette along my quarterdeck, and the two men on watch continue their stately march across the deck on opposite sides of the waist. I pause to sniff the scented air, listen for war drums, idly scratch at a flea bite, and my cutthroat *corps* pause as well, alert to my every breath, now that I am magical. I sigh and wave them back to their duty.

Once it was my habit under sail to prowl my quarterdeck at night, where the sting of salt spray and fresh breeze might harry my wits into better order. It's an altogether different experience aboard the gloomy *Rouge* with her canvas all reefed up, scarcely ever a breath of wind on the still water, and the unchanging Neverland stars as stationary as a painted scrim.

I've drunk not one drop of spirits tonight, despite the presence of all the ghosts Stella Parrish and I have unleashed between us. I thought my cabin would feel crammed to overflowing with them, that they would suffocate me. But loosed from inside me after so long, they evaporated into nothing in the night air. Indeed, my cabin felt vast and empty after Stella left it. A part of me is incensed that she beguiled so many secrets out of me, yet I confess I reveled in the gluttony of our conversation, came away reeling and glassy-eyed, like a bumpkin at a village feast. And therein lies the danger. I can't let her become indispensible to me, with her healing balms and her clever talk. I can't give Pan any opportunity to use her against me.

Surely naught but staggeringly poor judgment landed her here, as is the case with my men, indefinable yearning beyond all reason. Still, it's remotely possible that one of them, not a boy, as Stella thought, regrets coming here and longs to go back. Might that be what summoned her? Might that be the journey, the quest in progress?

One of the men on watch is Filcher, so I trot down the ladder and cut him off amidships for a private word while his counterpart at the opposite rail scurries gratefully off. If he is surprised that I inquire after the former lives of the men, he dares not let on.

"Well, they don't talk about it much," he begins hesitantly. "It ain't real, like, the time before." He frowns, absently scratches at the red rag around his head. "Flaxy might've got a girl in trouble and run off. Nutter, he's mad about football; busted up a few 'eads over it, I reckon. Burley were a fisherman. Lived with 'is mum all 'is life, then she died. Swab were a drifter, I guess, lived all over. Brassy come from council flats, 'is folk was foreigners. Gato were only a little bleeder in the Spanish war. Lost 'is family."

"And Dodge?"

"Bit of a toughie, that one," Filcher shrugs. "Fights and dice."

"And yourself?"

He scowls at the phantom memory. "The peelers was after me, wasn't they? It's the choky for me, next time."

History repeats itself with my men, so it seems. As boys and men, they only dream themselves here when the other world is closing in.

"Do any of them seem sorry to be here?" I venture carefully.

Filcher guffaws in disbelief. "Sorry? Where else would we go?"

Where, indeed? "What about Jess?" I force myself to ask, dreading the answer. Did that affable fellow send a dream to the stars, begging for release, which was answered by some mysterious power? Was it his destiny to go home, until I got him murdered on my quarterdeck?

But Filcher snorts again. "Jess? 'e loved it 'ere, Cap'n, more'n any of us! It was always 'appy days with Jess."

I thank him and send him below to fetch Burley. The square, solid shape of my bo'sun emerges from the forward hatch, and I join him at the rail as Filcher resumes his place on watch. Burley has brought up his pipe and lights it with relish. He never smokes below decks; he is seaman enough for that.

"I've heard how you tried to save Jesse," I tell him. "I appreciate all you did."

"Wish we might've done more," Burley sighs around his pipe, smoke curling above his head.

"I know." I gaze out at the vivid stars, the distant dark rim of the fog bank. The moon is not yet risen over the island. "Tell me, Mr. Burley, have you noticed anything... odd, lately?"

My bo'sun says nothing at first, although his expression is plain enough. What is not odd in the Neverland? Something completely unremarkable, that would be the odd thing.

"Something not seen before, out in the bay, perhaps?" I try again. "The sky?" I know not what form these other signs may take, if indeed they are any more than the sheerest whimsy, but fisher folk always have one eye on the sea and the other on the stars.

The Cornishman chews thoughtfully on his pipe stem. "Can't say as I have, Cap'n. Am I t'be looking for oonything?"

"No, no. It's nothing." And I thank him and send him off to the galley for another bottle of rum. I tell him I desire the men to drink a round in honor of Jesse, and watch him amble off.

Unpromising material for Stella's heroic journey, my men, in flight from a world to which they've severed all ties. Clearly, Stella Parrish herself is the only one on a journey here. But where will it lead? And what has it to do with me?

***

"We'll have you whittling again in no time, Maestro," Stella assures me in the morning, tucking in the tail of a fresh cloth bandage as I gingerly flex my hand. With my shirt cut open all down the front, I can keep half of it on while she tends me, and not subject her eyes to the wreckage of my entire body.

I note that she is down to a last few meagre bulbs and stems from her store of medicinal plants. "I can always go back to the Fairy Dell," she shrugs, scooping up these last few crumbs into a scrap of cloth.

"At the expense of your wits? I think not, Parrish."

But it might be useful to produce some sort of restorative against our next skirmish with the boys, as she has used up all her remedies on me. As she tidies up, I go into the galley, signaling Brassy to come with me and sending for Filcher as well. Cookie is clearing up after the morning mess, and we gather near the brick oven as I explain my purpose.

"Look for any sort of small glass vial, stoppered with cork or wax," I tell them. "A dark liquid inside, with a slightly purple cast when held up to the light." How to describe the scent, I wonder, the sweet, seductive allure of oblivion.

"Wot's it for?" Filcher asks.

"It's medicinal," I say lightly. "To ease pain."

"Like morphine?" suggests Brassy. "In the war."

The name charms me. Morphine, the gift of Morpheus, yes, exactly. "Our supplies have, ah, run low, but there might yet be a bottle or two secreted about the ship. Brassy, look to your cupboard, Cookie, your pantry, Filcher, wherever you happen to be. There are extra rum rations for any man who—"

A cry burbles up from on deck. "Boys!"

I bolt out into the passage. Already I hear a shriek of pipes, a far-off chant. "Hook! Hook!"

Damnation! I'm scarce given—what has it been, three days, four?—to recover myself, and now the little maniac is back to finish the job aborted last time by my untimely demise. I should have known he'd not rest until his boys cut down every last man in my crew. And not only men, not this time.

"Nutter!" I roar, as my head emerges above the deck. "Battle stations! Shields!" Gato is on lookout aloft, Swab and Sticks on watch, shouting at the sky. The rest are still below, although Nutter's red head shoots up the forward hatch at the first whiff of battle. "Men, to the magazine—"

"Captain."

The quiet composure of Stella's voice startles me into silence. She's in the shadows at the foot of the ladder behind me, peering up at me. "Tell him no," she says.

"Madam?" I gape.

"Peter. Say no to him," she says again. "Don't answer, don't go up. Send your men below and batten down the hatches, or whatever it is you do. Don't engage him."

By God's bleeding thorns, she's serious! "They will slaughter us all!" I sputter.

"Not if you don't play."

"But that would be the baldest cowardice!" I exclaim.

"It's idiocy to let him goad you into a battle you can't win!" she insists. "Why risk the lives and limbs of your men over nothing? To amuse the boys? Who must die this time to prove your manhood? It won't be you!"

My phantom hand aches to strike, the impulse bolts through my arm, I'm near enough to slash her wayward tongue out of her head. But that won't make her words any less true. What can more deaths possibly achieve? How many more must die? The circles of Hell already teem with my former crews, and yet my exile continues. I hesitate for a crucial instant, my hook half-raised. Stella stands her ground.

"Codfish! Codfish!" comes the distant wheedling of the boys.

Am I to lead my men into further bloodshed over the taunting of boys? They expect no less, Nutter halfway to Long Tom, bawling lustily for his crew, the others erupting out of hatches, diving for their weapons, itching for my orders. That's how it's always been.

"They'll think me a coward," I protest. How then shall I command them, protect them?

"Let them live to think it," Stella urges. "Prove you are stronger than all of them. Resist him. Refuse him. Change the game."

Can such a thing be possible? If she is wrong, my men will pay in blood, but they are dead men anyway if the battle goes on. "Deck, there!" I shout, still staring down at Stella. "Below with you! All of you!"

Their responses are shocked wheezes, profanity, blustery outrage.

"That's an order!" I spring up the ladder and out on deck. "Nutter! Gato! All of you below!"

They bleat as if I'm denying their rum ration, not protecting their sorry lives. It's plain they think me in an advanced stage of imbecility, but I herd them below as the cloud of boys approaches. All but Nutter, lingering at the gun, shaking with fury.

"Goddamit, Captain…"

"Damn you if you disobey me!" I rumble at him, fingers at my sword hilt. He wants to rage at someone; his golden eyes are feral with it. But it won't be me. Steel rattles in my scabbard before he backs up one step, but my fury is colder than his.

"The first man to come up," I shout, as he throws himself down the forward hatch, "will answer to me."

"Hook! Where are your men?" cries Pan from his flotilla of boys, gliding in amid the foretop yards. "Didn't you hear us coming?" He blows his war song on his pipes, as his boys take aim at the hatches with their arrows. They're keen for blood today.

"We heard it," I shrug. "The answer is no."

"No?" he gapes at me, so visibly startled, he drops an inch or two in the air, drawing out his short blade as if to bat away the word itself. In some confusion, the others turn their blades and cocked arrows toward me. "What do you mean?" Pan bellows.

"No, *thank you*," I elaborate, with mock formality, despite the tension crackling through every fiber of my body. "No games today, if it's all the same to you."

"But I want a game!" he shouts, shocked and angry. "What's the matter with you, Hook? You know the rules!" He shakes his sword, and the trigger-happy boys set to yelping and bandying about their bows and knives. Fairy light glints at Pan's shoulder, goading him on.

"Sorry," I gaze back at him coolly. "I'm just not in the mood."

Pan scowls down at me, as furious as Nutter, a sparkle of fairy irritation at his ear. "The pirates are afraid!" he bleats suddenly, and swoops down toward me with his blade upraised. I gesture in the air with my hook, more dismissive than menacing, and he wheels away.

"The pirates," I reply easily, "have better things to do." I turn, and with my back to them all, saunter aft toward the hatch.

I don't expect to feel their arrows peppering my back – that wouldn't be fair – although I listen for the hammering of their weapons at the hatch covers, the thumping of little feet onto the deck to swarm below. But I hear only confused chattering, swelling into an indignant new chant: "The pirates are afraid! The pirates are afraid!"

Gaining the hatchway, I see Stella in the shadows at the foot of the ladder. The boys keep it up a little while longer as I descend, adding various other whoops and insults as the spirit takes them: Hook is a codfish, the pirates are stupid girls, that sort of thing. But the chanting grows ragged, and the boys begin complaining.

Finally, Pan cries, "Aw, stop it, Kes! C'mon, men," he tells his boys, "There's nobody here worth fighting today." As the others rally, Pan shouts after me, "You owe me a game, Hook. And I won't forget!" Then he herds his boys off to look for redskins.

Stella retreats down the passage, her face drawn and tense, but I suddenly feel giddy with success. "B'God, I missed my calling! I ought to have mounted the stage, not merely the trollops who act upon it. Well played, Parrish." I bow to her.

She draws a shaky breath. "They are children yet," she murmurs. "As easily bored as children everywhere. And as quickly."

"I'll remember," I nod to her.

Only now do I notice the atmosphere of tension below, even though the boys have flown off. Knots of men massed in the forward shadows ooze onto the gun deck as I turn, glance round. I doubt they mean to thank me as their dark, furtive expressions emerge out of the gloom, peering at me from round the masts.

"Do what you like with the rest of the day, men," I sally, with determined cheerfulness. "Keep a weather eye out for boys."

Some mumble in assent, begin backing away. But Filcher and Nutter linger in the shadows, facing me.

"Mr. Filcher?"

He shifts where he stands, glances sideways at a couple of fellows still lurking in the shadows, works his mouth. It's Nutter who stands forward.

"We ain't afraid, Cap'n," he says quietly. Filcher and some of the others nod vigorously, and then all of them melt back into the gloom.

CHAPTER 17

INDIANS

"I unmanned them," I complain to Stella from the doorway of her cabin.

The atmosphere was so thick on deck after the boys flew off, I sent the men off to the beach for one of their football matches with the black and white leather ball Nutter brought back from the other world. They've been testing their insulted manhood against each other all day, and come back stinking, bloody and begrimed, in no less foul a humor than when they set out. Having spent my afternoon sweltering in the top, spelling Gato, I too am spoiling for a fight. "Thanks to you," I mutter.

"They're alive, aren't they?" she parries, closing her book. She too has retired from the field today, holed up with her Milton.

Lubricious yodeling wafts down from on deck, accompanied by Gato's mournful guitar-strumming. They're all awash in rum, tonight, drowning the memory of their wounded pride.

"What use is prolonging their lives in this place?" I shoot back, a question I've grappled with all day. Twice, now, I've protected the men from violence, with the result that my crew grows mutinous and Pan more determined than ever to torment me. "When they die fighting at least they have their honor," I grumble to Stella.

"Tell that to your Jesse," she bristles at me. "Much good his honor does him now."

"Much good our lives are to us here."

She glares at me through another volatile moment then smacks down her book on the bed. "Oh, I give up! It's hopeless. I was a fool to come here."

At last we agree. "You wanted to be a mother." I can't keep the sneer out of my voice.

"I thought I might have a chance to raise boys," she corrects me, "to help shape them before they grow into cruel, warmongering men."

"There is no creature on earth more cruel than a boy."

"But are they beyond all possibility of redemption?" she persists. "Can't they be taught compassion?"

"Like sums?" I suggest. "Like Latin?"

"By example. From someone who cares for them."

I shake my head. "Your teacher would have to be a saint. And they would have to grow up."

"Yes," she agrees, with a wistful sigh of her own.

***

No noise wakens me. But I am suddenly alert to the blackness, the stillness, the absence of any sound, not even the tread of the watch. There's something eerie afoot. Not boys, not at night. Fairies? I shudder and sit up, straining to hear. Then I think of Stella alone in her cabin, and my feet touch the deck. I creep out in my nightshirt, pausing only to grasp my sword, make my way into the absolute gloom of the passage.

I hear nothing on the other side of Stella's door, the silence portentous. I touch the door with the elbow of my sword hand. It gives way a fraction of an inch. I press it open another inch, then another. All is silence and darkness, yet I sense something alert and waiting in the dark, something more than Stella. Peering in, I make out the nap of buckskin only inches away, just inside the door, smell the mingled fragrance of cured leather and crushed grass and pine.

Indians.

Where is the watch? How have they come aboard? But the braves are stealthy as ghosts, and my men blundering fools.

An errant streak of late moonglow through the skylight illuminates shine on a long black braid, and a shine in the black eyes watching me, as the door yaws open in silence. He's tall and heavy-chested, a single eagle feather woven upside-down into his braid.

"Red Eagle," I breathe, straining to conceal my alarm.

"Your memory is strong, Captain." The voice is low, terse. The big brave nods once. "Red Eagle was my grandfather. I am Eagle Heart."

And I am Methuselah, but of course I don't say it. I know better than to raise my weapon or rouse my men, now the braves are already on board. How many of them stand in the shadows? Enough to hold Stella fast, a glimmer of white in the darkness. Enough to make painful mincemeat out of me. I glance at the pale smudge that is Stella. She found something to her liking in that trunk after all, a long white nightdress. I'm absurdly touched.

I've no prayer of fighting them off, but none makes any move toward me. It must be Stella they want. Did they mean to butcher her, they'd have done so already. They've bound her hands behind her, and tied a clout of buckskin over her mouth, I see it now, but her expression betrays no more emotion than the warriors' own. Eagle Heart stands implacable as an oak before me, face impassive but for his keen black eyes, awaiting my next move.

"There's no need to bind her mouth," I hear myself say quietly. "Who will she cry out for? I am already here."

Eagle Heart regards me a moment, nods once again. From the corner of my eye, I see the cloth fall away from Stella's mouth. She makes no sound, continues to stare straight ahead. I keep my eyes on Eagle Heart.

"Now you will let us pass, Captain," he says to me. He makes no move to grapple me out of his way nor raise his knife to me, but that doesn't mean he won't, if provoked. But for this moment, I'm still extended the courtesy of a parley.

"What do you want with her?" I ask him. "Have you not women enough of your own?"

Eagle Heart raises his chin a degree and glares down at me. "We do not need your woman."

"But…"

"She is not for us," he declares. "She is for Little Chief Pan." He makes another subtle move of his head, scarcely more than a shiver in his eagle feather; a blade snicks out of the shadows and up under Stella's throat. "And now you will let us pass."

How can I do otherwise? I back into the passage as they file out, Eagle Heart in the lead and four or five of his men behind, mustering Stella between them. It takes all of her attention to manage her bare feet and long gown over the door sill and up the ladder with the knife at her throat. She does not look at me.

My woman, he called her.

***

"Captain." Brassy stands in my cabin doorway. It's barely dawn, yet he finds me awake and dressed, my hook buckled in place, grim purpose in my eye. "The woman," he mutters, his voice low and wary. "She's gone."

"I know."

My men were not slaughtered this time. Gato and Nutter were on watch, the one half-drowned in sentimental ballads, the other capricious at best, and every man jack of the crew basted in rum. The braves didn't even bother to kill them; they must have been insensible already. Now, in the blazing morning sun, they swear and posture impotently to hear that redskins boarded the ship, give thanks they weren't scalped in their hammocks. Time was my men went about festooned in feathers from the war bonnets of the braves they'd killed, but those were not these men. Indeed, I disrecall the last time we skirmished with the braves at all.

For Stella to be in the possession of the Indians is not necessarily a sentence of death; she might be a pawn or a hostage. But she's not in their custody, or so Eagle Heart told me. They captured her for Pan.

***

"Oi! Call the cap'n!"

It's Nutter out in the skiff pulling for the *Rouge* as if pursued by the Furies of Hell. Dispatched to the creek for fresh water an hour ago, he leaves Swab in the boat, hauls himself up the chains and clatters straight over to me.

"Cap'n, look," he gasps, and hands me an Indian arrow fletched with a single eagle feather, a scrap of pierced buckskin halfway up its shaft. On the nappy side, a crude representation of a hook has been etched with a hot implement; on the reverse, an image of the waning moon in its current phase.

"Come out of the brush when I was at the creek," Nutter pants. "Shot into the dirt right beside me. Coulda nailed my foot to the damn bank."

"It would have, had that been its object," I assure him.

"Some kinda message, Cap'n?" Filcher asks at my elbow.

"I'll soon find out," I mutter.

***

It's hours past midnight when I tie up the skiff at the creek mouth and debark into the shadows. The late moon is on the rise, a lascivious green grin in the black night. My black coat renders me as obscure as possible, and I carry my sword, but I come alone. Did Eagle Heart desire to harm me, he had ample opportunity last night. The sender of this arrow has something to communicate to Hook at this hour, and I will hear it.

179

Aside from the unwholesome purple mist curling above the water, oozing out of the loreleis' fetid jungle, nothing appears to move, but I know the stealth of the braves. I set my hat so the feather cocks jauntily upwards and step out onto the creek bank. Without so much as a rustling of leaves, a tall, sturdy silhouette separates from the dark mass of the underbrush and steps out as well. Eagle Heart, himself, his expression stony, black eyes agleam.

"I am alone, Captain," he tells me.

"As am I," I respond.

Eagle Heart slowly spreads open his arms so I can see the only weapon he carries, a sheathed knife stuck in the beaded, plaited belt round his buckskins. I do the same, revealing the hilt of my sword. Our eyes lock; he moves very slowly to pluck his knife out of his belt and place it on the ground at his feet, straightens up, takes one step backwards. I again follow his lead, place my sword on the ground, out of my reach, back away. We stand unarmed, regarding each other. How like his grandfather he looks, although he does not affect the same long headdress of feathers. His face is scarcely lined at all. Hard to believe this youthful sprout is their chief, but for his imposing demeanor.

"You wish to speak to me?" I say in the pregnant silence.

Eagle Heart nods. "I am glad you have come."

Slowly he reaches for the medicine bag hanging from his belt, its brave beading worn away in patches, its leather fringe in tatters; I recognize it as the one Red Eagle once wore. My muscles tense, ready to dive for my weapon should something unpleasant emerge from that ancient pouch, but all the young chief withdraws from it is another scrap of hide. With a wary glance at me, he lays the thing on the ground between us, smoothing it more or less flat, rises again, backs toward the shadows, and nods at me to pick it up.

Slowly, I grapple out my spectacles, peer at it by pale moonlight. It's a map, burned into buckskin. There are simple renderings of points I recognize: a familiar stand of willows in the wood, a fallen log, an outcropping of rock. A path twists through them to a black spot in the center.

"Tomorrow she will face a council called by Little Chief Pan," Eagle Heart tells me. I don't have to ask who "she" is. "To answer for her crimes."

"What crimes?"

But the young chief will not be baited. "This is where the council will be held," he says, nodding at the map.

Pan's various lairs in the wood have always been protected by enchantment. On the rare occasions that I or my men stumble across one by sheer blind chance, the boy merely dreams a new part of the wood into existence that we have never seen and builds himself a new one. But never before have I had a map.

"Remember it," Eagle Heart intones, and when I've fixed the route in my memory, he rolls the buckskin back into his pouch.

I stare at him. "Why show this to me?"

"Our women," he begins, "my mother, they fear he will do her some mischief. He is only a boy. And boys can be... reckless." We regard each other in a moment of empathy I should never have thought possible. "We will very much regret an innocent life come to harm," he goes on.

Easy enough take the high moral ground, now he's delivered her to the Pan. And yet, he brings me the map. "Can you not advise him to be merciful?" I fence. "You are his allies."

Eagle Heart slowly shakes his head. "My men will not oppose him. We do not wish to lose our homeland."

Of course, the Indians can ill afford to anger the boy. Their crops would fail, the buffalo would die off, their villages would not survive. They'd be banished to make their way in a hostile world that's long since passed them by.

181

"You risk much coming to me." I eye him keenly. "Why?"

His gaze does not waver from mine, although another beat of time passes between us. "Our elders tell us that innocent blood must never be spilled in this place."

"That has never pertained to my men," I point out.

"Your men engage in warfare. My men, too, are warriors. When we pledge to fight each other to the death, we are no longer innocent."

"The boys make war," I protest. "How can they be thought innocent?"

"The boys do not understand what they do," the young chief replies. "They forget their actions and can not learn from them."

"They have license to murder at will," I say sourly.

He fixes me with his flinty gaze. "The wisdom of our elders is very old. Older even than you, Captain. It is said that if one innocent life is lost here, this place, the Dreaming Place, all of it will end."

End? Can such a thing be possible? No wonder the chief is desperate enough to seek my help. "But I am no barrister; I cannot speak on her behalf," I try to reason. "It will go much harder on her if the boy believes she is valuable to me."

The young chief does not ask me the obvious question, the one I cannot, dare not answer. What exactly is her value to me? But it's plain in his penetrating silence as he gazes at me.

"Well, what can I do about it?" I grumble.

"Our storytellers say you have lived for many suns and moons in this place," replies Eagle Heart. "The elders tell us that great age brings wisdom." He eyes me pointedly. "You must be wise."

I stare back at him.

"If you bring your men," he adds quietly, "we will kill them all."

CHAPTER 18

THE BOYS COUNCIL

"It's a trap!" Filcher insists, bug-eyed with dread, when I climb into the skiff under the larboard main shrouds.

Once again, Brassy found me sober and alert at daybreak, fastening my gold-trimmed scarlet coat, my habit de guerre. But this mission calls for a diplomat, not a warrior, so I've selected a less martial hat, my mahogany tricorne with its froth of gold lace and pink flamingo plume. I tell the men I am summoned to a parley with Pan, but I am not so witless as to mention the map.

"Don't go, Cap'n," Filcher wheedles, in a panic at having to command the ship in my absence. They all saw what happened to me in our last battle.

"Nothing can happen to me, Mr. Filcher," I remind him, with a show of cavalier ease, flipping back the tails of my scarlet coat as I sit. "And there's a great deal to be gained if I learn where the boys keep their lair."

At least no one can argue with this.

"What about us, then?" Nutter grumbles, at the tackles.

"Man your guns. Hold your positions." Do your worst, I narrowly prevent myself adding, for I've seen how little interest Pan takes in murdering my men if I am not here to see it, and today he'll be busy. "It's not every day I'm invited into enemy country," I point out. "If I can't make it pay, I'm not worthy of the name Hook!"

Now as I pull through another brilliant blue morning up the coast for the northernmost extremity of Pirates Beach, I'm not at all convinced that anything I say will persuade the Pan from whatever course of action he chooses. It never has before. Yet I was reckoned quite a wit in my day, and Pan is only a boy, as they all keep telling me. In a war of wordplay at the boys' trial, might not a seasoned wit prevail over youthful willfulness?

At mid-morning I stow my boat in the underbrush and claw my way up the cliffside trail to the wood. I make my way from the willows to the log, and finally to a tumble of ancient rocks, choked with high yellow grass and bristled shrubbery, where I conceal myself to peer into a little clearing. The council, as Eagle Heart called it, is already underway.

"The prisoner may not speak!" cries Pan, perched like a little lordling atop a high tree stump at one end of the clearing. The Lost Boys sitting clustered together to one side of the stump all cheer wildly. A row of stoic Indian elders, all male, sit opposite the boys, a line of chess pawns ready to be deployed: two boxy, big-shouldered fellows, one corpulent, a fourth arrow-thin, all wrapped in blankets, with long gray or white braids and furrowed, impassive faces.

Stella stands at the foot of the tall stump, her cinnamon-colored hair loose above her shoulders, hands still bound behind her back, watching it all with her lively eyes. An old blanket with a hole cut in the middle has been thrown over her head, so as not to offend the precious innocence of the boys, I suppose, with the sight of her immodest shift. There's something poignant in the sight of its dirty white hem, torn and muddy from the wood, peeping out from underneath the skewed edge of the blanket, but I'm relieved to see that someone has given her a pair of sturdy buckskin slippers to wear, beaded in the Indian fashion.

"But that's foolishness. I must speak if I'm to defend myself," Stella reasons. I cringe for her as I huddle behind the scrub; there is no reasoning with boys. Call them foolish, and they're goaded to ever more reckless acts of imprudence and perversity just for the delight of thwarting you. Boys are made of petulance and bravado; they do not respond to reason.

"You are not allowed to defend yourself," scowls the Pan, angry to be contradicted. "We all know you broke the law, and now you have to be punished."

"Punish her! Punish her!" chant the other boys.

"What law have I broken?" Stella fences.

"I'm the one asking questions!" Pan exclaims. But the redskin elders, sitting across the clearing from the boys, all look at him in expectation, so he heaves a great impatient sigh at this delay. "You came to the Neverland against my wishes," he tells her. "I said no, and you came anyway."

"But why was I forbidden?" Stella persists.

"Because you talk too much!" Pan explodes. But his angry face turns crafty in the blink of an eye. "There, that's another law you broke," he cries. "Girls talk too much, and ladies are worse."

He's on his feet now on top of the stump, arms folded across his chest, gazing down at Stella, secure in the triumph of his logic. She says no more, gazing up at him, just like all the saucy little Wendys who ever tried to prove their mettle, coaxing, even arguing with their beloved Peter. He doesn't like to be defied, but he never minds so much when the Wendys do it, for then it's only make-believe. He knows they adore him; that's what gives him power over them, however much they might protest and stamp their little feet. But Stella does not betray her feelings so easily. He can't be sure she adores him, and so he loses the power of allure over her. He always forgives the Wendys because they are children. But he'll not forgive Stella.

"What's the sentence for breaking the law, men!" he cries.

"Kill her! Kill her! Kill her!" the Lost Boys chorus happily.

Stella ignores them, watching Pan, and he chafes under her scrutiny. Would she fall to her knees or plead for her life or even bow her head, acknowledge his superiority, he might show her mercy. But she does none of these things, and her quiet courage, the thing he finds so laudable when the little Wendys are defying me, now irritates him almost to a frenzy.

Suddenly, Stella turns to face the gabbling boys. "Do any of you know what it means to actually kill someone?" she prompts. "You? You?" The boys she's addressed, a chunky little Hindu fellow with missing teeth and a squirrel tail on his belt, and a grimy, leaner boy with reptile skins knotted round his middle, shrink back as if lightning bolts had issued from her eyes.

In a fury, Pan launches himself off his perch to hover before Stella's face, blocking her view of his boys. "It means to win!" he cries savagely. "I always win. You'll see!"

I've never seen him so wound up. He might do anything in this state. The elders shift uneasily, murmuring among themselves in their private language, while the boys resume their lusty chanting. There must be braves hidden nearby, watching these proceedings, but they won't interfere. No one else in all of the Neverland is foolish enough to oppose the boy. Cursing myself for the fool I am, I rise from behind the barrier of scrub and stride into the clearing.

"Stop!" I roar, and the chanting and muttering give way to an awkward pause. Everyone's gaze swings to me.

"Hook!" cries Pan. All the boys scramble for their weapons, but I strike an accommodating pose and slowly spread my arms so they can see I've not worn my sword. My scarlet coat opens as well, to show I have no pistols stuck in my belt. I even peel back the lace cuff of one sleeve and hook back the other to show there are no knives concealed underneath.

"What are you doing here?" demands Pan, still on his guard.

"I assure you, I am quite alone," I tell him. "I only intrude in the interest of justice. Ladies...er, Gentlemen of the council, I must lodge a complaint. This trial is not fair."

"Not fair?" echoes Pan, utterly shocked.

"Your honor," I address him, with a deep bow, mustering off my hat with a flourish so low, the pink feather flirts briefly with the dirt. "May I beg your permission to be heard?"

That's the way to play the Pan. He regains his composure on the instant, cocks his head to one side, delighted I've come to join another of his games. Delighted at the chance to best me again.

"You may speak, Hook," he declares imperiously and zooms back to his lofty perch on the old stump.

My mind races through the meagre possibilities offered by what I've seen thus far. "The evidence in this case has not been thoroughly examined," I suggest.

Pan folds his arms again. "She came here against my orders."

"That is so," I agree. "But how?"

The boy frowns mightily. "That's right!" he cries. "Why didn't the fairies stop her? Why didn't the tigers eat her? Why didn't the braves shoot her down?"

No one attempts to offer any explanation. "There is something in the Neverland itself that draws us all here," I go on. "Is it not written in the stories? The Neverland must find you if you are to come here, not the other way round."

They all mumble and nod. The sacred text of the stories is not to be disputed.

"Perhaps there is someone in the Neverland who asked for a mother," I offer delicately.

"Who dares defy me?" Pan yelps, glaring down at the Lost Boys, who all begin to babble and shriek in protest. When they run out of their own number to point their grubby fingers at, they turn resentful eyes upon the elders.

"We have our own mothers," the white-haired leader of the elders responds with cold dignity. "And our own storytellers."

Then all look at Stella, who only shakes her head. "I don't know who brought me here," she says.

I turn again toward the boy, set my tricorne back upon my head. "Perhaps it was you," I ooze.

"Me!" he bleats, outraged, his little hand reaching for the hilt of his sword. "Are you calling me a liar?"

"By no means," I reply, warming to the subject. "But is it not possible that you might want a thing and never even know it?"

"Not me! I always know what I want. And I want her punished!"

Stella's face remains composed above the ratty blanket that covers her. In her nightdress, she scarcely looks any older than the Wendys, but for the fierce intelligence in her eyes. She neither weeps nor protests. Perhaps she believes it's only a game, that they won't see it through, that with the inconstancy of children, they'll tire of this game and find another. Or perhaps, despite all she said to me, she still craves the death that eluded her in her own world. Was this her plan from the beginning? Have I been part of her plan?

"This is when the prisoner must speak," I interrupt them all. "Final words," I explain loftily to Pan. "Marquess of Queensberry Rules, and all that."

And he nods, the little whelp. Anything to make the game sound more official.

Stella glances at me for the first time, but I can't read her eyes. "It's true, I came here against your wishes," she tells Pan. "But I wanted to escape the grown-up world, just like all of you. I thought I was needed here." She glances all round. "But I see I was mistaken. You've clearly done very well for yourselves without a mother."

The Lost Boys at this moment are sprawled all together in their reeking furs, their feet bound in rags or not at all, hands filthy, faces caked with mud and blood and snot, hair snarled with rotting vegetation, teeth blackened or missing in their gaping mouths. Irony is lost on the boys, of course, but a ripple of amusement passes through the elders, although none is so immoderate as to actually laugh.

"If I can be of no use to anyone," Stella concludes, with a brief glance at me before turning back to Pan, "then of course you must send me back."

Back. My blood is pounding.

"But you'll tell!" Pan glowers at her.

"No—" Stella begins.

"Yes you will! Grown-ups always lie, especially ladies!" he shouts. "Children never tell when they go back. But she's a grown-up. She'll give us all away," he appeals to the company. "If the grown-ups find out about the Neverland, they'll put a stop to it. They always stop anything fun. Then where will all the children go to get away from them?" Pan glares down again at Stella. "But no silly lady is going to make a man out of *me!* The sentence is death!"

And of course all the other boys take up the happy cry. "Death! Death! Death!"

Stella's expression betrays a hint of the cold comprehension I felt on the day Pan cut my hand away, the shock of a rational mind against a tide of childish willfulness run riot. The boys dole out death without a scrap of conscience, with no idea of the gravity of it, the horror, the rapture. They neither fear nor respect the death they wield with such delight. Their only adversaries have ever been my pirate crews, lumbering future versions of themselves. Killing is a game to the boys, but Stella has seen how real death is in the Neverland. Until this moment, however, she has never been its target.

She glances again at the tribal elders, but their faces have turned to stone. She won't look at me, will implicate me no further. But she's been a friend to me, as no one else on this benighted island ever has.

"You cannot kill a mother, you know," I protest to Pan. "It's unheard of in the stories."

"Why do you care?" He peers at me more intently. "You're trying to protect her! You hid her from me on your ship!"

"She was my hostage," I riposte smoothly. "I meant to ransom her. But as she comes from out there, she's of no use to me."

"Then why do you defend her?"

"Consider the bad luck it might bring to the Neverland," I extemporize. "Killing a mother. And besides, who is going to do it?"

This at least is something none of them has thought of. Killing in battle is one thing, but this demands a different sort of mettle.

"We are warriors," the leader of the elders injects, when Pan turns to him. "We do not execute."

Various Lost Boys begin to argue for hurling the prisoner off a cliff or abandoning her to the beasts in the wood. None wants to be the unlucky one called upon to use his weapon against her. A tremor of hope stirs at my throat.

"Silence!" Pan shouts, his eyes glittering again, his little teeth beginning to show. "We'll take her to the Mermaid Lagoon!" he orders. "Let them have her!"

My blood chills. The Mermaid Lagoon, that dark, seductive, troubling place within the steaming jungle. The place the boy fears most in all of the Neverland. As do I.

The boys are cheering, taking to the air like bats, swarming toward us. My phantom hand twitches with the urge to defend her, but I step away for fear they'll harm Stella trying to strike at me if I resist. The elders are all on their feet, and as the boys close ranks, hovering in the air round Stella, Pan rises up to crow in my face.

"I win again, Hook!" he jeers. Then he swoops back to glare at Stella. "Now, Lady, you'll see what comes of defying me!"

And they march her off, poking and prodding at her, driving her into the underbrush. I've not been wise enough to stop them. I have only to look into the faces of the elders, watching with grim impassivity, to know how completely I've failed.

I won her a reprieve, no better. There might yet be a way to intervene, but only if I dare enter the most lurid, monster-infested hellhole in all of the Neverland.

CHAPTER 19

SUITE: THE MERMAID LAGOON

1

For all my secret forays upon this river, even I have never dared disturb the loreleis at their sinister games. The Mermaid Lagoon has always been as hidden from me as the boys' secret lair. Why would I seek it out? Everyone knows how they lure mortals into the slimy depths and drown them for sport. My oldest, deepest fear, an eternity of bloated, airless misery in the bowels of the unforgiving sea, grips me like a choking fist.

Yet, I row with all my strength, near dusk as well, when the fair folk are up to the most mischief. It took the better part of the day to regain my boat and pull across the bay for Kidd Creek, but for once the fractious currents were with me. Stella is a grown-up; they can't fly her to her doom; they must walk her, or resort to some hidden water route, and I must be there when they arrive. My wounded shoulder scarcely complains during this activity, making me all the more anxious and determined on her behalf.

The creek has long since given way to the Mysterious River, a maze of fetid overgrowth and steaming, tangled vegetation, heavy with the sweet perfume of jungle blossoms. Tendrils of organic slime drift across my bows, mossy mounds thrust out at me from the banks as I plow into that lush, damp, and perilous canal.

I hear the lurid boiling of the lagoon some distance ahead, but evil vapors are already rising up from the water to protect its hidden entrance. I lose my heading in the mist; one tributary beckons me to starboard, another veers off aport, and I don't know which to follow. Which will cost me precious time, driving me in circles like the tide in the bay? Which will wreck my boat on unfriendly shoals? Which are merely phantoms? They seem to open and close at will within the shifting vapors, like mocking lorelei mouths. Yet I must choose one. I cannot abandon Stella now; she has no one else.

A splash, a spray of water, startle me in the vaporous humidity. I twist about and see a glint of vivid color, hear another splash just ahead, to starboard, something bursting out of the water, then sinking again. Expecting the tentacle or claws of some slimy thing, I crane round further to see. But it's only a fish arcing out of the water, scales a shimmering rainbow of gemstone colors, sapphire, amethyst, celadon green, as beautiful as the roses. As it dips back into the water, another as vibrantly colored rises in formation close behind, and dives, and then a third leaps out in the others' wake.

In a heartbeat, all three break the surface again, just beyond the starboard bows, trailing long, gossamer fins, splash again into the water, rise up some little distance further on, making for a single green lane amid all the shifting entrances that tempt me out of the mist. Rarely have I beheld such exotic looking flying fish, and never in the river; they are creatures of the deep sea.

A sign from out of the sea, that's what the Indian shaman said. Squelching my unease, I row after the gorgeous fish through the obscuring mists and into the deep green passage. The channel narrows, and I keep close to the river bank. Bending low on the thwart, I work up under a canopy of ferns and the long limbs of ancient trees, stretching out to trail their fertile green foliage in the water. And beyond them, the Mermaid Lagoon spreads open before me, hissing like steam from a kettle, despite the chill in the air. My phantom fingers ball up for warmth, but my hook holds steady through its hole in the oar shaft as I work into the vertiginous tunnel at the mouth of the lagoon, sweating with apprehension in the clammy cold.

Smoky clouds edged in pink stretch and dissolve overhead, revealing a first faint scattering of stars in a lavender sky. The lagoon seems to pulse with its own unearthly glamour, while the water, as black as pitch, laps and eddies round the narrow wedge of Marooner's Rock, thrusting up in the middle. It takes a moment for my ears to pick out another kind of lapping, paddles dipping almost soundlessly into water; I freeze, hug my skiff to the bank, as a canoe powered by half a dozen braves glides past the mouth of my green tunnel and back out into the river.

I see them now, a cloud of jeering, whistling boys harrying Stella along the fetid marshes at the edge of the lagoon, about a quarter way round from my hiding place at the river mouth. The stark silhouette of Marooner's Rock stands off to westerly from both of us. They're all in a hurry now; the boys know what an evil place this is at night. Pan orders them to strip off the blanket, and four boys gingerly grab a corner each and fly it off over Stella's head. Her hands are still tied behind her, but the hint of her womanly body under her shift troubles the boys, who fall back on instinct. Pan alone goes boldly forward, fluttering up to her face.

"It will be a gruesome death," he promises eagerly. "You'll sink under the water, and the mermaids will tear you limb from limb!"

"Why would they do that?" Stella asks mildly.

"Because that's what mermaids do!" he snaps back. "Everybody knows that!"

Stella gazes out at the water, faintly rippling now with dark activity. A fishtail gleams just below the surface out near the rock, and my flesh crawls. How can I intervene? I haven't even brought any weapons, but when have my weapons ever been any use against the boys or their allies? My groping fingers close on something damp and gritty under the thwart, and I withdraw the object the lorelei left in our boat; I once compared it to a bagpipe. I raise the reed to my lips and blow. The amphibious pocket expands the slightest bit, holding the air. I blow again.

"Of course," Pan goes on, rising a little in the air, "I might be merciful. If you begged me."

Stella gazes up at him. "Beg you? For what?"

"For your life, Lady. I caught you fair and square, and you deserve to be punished for your crime. Still, I could show you mercy. I could let you live. But you'd have to follow my rules."

"Which are?" I hear the incipient smile in Stella's voice. Their words carry wonderfully on the water.

"You could stay with the Lost Boys. You could cook our meals and mend our clothes. You could tell us stories, just like the other mothers." Pan flutters in the air before her, buoyed by his own magnanimity, then leans his face a little closer to hers. "But you wouldn't be allowed to think any more grown-up thoughts!" he declares. "And you must call me 'Master.'"

Stella bursts out laughing. "Oh, don't be silly!"

Pan's feet hit the ground with a thump; it was almost his backside. He has to claw furiously back up into the air again. The Lost Boys are all whimpering in the shadows behind him, all of them grounded just as suddenly and scrambling to follow his lead and rise up again, their alarm as palpable as the mist on the water.

Something splashes out by the rock; with sick dread I see one of the loreleis emerging from the water. Her

195

long, webbed fingers come first, securing handholds in the mossy rock as it angles steeply upwards. Then her arms, translucently white, and her head trailing its mane of seaweed hair, iridescent black and green. The flesh of her spine curves down to the glistening scales of her rump as she rises above the surface, pert, naked breasts exposed as she twists on the rock to look toward the shore.

The boys draw back further still, but Stella stands transfixed, as beguiled as any Wendy. They stare at each other, Stella and the mermaid, as panic pounds in my blood. Don't look, I beg Stella silently, turn away. She will enchant you. She will kill you.

Pan boosts himself to a more authoritative position in the air, cups his hands round his mouth.

"Look what I've brought you!" he calls out to the siren. "Tell your queen!"

The mermaid lifts her head, angles it curiously to one side, and I dare to draw a breath. If they engage in some parley, the way Pan always likes, then Stella may yet have a chance to gather her wits and flee. The boys are far up the bank now, and—

Without a word, Stella steps off the bank and drops into the water, which closes over her head. The lorelei lets go her perch and slides tail-first under the surface with the speed of an eel. The boys are as astounded as I, even Pan. He flies out to the still-rippling water and stares down in dismay.

A low vibrato begins to boil up out of the depths of the water, dissonant siren voices rising in a lurid crescendo to speed the boys off to their beds perhaps, or praise their profane gods for this succulent morsel so callously thrown their way. Whatever it means, Pan composes his features into a scowl and turns back to the others.

"Let's go, men!" he cries, "she's done for!" And off they fly.

I'm out of my coat, scrambling over the wales, still clutching my inflated pocket, even though every fiber of my flesh and blood and bones recoils at the black water. As horrible as it may be, I know I can't die.

But Stella can.

The water is cold and deep, the darkness total. My wide-open eyes perceive no light, no movement, only black. I hear nothing, so instantly numb from cold that I don't even feel the wet, aware only of my blood pounding in my ears, and the speed with which I'm spiraling downward. It's black all around me, as black as the tomb I've always craved. Will this become my tomb? Will blackness swallow me up at last? But Stella is bound and helpless somewhere, alone in the blackness, and I plunge deeper still, thrusting with my hook. I wait as long as I dare before pressing the reed to my mouth for more air, a sip only: I must save some for Stella.

Something glimmers in the dark below, not the gloss of fishtails, but a smear of white. I claw after it against the pressure of black water. The white disappears just as my hook touches hard, solid rock, sharp, crusted with barnacles and ridged by the tides, but I find purchase and crawl downward along its surface, fist over hook. My lungs are some foul, heaving fish I've swallowed whole, the urge to spit it out all but irresistible, yet I drag myself down to a ridge of the crusty rock. That's where it went, the white apparition that must be Stella, and I hurl myself over the edge and downward, kicking clumsily, into absolute black.

My lungs strain, the ache of holding my breath spreads from my chest up my throat into my nose. What would happen if I let go, empty my lungs, my mouth, my nose, suck in black water? It should be easy to let the blackness take me. My blood thunders to escape my flesh and become black water, my brain is giddy with the struggle not to breathe, as I'm propelled through weightless nothing. This must be what it's like to fly. This must be what it's like to die.

Purple, green, orange, vermillion explode before my eyes and I touch sheer solid rockface again, feel my way down to the edge of an open archway. I poke my head over the edge, see a deep underwater grotto, all a-shimmer with a pulsing spectrum of light. But she's not here. Did I follow a phantom to this place? My mouth forms a single mournful word,

"Stella."

It escapes in a forlorn bubble and drifts into the grotto.

Out of the riotous colors something comes wriggling toward me under a cloud of dark, greenish hair: pale arms outstretched, round breasts bared, serpentine tail reflecting all the rainbow colors snaking back and forth as she hurtles up to me, the lorelei I saw above, or her sister. Her eyes are turquoise, like the water of the Indies. I'm too exhausted to struggle, my hook too heavy to raise in the water. She takes my face in both her long-fingered hands; I feel rubbery webbing and the grit of sand against my cheek, open my mouth in a useless cry, and air explodes out of me, the last I'll ever taste, as she thrusts her face to mine and opens her wide, gleaming mouth to suck the life out of me. My last thought is for Stella.

But when her wet lips press to mine, she breathes air, warm, dry, blesséd air into my mouth. I inhale it hungrily into withering lungs, and she gives me more. I'm almost clear-headed again when she peels away and dives down under the arch into the grotto with a snap of her tail. I clamber after her in a fever of need, my hand fisted round the air bladder thrust awkwardly forward, my hook dragging behind. Then my hand runs into thin, slippery mesh I can neither claw past nor through; I try to back away, and more of the stuff drops over me wrapping round me like a spider's web, cocooning me like a moth.

I am netted.

2

It's no use wriggling or squirming as I'm dragged into the grotto. Through a haze of colors, my captors' fishtails flicker on either side of me; the water thrums with their language, or their laughter. I taste wet lips, salty tongue, as one, then the other press air into my mouth, yet I am scarcely conscious as I'm drawn into a dark passage, unceremoniously scraped against a jagged wall, feel a vibrato in the water like a remonstrance, and a softer ripple of apology. Through the passage at last, an aurora of lights pulses far overhead, I'm flying into a starry sky, toward the arch of a rainbow. Then my head breaks the water's surface.

Air! So much, I gag on it. Wet mesh clings to my face, but I throw back my head and slurp in air, choking and spluttering, my lungs heaving as I'm dragged to the edge of a pool, hauled onshore, where I lay coughing and panting, sucking in the abundance of air. The shock of it is like the finest spirits; my brain reels, intoxicated, exhausted, slipping in and out of sense.

***

Hard rock beneath me, neither sand nor mud, this is my first sensible thought. How long have I lain here? Long enough for my joints to ache, my muscles to cramp. I'm still bound in mesh, my clothing briny-stiff. It's not a dream. I open my eyes to find myself discarded like an old boot on a ledge of hard shale that rings the pool I came up in. The sirens who dragged me here maneuver themselves across it, sitting up on their tails like sea lions, rotating their after-fins like rudders.

We're in another grotto, hidden behind the first, but this one full of air above the pool, under a ceiling of rock as high as a cathedral. Clusters of glowing, incandescent crystals, unimaginable in the world above, thrust downward from the rock ceiling like gaudy chandeliers, bathing everything in rainbow hues: turquoise green, cobalt blue, ruby, violet. Soft, dark shadows gird the perimeter of this enclosed space so far from the sun, but a luminous mineral haze hangs in the air, and the water glows velvet green. And in every direction I peer, twisting my head around, are mermaids, a score at least, some idling along the surface of the water, others hauled up onshore, murmuring together in pairs or lounging on thick mats of seaweed and grass and kelp plumped into crevices of the rock.

Their variety amazes me. In the water they glimmer blue and green and purple, but others on shore are chocolate brown or pink or caramel above their fishtails, like human females on land. One elderly, dusky-colored dame, hair knotted into a sunburst of snow-white tufts all round her head, strands of shells and sea glass clattering on her bony breast, sits up on her coiled tail higher up the bank, amid thin spires of crenellated rock. Others have distended bellies above their scales, or cradle infants who flap their shiny little tails. Most wear shells round necks or waists, or in their hair. None are modest.

As I attempt to shift my sore body, they quiet their chatter and peer at me. Twisting up my head, I see an opening like the mouth of a small cave not far from me, set back along the rocky shore. Something stirs in the shadows within, a whisper of white fabric.

"Parrish!" I croak.

The white thing moves, grows larger as she comes crawling to the mouth of the cave like a child, on her hands and knees, her wrists no longer bound. She's breathing, alert, alive. Her dark eyes widen with surprise.

"Captain!" she exclaims. "But...what...what in the name of God's spleen are you doing here?"

"Looking for you, looking for you, looking for you!" chants one of my captors, materializing from behind me, the dark-haired jezebel who filled my mouth with air, then lured me into this trap. Her inky-green seaweed hair is plaited back in dozens and dozens of long, snaky coils trailing down her back. She wriggles up to Stella, balancing something liquid and luminous on upturned fingertips, which she bats delicately upward: it's a bubble. It breaks in midair with a tiny pop, and a sound like a far-off echo bursts out of it.

"Stella."

It's my own voice, or a ghost of it, forlorn with defeat. Stella climbs to her feet, peering down at me without a word to say. My captor is looking very pleased with herself.

"What has he done?" Stella asks anxiously. "Why is he tied up?"

"He's a man," the fish-woman caws triumphantly.

"That's a crime?" Stella rejoins.

"And a thief!" the pale lorelei insists, and she produces the marine bladder that brought me here, wrested from my hand, and hurls it down to the rock beside me. "He's come to hunt you!" the minx explains to Stella. "That is what they do! The legmen, they hunt us, capture us in nets. They will eat us, or put us in cages, force us to bear their children."

"But that's nonsense," Stella begins, but her voice trails off into a sigh. She's surely heard the old tales as often as I have, lonely fishermen and their captive mer-brides, although I've never heard of one served as an entrée. In the court of the Sun King, perhaps, or the decadent palaces of the Turks. "Well," Stella tries again, "it may be true out there in the other world..."

"Of course it is true," a voice wafts out from inside the cave, and another mer-female hefts herself into view. Her complexion is twilight blue, her face as broad as the moon under a quivering cloud of kinky hair, granite-grey and silver. Of all those watching us now, she seems to command the most authority, rising up on her tail to gaze down at me. "That is why we come here," she says to Stella. "To get away from the men. They are everywhere in the world, in every ocean. Everywhere but here."

"This man means you no harm, I swear it," Stella insists.

"No male ever enters the lagoon, not even the Boy King," declares my fierce captor. Her fingers are working a mollusk shell off a seaweed rope round her middle. A weapon, by the way she hefts it. Now, too, I notice teeth marks of some savage marine predator branding her pale shoulder. A wicked shark's tooth pierces her ear lobe like a trophy. "Why else would he come all this way?"

"Looking for you," muses the blue woman, with a speculative glance at Stella. They all heard my voice in the bubble.

"But not to hurt me," Stella declares. "Please let him loose."

Does she think to move the loreleis from any course of action but their own desires? Hasn't she learned from the Boys Council how heedless and willful all creatures can be in the Neverland? The blue fish dame gazes at Stella a moment longer, then moves between her and my captor down the rock toward me. If one could be said to wriggle majestically, that is how she comes at me, smoothly muscled arms pulling her forward, her rotating tail propelling her from behind, unhurried, her head erect under its cloud of quivering corkscrew curls. A thousand colors shimmer in the scales of her undulating fishtail, and when she stops to bend over me, the wine-colored aureoles of her blue breasts dangle nearly to the rock. I cannot say she sniffs at me, exactly, but her face hovers above mine as if she's taking some measure of me, pitiful sight as I must be.

"Mica. Amber," she says mildly to my dark-haired captor, and a brown-skinned, golden-haired female who must be her partner. "Release him."

Astonishment gushes out of me like steam from Mount Merciless. Her eyes above me are dark marine blue, like sapphires, bright with curiosity, like all glamorous creatures, but calm and intelligent as well. I nod my thanks, and the sirens who captured me slither up alongside me. Each carries a shell honed to a blade-like edge, and they set to slicing through the strings of mesh, so close, the hairs on my body rise to the whisper of their blades. They peel the wet mesh off of me, and I sit up slowly, my arms still shaky from confinement. I shove wet hair off my face, throw the sodden length of it behind my shoulder, every atom of my person and my clothing soaked and sullenly dripping as Stella comes down the rock toward me. Over her shoulders she carries a matting of long, dried, pliable sea grasses woven together, like a cloak, and as she crouches beside me, she slides it off her shoulders and over mine. It's blissfully dry, and warm from her body. However long we've been here, she's not much worse off for her ordeal. Her cinnamon hair falls in a tangle of damp, stiffening curls, her dark eyes are alert with concern, as comforting as the dry grass cloak.

"Are you all right?" I demand, more brusquely than I intended, ashamed for her to see me exposed in all my failure.

"I'm not the one who dreads water, Maestro," she reminds me.

I peer into her face, close enough to mine so that we might not be overheard by the curious sirens still watching us. "Why did you jump in?" I whisper to her.

She blinks at me; of course she can't know I was watching her from my hidden boat. With a discreet movement of her dark eyes, she indicates my former captor, the tooth-branded lorelei called Mica who climbed out on the rock in the Mermaid Lagoon.

"She told me to come with her," Stella whispers back. "She just looked at me, and I knew. Said I'd be safe here. The boys are terrified of the lagoon."

"Of course they are," agrees the blue grand dame, coming up again beside Stella. "That is the way we prefer it. Boys can be such a nuisance sometimes." Her sonorous voice is low, marshy, faintly damp, but her words are clear, and her English excellent. A murmur of agreement bubbles up from the others all round the pool in tongues of which I'm far less certain.

"For that matter, Captain Hook," the blue woman addresses me, "we have never seen you near the lagoon before."

I suppose the wretched stories have penetrated even here. Perhaps I'm part of their folklore, passed down through their generations, the wicked legman who lives above.

"Please forgive my poor manners, Madam," I reply, with a feeble stab at chivalry. "Have I the honor to address the queen of this place?"

But she bats away my flattery with a wave of her blue hand. "We have no queens here, Captain; that is a fantasy of the Boy King. But it is my duty to preside over this place, yes. I am called…" and she makes a lubricious sound, not unpleasant, but impossible for me to decipher. Something humorous stirs in her plump face as she awaits my response. "The closest word in your tongue," she offers, "is Lazuli."

"I am enchanted, Madam Lazuli," I reply, with all the formality I can muster, half-drowned and shivering on my knees. "The fact is, I…I never expected to find hospitality in the Mermaid Lagoon. There are few enough places in the Neverland where I am welcome."

"Because they are all controlled by the Boy King," pipes up my captor with the shark tooth in her ear.

"But not here?" Stella wonders, turning again to blue Lazuli. "Do you mean you are immune somehow to his will?"

The blue mer-woman chuckles, like water gurgling softly over smooth river stones. "We are all women here, you see."

I glance round the pool again, where the females are all watching us, and notice what I'd lacked the wit to appreciate before: the large-bellied women, the infants, the elders, the fierce armed guardians protecting the outer grotto.

"It's a temple of witchcraft!" I cry.

They all burst out laughing, a rolling, musical sound with sharps of high hilarity and bass notes of scorn that echoes all round the high rock walls. Even Stella smiles, her hand touching my sleeve in gentle reproof.

"I believe it's a birthing pool," she corrects me.

"Yes," Lazuli beams at her. "But it is all the same to the boys. Female cycles are very mysterious to males. It is the difference between the bold and constant sun, and the dark, ever-changing moon. They cannot quite grasp it."

"And what they can't understand, they fear," says Stella.

"Peter is so innocent he does not even know what a kiss is called, but he knows to fear it beyond all things," Dame Lazuli agrees. "He senses it will corrupt him in some unfathomable way, change everything. It is almost always wanting a kiss that gets the young girls sent home from the Neverland. Imagine how frightening an entire community of females must seem." The blue merwoman smiles and nods toward me. "Ask your friend, the Captain."

"But...there have been mermaid stories since the beginning of time," I protest. "I didn't invent them. Every sailor knows them. The lorelei, the succubus whose love is rash and all-consuming, who will drain away your soul and drown you for sport..." My words trail away to a fresh bubbling of female giggles. How absurd they sound.

"Fear itself is a powerful force, Madam." I speak to Lazuli, but my words are meant for Stella, whose glance answers with a flicker of understanding. Here is an entire district in the Neverland beyond the Pan's control. A place he fears.

"But in the stories," Stella pipes up, "Peter is great friends with the mermaids. He lolls about with them on Marooner's Rock and teases them and sits on their tails. He is the only one the mermaids allow to play their games with them in the lagoon. All the other children are jealous of him for it."

More peals of amusement chime round the pool. Even I laugh at the notion of the Pan frolicking in the water with the loreleis and treading on their tails. He might as well sleep with the savage tigers in the wood; indeed, he's far more likely to do so than ever sport with mermaids in the lagoon.

"But consider the source," I say to Stella. "The Scotch boy adored Pan. He would never portray him in a less-than-flattering light or admit there was anything his hero feared."

"Exactly so, Captain," Dame Lazuli agrees.

"But," Stella begins again, "if you have regular female cycles, the same as…as any woman, and you, well, mate and give birth in the usual way, where are your men?"

"They are off shepherding our colonies in the sea," says Lazuli.

"Colonies?" I echo. I've sailed the seas of the world, and never encountered a single member of the mer-race except in this lagoon.

"You cannot think we live all of our lives in this tiny place?" the old mer-dame replies. "We must make our annual migrations out in the great sea. That is how we survive."

The great sea. My blood quickens. The merfolk migrate out into the other world every year. They know a way out.

3

"We are a nomadic race. We follow the currents that have boiled beneath the sea since the beginning of time, to places where the food is more plentiful, the climate more friendly." Dame Lazuli settles down on her tail and pushes back a handful of her springy grey-and-silver spirals.

Wine the color and texture of squid ink dares my courage from a vessel of shell. But it's dreadful bad form to decline hospitality, and Stella sips at hers with stoic aplomb, so I ignore the faintly marine fragrance and hoist away. It's a cold, rich, mineral taste on the tongue, with assertive notes of copper and plum, like drinking the blood of the sea.

"We meet other migrating colonies and feast together and share our stories," the blue dame continues. "Pods of our young males and females mingle with the youth of neighbor colonies, and pair off together, swimming with one parent colony for half the season, and then the other. But the waters are more dangerous now than they have ever been." Her sigh extends all the way to the muscular fins at the end of her coiled tail, which quiver against the rock. "It takes the strength and cunning of all our men to protect our colonies."

"From the men, you mean," Stella injects. "On land."

We sit on seagrass mats, Stella and I, our legs thrust out before us like little children. The mer-dames have no furnishings for legged creatures, neither chairs nor tables. Our shell vessels stand upright on their coralline prongs upon the pitted surface of the rock; Stella's soaked moccasins are drying in the air further up the rock, outside the cave. Several of the young mer-mothers have carried their newborns into a deep recess of the pool under a volcanic tunnel; their soft lullabies, more melodic than I have ever noticed before, echo up through the porous rock into the Neverland night.

"It was long ago, time beyond reckoning, when the first of our brethren grew limbs and walked upon the land," says Lazuli. "The songs of our bards tell us we lived in harmony with the legmen for ages. The world was huge and bountiful then, with room for all. There were fertile deepwater plains for planting, unspoiled pools for fishing, broad sand beaches beyond counting where we might sport and play in peace, quiet lagoons for birthing our young. But the legmen are greedy. They want the world for themselves. They've swarmed over all the land, and now their ships of fire disturb every sea."

"Except this place?" asks Stella.

The blue woman nods her springy head. "We are protected here. Only children find their way here, and when they go back and grow up, they forget. This is the safest place in all the waters of the world to birth our young. The mothers stay until they and the babes are strong enough to rejoin the colony the next time it returns on the current."

"And he allows it?" Stella marvels. "Peter? The Boy King."

"The Neverland is the dreamworld of children," Lazuli replies. "All manner of fey creatures make their home here, as well as the beasts in the wood, because children love us so. The Boy King is immensely proud to have such exotic and dangerous creatures in his world, to show off to the children who come here. Especially the girls. They fly overhead to view us, and we appear in the lagoon for that purpose, so he will trouble us no further. It's a small enough price to pay, amusing the boy, chasing away his sorrows, to preserve our sanctuary here."

"Sorrows?" I rumble. "This is his Paradise."

Lazuli peers at me, surprised. "Life brings sorrow, Captain, and his life has endured for so many suns and moons. So many losses, so many children gone, leaving him alone. His losses haunt his dreams sometimes, in spite of all our singing, my sisters and I. It is a delicate thing, keeping him happy, protecting him from the memory of all he has lost. Preserving his innocence. Our bards sing of a time when this place was in fearful peril, when the Boy King nearly succumbed to his sorrows, but for the heroic chanting of our singers. Now harmony is restored."

She sits up a little taller on her coiled tail. " Of course," she adds delicately, "he does not guess what our true purpose is within this grotto. Indeed, our own men, who would gladly shed their last drop of blood to defend this place, do not like to come in here. They know perfectly well what we do here, play no small part themselves in the cycle that brings us here, and yet they prefer to keep off, to let us do our work in peace." She lifts her blue shoulders in wistful resignation. "That is how men are."

And her sapphire eyes shift again to me. "It's a matter of no little concern to us, Captain, that you have found your way here."

I set down my wine vessel abruptly. They are looking at me from all round the pool, as if awaiting judgment against the wayward man foolish enough to penetrate their sacred circle. The two warrior sirens who captured me loom nearer. I have very little desire to be flung back into the water like a disappointing fish; it's a long, long way back to the surface of the Mermaid Lagoon. My fingers inch across the rock to where my expired air bladder still lies, which I lift to show Lazuli. "I was trying to bring this to Stella."

"Thief!" hisses Mica.

"Why was it placed in my boat?" I ask them.

"For the journey, I was told," Stella pipes up.

The blue merwife nods up at the ancient mer-dame I spied before, with the aureole of snowy white hair, perched up in a higher elevation of the shore. "Our sibyl throws sand collected from the shores of the seven seas into her water-glass and reads the patterns," says Lazuli. "She saw an image of your ship, and we knew we were meant to aid the land folk the only way we can—a safe passage through our element, the water."

"But why aid your enemies?" Myself, I mean.

Lazuli smiles patiently. "Not enemies, Captain. Yours and mine were the same race, once upon a time. We knew not whose passage it was, nor for what purpose. Nor do we know what the journey is. The old songs tell us only that it begins with the signs."

"Three signs," Stella whispers, with an eager glance at me.

The old woman, their sibyl, wriggles up higher upon her shiny tail and mimes at what must be another, much smaller pool of water amid her spiky volcanic peaks. Her voice is soft with age, but it rumbles across the water with authority. "The journey has begun!"

***

The three elegant fish I saw before, with their jewel-box colors and silken fins, leap across the surface of the water-glass. It seems an ordinary pool of dark water, the circumference of a large platter, formed within a circlet of coralline spires on this crag above the birthing pool. Lazuli worked her way up a terraced path hewn out of the black rock, kept moist by a trickle of water from some hidden spring, while Stella and I were obliged to claw our way up the rocky incline to this plateau, where the sibyl keeps watch over her oracle.

"The sign of Mother Sea," the mer-sibyl announces, gesturing to the image of capering fish in her water-glass.

"I saw them in the river," I say to Stella, and feel every other pair of eyes in that vaporous cavern turn upon me. I turn again to Dame Lazuli. "They brought me here."

"The blessings of two mothers smile on this journey," the sibyl intones, bright-eyed under her tufted white hair.

"Mother Sea," Stella murmurs at my elbow. "Mother Earth."

The sibyl beams at her and stretches knobby fingers into a large, upturned clam shell full of sands of every hue: black, white, red, honey-gold. She sprinkles a handful over her water-glass, peers into it again. "One journey ends, another begins."

210

"There are more than one?" I frown.

"It may be like a birth," the blue merwife suggests. "A change from one condition to another."

"But whose?" Stella asks softly.

"Whoever earns it," Lazuli replies. "So our bards sing. But if all three signs are not seen, the chance to take this journey will never come again. Never, ever."

"So you called Stella here?" I venture. "To placate this oracle?"

But Lazuli gives an adamant shake of her head. "We are very distressed that you are here at all," she says to Stella. "None of us would ever call you. It is much too dangerous for you."

"I've no wish to cause any more distress," Stella sighs, shoving back an unruly wisp of her own hair. "Ma'am, the route you spoke of, the one that leads to the great sea. Can you show us where it is?"

A conflagration of feeling crashes against my ribs. But Dame Lazuli sighs, shakes her head again. "It's a very long way under the sea. Our air bladders would be no use; your human lungs could never endure it. We of the mer-race have sea lungs. They serve us much like yours when we are in the open air, but they extract the air we breathe out of our blood and muscles when we are long underwater. Forgive me, but I am senior midwife here; I know how our bodies function."

"Yes, I'm a nurse," says Stella.

"Then you understand that the distance is too far and the pressure of the sea too great," rejoins Lazuli. "But if you are skilled at nursing, we might make a place for you here with us."

"Why…" Stella falters, "that is…a very great honor, Ma'am."

"She is exceptionally skilled at healing herbs and the like," I offer eagerly. A refuge from the boy!

211

"It is calm just now, but at some seasons we have great activity here," Lazuli tells her. "Another pair of hands would be useful."

"But...my experience has mostly been with male patients," Stella confesses. "I have little knowledge of... birthing."

I hear the sadness she tries to mask in her voice. How might it affect her, all these females birthing healthy young?

"We can teach you what you need to know," says Lazuli. She tosses back her explosive curls, wriggles a little closer to Stella. "I would prefer to have you here with us than to leave you above and vulnerable to the Boy King."

Stella looks at me. I nod heartily.

"I regret," murmurs Lazuli smoothly, "that I cannot offer the same hospitality to you, Captain. You are a legman, an object of great wonder to us, but disturbing to my women at this delicate moment in their cycles. As it is beyond our power to send you anywhere else, you must return."

"Return? To where?" Stella demands.

"To his ship," says Lazuli patiently. "Back to the Neverland."

Back to my eternal torment. Stella will be useful here, the thing she most craves, and safe. But there is no mercy for Hook.

"So be it, Madam," I say, coolly enough. I step out to the edge of the plateau and gaze down at the water in the pool, darker now, less green and friendly. If Stella's journey ends here, let her at least remember that I'd not stood in the way of her good fortune.

But Stella rustles to my side. "Then I'll go with you."

Thus she makes hash of my attempt to accomplish one honorable thing in my life. "But you're safe here," I tell her. "You've nothing to fear from Pan if he believes you dead."

"And what about you?" she counters.

"He can't hurt me," I say grimly. "But if you return to the Neverland now, you will be an outlaw. He'll believe himself justified in hunting you down like an animal with his wild pack of boys."

"We can do nothing at all for you, my dear," Lazuli speaks up, "beyond the protection of this grotto."

"The signs appeared to you," Stella persists, still looking at me. "You had the Dream Vision. It must be your journey, Captain. This must be the chance your witch told you about."

"This is no game, Parrish—"

"But what if I'm part of the journey somehow?" she goes on eagerly. "What else can I possibly be doing here? Suppose we're on this journey together?"

Something long dormant stirs inside me. Dare I call it hope? It is a reckless thing.

**

"Take this," Dame Lazuli bids Stella, emerging again from the mouth of her cave. She hands Stella a small spiral of pink shell strung on a seaweed thong. "Our sisters are posted in every island waterway, conveying information on currents, tides, and boy activity, for the protection of our grotto. If you change your mind, blow a note on this shell over any body of water in the Neverland, and we will come for you."

Stella wears the little shell round her neck. It floats above her nightdress as we make our ascent through black water back to the Mermaid Lagoon. The merwife gave us fresh air bladders, puffed up like pastries when properly filled with air; a ready supply is kept for the mer-babes' first long migrations underwater to rejoin their colonies. Mica, the shark-wrestler, escorts us, although I'm not at all certain she has our best interests at heart. At least not mine. But Stella guides me through the water even when we lose sight of our escort.

Stars scatter like diamonds across the black sky when we finally break the surface of the lagoon. All is still but for a lazy chittering of insects. Stella and I grope for hand-holds in the volcanic mass of Marooner's Rock, gulping air before swimming for the shore, as Mica disappears again beneath the water.

"Let's get out of this lagoon, in case there are any spies about," I suggest.

Stella wrapped her gown with sea vines in the loreleis' cavern to prevent it filling with water, and she strokes ahead for the shore as I paddle behind. She pulls herself out by a tangle of roots at the water's edge, the wet skin of her gown clinging to every curve of her breasts and rump—pear-shaped, I notice, now that she's out of those damned trousers. I was lately surrounded by exotic, bare-breasted sirens of the ripest carnality, the private dream of every sailor, however much he fears them, but none excited in me the same quickening as the sight of Stella sprawling on the bank in such artless abandon. In my day, women of her matronly years took pains to conduct themselves with dignity, real or imagined. But Stella flops over, flushed and giddy, without an atom of self-consciousness. And why not? There's no one to see her but me.

I splash in closer to the shore, stretching for something solid to grasp onto. "You might lend a hand," I carp.

"Sorry, Captain. You're so full of surprises tonight, I thought you might walk on the water," she blasphemes merrily.

But my clever rejoinder dies as a distant percussion I'd taken for insect clacking becomes louder, more insistent, a steady rhythm like a heartbeat. Like a ticking clock.

He sent a spy, all right.

CHAPTER 20

CROCODILE

"Captain, what is it?" Stella is staring at me.

"Listen!" Above my desperate paddling, I hear the squishing of wet leaves and grasses beneath its lumbering weight. The ticking grows louder. "It's coming closer!"

Stella scrambles to her feet in confusion, peering about. When she sees it, her whole body jolts.

"The crocodile!" she gasps. "But I thought that was just a…a metaphor!"

My phantom hand already burns with remembered pain. I see it now, low to the ground, its massive grey-green head and snout aloft, black eyes agleam, crashing through the scrub and into the wetlands of the bank. But Stella freezes, crouching, her wet skirts gathered in her hands, watching the vile monster plowing toward her. "For Christ's sake, woman, run!" I bellow.

She rises up a little higher on her haunches, but every move she makes to feint to one side or the other is mirrored by the beast. Yet the crocodile slows its advance, making for Stella with unusual caution. Possibly fear.

With sudden inspiration, I plunge my hook into the thick muddy bank, drag myself halfway out, grasp Stella by the elbow, and fall back into the water with her. The splash breaks over our heads, we both come up spitting and spluttering and I catch her by the waist and pull her farther out into the water.

"You call this running?" Stella cries, kicking furiously for her bearings.

"Look!" I gasp, flailing beside her. The great beast plows to where Stella was on the bank, swings its head from side to side, snapping its jaws at the empty air. But it does not pursue us.

"It's Pan's creature," I exult to Stella. "It won't come into the water here, see? The power of the loreleis is too strong."

The monster puts its snout right down to the water, lifts its head, and turns one glaring eye toward us. But it stays onshore.

"Did you know that for a fact?"

I shake my head, trying not to actually pant with relief that I guessed correctly. We're both paddling upright now. With a low rumbling noise, the beast onshore lowers its belly placidly to the muddy bank. To wait. The wretched ticking goes on and on.

"Now what?" Stella whispers.

"This way." I point about a quarter of the circle of the lagoon away from where the crocodile lies, then breast the water with a mustering of strength born of desperation. With Stella close behind, I listen for the sigh of moving water, paddle to the bank in that direction and pull myself along by slimy vegetation. At last my outstretched hook lands on something solid. Not mud, not weeds. Wood. The prow of my boat, still rocking patiently at anchor at the river mouth, hidden in the tunnel of drooping branches.

"Captain!" Stella cries behind me. The ticking thunders along the bank above us. For its size and girth, the damned thing is as nimble as a snake along the muddy shore.

"The river!" I rasp to Stella. "I have a boat."

Stella sees it now, the tip of the bows poking out of the underbrush where the river flows into the lagoon. She paddles to it, feels for the painter like an old sea hand, but I fastened it to some jutting portion of the rock on the other side of the bend.

"We'll have to swim for it, Captain," she pants, sounding for all the world like one of my old crew.

"Under the hull and up by the stern," I agree. "Can you see?"

Stella dives for the boat, a ghostly glimmer of white in the dark water. A rustling of bramble answers almost directly above me, and I look up to see the crocodile's mighty jaws gape open in silhouette against the pattern of stars, as if it were sucking in every scent, every taste, every sound that might lead to its prey. I thrash out to the bows, gulp one last breath, force myself under the water.

The keel jerks against my hand, the boat lowers in the water, and I know Stella is aboard. Hand over hook, I pull for the stern, and out to the larboard quarter furthest from the bank. I poke out my head, and ticking as urgent as hailstones assails my ears, then a splash, and the water rocks around me.

Stella's frantic voice shrills as I clutch at timber, the monster rushing toward me on the water's surface; it's entered from the river side, rounding on the boat, coming for me with the speed of an arrow. I throw my hook up over the gunwale, but there's nowhere for my flailing feet to get a purchase, no time to swing up a leg. In a frenzy of ticking, the beast's jaws yaw open behind me as my fingers close on the gunwale. Struggling to drag myself up, I see the underside of its giant mouth pocked with scabs and sores, feel a gust of its nauseating breath. The boat rocks and I brace my flesh for the piercing of razor teeth.

Something solid shoots past my cheek, and the beast jerks violently in the water and falls away behind me.

Reprieved for an instant, I clamber up over the wales, Stella's hands clawing at my shoulders, my back, dragging me in. Looking back out over the gunwale, I see the monster paddling its short, stout legs in the water and thrashing its head wildly from side to side, its jaws still half open, gagging on some stick-like thing protruding from its mouth: the flat paddle end of an oar thrust shaft-first down its throat.

Stella crouches in the stern beside me, glaring out at the creature, her gown befouled with muck, her hair a wet, tangled mop, her expression fierce, her body alert as her fingers inch backward for the other oar.

"Wait," I rasp. "We still have to row." Her searching hand pauses. "Besides, I believe you've done for him, Madam."

Thrashing vigorously, its scabrous body still shuddering, the monster sinks below the surface to spit out the rest of the oar or choke on it. The ticking has ceased; the rippling water stills.

"You're an excellent harpooner," I pant, crawling onto the thwart. "Let's see how you fare as a coxswain."

"Aye, aye, Captain," she responds smartly.

I go forward to cast off the line. Stella passes me the oar and I use it like a barge-pole, thrusting the boat off the bank beneath the high canopy of branches. When we've backed into open water again, I manipulate my oar Indian-fashion, this way and that, nosing us into the tidal current, flowing now away from the lagoon. No phantom tributaries confound me in this direction, although I glimpse the vapors closing in around the lagoon again behind our departure. The coat I discarded earlier tonight is still in the bottom, and I hook it up and toss it to Stella; she's shivering now in her flimsy gown, while I'm actually sweating from my labors.

But the night is mild, and after a while, the coat falls from Stella's shoulders. I pole the oar to steady our course. I'm in more familiar waters now, know these currents like the flow of my own blood. Reeds, ferns, tangles of wild berries stretching their ferocious points in all directions, riotous night-blooming jasmine, pass by on both sides. Palm trees line the banks, with shadows of pines, firs, oaks, maple looming in a jumble beyond. We pass an enormous weeping willow trailing forlorn leaves along the surface. Even the insects have quieted; the only sound is the music of the water.

"Why did you refuse the lorelei's offer?" I ask, at length.

Stella gazes out at the water. "I told you why."

"The mermaids would have provided a haven for you."

"But a cold and watery one." She rubs her arms in a mock shiver. "I suppose I might be safer, but I'd miss the flowers and stars, and the music of a lovely night like this. I'd miss the sun." She turns her frank gaze again on me. "I would miss you."

My attention is demanded rounding a bend at the entrance to Kidd Creek, whose outbound current flows to the sea, where the *Jolie Rouge* lies. But I work our boat across to the opposite bank and pole along for the hidden gap in the foliage I know so well. Instantly alert, Stella takes the measure of our situation.

"We're not going back to your ship?"

"That's the first place he will look," I reply.

A pair of oars should make the work easier, but I'm in no position to complain about how we lost the second one. And I've made my way into these neglected waters in all tides and conditions, hundreds of times, thousands. I work us through the gap concealed by brush and ferns, into a narrow tributary. I stand, planting my feet in the bottom while poling us off the larboard bank. The mud bank gives way to higher elevations of brush and rock and greenery until we're making our way under the lee of a moderate cliff. A lively pattering of water against water sounds up ahead, and we come round the last bend in the tributary to face an apparent dead-end, a modest waterfall sheeting down from the cliff above. Stella gapes as I pole us toward the pool at the base of the falls, but it's clumsy work with only one oar, and I can't manage the turn into the narrow channel behind the curtain of water without earning both of us a thorough drenching from the falls we're meant to pass behind.

Stella whoops like a girl, throws back her head to let water wash all over her, while I press on with the oar to set us back on course. I rake long strings of wet hair off my face, as she shakes out her own locks, her arms, coughing, laughing.

"You did that on purpose!" she accuses me, her eyes merry.

"I generally manage the turn with more finesse." I muster the oar inboard and sit beside her as she bends over the hem of her gown and wrings it out. Grasping her hem in her hand, she turns impulsively toward me with the thing upraised, as if to pat me dry. We both stare, not at her alarming immodesty, but at the garment she clutches with which to clean me, the once-white fabric blackened with dirt from the road and muck from the lagoon. And we erupt together in laughter, raucous, helpless, intoxicating.

Wiping my eyes and smoothing back my hair with my own wet sleeve, I reach under the thwart and hook out my coat, still relatively dry inside, and offer it again to Stella. Still snickering, she pulls it on over her gown.

Only then does she begin to look about to see where we are.

CHAPTER 21

LE REVE

Beyond the waterfall, around another bend, the tributary widens into a deep, placid pool, glittering like shards of emerald under the canopy of Neverland stars. A strip of black beach nestles in the lee of a high cliff overhung with jungle vegetation. Nothing can be seen beneath the cliff, in the shadows, but I work the boat around until a proud black silhouette becomes plainly visible against the riot of stars and their reflections in the middle of the pool.

My beauty. My pride. My sanity. *Le Reve*.

She's sloop-rigged, her canvas below, the naked spine of her mast and lines exposed to the night. Her elegant prow thrusts forward, her stern is pert, but low, for faster sailing. Her brave paintwork gleams, black trimmed in green to blend in with the black beach and surrounding jungle foliage. Her deck, less than a third of the length and width of the *Jolie Rouge,* is uncluttered and tidy, everything properly stowed and secured. She rides to anchor, poised and alert, ready to spring, ready to fly. She is everything the *Rouge* is not.

I've fallen silent as I work our boat round her stern, beneath the name *Le Reve*, in green. It's another moment before I remember Stella sitting beside me. She too is rapt as I paddle us round in silence to tie up to the starboard quarter. I grasp the cable; by now it's no surprise that Stella throws her skirts round her hips and climbs up like the hardiest old salt. I follow her up, and we stand together on a deck that shines with ghostly elegance in the starlight.

"Welcome aboard *Le Reve*, Madam," I say.

Stella turns slowly, her eager gaze sweeping the deck, from graceful stem to clean, slender waist, to the polished wheel in the stern. There's no stern castle, only a low rise of cabin top between the mast and the wheel.

"This was never in the books," Stella breathes at last.

"No. It's my secret," I agree. "I built her."

She turns to me in astonishment. "By yourself?"

I nod. "Mostly. Otherwise it should not have stayed secret for very long."

Stella's inquisitive fingers stroke the polished gunwale in her eager way of knowing a thing by touching it. Admiration shines in her face as her glance rackets all round the deck. It's as if I've peeled back my skin and laid myself bare for her, a thing I've never done for any other living creature in the Neverland. When her vibrant gaze returns to me, I see she does not take the moment lightly. And in the perverse way of the human race, when I see how deeply she understands, the more uncomfortably exposed I feel.

"However did you manage it?" she asks, her voice hushed.

"Plank by plank. Spar by line."

The toe of her moccasin slides along the deck, she crouches down to stroke a hatch coaming, sanded and buffed to a soft sheen. "It must have taken you ages," she breathes.

"Fortunately, I had ages to spare," I remind her. "I spent years on each section—the hull, the deck, the cabin." I'm warming to the topic in spite of myself. "I scavenged what I could from the stores of the *Rouge,* instruments and supplies we plundered from other ships. I built the rest from timber my men have taken from the wood over time. The wood is never depleted, you know. There is always new growth to accommodate the boy. They did most of the sawing and cutting, my men, so many...willing hands...to do the work." Now I've plunged in, I can scarcely stop myself. "It kept them from idleness. I did the finish work myself, planing, sanding, carving. Generations of former Lost Boys picked oakum and spliced new lines from our stores of hemp and junk. It was no business of theirs how I chose to dispose of the fruit of all their labor after they were gone." I've rigged up a tackle to lower away the boats from the *Rouge* by myself, hauling boatloads of tools and materials to my hidden Black Beach during those long periods when I had no crew.

"There is full running rigging stowed below," I go on. "Extra spars, sails. Best to keep 'em out of sight. There's a galley, a small salon, a cabin, all with furnishings pilfered from the *Rouge.*"

Stella climbs to the cabin top, crosses its planks, steps down to the wheel, inspects the binnacle, savoring its clean lines and smooth finish with her fingertips. The compass I pried loose from the *Rouge*; none of my crew were ever mariner enough to notice its absence.

"Will she sail?" Stella's raises keen eyes to me.

"She might, was there anywhere to go," I sigh. "She's no more practical use than a ship in a bottle, although she took a great deal longer to build."

Stella gazes at me still, her dark eyes as vivid as the starlight. "I've never seen anything so beautiful, Maestro," she says earnestly.

I look away, more discomposed than if she'd ridiculed me. "Her chief virtue now is her privacy," I declare, motioning Stella toward the ladder. "No one alive in the Neverland knows about this place. You're safe here, for now."

***

I peep into the galley below to see if anything edible remains from my last visit, and when I emerge empty-handed, I find Stella sunk into a motley pile of plundered cushions on the bench in the salon. Her long ordeal catches up with her at last: she lies in a stuporous sleep, still wrapped in my scarlet coat. I meant to show her into the cabin and claim the salon for myself, but I won't wake her now. So I stoop under the deck beams and go into the little cabin, shutting the door behind me.

Striking a spark off my hook to ignite the tinder, I light the candle inside the lamp by the bed. Its trembling glow does not extend far into the room, but it's a beacon of warmth and comfort after the dark and wet of the lagoon. I plunk myself down on the bed, a proper mattress in a wooden frame that fills most of this small compartment. With a deep groan, I drag off my sodden boots and soaked shirt, cold wet hair snaking down my back. The leather straps that bind my hook in place have seized up like a torture device from their soaking, biting into my flesh all up my arm, over my shoulder, around my chest. My phantom fingers clench with cold and discomfort as my actual fingers pluck clumsily at the buckles holding the straps in place. At last I peel the harness away, shaking off my heavy hook until iron and brace and buckles all clatter in a heap to the deck.

My maimed arm looks even more gruesome than usual in the lamplight, criss-crossed with red welts. With irresistible morbidity, I touch one red stripe, feel the depression in my skin. My fingers move up my arm, feel similar gouges over the saddle of my shoulder and across my chest. Rubbing does little either to ease or erase them. Finally, I grope behind me for the spare shirt I keep stowed among the bedclothes. My fingers close on linen, soft with age, and I wrestle the shirt on over my head, fastening neither yoke buttons nor sleeves, craving only concealment from my own eyes.

I peel off what remains of my grimy stockings; it seems a lifetime ago that I drew them on to go play advocate at the boys' council. Undoing the buttons of my sodden breeches,

224

I roll them down, and kick them aside next to my hook and harness. Nothing should please me more than to sink into oblivion now, but for a persistent humming in my blood; my body is still too stoked up on the day's adventures for sleep. Time crawls, and I sit up again, wishing I'd thought to stow a supply of black drops in this cabin, to prevent myself thinking too deeply. For all my half-wit gallantry on Stella's behalf, I've only delayed the inevitable, once the boy finds her out again. She'd have been far better off with the loreleis.

But I'd be more alone than ever.

How could I ever bear to lose her again?

Flame flickers in my lamp, as if on a draught. The door gapes slowly open, and something alive, not ethereal, rustles into the shadows of the cabin. My weapons are back aboard the *Rouge*. My hook is out of my reach. I sprawl, bare-legged, on the bed dressed in only a shirt, as trapped as I was in the loreleis' net. Brass glitters in the dark as the crouching figure nears. I recognize my own coat by its gold piping. Stella huddles inside it, holding it round herself with both hands.

She emerges out of the shadows, a glimmer of flotsam on the tide, and as she comes into the light, I see she has not a stitch on under my scarlet coat. Her crossed arms cover her breasts, but I'm mesmerized by the little thatch of dark fur between her legs as she perches herself uninvited on the edge of my bed. Her face is in the light now, her dark eyes intent, looking into mine.

"That was a very brave thing," she says, "coming after me."

Frozen by the shock of her nearness, I inch my damaged arm into the folds of my shirt, phantom fingers groping for cover. "You may speak plainly," I mutter. "It was an act of utter foolhardiness. I had no more sense than a boy—"

"No," she interrupts, her eyes serious, her agile fingers stretching impulsively toward me. "No boy would ever have

225

done it, cared so much. Felt so much. Risked so much. I've never been worth so much to anyone before."

Her fingers land on my forearm, below my elbow; the muscle clenches with anxiety as her fingers slide down with agonizing, intoxicating slowness. I can't stop them. They close round my wrist, withdraw my ruined limb out of the folds of my shirt into the light. She cradles my hideous stump in both her hands, gazes at it without flinching. Fetishist! Pervert! I'm furious that she's found me so naked, shuddering with rage, yet too spellbound to move. I watch in horror as she lifts my stump to her mouth, presses a kiss I can't feel into my deadened flesh. Were my hook in place, how I'd love to tear her mocking lips from her face! Her eyes remain on mine as she presses her mouth again to my ruined flesh. And something stirs within me, a thing I thought as dead as my stump, so long buried I can't even give it a name.

"James," she whispers to me.

Can some withered, mottled remnant of James live still inside this rotting hulk that is Hook? Never. Impossible.

"You mistake me, Madam." I mean to freeze her with my coolness, my fabled *sang-froid*, but I scarcely keep the tremor out of my voice. She feeds on my weakness, growing bolder still.

"Do I?" She holds my stump against her cheek, her other hand stretches toward me. The coat falls away from her shoulders as her fingertips light on my exposed chest. I jump at their warmth on my skin. What is this staccato in my chest, beneath her touch? This is no phantom; it's the hammering of my heart.

My hand twitches up at last. She doesn't pull away, caresses me still, bold eyes fixed on mine. I might slap her hand away, strike her face; even I don't know what I might do. My hardened fingers brush her soft cheek, curl in her hair, curve round her neck, and I pull her to me with sudden force; it's not yet too late to take charge of this game. I'll show her my mettle, if that's what she wants. I expect her to cry out, claw at me, but instead her mouth opens under mine, and I taste hunger as raw and ravenous as my own, magnetic, irresistible. Then she pulls away, of course, her fingertips rising to my lips, pressing me back. But before I can sneer over my victory, she takes my face in both her hands, kisses me again, slowly, deeply, soundly, until I am reeling inside. I've had saucier kisses, before, craftier, but never anything that seared so deeply into the very heart of everything I thought I knew, everything I thought I was.

Her trembling body settles in to mine. She's not so composed as she pretends. I'm shaking like a schoolboy.

"I..I know I take liberties..." she murmurs against my cheek.

"Oh...Stella," I riposte; I have no other words at my command, much less wits. I can only cradle her to me, my maimed arm curling round her back, my fingers in her hair. Her fingers slide over my hand; she draws it down over her breast, her nipple smooth and swollen as a grape under my palm. I caress her slowly, gently, and she moans with pleasure at my touch. Mine. Her skin is unbearably soft, her body ripe and firm for a woman of her years, a miracle for a man of mine.

I cup her breast in my hand, lower my face, tease her nipple with my lips, my tongue. She sways closer, fingers in my hair, chafing down my back, keening softly. My phantom fingers yearn to glide over her body, but my ruined arm is awkward against her soft skin.

"I'm sorry," I whisper, "I've never done this one-handed."

"It's all right," she murmurs, tilting up my face, her eyes glistening in the warm light. "All it takes is practice."

And she nudges me back across the bed, slides up my shirt, takes inventory of my ruined body with her sweet mouth and probing fingers, bringing warmth and life to parts of me that have felt nothing, nothing, for centuries. One-handed or not, I would consume her in a fury, like a hurricane, but she slows me down, savors every part of me, soothing and tormenting at once. It's like the rhythm of the sea, the way our bodies rise and fall, rise and fall, the little trembling swells of desire, the furious surge of release, my incoherent cries, the sweet music of her laughter.

Never in my life has any woman ever loved me with such tenderness. As a rakish young coxcomb, I was all hot blood and fire, brimstone and gall indeed. I'd have rejected tenderness were it ever offered me. But I am young, cruel, heartless no more. It's not Hook Stella loves with such slow, shuddering abandon. It's me.

What unholy force do we release into the Neverland this night with our forbidden passion? Thus was the Fall of Man perpetrated; Eve tasted the forbidden fruit and transmitted all she knew to Adam in a kiss. But what if Eve forsook Adam and kissed the Serpent instead? Is it enough to corrupt the boy's precious Eden of innocence? Perhaps Stella gives me a greater gift even than herself. Oblivion eternal.

Has my Angel of Death come for me at last?

CHAPTER 22

IDYLL

Hell could never be so pleasant, but Stella's gentle, searching fingers make me less sorry than usual to wake to another day.

***

"Has no one ever discovered this place?" She sits beside me on the thwart, twining my long hair into two plaits, Indian-fashion. Green ferns explode from the top of the distant ridge against a bright blue sky, throwing lacework patterns across the water. I unearthed a bottle of rum from the galley and a spare oar, and we've rowed out into the channel and catch fish to cook over the galley fire, although neither of us hungers much for food.

"Lake Hypnos, as I have christened it," I tell her, with a cautious tug at my line. "Which continues to slumber out of sight of the boy. Perhaps all water belongs to the loreleis, and the boys steer clear of it. Like the crocodile."

"Ah. That explains why Peter made the braves paddle me in a canoe to the lagoon. The boys wouldn't go on the water."

I glance at her. "A water route from the wood to the lagoon?"

She nods. "Through a deep ravine, until we got to the big river. Incredibly gorgeous, like drifting through the center of the earth."

She must mean the Terraces, the steep blue hills in the interior of the island that rise from Pirates Beach at sea level to the high plains of Indian country. A channel that waters the wood and connects to the river, hidden from me for centuries.

"They had to stop and perform a ceremony along the way," Stella recalls. "The offering—that was me—had to be purified. They drew circles and burnt sage leaves, and there was a lot of chanting. It took hours. Not even Peter could speed them up."

"Perhaps they hoped the boys would give up and go off on some other game," I suggest. Or perhaps the wily chief was buying time for me to get to the lagoon and intercept them. Astonishing, the confidence he placed in me.

Stella only shrugs, ties off the second braid with a bit of vine. "Peter was pretty determined this time. It drove him crazy when the village elder, Grandmother Owl, they call her, kept me secluded one whole day before the trial. She said a council was a serious thing, and the prisoner must spend a day reflecting on her crimes."

"Do you mean the Indians disobeyed the boy?"

"No, they compromise," Stella corrects me. "Give and take. Their chief is quite the diplomat. No one in the village contradicts Grandmother Owl, not even the chief. Peter made the braves play war games with him all day, because he had to wait. That's when they gave me these," she adds, nudging out a foot in its buckskin slipper.

She sits back, shades her eyes with a hand, squints briefly up at the blue sky above the rim of foliage. "Peter doesn't fear the sky, you know," she observes. "That's his particular element. I wonder he's never seen this place from above."

***

Aboard *Le Reve*, we answer to nothing but the ebb and flow of our own desires. The Neverland, the boys, the fairies, my men, all might as well be on a distant star for all the difference they make to us now. Stella wears my linen shirt above, the one she peeled me out of so shamelessly that first night. Below, she parades about in nothing at all. I go barefoot in my breeches, sometimes in my other filthy shirt, sometimes without. Stella is as undaunted by the scarred wreckage of my body, even in broad daylight, as she was by my ruined arm, so I forget my hideousness for a while.

Below, at night, Stella is a symphony in pink, *rose,* as the French say, her cheeks aglow in rosy lamplight. The merwives' pink spiral shell dangles between her breasts, glistening against her damp skin. She's got hold of my tricorne hat with its luscious flamingo feather, plops it on her head, pretends to preen in the dark cabin window.

"Peacock!" she giggles at me, glancing over her shoulder. There is no cruel glass in which to view myself here, only the tender sheen in Stella's eyes.

"I feel a perfect highwayman," she declares, as I unhook the last buckle and peel the harness off my arm. She whirls about, sweeps my hat off her head, points the extravagant pink feather at me. "Stand and deliver!"

My body complies on the instant, yet I come about, disarming her with a single swift feint, sending her scurrying backwards into the bed pillows. "No silly lady is going to make a man out of me!" I declaim, grappling my hat about so the soft flamingo down grazes her cheek. "First, Madam Outlaw, a taste of your own cruel justice."

I slide the feather slowly down. She lifts her chin, exposes her throat to its whispery touch. "Oh sir, I'll reform," she murmurs.

"I certainly hope not, Madam," I parry. "At least, not yet." The fronds of the feather slide up and down her collar bone, rise up over the mound of one breast, part round a plump pink nipple. Her protests are less coherent as I move the feather over her body, across her belly, slowly, gently down between her legs, until she is squirming, and I am no longer master of myself. "Permission to come aboard Madam," I rumble.

"Aye. Aye. Captain," she breathes.

***

I'm accustomed to women begging for my favors, practiced whores well-paid for their cozenage, or ordinary women desperate to exchange their bodies for mercy.

Please Captain, for God's sake, take me, spare my husband, my daughter, my child...

Their voices blur together, a single lament that creeps into my dreams sometimes like the mournful tremor of a bass viol beneath a bright quartet. I did what they asked if it suited me and pleased myself the rest of the time. It was my power over them that pleased me most. But it's not like that with Stella. She begs for nothing, and I surrender everything to her.

***

We've put out the galley fire and hauled a few mismatched pillows and bolsters up on deck to lie gazing up through the rigging at the rising Neverland stars. The moon has disappeared from the night sky, so the stars are more vivid than ever.

"The tribes have names for them," Stella tells me. "The women told me. There is the Hunter, and the Hawk, just rising over that ridge. That column of three vertical stars, with the little ones above it, that's the Sheaf. And, see that circle?"

I peer up at a ring of tiny stars. "Yes?"

"The Medicine Wheel. Most cultures have something like it, the Wheel of Fortune, the Circle of Life, or some such," she expounds. "One day, they say, the wheel will turn."

I glance at her skeptically. "Surely their pattern is fixed?"

"It's just what they believe," she shrugs, and settles back again.

The loreleis' crooning to their mer-babes is a soft, graceful *adagio* tonight, dipping and soaring as gently as mist along the river. "What a magical place this is," Stella sighs. "No wonder children love it so."

"Magic is overvalued in your world," I remind her.

"It can be abused, like any intoxicating thing," Stella allows. "But children must believe in magic."

"Must they?"

"Absolutely! The world needs magic, now more than ever. If there is no safe place for children to dream, how will they ever dream themselves a better world?" She shifts around a bit among her cushions. "My dreams of Neverland sustained me through some very dark times. I even wrote a story about them once."

"A story? You said your dreams were shapeless things."

"Well, yes," she agrees. "But all writers hear voices in their heads, you know, talking to them. I'd hear bits of dialogue in my head, and I tried to make sense of this feeling I kept having in my dreams, this elation, this...connection. It felt so important."

"Do you recall what you wrote?" I ask her.

"Oh, yes. It was called *The Girl Who Made Friends With Fear*. Very Freudian," she adds, and when I shake my head at this foreign expression, she smiles. "Very symbolic. It was my attempt at a modern fairy tale. A little girl is lost in a deep and frightening wood and trying to have courage. She knows if she gives in to fear, she is lost. She meets a mysterious stranger in the wood – he might be Death, he might be the Devil, she doesn't know, but she doesn't run away. To her surprise, the stranger treats her like a friend, and the wood becomes a beautiful garden."

"A garden?" I interrupt. "Not a golden palace with a handsome prince?"

"Well, I didn't want to overdo it," Stella grins. "It's enough that she suddenly finds beauty and peace in a place she had thought was so terrifying. Her courage is rewarded, you see. Now she can face anything."

"And?" I prompt her. "What happens next?"

Stella shrugs. "She wakes up back safe at home. Ready to take up her life again, I suppose."

"That's all?" I frown. "Hardly a thrilling climax."

"I guess not," Stella laughs. "Maybe that's why I couldn't sell it!"

She sits up to pummel the pillows into a more forgiving shape behind her, then lies back again, bare legs cocked up at the knees, myself stretched out to full length beside her.

"What does it take to fly?" she asks suddenly.

"The approbation of the fairies, for one thing," I sniff. "They provide the magic dust."

"But why fly the boys and not you?" she demands. "Why not even the odds? Wouldn't that be more fair?"

"Only children fly in the Neverland."

"Then it must take more than fairy magic," Stella insists. "Something only children possess."

"Happy thoughts?" I suggest drily.

"Oh, it can't be as mundane as that." She sits up, turns lively eyes on me. "Even you must have had one happy thought in all the centuries you've been here."

"I'm having one now," I grin, reaching out to gently stroke the curve of her thigh, so ill-covered by the hem of my shirt.

She swallows a renegade smile. "And?"

I roll up on my elbow. "Hmmm. I do detect a certain... elevation—" But she grasps a corner of a pillow and claps me across the chest with it. I lunge up, grab her by the waist and pull her back down with me. She doesn't put up much of a fight.

"Is it their youth, do you think?" she goes on with maddening tenacity, once we've settled again.

"I suppose so. My men were all flying boys once, but the fairies have abandoned them. They are fickle in their affections, the imps."

"But what do you actually know about them?" Stella's head pops up from my shoulder. "Do they conjure, turn men into toads?"

"They are allies of the boy," I say firmly.

"Are you sure? What about this ship?"

I stare at her.

"You say you built it yourself, and I believe you. You've a deft hand, I can vouch for that," she adds, with an impudent tilt of her mouth. "But swaying up the mast? Alone? Somebody must have helped you."

"There are...gaps in my memory. I am more prone to drink when I am entirely alone here," I confess. "I awoke one day, and the mast was stepped. But I must have done it in a stupor of passion, don't you see? Drunkards are often capable of the most stupendous feats they can't even remember."

"True," Stella muses. "But what about that fairy who came to your ship when she heard the bell?"

"Do you not recall how she lured you to the Fairy Dell?"

"I remember it very well," Stella says softly, lowering her head again to my chest. "That was the first time you were kind to me."

I've not thought of it in quite those terms.

"They know a way out, don't they?" Stella murmurs. "The fairies."

"But no one ever makes the journey out but Lost Boys and..." I pause, eye her. There's no longer any point in trying to trick an answer out of her. "You were never a Wendy, were you?"

"What?" Her head pops up again.

"Well, think about it, Parrish. It might account for you dreaming your way back with such ardor."

"To cook and clean and mend for the boys?" Stella exclaims, sitting up. "A lifetime of drudgery, you think that's what called me here?"

"You once spoke of teaching them compassion."

"But at what cost?" she counters. "To obey Peter like the little god he thinks he is? What do the Wendys do here? Scrub and mend and pick up after the boys, exactly as they did at home, while the boys go off on adventures. No woman needs the Neverland for that. It's no wonder the Wendys never come back here!"

"But, the stories—"

"Your Scotch Boy knew nothing about women," Stella insists. "Contrary to his fantasies, Wendys cannot possibly long to return. Maybe for some of the more spirited, their taste for adventure, for flying, stays with them. In my world there are women who fly in airplanes. Aviatrixes, they are called. Those are your Wendys."

"So that's why you turned Pan down at the lagoon," I venture.

"I'd come to my senses by then," she agrees. "No more grown-up thoughts, he told me." She smiles down at me, slides one fingertip lazily down my chest. "Too late for that, I'm afraid."

She bends over me again and follows the line she's drawn with a series of kisses. "I love you, James," she murmurs.

"You are a madwoman," I remind her, which discourages neither of us when she burrows again into my arms, and we give ourselves up to the fragrant night, the mermaids' swoony lullaby, and each other. Once I should have called myself unmanned, but not now. Never have I ever felt more like a man than when I look into Stella's eyes and know she loves me. Against all the laws of Nature and reason, Stella loves me.

***

We lose track of the days we idle aboard my sloop. But one morning, Stella jerks out of my arms and rolls apart from me in the bed.

"What is it?" My phantom hand clutches for a weapon.

She lowers her eyes guiltily. A splotch of red smears the rumpled Holland sheet between us. Another little tributary of blood trickles down her naked thigh.

"You're hurt!" I gasp, jolting upward.

"No. Oh, no," she says quickly, shrinking away from me.

I frown at the sudden maelstrom of possibilities. "But… good God, I'm not…I mean, your marriage—"

"I'm thirty-eight years old, James; you're hardly the first man to ever make me bleed," she assures me, with a brief smile. "It's only…it's my monthly cycle."

I'm horrified, of course, although it would be churlish to let her see it as I edge away from the spot between us.

"It's just…unexpected," she goes on. "I haven't bled for a long time. Maybe since I became a governess."

I have no interest at all in speaking about such things. But she looks so forlorn, I reach out to cradle her face. "Does it hurt?"

My answer is the stoic way she sighs and shrugs. In her haste, she's rolled over onto my castoff linen shirt. I spy a fold of it beneath her as she shifts about, smudged with red.

"I'm sorry," Stella whispers, "I've stained your shirt."

"Never mind, *cara,*" I tell her. "Take it. Rip it up into rags if you like. I'll get another. It's high time I returned to the ship to see how the men are faring, in any case," I add briskly, ashamed at how grateful I am for an excuse to leave her to her business. "Will you be all right?"

Her mouth tilts up. "It's not a disease."

"No, but you should rest. Stay below. I'll not be long."

She's watching me with perfect comprehension. Her wry smile broadens. "It may take a few days," she warns me.

"God's eyeteeth, Stella, do you think I would leave you alone for one moment longer than I have to over such a little thing?" I demand, struggling to sound wounded. "Do you take me for a boy?"

Her smile warms. "No. No, I don't."

Blood or no, it's hard to leave her when she looks at me like that. I lean across and kiss her. "I'll be back by evening," I promise.

***

I can't say I expect my men to cheer like the mangy boys upon my return to the *Rouge*, but they might at least muster some feeble sign of welcome. When I row out of Kidd Creek and pull up alongside the *Rouge*, however, absolute silence is my only greeting. The men on deck either freeze in place or stumble to the rail to stare at me, eyes wide, jaws agape. Gato wriggles down the backstay, signing a hasty cross over his chest. Men clutching tools in the waist stare in wordless astonishment as I climb the chains to the deck.

"Well, men, what news?" I hail them pleasantly, for Stella has put me in a high and forgiving humor. Yet I chafe under their eerie silence. The dry spice of sawn wood hangs in the air. A planked workbench is set up amidships with a little tumble of sawdust on the deck below. Sticks stands beside it, guiltily fingering a handsaw. Flax braces himself behind the bench. The fruit of their labors sits on the bench, a little wooden box, pink and freshly made, perhaps a foot and a half square. A sea chest for an infant, perhaps.

Or a coffin.

CHAPTER 23

THE FUNERAL

"Has no one a merry word to say to your captain?"

"Cap'n," Nutter finally rasps, then flinches at breaking the silence, his big hands still fisted in the lines where he and Burley and some others are making ready to lower the gig boat.

"Mr. Nutter," I greet him equably. "Pray, what goes on here?"

No one wants to tell me. They cast their eyes recklessly about and downward, as if the fugitive answer were hiding in the planks of the deck. Filcher is nowhere to be seen, so I address myself to my bo'sun. "Mr. Burley, you are making ready the boat. Why?"

"A funeral," he mumbles, so low I scarcely hear him.

Has there been another battle in my absence? Again I eye the tiny box. A fairy? They could not have killed a boy.

"Whose?" I prompt them.

All eyes turn to Burley, who squares his bulky frame as if shouldering into a headwind. "Yours, Cap'n."

How must I appear to them? Grimy clothing befouled by the Mermaid Lagoon, my drooping red coat reeking of bilgewater from the bottom of the boat, plumed tricorne in disarray over my loose and tangled hair. Now that Stella has brought me back to life, they take me for a ghost! It makes me exceedingly merry; I can't repress a laugh, which horrifies them further, Hook's vengeful ghost laughing in their faces.

"I fear your labors are in vain, my bullies, for as you see—" My gaze falls again on that forlorn little box. Oh, it's like a comic opera! I expect the chorus to march in, singing *fol-de-rol, fol-de-rol, folly, folly, folly.* "And what portion of my anatomy were you planning to ship over the side in that?" I ask in giddy astonishment.

"Er...they said...there wasn't nothing left," Nutter offers, still clutching the lines. "They said you was drowned."

"Who would say a thing like that?" I ask coolly.

At that moment, Filcher bounds up out of the hatchway carrying my splendid indigo hat, beribboned in red and gold. He stops dead in his tracks at the sight of me, his small, shiny eyes rounding with shock.

"Bloody 'ell!" he stammers. He stares down at my hat as if it's come into his hands of its own accord, looks at me as if I've caught him making off with the bloody crown jewels.

"Eager to assume my badge of office, eh Mr. Filcher?" I sally.

"We was going to bury it," he murmurs to the hat.

"Out of respect," Burley chimes in hopefully. "Swab said we had to put it in a box or it wouldn't go down."

I nod at Burley, sweep my gaze back to Filcher, quaking before me. "And who told you I had drowned?"

He seems unable to account for it, shoots an uncertain glance at Nutter.

"It was the boy," Nutter declares, making a decisive movement to coil the line back in place that the others follow.

My blood chills. Did Pan see me at the lagoon? "You spoke to the boy?" I demand of Filcher.

"Not just me, Cap'n," my first mate hastily rejoins.

"They came two days ago, Cap'n. For a parley." Nutter takes up the tale. "Him and his fairy. Asked where you were.

We didn't know. He said he'd beaten you, and got rid of the…new mother…in the Mermaid Lagoon."

"Wot was we to fink?" Filcher pipes up.

"And then, when you didn't come back…" Nutter shrugs, and Filcher nods enthusiastically.

"That's right, Cap'n, that's how it was," Burley agrees.

Hook would snarl that he was back, and they'd all better look lively, but my brain is racing. The boy is not so easily gulled as my men, but if the rumor goes round that I am dead and Stella as well, drowned in the Mermaid Lagoon, might we not gain the advantage? If Pan had to come sniffing round my men to learn my whereabouts, perhaps he doesn't know for certain I was ever at the lagoon. His spy, the crocodile saw us emerge, but what if it didn't live to tell the boy? Pan forgets those he kills, and if we disappear from his sight, Stella and I, drowned in the lagoon, might he not forget us both? This might be my quest, a rebirth, as the merwife called it, if not a victory over the boy, at least a means to wriggle out from under his control. To abdicate my command here at long last, retire from the field. It's worth a try. Indeed, it's in the best interest of my crew if I am not here to draw the boys' fire. I have only to invent some plausible story to pacify them.

"Well, men, I was at the Mermaid Lagoon," I confess, gratified to see the shudder that pulses through them all.

"And the woman?" Filcher asks sullenly.

"I meant to snatch her back if I could. She was a valuable physician whose skills would have been useful on this ship," I tell them. "But the boy condemned her to death, and there was nothing I could do." Let them construe what they will from this. The fewer people who know Stella lives, the safer she'll be. "I scarcely escaped from the place myself," I continue. "I was driven into the water and had to fight for my boat. One of the loreleis gave chase; tenacious as a bloodhound, she was. Pursued me downriver." I struggle

241

not to laugh aloud over this inspiration; if the men believe the loreleis inhabit the channels as well as the lagoon, they'll be far more likely to stay out of the waterways altogether. "But I routed the creature and sent her sniveling back to her sisters."

I'd better play Hook to the hilt if my ruse is to succeed. I eye each man in turn to see who dares dispute me. None do. My grimy appearance does nothing to dispel my story, and most of them gaze upon me with renewed admiration.

"Now, men, we mustn't contradict the boy." I beam at them. "If he believes me gone, he'll be off his guard. So I think it's best if we carry on with this funeral." I nod at the wooden box. "Although, Mr. Filcher, I'd appreciate it if you'd spare my hat."

With an audible gush of relief, Filcher hands my hat to me.

"My time among you must be brief if we are to maintain this fiction," I counsel them as they all hop back about their business. "Filcher, you're in command when I'm gone. Keep the larder stocked and the weapons in trim."

"But Cap'n, where'll you be?" Filcher grunts, grabbing a line beside Nutter to lower the boat again.

My malicious grin cheers them, and they bend eagerly toward me. "I will be in the skiff on the river. Scouting a passage to the boys." The hauling and hammering still as they all swivel their faces toward me. "The redskins have their lakes up in the high country, and the loreleis their lagoon in the south. There must be a channel connecting them that flows through the wood, and I mean to find it. Now that I've survived the Mermaid Lagoon, the whole of the river is ripe for exploration. The boys council I attended was held in a public place, but how much more likely are we to find their secret lair by cunning, from their private waterway? Think of it, men! Why should we constantly wage a losing war of defense when we might enter into the heart of boy country by stealth, launch a pre-emptive strike on their own turf? Murder them all before they have the wit to fly!"

Now the men finally open their lungs and cheer. How like the boys they are. *Kill, kill, kill.* Stella is right; we men are a sorry lot.

What ever possessed her to love me?

This unwelcome thought steals in upon me like a sudden frost in the middle of my triumphant charade. But I shake it off, order the burial party over the side with Burley in command, and a brick from the ballast in the hold to weigh down the box. I give my abused scarlet coat to Brassy and go into my cabin to collect fresh clothing for my presumed voyage of exploration, my French cutlass and an extra dagger. With Brassy off in his cupboard with his brushes, and Cookie packing the victuals I requested from the galley, I steal into Stella's cabin to purloin another shift out of the chest I gave her, along with the clothes she wore here, and the volume of Milton that gave her such joy, all of which I stuff into a pillow sleeve.

Back in my cabin, I return my ribbony hat to its peg. My plumed and lacy tricorne is so unsuitable for skulking about in shadowy places, even my men might notice, so I hang it up as well, pluck off the black hat, and draw on my black coat. But at the last moment, I find I cannot bear to leave behind the frothy pink feather, still redolent of Stella. So I snap it out of the brim of my tricorne and slide it inside my shirt, under my black coat, next to my heart.

***

I scarcely step foot upon *Le Reve* when Stella comes bounding up the hatch and across the deck to kiss me.

"You must be sweltering in that thing," she exclaims, pushing my black coat off my shoulders.

"If you are going to undress me every time we meet, Parrish, we'll never get anything done," I protest, making no attempt whatever to move away from her busy hands.

"Well, you look like an undertaker!" she laughs.

"How fitting, as I've just come from a burial." And I tell her all that transpired aboard the *Rouge*. "I need only go back now and then to hear news of the boy. Only think, if he forgets about me, about you…" I'm arrested in the act of shrugging entirely out of my coat. "Perhaps they will all forget," I breathe. "The boys, my men, all of them. The Neverland. They might forget all about us, Stella. They might leave us here in peace."

But Stella frowns. "Here?" she echoes. "We can't stay here, you know that." Her hands clasp my shoulders, her dark eyes are vivid. "I'm going home, James. And you're coming with me!"

CHAPTER 24

THE REDEEMER

"Home? The world of men and war you were so eager to escape?" I suck on a stringy piece of salted wild pig purloined from the galley of the *Rouge*, along with a bottle of port. We've removed ourselves below to the salon as dusk creeps over the Neverland. "Have you changed your mind?"

"Coming here changed everything," says Stella. "I never realized how much I'd miss all I left behind. Little things. Daft things. A snug home, a fire in the grate, and a rattling good book. An excellent glass of port." She raises an empty hand in mock salute; we must pass the bottle between us, as all my goblets are back aboard the *Rouge*. "The changing of seasons, the company of friends, the healing cycles of time, grown-up pleasures, I crave them now." She sits back a little, sighs. "Running away doesn't solve anything. It's time to go back and rebuild the world we've got."

I reach out to stroke her hand. "Stella Rose, my sweet outlaw, my tumbling star. There is no way back from the Neverland. I prayed for centuries. I should have found it by now."

"*Prayed*, is it?" She cocks an eyebrow at me. "Perhaps you invoked the wrong gods."

"In my day you'd burn at the stake for such talk," I note admiringly.

"It's not witchcraft," she says. "Forces exist in the world far older and more compassionate than the gods of

245

men. Or boys. The miracles of nature are more powerful than anything church or science can imagine. Mysticism is as old as time. The shaman spoke of a dreampath—"

"Poetic metaphor," I protest.

"All right, but he said the quest belongs to someone brave enough to follow the dreampath the *other* way. Out of the Neverland! Lost Boys and Wendys go back all the time. Peter flies in and out all the time. The merwives go back and forth underwater."

"I mean there is no way back for *me.*"

She shakes her head, her bouncing hair nearly the color of the port in the warm lamplight. "But it's all different now. You yourself have visited the fairy queen and the mermaids."

"Only because I was witless enough to follow you."

"And why didn't the fairies stop me, as Peter asked that day, remember?" Stella counters. "Why didn't the Indians shoot me down? Why didn't the mermaids drown me? Because the signs appear in all their folklore, and I must be part of it, somehow."

"It may be your journey entirely," I agree. "But not mine. Eden must have its Satan."

"But surely you are the sacrifice here, not the Devil," she exclaims. "You are the redeemer."

I stare at her. "Madam, in my time I've been accused of many things—"

"You're the one who suffers for their games," she insists. "You are the one who dies over and over again so children may have their innocent Dreaming Place. So Peter can win, over and—" she pauses, wide eyes gazing inward, then gapes again at me. "His dreams are freighted with centuries of losses, that's what the merwife told us. How can he not explode? He has to take it out on someone. Then you come along, the dark and sinister man, the pirate, symbol of the cruel grown-up world that has stolen so much from him. But this is the world where children prevail, where Peter

246

always wins!" She is eager now. "Maybe he doesn't even know why, but it must relieve the sorrow somehow, all his victories over you, the sorrow he can never be allowed to remember. That must be why she sent you here! Your witch, your voodoo queen."

"Why would she care if the little whelp has bad dreams?"

Stella shrugs. "Might *she* have been a Wendy?"

I frown. "If so, she would have no memory of this place, would she? But…she did commune with spirits of the dead." *Bienvenu, Mama Zwonde.* It chills me still to think on it.

"Maybe she didn't care anything about Peter," Stella suggests. "But she cared a great deal about you."

"To curse me to eternal torment?" I gape. "By God's hamstrings, it's lucky she didn't dislike me!"

"A curse *and* a chance," Stella persists. "Lazuli told us the Neverland was in grave peril once because Peter was on the verge of giving way to all his sorrows. What if it was you coming here that put things right? However awful your other crimes, your witch must have known this would outweigh them all. Preserve harmony in the Neverland, keep this place safe for dreaming children everywhere. Redeem the Neverland and redeem yourself."

And it comes to me again, what Proserpina said that day about my future, a violent end, my unshriven spirit forbidden to rest in peace. I took it for a curse flung at me in anger. Was it a warning?

"But…it's fantastic," I mutter. "Why would she bother?"

"She must have loved you," Stella murmurs. "As much as I do."

I am stunned to speechlessness.

"It just wasn't supposed to take so long," Stella adds.

"Perhaps my crimes were greater than she imagined." I'm shaking my head against a floodtide of grim memory. "I should have faced the charges against me like a man, stood up to my accusers, removed the stain from our family name. But I chose to run away, take it out on the world, like a fool. Like a boy." I draw a heavy breath. "My father might have lived."

Stella grips my hand in both of hers. "Your witch knew what you were. She knew how much you had to answer for. But she expected you back in her lifetime. She wanted you back, I'm sure of it. What prevented you?"

I shake my head. "That was centuries ago. My memories of that time are naught but a blur of one fruitless campaign after another. After Pan slaughtered my original crew, he started bringing in replacements, former Lost Boys with no better sense than to dream themselves back. I would find them dazed and helpless in some forgotten corner of the island or other, de facto outlaws in this fairyland of children. How could I not—"

"They never came back before?" Stella interrupts. "The old Lost Boys?"

"Well, before I came, I cannot say, but I never saw evidence of any other grown men, save the braves, until after all my original crew were killed. And why would there be? If Pan so despises men, why would he ever bring them back?"

Her expression is all the answer I require. To fight and kill, of course. So they might join my crew, die under his blade, hundreds of them, thousands, so he might have his revenge on the grown-up world and spend his sorrow. And I am his accomplice, his high priest, his bawd, leading his victims to their ritual slaughter, over and over again. *How many more must die?* "By Christ, I will never go back," I whisper. "I am irredeemable."

"No," Stella says firmly, twining her fingers through mine. "You've done all that was asked of you. Peter and the Neverland thrive! There are other men to take up the battle now, and there always will be."

"Yet more pointless deaths." I sigh. "That can't be what she wanted."

"Perhaps not," Stella agrees, considering. "But nothing turned out the way she planned, did it? You've had two centuries to pay for all your wrongdoing, James. That's long enough. And now the signs are in play."

I sit back, my wits harrying her notion for its hidden flaw. There must be one. "The shaman spoke of three signs," I remind her.

"There hasn't been a third sign, in the sky, yet," Stella agrees. She gazes up the hatchway, out to where the first of the stars are winking to life. The moon is waxing now, the merest sliver of light in the evening sky, everything the same as it always is.

"There's something we haven't said or done yet to get you out of here, James. We must find out what it is."

We, she says. We're on this journey together.

"But what?" I sigh. "Some offering, perhaps? Incense? Animal bones? You've already been purified. What do your books have to say on the matter?"

"Well, curses are broken all the time in the old tales. Sleeping Beauty. Snow White. Beauty and the Beast—"

"How?"

Her mouth quirks up. "True love's kiss."

I lean across the table obligingly and kiss her piquant mouth. But no thunderclap, nor tidal wave, nor volcanic eruption from the bowels of the earth disturbs the placid Neverland evening. "Well?"

"It can't happen just like that." Then her expression brightens. "Your witch! Didn't you see her in the Fairy Dell? We must go back to the fairies, find her again!"

I do not dignify this hare-brained suggestion with a reply.

***

249

How can it be true, any part of it? Yet Stella so ardently embroiders this fantasy of escape, I cannot help but be buoyed up with each new stitch; her hope is as contagious as the pox.

"Where will we go, when we are free?" I prompt her that night as we prepare for bed. I so want to believe her.

"Trescoe Island in Scilly," Stella replies eagerly. "My aunt's cottage – well, it's mine now. Such a fine prospect, a thousand isles, gilded by the western sun. A huge panorama of stars that change with the seasons, tumbles of rock and stone like ancient castles, a wild, abandoned, beautiful place, James. You will love it so much."

How I crave to hear the pounding of restless, living surf, the scree of gulls; the Bay of Neverland is so eerily calm. "I wish I could believe it will be as rapturous as you make it sound."

"Well, it won't be all that rapturous. The cottage is half ruin inside, and we'll have to hack it out of the overgrowth. The islands are battered by fierce winter storms. And there are all sorts of… modern conveniences…to contend with," she adds with asperity. "Automobiles. Jet planes. Telephones. You may find them a very great nuisance, as I do."

"Since I've no notion what any of those things are, I'll reserve my judgment," I promise her. "What are we to do there?"

She regards me, chewing on her lower lip. "You'll laugh." I gaze back at her with my gravest cardplayer's face. "Well, the great age of smuggling and murder is long past," she says wistfully. "Now the islanders are mostly devoted to flowers."

"Flowers?" I laugh.

"See?" she reproves me, but her eyes are merry. "Yes, flowers, growing them, tending them, harvesting, packaging, hauling them to the mainland. That's their industry. That's how they all live."

"So the ferocious Hook will finish his days gamboling among the posies," I muse.

"A skilled carpenter is employable anywhere," she nods at me. "You'll be able to get work in Hugh Town on St. Mary's, the big island."

How easy she makes it sound. "When I left, I was a wanted man on three continents," I sigh. She's scooted up beside me on the edge of our bed, and begins unhitching the little buckles of my harness. "Suppose your world won't have me back?"

"It's a very different place now," she replies, peeling the straps off my arm. "Everyone you wronged, or who ever wronged you, they're all long gone." She slides the apparatus gently off the end of my truncated arm, sits gazing for a moment at my hook in her hand. "Your crimes are mere trifles next to what the world has seen since."

"The world war you spoke of."

She nods. "One man, full of hate, he was the start of it all." She sets my hook on the shelf beneath the window, straps dripping over the board. "He rampaged across Europe, murdered millions, men, women, little children, entire families, whole villages destroyed. Other countries joined in. It doesn't take much to goad a fellow into making war on his neighbor."

"No," I agree.

"He had to be stopped. The good war, they called it."

"Wars of aggression will always meet with passionate defense," I reason.

"But even a 'good' war, a 'just' cause becomes its own tyranny after while," she says. "And why should men willingly turn into monsters, torturers, aggressors, just because their leaders tell them to? Shouldn't there be a point where each man says 'enough?' When a madman's ranting is laughed off for the insanity it is?"

"Impossible," I mutter. "Persuasive ranting is the chief office of leadership."

"If leaders were made to fight their own battles, wars would cease." says Stella.

"Bugger witchcraft, my dear, they would hang you for sedition," I tell her. "My men do not guess where they are, or why, when they come here. But no sooner do they spy a fighting ship in the bay, hear the first tattoo of war drums, than something primal stirs inside them. They surrender completely to this place, this war, crave battle above all things. It is their nature."

"If men gave birth, they would understand how precious every life is," she murmurs. "And how fleeting,"

She has slid back among the bedclothes, taken up a pillow which she cradles to herself absently, her expression suddenly bereft. I pretend to fiddle with my harness, coil it away.

"I did kill him," comes her soft, desolate voice. "My son."

I would speak, but her face silences me.

"Damaged, they said. Not enough oxygen to the brain. Unresponsive. Unfinished." She gazes at her pillow. "It happened so fast. They had to get everything ready, tubes, wires, machines. They let me hold him. He looked at me. He knew me, I'm sure of it." Her eyes are dry, her expression unbearable. "He was so beautiful, my tiny, damaged boy. So wise. He never even cried. All those months I carried him under my heart." She draws a quavering breath. "I must have known he was leaving me. How could I not see it?"

"You couldn't know that."

"As surely as if we still shared the same heartbeat." Her voice is empty. "It happened so fast. I should have screamed for the nurse sooner, made a fuss. They might have saved him."

"Or there might have been nothing at all they could do," I tell her. "You might have only prolonged his misery. You can't know, Stella; you can't say for sure what might have been."

Her stark gaze meets mine. "I let him go."

I struggle for the right words. "You were merciful."

"I was a monster. There must have been something more I could have done."

In my mind's eye, I see my father's face, imagine him cursing me from his deathbed as clearly as if I had been there. I know what is to kill someone you love.

"He died in the arms of someone who loved him," I say carefully. "A good death. Better than most of us will ever know."

She gazes down at her twisted pillow. "I couldn't keep either of them," she whispers. "I couldn't love them enough."

"Stella, don't—" I reach for her, but she shrugs away, hugging the pillow closer to her ribs.

"Some things are beyond forgiving," she whispers to it.

I blow out the light, curl up nearby. It's a long, long time before she lets me hold her.

***

We search the skies, day and night, for any unusual activity, but see nothing out of the ordinary: sun, blue sky, the occasional wispy cloud, a full complement of Neverland stars, and a nearly quarter moon, cracking on for her next full phase. But neither do the boys trouble us. Stella is more restive than ever, but I've hit upon a plan to test my theory: if the Neverland has forgotten us, surely it will begin with my men. Perhaps they are already addressing another man as captain in my stead.

I am in the skiff, rounding the last bend in Kidd Creek, near the fertile place where we keep our garden, before I feel the first internal pang of dread.

"Hook!" caws the Pan triumphantly, vaulting up out of the foliage. "I knew it!"

253

CHAPTER 25

A PARLEY WITH PAN

He emerges from a giant overhang of leafy ferns, sails out over my boat, malicious fairy glitter humming at his shoulder. He has obviously not forgotten me.

"Pan," I nod, and still my oars.

"I call for a parley!" he cries.

What choice have I? He descends into the stern and perches on the after thwart, facing me, but out of my reach. His imp sparks warningly between us, throwing off powdery bursts of light in iridescent shades of green and rust. At this range, I glimpse a flash of her golden hair.

"I know the rules," I sigh, and spread wide my hand and hook, still gripping the oars. The fairy springs for the hilt of my sword, magicks it out of its scabbard in another volley of scintilescent light, drops it on the empty thwart between us. I don't bother to ask for his blade; it wouldn't be fair for him to draw against me unarmed.

"They tried to trick me, you know. Your men," he sallies, sitting himself cross-legged in the stern, patting out his motley of leaves. "They said you were dead."

"Perhaps they thought I was."

"But I knew it was a trick!" he crows, thumping his scrawny chest. "I knew you were alive. I can always tell." He leans closer to me, his grey eyes bright. "And so is she!"

I dare not betray any flicker of feeling at all, now that Stella is alone and unprotected. "Well, what of it?" I reply easily, pulling my oars inboard.

He sits back, frowning. He wants me to defy him, wants a new game to begin. "She's an outlaw!" he challenges me.

"There's nothing she can do to hurt you," I say reasonably. "You are master here."

"She is condemned to death!" he insists.

I don't remind him that his sentence was carried out to the letter with results that were beyond his control. I decide instead to turn the conversation in another direction. "Do you never tire of being captain?" I ask him.

The question surprises him, but he furrows his brow in elaborate rumination. "Well, it's hard work sometimes," he concedes loftily. "They take a lot of looking after. But when they get to be too much trouble, I kill 'em!"

"Your own Lost Boys?" This shocks even me. "How?"

His grey eyes glisten. "I send 'em back! Make 'em go back and grow up."

Blood pounds like a blacksmith in my head. "Then why not send her back too?" I hear myself say calmly; send her back, my bully, and show old Hooky how it's done. The fluttering of the fairy grows more agitated, as if she can hear the din in my head.

"She's grown up already," Pan declares. "She has to die here."

I will my hammering heart to silence. "You might pardon her, you know," I say evenly. "It would be very grand of you."

"She doesn't belong here!" He folds his arms in defiance. "Everything's changing, can't you feel it?" He leans toward me again. "You have changed!"

I gaze at him impassively. The water of Kidd Creek babbles happily round the boat, sunlight glows a hundred shades of green in the rustling trees, shrubs, ferns and reeds. How can I argue, with the memory of Stella still so sweet inside me? Pan scowls, studying me.

"Of course, *my* mother was prettier and cleverer and so much more fun!" he proclaims with the absolute confidence

255

of ignorant youth; I know he has no more notion of who his mother was than an egg in a henhouse.

"She's not my mother," I say simply.

He peers at me, his eyes suddenly rounding in pity and horrified delight. "You like her!" he squawks. "Hook likes a lady!"

Let the boy jeer. Let him be the one left out of the game for once. And as soon as he sees my indifference, the glee leeches out of his expression.

"She can't have you, you know," he says more darkly. "You belong to me."

A riot of fairy light pulses between us. My mind closes instinctively to the shrill grapeshot of the imp's language, yet from her tone and movements, I might almost think she's upbraiding him.

"Stop it, you silly thing!" Pan cries in real irritation. "We're talking! If you can't behave, you go home!" He dismisses the creature with a wave of his hand, yet she sparks in the air beside him, gabbling in protest. "I mean it! Go on!" the boy shouts. Then her glittery trail speeds away.

Pan peers at me again. "That lady can't win against me."

"She is stronger than both of us," I reply.

"You, maybe," he protests. "You are old and weak and stupid."

"True," I agree mildly. "I'm no use to you any more."

He scowls again. My mildness enflames him more than my wrath ever did. How did I never notice before? Watching him, I try another tack. "I propose a new game," I suggest. "Pretend battles between your men and mine, like you wage with the tribes. It will be just as much fun," I promise, thinking of the ferocity with which my men throw themselves into football.

But he screws up his face in disgust. "That's stupid!" he cries. "How can I win if it's all pretend? I want to win!"

By God's blood, that part of Stella's theory must be true. Beating me is all that matters to him, all that ever will. Look at the predator's glint in his grey eyes, peering at me. There is no appeasing him, no cajoling him. There is no compromise, not for me. He's like the most savage hunting dog; he smells me by my fear. Soon, very soon, he will make me pay for my foolish dreaming in the coin I can least afford.

His expression intensifies. "She'll make a fool of you, Hook," he needles.

Where does he get such talk? From one of the more forward Wendys? I gaze out at the water without responding, but he has the instincts of a shark when it comes to drawing blood.

"My best hunting knife says she will leave you all alone," he presses on. "What will you wager?"

Only my heart, although I do not say it. His little animal face flushes with cunning, even as I resist his game. "She doesn't really care for you, you know," he says airily. "There are probably a hundred men out there, a thousand, that she'd like better. It's only because she's stuck here with you."

I keep my features composed, imagine myself with the stoic visage of Eagle Heart, as a tide of dread steals upon me. Which is worse: my anger that the boy so skillfully plumbs the depths of my darkest thoughts, or my shame at having such thoughts at all?

Suppose now that Stella regrets coming here, she means to exploit the signs and this curse against me for her own ends. No wonder she was so eager to seduce me, if she believes I am destined to find the way out. She came after me as soon as the merwives told her the journey had begun, I remember now. Suppose that's all she wants from me, a way out of the Neverland. And I was glad enough to be duped. Hook, the gull. Hook, the fool. But, no, a tiny, sane, stubborn voice argues within me, this is Stella, my Stella. Am I really so gullible? Or is Pan a more formidable opponent than even I ever suspected?

It takes all the aplomb I can muster to shrug him off. "I can't expect a boy to understand."

That irritates him, of course. "I'm not just any boy!" he cries. "I'm a warrior, just like you, Hook!"

In heartless cruelty, in self-absorption, in the easy way he can dismiss everything valuable in life, yes, he is much like the Hook I was once. But I am Hook no more, I tell myself.

He leans closer still, his grey eyes shining and eager. "And you are *just* like me!"

***

The newly sanded deck of the *Rouge* fair crunches underfoot. Below, I find fresh stores of small game from which to choose my supplies. The men still know me, but in the face of my negligence, someone else is taking pains to keep the ship in trim, or at least defensible. Defense, the only possible weapon there is against the boy in this benighted place. On my obligatory tour round the deck, I see the gig, our larger boat, has been scraped free of barnacles.

"Careened her yesterday, Cap'n," Burley tells me when I seek him out, where he leads a party of men in knotting new lines into the lower fore shrouds.

I turn about as Nutter lumbers up out of the hatch, pinked with exertion. "Oi, Cap'n! What about your boat, then?" He gains the deck, wipes a blue and white striped sleeve across his forehead. "Since you're here, what say me an' the lads take her off to the beach and set her to rights? Bit of the ol' spit an' polish, eh?"

Rarely have I seen Nutter so eager for work. "Pity it's so late in the day," I reply. "Next time—"

"We'll be done before dark," he persists. "You can be off again in the morning."

How long can I keep on like this, pirouetting from Hook to James, divided from myself? The men deserve a more constant captain, but I am too eager to get back to Stella and forget the boy's poisonous words. "Next time," I say more firmly.

***

It's near dusk when I return to *Le Reve*, freshly provisioned with wine and victuals, and an ugly layer of doubt larding my heart. I scold myself for a fool when Stella welcomes me home with a warm, loving embrace; how unfair of me to give the boy's cruel words any credence. Yet I can scarcely bear how vibrant and lovely she looks as sunset fills the salon, bustling under the deck beams, stowing our supplies, teasing me with her musical laughter. Her proprietary touch delighted me this morning, but now I can't help but feel something cunning in it.

"Are you all right?" she murmurs at last, reaching across the salon table where we sit to lay her hand on my arm.

"The boy has come back looking for us," is all I say.

She sits up, worried. "He knows where we are?"

"Not yet." Did he know for certain where we shelter here, he'd not have had to lie in wait for me at the mouth of Kidd Creek.

Stella sighs. "But he soon will. We must find the way out."

If only I could be sure of her. "I suppose," I mutter.

Her hand slides off my arm. "What is the matter, James?"

"This body of mine is very old," I improvise, glancing away. "It has supported me for centuries. If I set foot out into the natural world, what's to prevent the ravages of time from catching up to me all at once? Suppose I crumble to dust upon the spot, like the ancient artifact I am?"

"But you won't," she insists.

"We could stay here, Stella," I urge her. "Stay here with me."

"Absolutely not!" she cries.

"You would grow weary of me," I suggest, as petulant as the boy.

She stares at me, and I'm instantly ashamed. Perhaps I'm not ready to leave the Neverland after all. I reach across the table and knot my fingers through hers in apology.

"You would be far more likely to tire of me, as I age into a crone while you remain the same," she says softly. "I couldn't bear to watch your feeling for me fade over time."

That complication has not occurred to me. "But," I begin to bluster, "I would never—"

She waves away my protest. "For another thing, he will never, ever let me stay to make you happy. He'll find a way to thwart us."

Of course, I know this is true.

"Anyway, he has made the journey back and forth innumerable times. Has he ever crumbled to dust by exposure to the other world?"

"He is never there long enough," I suggest.

"Exactly so," Stella agrees. "Were he to stay too long, he might fall prey to the natural cycles of life. He'd lose his baby teeth, grow hair on his privates, all the things he most fears." She leans closer to me. "The normal aging process would begin. Why should it work any differently for you?"

Her arguments are utterly sound. Her enthusiasm buoys me up a little, for I begin to believe anything is possible with Stella. The warm flush on her cheeks in the gilded light rouses me to amorous expectation. The only sour note is the voice of the boy yammering away in a deep recess of my heart: if she really cared for me alone, mightn't she at least have offered to stay in the Neverland with me? Even if she didn't mean it, even if only to humor me, might she not have said it?

CHAPTER 26

SUITE: FAREWELL HOPE

1

"This is madness!" Stella insists.

"This is war. It's madness to believe otherwise."

The oaken panel is heavy in the inner curve of my hook as I stand midway up the companion ladder, lining up the teeth of the hinge. It was the stoutest board I could find on the *Rouge,* thick enough to resist the boys' blades. It took some sawing to fit it to the hatchway; all of *Le Reve* reeks of sawdust still. Its innovation is it will swing up into place from underneath the hatchway. The boys can pry open the coamings on deck, but this can be sealed from below.

"We will always be at war here," I tell her.

"Then don't play—" she begins.

"This is not a game! He knows we're alive. He will find us again. We must be ready."

There is no escape. The heavens have not cracked open to disgorge another friendly sign. Even my old dream of release has abandoned me; the comforting stranger in a garden, escape on the phantom ship, I've not had it in weeks. Our seclusion and safety on board *Le Reve* are but illusions, I know that now, tricks to make his next victory even sweeter. That is the way of things here, to play out the line a little, let me delude myself that I have earned some infinitesimal measure of peace, respite, happiness, before all is wrenched from me yet again.

But Stella's expression is tragic as she stands below in the salon, amid the litter of boards and tools and hardware, gazes with loathing at the extra sword and shields I've also brought back from the *Rouge*.

"Don't do this to *Le Reve,* James," she begs me. "This is our only refuge. She was never made to go to war."

I do not like to see her face like that, cannot bear to be the cause. But I did not begin this war, and I'm damned do I not defend what is mine. My men know this much, even if I have forgotten.

"This is the world where Pan always wins, you said it yourself," I remind her, and drive in the pin that joins the teeth, securing the panel to its new hinge in the deck above. It hangs there forlornly alongside the hatchway, blocking out the sun. "I can't let him hurt you, Parrish." I am all but pleading, as well. "I must prevail, this one time!"

"And then what?' she demands. "Will you become the new tyrant of the Neverland? Rule over your enemies, bend them to your will, until you become the new despot they're all plotting to destroy? Don't you see that it never, ever ends?"

"How can I stop him? What else can I do?"

She sighs. I sneak a glance at her, see her turn away into the gloom. I know what she wants to say. I do not want to hear it.

"They can't all be as perverse as their queen," she murmurs at last.

"They all do her bidding."

"But they must know the laws of magic that govern this place," she urges me. "Someone will know what we must do. Or maybe we can find one to show us your witch again."

"The fairies have never been friendly to me, Stella—"

"What about the one who came to your ship that day? She told you it was your last chance."

"A taunt, nothing more," I reason. "I know now the terrible Hook can expect no mercy here."

Another brush with the imp queen could only erode what's left of my sanity and rob me of the only thing of value I possess—Stella's love. If, indeed, it's still mine.

***

Apocalypse wakes me in the morning; I come to my senses thrashing in Stella's arms, blood thundering in my ears, brain exploding with images of fire, tempest ruin.

"Easy, baby, easy," Stella croons, her arms sliding round me in the cold chill of dawn.

"You think me an infant," I rasp.

"It's a term of affection where I come from," Stella smiles slightly, curls up alongside me. "What were you dreaming?"

"The end of the world." I can't even name what I dreamt, sinister foreboding beyond all imagining. I slide out of her embrace, sit up on the edge of the bed, reach for my trousers, too agitated now for sleep. With a sigh, Stella too throws off the bedclothes.

"We must get away from here, Maestro," she murmurs.

Another miserably bright blue boy day is dawning, a quarter of an hour later as I finish buckling on my harness. Stella brings me a shirt.

"We've got to ask the fairies—" she begins.

"No!" I snap, still raw from my dream.

"But, James—"

"Maybe it doesn't matter what happens to me, once you complete your journey." I cannot stop my bilious words as I haul on my shirt. "Think of the adventure! You can put it in a book."

"What?" Stella gapes.

"Why else subject me to the fairies a second time? Or perhaps Pan is right, and you've no intention of—"

"Pan? You spoke to him? About me?"

"Perhaps it makes no difference to you if I dissolve in a pillar of salt or wither away in the sun, once you're free of this place," I press on guiltily, daring her to prove me wrong. I am beyond all prudence, so desperately do I need her reassurance. "All you want of me is passage out of this hellhole!"

"You know that's not true!" Stella cries, outraged. "Since when does his word count for more than mine? You're as bad as the damn boys!"

Wounded, I snap back, "Trade me to the fairies for your freedom if that's all the more I mean to you. Or perhaps you'll simply let me slip away when you're done with me, like your child—"

Her expression checks the volley of my terrible words; even I am shocked to hear them. They are like a thousand laughing demons exploding out of the air, digging a chasm between us that can never be bridged, never ever. It's another frozen moment before I realize what I take for the pounding of my heart is the distant report of real cannon fire echoing in from the bay.

Just because Pan has not found us out doesn't mean he's not up to mischief elsewhere.

"Damn and blast, that's the *Rouge*," I bluster, grateful for the interruption, turning quickly away, as if rapid movement might reverse the flow of time, erase these last few, fatal seconds. But Stella's face tells me otherwise, beyond pain, beyond any rage that even I have ever known, blistering as the sun.

"That's right, run away," she says tersely. "Go back to your ship, your men, your precious boys, back to your stupid war; that's all you care about. You're just like all of them! Stay here forever, if that's what you want. God forbid you should ever grow up and be a man!"

The wan apology that had struggled to my lips curdles on the instant. Without another word, I grab my black coat, launch myself up on deck, and clamber over the side for the boat, awash in fury and shame.

2

But the *Rouge* lies to anchor placidly enough as I round the last bend of the creek and pull out across the bay. The intermittent booming of shot has punctuated my journey, and I'm near enough now to smell acrid smoke and see a smudge of grey adrift above the *Rouge*. Yet I see no war canoes, no flying boys, hear no echoes of jeering laughter, only a hollow percussion of footfalls, a distant staccato of barked orders conducted over the water. It's some sort of drill, but with real shot, a foolhardy waste of supplies and energy. And upon whose orders?

I tie up astern and climb the chains, but all activity is on the foredeck where Nutter is bawling orders to a ragged line of men making clumsy efforts to obey, hauling up powder-filled breeches wrapped in flannel from below.

"Aw, c'mon *ladies,*" he yelps, as the others scramble about their work. "You look like a bunch of faggots. Let's go!"

"Who gave the order to fire that gun?" I ask Filcher, when I've herded up the men to attend me on deck.

Filcher glances sideways at Nutter.

"The boys respect the gun," Nutter chimes in. "They keep their distance."

I don't say the boys keep away because I am not on board for them to humiliate. "Until you waste all your powder firing at nothing. Drill all you like, men, but save your live ammunition for the boys." Still, I praise their martial enthusiasm and set them to stowing the rest of the shot back in its magazine below. Someone in the Neverland, at least, has the wit to keep their enemies at bay.

"More grape for Long Tom," I bellow into the hatchway at the men clattering down to the hold.

"Captain." I come about to find my steward poised gingerly at my elbow. "We—"

"Brassy!" I hail him. "A pot of your worst, if you please. Bring it to my quarterdeck." It will take a tankard or more to burn off the edge of my rancor.

But I chase the first with a tankard of rum shared with the men in the mess room after their morning labors. It's brutal hot on deck, but pleasant enough down here. Nutter fetches me another, and whatever sense of urgency I came here with is fast ebbing away. I can scarcely recall now what it was that so troubled me earlier. But whatever it was I had to do can surely wait. We've nothing but time in the Neverland.

***

A faint, brash piccolo, or perhaps a tiny bell rouses me out of deep, dreamless torpor. The next thing I know, an agitation like furtive bees snags my attention once more, another high piping, echoing down as if from some prodigious height. My wits are uncommon sluggish; the voices, if such they be, are out of harmony with each other, one lugubrious, the other harsh, fleet, rattling.

"What do you get out of it?" rolls the first.

"The destruction of my rival," spikes the other.

I must be dreaming, after all; it can't be fairy speech. But thought of fairies bursts the dam so painstakingly built up out of rum, anger, and oblivion, and my argument with Stella comes flooding back to me in all its naked viciousness. I groan, sit up, grapple for my coat, and the dream voices vanish.

Blinking about, I see I'm in my cabin aboard the *Rouge*. The sun is westering toward the distant fog bank; the golden light of afternoon slants across my stern windows. How can I have been here so long, the day all but gone? What must

Stella think? My bruised, defiant heart cares nothing for her thoughts, but now my wits are ticking back to life, I'm more ashamed than angry. We spoke terrible words to each other, and now I must go back and face the consequences. It is all that separates me from the boys. Otherwise, I prove her accusations true.

At my cabinet, I select two crystal wine goblets, which I wrap up in another linen shirt and conceal inside my coat. I stop in the galley for another bottle, not rum, a seasoned port. Stella's favorite.

"But Cap'n, you ain't leaving us?" Nutter protests, clawing up on deck as I march astern for my boat.

"My work is best done at night, while the boys sleep," I tell them all, and climb down the chains.

***

Stella does not come on deck to greet me when I tie up and climb aboard *Le Reve*. Small wonder, after our bitter words. The golden afternoon has given way to violet dusk, and the gloom below decks is total. I pause, blinking, at the foot of the ladder to get my bearings until the shadows arrange themselves into the familiar shapes of cookpot and bricks in the galley, heaps of tools stowed away in the salon. But none are Stella. The cabin too is empty, and the hold. In a panic now, I race above again, but discover no fallen form, collapsed in a swoon or worse, behind the cabin top or in the bows. Stella is an excellent swimmer; she can't have drowned in the lake. Swum off to the beach? But I don't need my glass to see the whole of the black sand beach is empty.

She is simply gone.

I can scarcely breathe for the fear clutching at my insides. The boys, it must be, made off with her at last. But there is no evidence of struggle. The hatch cover hangs complacently where I left it, unlatched, not hacked to bits. There is no toppled furniture, nor stray arrows poking out of planks, nothing disturbed or out of place. Nothing at all is the matter with *Le Reve* except Stella's absence.

I grasp the rail, heart pounding. She's run off. Abandoned me to this living nightmare for all eternity. She didn't get what she wanted of me and now seeks it elsewhere. She is either the falsest, cruelest woman to ever draw breath, or part of some vast conspiracy in the Neverland to wound me beyond all enduring. Both explanations are equally repellent. Hook, the gull. Hook, the fool. Rage boils up inside me from some deep, rank place, blotting out the day, the beach, my sloop, the feeble bleating of my ruined heart. Rage, my oldest ally and only friend, hotter even than the bloodrage of battle, seductive as black drops, an inferno of consuming, unthinking rage; take me my old friend, use me.

I storm below again, desperate to stop the spinning of the world and all its mockery, trembling with the urge to destroy some thing of hers as she has destroyed me. All is fearfully shipshape in my cabin, bedclothes straightened under the coverlet, a little pile of her garments folded neatly on the bed. The lantern hangs on its peg; candle stubs and flints are arrayed upon the shelves beneath the window, alongside her precious Milton and the long, curling pink flamingo feather. This last I grasp, but it seems to hum against my skin like a kiss or a sigh, or a butterfly's downy wing, sensation more potent than memory, fraught with all we shared. Once.

I slam the feather back on the shelf. Damn her and all her kind! I never claimed to be aught but the monster I am. I challenged her to love me, and she failed that challenge. If she thought to reform me, like some coy little Wendy, with her laughter and her clever talk and the sweet refuge of her body, she was sadly mistaken. I've been cozened and betrayed by women all my life. Why is this one so remarkable? Perhaps it's the precision with which she cut through my defenses, found the part of me kept hidden even from myself, dazzled me with the falsity of hope, and then destroyed it all. Devastation will consume me for the rest of eternity. Infinite wrath or infinite despair? Which way I fly is Hell.

Thus paralyzed I remain on board *Le Reve* as night falls, hoping against all reason that Stella might yet come back to me.

***

Blue moonlight bathes the frothy carrot tops, the corrugated cabbage leaves, mutes the vivid hues of my irises until all resemble an eerie, phantom landscape on the bottom of the sea. The pealing of a tiny bell, and a presence rustles up beside me, so near I could touch it, a voice as soft as the moonlight.

There's always a way. We can find it together.

I turn slowly; the shadows fall away. My hand stretches out as the figure comes closer still. At last, I see my companion, my redemption, a woman's pale face under cinnamon colored hair, dark greenish eyes, mouth tilted slightly up in heartbreaking intimacy. My heart soars. Stella.

Take my hand.

A grazing of skin, a surge of joyful relief. And then consciousness glimmers and all of it, redemption, release, Stella's warm, forgiving smile, all spirals away from me like sand in a hurricane. Clutching madly at nothing, feverish with remorse and despair, I come awake alone on board *Le Reve*, reeling, heartsick, my sex so hard I have to relieve myself with my hand like a green youth. My agony is complete when in the very instant of self-release, I moan for Stella. Never, not once in over two hundred years I've suffered in the Neverland, never, ever have I so wanted to die as in this moment.

3

"She's dead, Cap'n."

Filcher blinks at me with rabbit-like sincerity, but the shock his words produce must tell in my face, for he melts back another step. "That's wot you said, i'n'it?" he falters.

Recovering myself, I nod to reassure him. "So I thought."

The sky is murderous blue today, back aboard the *Rouge*. Stella did not come back to *Le Reve* last night. Run off to the loreleis, perhaps. Had she any intention of coming back to me, she'd have done so at night, while the boys slept.

But had the boy himself or any of his allies captured her, he'd waste no time coming to me to trumpet his victory. For this reason, I've returned to the *Rouge* at first light. I know not which I dread more, that Stella has deserted me or been made off with by some enemy, but either way, I must know.

"She never came back here?" I quiz Filcher.

"Blimey, Cap'n, what for?" he exclaims.

Why, indeed? To beg my forgiveness? Not likely, after what I said to her. Or to launch a new plan of escape, for another grim thought has stolen upon me in the bleak light of day: that the signs and the quest have nothing at all to do with Proserpina cursing me. It was only Stella's insistence that led me to imagine they were connected. What if I am still here because my eternal curse can never be lifted? If Stella realized it, she might have even gone off in search of some other man whose journey the signs foretell, some renegade Lost Man, ready now to go home. Perhaps she's already found the way out, the path, the lover's kiss that was truer than mine.

I must know, must feed my anger, stoke up my flagging rage; I will be a sniveling, broken thing forever if I don't steel myself against the anguish of losing her. Did she find a more compliant ally among my crew, I must torture myself with knowing to which man she's transferred her pinchbeck love, which body she prefers to mine, quell the whining of that simpleton, James, within me, before he can point out how little rage, revenge, or even the phantom hope of escape can ever mean to me without Stella.

There's no more reason than ever to assume one of my men is on this prophetic journey. Except for the trouble someone took to keep me aboard the *Rouge* yesterday, for if I know my hook from a handsaw, I recognize now the hypnotic effect of black drops. Someone must have found an old vial of the stuff after all. I will know soon enough by whose orders they were placed in my drink. And why.

I peer again at my first mate, so gifted at lurking in the shadows. Those voices I thought I heard yesterday: product of my delirium or something more sinister? Did anyone else hear them?

"Filcher, you didn't happen to be anywhere astern yesterday—" I pause, trying to recall the angle of the setting sun through my stern windows. "Say, an hour before twilight?"

Filcher's shiny eyes round in apprehension; he's not sure whether 'yes' or 'no' is more likely to satisfy me.

"I...don't rightly recall, Cap'n."

Surely, had he overheard anything remarkable, he'd have been eager to tell me. I wave him off with my thanks, and he melts gratefully away.

The idlers are still below at their morning mess. Going above, I mark Gato in the crows nest, and Sticks and Swab on watch. Filcher assured me Burley went out in the gig with Nutter and young Flax to manage the nets, and I go to the larboard quarter to watch as the fishing party pulls in. But all three men are there in the boat, Burley in the stern, Nutter and Flax on their feet, fixing the dripping net with its cargo of fish to the tackle Filcher sends down.

Flax is up the side first, after the fish are hauled in.

"Handsomely done," I tell him as he clambers in over the wales. "Oh, and, Flax, where were you yesterday, an hour or so before twilight?"

Nothing seems to alter in his open face. "Dunno, Cap'n," he shrugs. "With the lads, I reckon."

Nutter is lumbering up over the railing, and I ask him the same question.

"Dammit, Cap'n, we got a ship to run," he blusters. "I don't know where I am every minute of the day."

I gaze after them both. I'd make a jest about how the River Lethe appears to be flowing into the Bay of Neverland, but only Stella would understand it.

I turn to the tackle, where men are beginning to haul in the boat, absently take up a line. Perhaps she didn't need any help from my men to effect her escape. Yet, how—I freeze in the act of winding the line round my hook. Suppose it was Stella's voice I overheard yesterday, bargaining with a fairy. Ridiculous! What would either one of them be doing on the *Rouge*? Those voices were hallucination, nothing more, I convince myself, as we sway up the boat. And yet, Stella was the one so keen to talk to the imps.

Was she so angry with me yesterday, she made some unholy bargain with a fairy to leave the Neverland in my stead?

Is that why they drugged me? *The destruction of you rival.* Suppose Stella discovered that she and I were rivals for the escape route foretold in the signs. And then we quarreled. I must have made it so easy for her. I even dared her to trade me to the fairies to make good her escape. What if she did? Hook sacrificed on the altar of the boy's pleasure, left behind for damnation eternal in the Neverland, was that the price of her freedom?

I scarcely notice water cascading across my boots from the streaming boat until Burley good-naturedly pulls me aside and takes my place at the lines. The shouting of the men swaying the boat in to her blocks seems as distant as the moon, as a rift of pain tears open my heart. Did my cruel words make Stella hate me so much?

Then the shouting of the men grows more urgent. The sky darkens above Pirates Beach as they come yelping and hollering toward us, a swarm of boys racketing along to the screech of Pan's war pipes. Nutter stumbles over the tails of the lines he's coiling on the wet deck, charges late round the deckhouse for Long Tom in the bows, bawling for his gun crew. But they are scarcely to the ladder before the boys gain the starboard rail. One grimy little fellow with a snakeskin across his middle lights on the foot of the gun near the touch hole and draws an arrow through his bow, a perverse little Cupid aiming at Nutter, who has sense enough to halt at the top rung.

"Hook!" cries Pan, from his perch in the center of the others along the rail. "I knew you'd come back!"

"What do you want?" I bark, steeling myself for the news that Stella is his captive, or worse.

"She's gone, isn't she?" He's positively beaming. "I told you!"

My first response is relief, followed by an agony of loss more bitter than I have ever known plunging through my vitals; it takes all the willpower I possess to conceal it. "Well, what of it?"

Pan frowns at me as if I am a stupid child, then his eyes light up. "So I am the true captain of the Neverland!" he crows, exuberance lifting him high off the rail. "And you are nothing!"

He actually feints backward in the air, grasping the hilt of his sword, anticipating my furious charge. The boys too loom up expectantly, threading their bows, drawing their weapons, eyeing the men. I myself tremble with the urge to go roaring after him, a target at last for all my renewed misery, and my men would not fail me. It's what they all want, men and boys, all of them.

But my imagination gambols on ahead to the aftermath of my decision: the deck of the *Rouge* strewn again with the corpses of my men, unprepared for battle, without even Long

Tom for cover, flesh sprouting arrows, stab wounds gaping blood. I can drive them to a brave and glorious death, as commanders have done since the beginning of time, and they are sheep enough to thank me for it, but why? The whole business revolts me, our battles to the death over nothing at all, Hook's pompous pride, so easily ignited, the boy's childish imperatives.

The boys shriek with pleasure as I yank my French sword from its scabbard, but they choke on their hurrahs when I throw it to the deck and stride across the waist, leaving the men in a knot on deck, Gato in the ratlines, Needles peeping out of a hatch, Nutter teetering on the balls of his feet, all of them staring at me as I march to the center of the boys' line and glare up at Pan.

"Go home, boy."

His grey eyes sparkle, his sword is in his hand, but as I am unarmed, there's naught he can do but brandish it menacingly about my head, each thrust a little closer, so I feel a scurry of air against my cheek, a flutter of blade in my hair. It's as if he were trying to coax a cat into swiping at a string, clucking and simpering at me. Flat steel slides against my cheek, a point glances off my shoulder. A stout little fellow in raccoon furs nervously fingers his bow and arrow behind the Pan. Agitation boils across the whole of the ship.

"I am master here!" Pan yelps, his little teeth bared in a grin a jackal might envy. "Say it, Hook! Say it!"

But I stand like a block of stone, ignoring his whooshing blade. This time, for once in my life, it's myself I refuse to betray by giving in to the mob. I am done with his games. Let him scalp me if he wants, mutilate me again, prick out my eyes; how I wish he'd prick out my eyes so I might never have to see the Neverland again. He scowls, mouth compressed into a line, flourishes his sword, and the other boys swarm in closer, rattling their weapons, growling.

A larger shape looms up to my left, tall, solid, reeking hot sweat. Another weapon clatters to the deck, and the boys paddle about in confusion as Nutter plants himself beside me. The snake boy on the gun has to rustle up and follow to keep Nutter in his sights. The big redheaded fellow stares straight ahead even as blade points and arrow tips jab in the air round his face. The tide of the boys' attention turns again when Burley heaves up on my other side, square and stony-faced. Gato's knife rings against the deck as he drops out the ratlines to stand beside Burley; Flax, then Swab, even Filcher join the line, all of us unarmed and resolute in the face of the boys' chivvying.

"I am master here!" Pan tries again, but his voice falters with frustration. His boys begin to chorus, "Pan! Pan! Pan!" but more out of habit than zeal.

An arrow gripped by its shaft grazes Nutter's cheek, but his amber glare sends the assailant reeling backward. One little fellow cries "Codfish!" and a few others take up the chant, but even that feeble jeer dies off. The boys paddle more strenuously now in testy confusion. They can't call the pirates afraid, not this time.

Pan darts to me, his face as dark and furious as I have ever seen it, snorting through his teeth like a little terrier, trying to perceive what part of me he can no longer control. With an abrupt movement, he snaps his blade back into his belt.

"C'mon, men!" he cries to his boys. "We might as well fight a bunch of *girls*!" The boys hoot with laughter, scrambling to close ranks behind him as they all rise in the air. "But we'll be back!" Pan exclaims, drawing a few random cheers from the boys. Irresistibly, Pan zooms down once more to me. "That's two games you owe me, Hook," he growls. "Maybe you don't have enough pride to fight for yourself. But I bet you'll fight for *her!*"

"But she's gone," I remind him.

"Not yet," he hisses at me. "Not unless I say so!" And off they all fly, an erratic pattern in a sky newly besmirched with sinister grey clouds.

My men neither guffaw nor congratulate themselves, shocked to sobriety by their newfound stature, dispersing their line in silence. Only I remain rooted in place.

She's not gone yet. Stella is still in the Neverland.

***

"Cap'n's acting funny."

I pause at the foot of the ladder, hastily stuffing a strip of dried salt fish into my coat pocket, as Flax's covert voice drifts past the hatchway above.

"He's just smarter than you, is all," answers Nutter.

"It was smart not to fight?" Flax prods.

"Little bastards had the advantage," Nutter points out. "We wasn't ready. Cap'n played a smooth trick on 'em, though."

"Yeah?"

"Sure he did. Next time they come back, they'll think we've all gone soft. That's when we'll give 'em what for."

I'm astounded that Nutter thinks so highly of my methods. One impulsive act of bravado and Hook is reborn, his despair taken for tactical cunning. Thus are military legends made, of hot air and delusion. I creep up the ladder, behind them. As the voices move off toward the deckhouse, I hear Flax make a derisive click of his tongue. "If you ask me, he's soft already."

"That's why nobody's asking you, old son. Cap'n done the right thing—this time."

"Who's to say he won't turn yellow again?" says Flax.

"Oh, there's a fight coming, I promise you," Nutter chuckles confidently. "And next time we'll win!"

CHAPTER 27

SUITE: FAREWELL FEAR

1

She's not gone yet. But Pan may be rallying his murderous boys to hunt her down at this very moment. Certainly, if she were already in Pan's possession, he would have brought her on board the *Rouge* today to start a battle. I must find her before he does.

It's dreary work rowing once more down Kidd Creek, but if she is still at large, sooner or later, she must return to our only place of refuge. Where else can she go? I maneuver behind the falls, stroking for the shelter and solitude of *Le Reve*. By the grace of whatever powers rule in this place, let Stella be aboard. Ahead lies the strip of black beach in the lee of the familiar cliff crowned with ripe foliage. Every palm, every fern, every dripping succulent is just as it was, a silent chorus of tranquil beauty welcoming me home.

One thing alone is missing. *Le Reve* is gone.

Irrational panic grips me; I must have made a wrong turn, followed the wrong route, although I could row here in pitch blackness, even drunk or asleep. It's an illusion, some unrecollected rock or outcropping of vegetation standing between the sloop and my vision. But there is no such phantom impediment. The entire surface of Lake Hypnos stretches before me, and *Le Reve* is nowhere on it. All that labor, long, exhausting decades of my life lavished over every detail, my fond memories of peaceful industry away from the boy, all of them destroyed. My absurd pride in my work, blasted now to atoms, my only solace wrenched from my grasp. *Le Reve* is gone.

Why did he do it? For spite alone? Did he send her to the bottom, or did he simply command my beautiful sloop to disintegrate, the way he commanded the roses to die, to dissolve into particles and whisper away on the wind? Yet another victory over me.

I get a firmer grip on my oars and my wits. If our sanctuary has disappeared, where else in all the Neverland might Stella go?

***

It's as green as ever on the Mysterious River, tropical foliage waving idly in the breeze, dripping along the water with serene indifference. All is mist and humidity as I row, beyond feeling, beyond weariness, beyond any other consideration but Stella's welfare. Grant me her safety, and I'll do anything you ask, I beg of the limpid atmosphere itself. But I receive no reply that my poor wits can discern.

One place alone might offer Stella refuge. At the very least they might be able to help me find her. Their scouts inhabit every waterway in this island; perhaps one of them has heard something, seen something. If I am not too late.

Still some distance downriver from the place where phantom tributaries obscure the entrance to the Mermaid Lagoon, I hear something splash off my port bow. Hoping to spy again the flying fish guides, I peer over my shoulder to see a vision out of a nightmare, long, webbed fingers closing upon the wales, a dark head rising up to stare at me. A pale face under a tangle of greenish-black hair in long, dripping coils, turquoise eyes, an ear with a shark's tooth through its lobe; a face I know. I still my oars and nod to Mica, the warrior siren.

"Captain," she murmurs.

Letting go one oar, I reach slowly for my sword, which lies in the bottom at my feet. I lift it gingerly by the blade and offer the hilt to Mica. She takes it. I peel back the flap of my coat to extract the knife from my belt and hand this to her as well. She slides it into a length of plaited seaweed round her waist.

"I come to you unarmed," I tell her. "Please, I beg an audience with Madam Lazuli."

***

Sand swirls in uncanny patterns across the surface of black water in the old sibyl's water-glass, within its coronet of volcanic spikes. There is not yet any recognizable image, like the fish we saw before, but the sibyl nods her sprigged white head with satisfaction.

"We will find her, Captain," the formidable blue merwife, Lazuli, assures me, coiled up on her tail beside me on the rock plateau before the water-glass.

I am too late for Stella; she has come here and gone again, so they tell me. Not off to collude with some other man or fairy for her release, but here to the safety of the merwives after I abandoned her. She blew her shell whistle over Lake Hypnos and was borne to this lagoon by a mermaid escort yesterday, whilst I wallowed in oblivion on board the *Rouge*. This morning, scant hours ago, she left them again, and we have climbed to the water-glass to find out where she went.

I nod, squeezing out my hair, still wet from my watery descent, and lean in closer to put myself in the way of the draft of cool air that enters the grotto through a channel in the rocks directly above the sibyls' oracle glass. They have treated me generously thus far; dozens of Mica's sister warriors swam on either side of my boat and in the vanguard, creating a current with the strength of their bodies to speed me downriver to this place. The air bladder they provided rendered my descent into the lagoon as tolerable as possible, yet disquiet grips me do I allow myself to recall the fathoms of water under which we are buried here.

"She begged us to send a messenger to a certain elder woman of the tribes," Lazuli goes on.

"She's gone to the Indians?" My heart sinks another fathom still. A brave on a quest, a far more likely means of escape than any of my men.

But the blue merdame shakes her head. "I believe she wanted their help to guide her into the Fairy Dell."

I am chilled by more than wet. Of course, the Indians know the wood better than anyone but the boys. "Surely, they would not agree?" I protest. "It's too dangerous."

"I cannot say what the answer was," Lazuli confesses. "Our messengers relayed her request through the network of waterways that connect our lagoon to the Indian territory. The response that came back was not in words. The tribeswoman sent her a packet of dried blossoms."

I frown at her. "Dream Flowers?"

"So she called them," Lazuli nods. "Her answer was to come in a dream, and since it was evening by then, we persuaded her to stay the night here, with us, where she would be safe. But her sleep was troubled, and something had changed by this morning. When she awoke, she was desperate to go back."

"Back?" I echo. Can the boy be wrong? Has she gone already?

"Back to you," the merwife elaborates. "She said there was something she had to tell you."

My heart clenches. "She didn't say what?"

"She was in too great a hurry. Our women guided her back to the lake behind the falling water."

Dare I mention *Le Reve?* But if Stella called the sirens from on board yesterday, they must know by now my sloop exists. "Back to my ship?" I ask. "My sloop, I mean."

The blue siren nods. "That is the last they saw of her."

Only I was not aboard to greet her. What did the Dream Flowers tell her? If it was the secret to getting out of the Neverland, why didn't she go? Unless she flew off to London without me, on my ship, like in the stories. I almost hope she did, rather than imagine all the mischief that might have befallen her since then in this wretched place. "They are both gone now," I tell Lazuli, "Stella and my ship."

The merwife sighs, scratches thoughtfully at her springy, silver-grey head. "She was safe as long as she was with us," Lazuli tells me. "She has not called again for our help. We do not know that she's come to any harm..."

Again I find myself angling nearer the air shaft, as if to escape the miasma of dread rising to suffocate me like steam from the lagoon. "How can there be so many harmful things in this place?" I groan. "How can it be a haven for children?"

Lazuli regards me with patience in her sapphire eyes. "The Neverland must have its wildness, its terrors," she tells me. "Here, children must find not only their happiest fantasies, but their most violent and terrible nightmares. They must face their demons and laugh at them. They must conquer fear. That is the key to growing up."

The old sibyl scatters more sand over the water in her oracle glass. "Yessss..." she hisses, and Lazuli motions me forward to gaze into the water. The sand drifts apart on the surface, revealing a green image, foliage along a river bank. Falls thunder nearby; I can hear them. It's like watching a play on the surface of the water. An offstage voice cries out,

"Are you there, Madam? Come out. I need you!"

It is my own voice. But even as I stare in confusion, the last of the sand sinks away and I see Pan calling out through his cupped hands, calling out in my voice. The waterfall is visible now, and my heart catches as another voice answers,

"James, is that you?" Stella emerges from behind the falls, hurrying along the bank, shift clutched up in both hands, her expression eager. "Where are you? I've been so worried!"

And the wretched boys swarm up out of hiding, fly across the water to surround her.

"Your codfish *James* can't help you now, Lady!" crows Pan.

I watch in impotent horror as Stella tries to out-maneuver the boys. Twisting away, she grasps the shell whistle round her neck, but Pan rips it out of her hand with such violence that the seaweed thong breaks, and he throws the shell into the river. In an instant of inspiration, Stella feints away from the boys trying to herd her and plunges off the bank into the river herself. My heart surges; the boys fear the water!

But as she strokes out into the river, the boys shouting and heckling her from the air, Pan rises up and whistles through his two fingers. An ominous splash answers up ahead, and the nightmare shape of the crocodile comes speeding along the surface of the water, straight for Stella. She sees it, paddles in place for a frantic moment. There is nothing she can do but scramble back up onto the bank. The evil reptile might yet give chase, were that its purpose. But at Pan's signal it sinks obediently back into the water, waiting, while the boys charge Stella with a length of rope, winding it round her arms and shoulders, despite her flailing and wriggling, until she can only kick out uselessly at boys hovering several feet off the ground.

"You're wasting your time," Stella challenges Pan, shaking back her wet hair, determined. "He doesn't care anything about me."

I am stabbed to the heart to think she might believe it. Yet how gallantly she fences not to lure me into a trap. A trap for both of us, it must be, or he'd have let the crocodile rip her to pieces.

"We'll find out!" bleats Pan. Then he turns to his sparkling fairy. "Shut her up, Kes, so she won't be any more trouble." A shiver of light envelops Stella, and her kicking and squirming cease. "Glimmer her back and wait for me," Pan instructs his fairy. "We have work to do. C'mon men!"

But now the image is fading into black water once more.

"Where has she gone?" I beg the old sibyl. "Is she safe?"

The crone shakes her snowy head. "The glass cannot see where she is," she murmurs in her whispery voice. "Only where she was."

I can only guess at my ghastly expression from the sympathy in Lazuli's, scarcely notice the gentle hand the merdame lays on my arm as I struggle to collect my wits.

"As long as you are here in this grotto, the Boy King cannot detect you," Lazuli tells me.

I nod. Merely obtaining bait is no guarantee the trap will be sprung; that takes patience, and time to do properly. As long as Pan can't find me to demand a reckoning, Stella must be kept alive. I must find a way to free her without springing the boy's trap.

"Stay here with us tonight, Captain," Lazuli offers graciously. "We have many empty chambers at the moment. And no more harm will come to her while the boys sleep."

By the time we've climbed down from the craggy rocks that support the water-glass, two warrior guards have surfaced in the pool with a messenger siren from the river. She pulls herself out onto the shale bank with sturdy arms, her pale skin freckled faintly green, with long, wet coils streaked in gold, copper, pewter down her back. She wriggles to Lazuli, hands her some things she's withdrawn out of a net pouch at her waist. The blue merwife gazes at them only a moment before holding them out to me; with a pang of longing, I recognize Stella's two soggy moccasins and the pink shell once given her in this very grotto. My hand trembles as I take the shell on its broken thong, hug it to my breast. A feeble spark of an idea fizzes in my brain.

"Is there a body of water near the boy's lair?"

"A freshwater spring," says Lazuli.

Pan is not yet aware that I know he's captured Stella. The boys' lair and surrounding wood are well-fortified against any warlike assault, but Pan will never expect me to come alone, by stealth, without my fighting men, before Pan has even issued his challenge. It's my only chance to get Stella away before she's made a sacrifice in the boy's deadly game. I should go now, this minute, while the boys sleep, were my arms not already thrumming after the day's rowing. Besides I'd be at a fearful disadvantage, alone, in the dark, with no idea where the boys keep their lair. But others on this island do know. "If she is imprisoned in boy country, I ask only one favor," I say to the merwife.

Lazuli sighs. "We cannot guide you there. The wood is an unfriendly place to the waterborn."

"But if I blow this shell over that spring, you will hear it?" She nods her head, and I go on. "When I sound a note on this shell, will you and your women sing the boys to sleep? At whatever hour of the day it might be?"

She is silent, regarding me. The cooing of mothers and mer-babes around the pool grows still. I fancy I can hear an ominous stropping of Mica and her warrior sisters' shell blades.

"I will go into the wood unarmed," I go on stoically. "I have no desire to harm the boy or the Neverland. But I will not leave her there at his mercy." I draw another breath. "Please help me."

"Of course, Captain," Lazuli agrees.

***

The grass mats beneath me are surprisingly dry and soft on this bed of kelp arranged for me in a guest chamber of the rock that rings the pool. This is where Stella slept last night,

284

still fitted out for company, although I fear I'll never sleep in this eerie place, with the sirens' lullabies wafting round the grotto and the miasma of softly shifting mineral colors above the water. Yet I must have slept, for I'm wakened in the deep of night by a feminine voice gasping and crying out in pain. Past the mouth of my cave, I glimpse blue Lazuli waist-deep out in the pool with a younger female, who is supported by others. A murmuring of hushing, cooing, urging, flutters across the water; a last crescendo of pain gives way to the thin wail of a tiny new creature, flapping a sticky tail and shaking its little fists in the crook of a blue elbow, crying for its mother's tit.

 I roll over on the mat, plump up the grass under my head, and my fingers brush some small solid, knobby thing. Pulling it out, I recognize one of the Indians' Dream Flowers, such as Stella fed me once on board the *Rouge*. They tell you what you need to know, that's what she told me. Hoping to see the same vision that sent her away from the grotto in such haste, I swallow it down, close my eyes again, and give myself up to Morpheus, here in the heart of the loreleis' lagoon, on the banks of the birthing pool.

2

 The chiming of a tiny bell and a rustling in the bushes startle me.

 I had thought myself entirely alone in my garden, among my lavishly blooming irises and green vegetable rows. My head and shoulders draped in a length of gauze to keep off the sun while I work, I've even stripped off my hook so as not to damage the delicate blooms; it lies nearby in the crate under a brace of cabbages destined for the *Rouge*. The boys never come to the garden, it smacks of mundane, worldly things. That's why this sudden activity in the shrubs that protect this place makes me jump where I kneel.

Peering around my makeshift gauze hood I spy a child, a girl, emerging from the bushes. Her dark, reddish hair is cut short in a bob, long fringe in front over her forehead. She wears the kind of shapeless nightdress the Wendys always wear; the fashions of the nursery do not change much over time.

"Don't be afraid."

Thus she speaks to me: Hook, the terrible, Hook, the nightmare.

"You take me by surprise." I surreptitiously shake my shirt sleeve further down over my stump, under the length of gauze. I hadn't realized how late it's grown while I've been about my work, shadows are lengthening across the ground, an icy moon already on the rise in the blue sky.

"I didn't know anyone was here," says the girl.

"No one is," I promise her.

She scrutinizes my oddly cloaked figure. "Are you some kind of hermit?"

I make a noncommittal grunt and return to my work. If she doesn't recognize me as the terrible Hook, why should I bother to enlighten her?

"You have a beautiful garden," she says. "May I help?"

Not that she waits for my invitation. Everything in the Neverland exists but for their pleasure, as they all assume; she is on her knees prising out clover and dandelions with practiced fingers before I can even respond. Still, it's a rare enough child who finds pleasure in such things. She goes about it with far more skill and enthusiasm than any dozen of my men.

"Will they not miss you?" I suggest, as we work together. "The boys?"

"I'm fed up. All they want to do is wave their swords around and make a lot of noise."

"That is the entire point of being a boy," I suggest, and she giggles artlessly.

"But it's so boring!" she goes on. "They never want to do anything else!"

"So he gave you leave to just...walk away?"

"I've given 'em the slip." She gives her boyish bobbed hair an expressive little toss. "Peter doesn't know everything."

I steal a glance at her round the edge of my hood. Does he not?

"I suppose you're off to join the pirates, then," I suggest, with an inward sigh. She's making it so easy, the inevitable next step in the eternal scenario. Too easy. I'd have the playwright flogged for such obviousness.

"Why?" she snorts. "They're as useless as the boys. They never even sail anywhere. Have you seen their ship? She's like the Flying Dutchman. I'll bet she's rigged out of... out of cobwebs and rags!"

And crewed by the damned, I think, as good as ghosts already. From the mouths of babes.

"I'm looking for the way out," she tells me.

"There isn't any," I sigh.

"Well, of course there is," she says stoutly. "There's always a way to do anything. You just have to find it."

Spoken with the utter confidence of youth. But the little creature has salt, I'll credit her that much.

She drops a fistful of long-tailed clover in the gravel path outside the flower plot, sits back, gazes out at the leafy green vegetable rows. Then she peers up at me. "You've probably been here a long time. Maybe we can find it together," she suggests.

There is a way out of course, for her and the boys; it begins just about now, when the fairies steer one of them into my path and I'm obliged to take her hostage. Another excuse for the boy to come and slaughter us all.

But what if it doesn't play out like that? Pan doesn't know everything, she says; her being all the way down here, at the end of Pirates Beach, is proof of that. Generally, I find them wandering in the wood.

A part of me would keep her here talking forever; how long has it been since anyone in this vile place has spoken one single syllable to me unburdened by fear or cunning? At the very least, I might compel her to tell me how she's managed to slip away from the boys and the fairies' notice to be out here all alone, unprotected. But the first sour notes of the loreleis' nightly yowling have already begun, and an unwholesome hot, sulfurous tang is creeping into the air. In a moment or two, the little thing will be asleep, and utterly in my power.

No more boring games. No more bloodshed over nothing. She has earned her freedom. I can see she gets it.

I slide out my hand from the folds of gauze. "I'll wager we can," I tell her. "Take my hand."

She hesitates for an instant, glances at my proffered hand and up toward my hooded face, but then she grins. "It's a deal!" she chirps, and slides her little fingers round mine. A bracelet of tiny silver charms, one a perfect miniature bell, tinkles on her wrist.

We rise together, and I lead her some little ways down the bank to where my skiff bobbles placidly in the reeds.

"You have a boat!" she cries eagerly. "I love boats!"

This surprises a grin out of me. "So do I."

I hand her in over the thwarts, but it's just a formality; she knows exactly where to step and how to balance so as not to tip the boat. She steps down to the bottom, and in the act of seating herself on the thwart, turns to beam a radiant smile at me. In the next instant, she sinks all the way into the bottom, enchanted to sleep.

I watch for another long moment, to see she does not wake again, then trudge back up the bank to where I left my hook, near the cabbage bed. I'll need it for rowing.

***

Purple dusk is falling in earnest now, the moon high, white, and full, as I row the skiff out of the reeds at the mouth of Kidd Creek. Heeling about, I can see the lumpen silhouette of the *Rouge* out in the bay. It will be long, arduous work, pulling all the way to Indian Beach at the north end of the island, and yet I feel strangely elated. Not merely the rare pleasure of thwarting the boy at one of his games, but something more; I might call it a lessening of the tension that always oppresses me here, a momentary relief of my usual misery. It's a heady feeling.

I glance over my shoulder to see that the child still slumbers peacefully in the bottom of the boat. I have set my gauze all round her to cushion her from the hard, damp wood. I hope the rowing doesn't take all night; I would hate for her to wake and know me for who I am.

"Can't we get there a little faster?" I mutter aloud to myself, as if there were anyone else to hear.

And seemingly in the next heartbeat, I find myself, dazed and disoriented, clutching the oars, my skiff positioned near the shoals off Indian Beach. It takes a moment to get my bearings, but I am more eager now than ever to be about my task and be gone again. The braves guard their beach at all hours, but I am not a war party, and so I forge on, paddle into the shallows, then climb out and haul the skiff up onto the beach.

I can feel watchful eyes on me, so I hasten to reach into the boat and lift out the sleeping child, still swaddled in her nest of gauze. I carry her a little way up the beach to where the sand is soft and powdery and set her down. She rolls over with a soft, audible sigh, and I tuck the gauze more snugly round her and step back. There is no need to speak to the stealthy sentinels watching me; it has ever been the duty of the tribes to take charge of the children who are ready to go home and escort them to their fairy guides.

And so with a glance all round the craggy bluffs that surround the beach, and the merest nod of my head, I turn to march back down the shore, and shove my boat back into the water. Climbing in, I paddle carefully through the shoals for deeper water without a backward glance, but alert for any sounds of pursuit. But no one follows. And as I heel about for southward in the open water of the bay, a sense of elation grips me once more, greater than the triumph of a victory, a surge of something like hope that I have never felt before in this place.

Until the night goes eerily dark and I glance up to see the brilliant moon gone as red as a pulsing heart. I can scarce keep hold of my oars. What cataclysm can this portend? A red eclipse, common enough in the old world, but a rarity here. Only once before have I ever seen its like in the Neverland.

It was on the night Bill Jukes died.

And I am back aboard the *Rouge,* taking a brace of bottles straight to my bed, intent on burning away this troubling memory for good.

No daylight leaks into the merwives' grotto, but I come awake to the sounds of quickening activity round the pool that suggest morning—a clattering of shell goblets on coral trenchers, the animated cooing of infants, a soft hum of female voices. Yet my dream vision clings to me like the persistent tang of smoke after a bonfire. I am all but trembling with it: the pealing bell, the garden, a companion I could never name, a fleeting bond of friendship I have longed for ever since. Not a dream at all, but a memory.

Something called her back to the Neverland, she said. Was it me?

3

The new day is bright and blue with foreboding, as I row down the creek in shirtsleeves, under my black hat. A pod of loreleis accompanied me all the way to the juncture of Kidd Creek, opening a swift channel for my boat. But the creek flows into the bay, and from here I make my journey alone. One person on this island has the knowledge of boy country I seek, and it will take some time to row myself to Indian Beach. But evidently, I have done it before. Stella dared to ask for the Indians' help, and she received it. Can I do any less on her behalf?

The pink shell whistle, on a new thong, lies against my chest under my shirt. Stella's moccasins sit in the bottom of the boat. I pause my rowing, reach down to tuck them more securely astern. And doing so, I notice some crumpled white thing, soaked with bilgewater, also stowed under the stern. Memory stirs; I draw in my oars and lift it out of the bottom. It's an old shirt, and as I unroll it, its contents spark in the sun: a pair of crystal goblets. I smuggled them off the *Rouge*, millennia ago, only to be forgotten when I found Stella gone. Remarkably, they are undamaged, sturdy stems supporting inverted bell-shaped bowls.

What did Stella say about bells and fairies?

None but a raving Bedlamite would try it. But only Pan and the imps know the way out, I said to myself. Stella risked all to try to contact them, and my refusal to listen, to even consider her plan, has put Stella in unspeakable danger. What did Lazuli say about conquering fear? And so I screw up my vitals, clamp hold of what remains of my sanity, and chime the two delicate rims together.

***

It might be no more than a speck of sunlight off the water, but for the way it speeds toward me out of the thin air. Instinctively, I draw back, close my eyes against another scorching, raise my hand to ward of the corrosive terror of fairy language, but a scent reaches me first, along the breeze. Sulfur and allspice. I have smelled it before, aboard the *Rouge,* I remember now. *Seize your chance.*

Opening my eyes, I see her hovering before me, perhaps an armspan away. Her wings buzz too quickly to be seen, her person but a blur of lavender-blue and dark hair. She is not the queen, nor is she Pan's belligerent imp, with the fair hair and greenish habit. This one makes a formal movement of her head while the insane scree of her speech peppers the air. With a tremendous effort, I unclench my ears, allow the tiny peals of sound bubbling through my head to resolve themselves into words.

"Captain Hook," she flutes at me.

"Thank you for coming," I whisper. "Madam…?"

"Call me Piper," she says, with another little nod. "Thank you for inviting me. I thought you never would."

She hovers there, and I grope in the pocket of my coat across the thwart for my spectacles to see her more clearly. The rags she wears are the color of morning glories; strands of dry beach grass knot up her glossy black hair into fanciful loops and swirls. She peers curiously back at me.

"You once spoke to me about a chance," I hazard.

"Twice," she corrects me.

My throat constricts to recall how I chased her around Stella's cabin, too afraid to listen. "The woman you spoke to on my ship that day. She is in grave danger."

"I know she is," the imp replies.

I suck in breath, all but crushing the goblet still clutched in my hand. "I must find her, free her, somehow. I will do whatever you ask, give you anything I have, if you will help me."

Piper regards me in a curious manner. "You have only to ask me, Captain," she says serenely. "How may the Sisterhood help you?"

"Sisterhood?" I echo, glancing about fearfully for an onslaught of tiny, scintilescent beings.

"The Sisterhood of the Bells," the imp explains. "We are the order of fairies pledged to stand guard in the Neverland. We are sworn to protect the mortals here."

"The boys, you mean."

"Every mortal," she corrects me. "Every mother, child, brave and elder in the First Tribes. Every merwoman and infant in the lagoon. Every boy and girl Peter brings here, Sisterhood guards attend them all. That is the bargain by which the Sisterhood and all of our race earns the right to live in this place. We protect the innocent."

"Stella, my friend, is innocent," I point out. "Cannot the fairies, your sisters, protect her until I—"

But the little creature is shaking her head sadly. "She is innocent no more, not as she was when she first arrived. It is no longer a matter of urgency to the Neverland if her blood is shed."

"But…why?" I sputter. "She has harmed no one!"

"There are many ways to lose one's innocence, Captain."

The goblet has slid from my fingers. "But she does not deserve to be murdered."

"No, but fairies cannot interfere with the boys," the imp sighs. "We can urge and suggest, but we cannot prevent them doing what they please."

"I ask for no one to act against the boys," I tell her. "I am going there without weapons, myself. I will ask Chief Eagle Heart to show me the way."

"Very wise, Captain," Piper says approvingly.

I draw a steadying breath. "I pledge by the love I bear for Stella that I'll not harm the boys—"

"Oh, excellent pledge!" the creature sparkles avidly at me. "The boys pledge their rusty knives, their sour furs; their pledges are worth nothing!"

"I only beg you, your sisters, not to oppose me should I find the opportunity to release her," I finish.

The imp sobers, alights upon the thole pin, regards me. "Of course not. We are sworn to keep the peace here."

I peer at her. "Some of your sisters have been derelict in their duty," I mutter. "I have lost hundreds of men, thousands. Brutally. Savagely."

She gazes back at me with perfect equanimity. "I too have lost many sisters in our battles, to the iron in your pistols when your men still knew how to use them, to the tiny tearing missiles you call grape. We will fight to the death to protect the innocent. But no fairy will ever use magic against you so long as you offer no harm to the boys."

The brutal simplicity of it stuns me. How could it have taken me two centuries to understand?

"But how are my men to perceive such subtleties while under constant attack?" I protest.

"If they are under attack, it is already too late," Piper rejoins. "Your men return here in a state of reclaimed innocence, their dreams pared down to a single longing for lost childhood. But as soon as they make war on the boys, they forfeit their innocence. They understand perfectly well what killing is. They must be guided by a wise leader who understands that their battles can never be won."

"Eagle Heart," I murmur.

"The First Tribes were the boy's enemies once," Piper agrees.

"But my men will never stand for a truce," I sigh, even supposing Pan would grant them one. "Battle is the only vestige of manhood they possess."

"Then they must die."

"And Pan's fairy?" I venture. "Does she obey your rules?"

"Kestrel is a rash, strutting, wayward little thing, with no more sense than a flea, and just as irritating. And she is foolish about the boy." Piper huffs as deep a sigh as her miniscule lungs can emit and flutters up again to look me in the eye. "I may say these things because she is my sister. My blood sister."

By God's vitals, I've just revealed my intentions to the sister of Pan's ferocious imp! Have I cost Stella her life?

"But she is a fierce and loyal caregiver who takes her duties very seriously," Piper goes on. "We are of the Zephyrae clan, Kes and I, as old as the West Wind. We will never dishonor the laws of this place. Offer no harm to the boys, and Kes will not oppose you."

I grasp one oar and hook up the other. "Then I'd better go."

The imp flutters up out of the way of this activity, watching me. "Kestrel cannot injure your friend, but she will do as the boy commands," Piper tells me. "If you find the woman bound by fairy magic, this will break the enchantment: say something to her that stirs the heart. The mortal heart where fairies have no power."

I nod in gratitude, dip one oar to come about, but the imp continues hovering just above me.

"You cannot mean to go all the way to Indian Beach in this clumsy mortal device," she scoffs.

"I have no other," I point out grimly.

"I can get you there faster," Piper suggests.

My arms convulse with longing. "What must I do?"

"You must trust me, Captain."

***

It's like dreaming, an effusion of random sensation: tinkling laughter, points of sunlight dancing crazily on the sea, a tang of salt and allspice in the air, a constant, shuddering vibrato, deeper than normal hearing, like a huge swell just before it breaks, or a gust freshening into a gale. Then silence, and the warmth of the sun on my face. Glimmersailing, she called it. And I sit up woozily in my skiff, in the shallows off Indian Beach, the sun scarcely any higher in its vault toward its zenith than it was moments ago when I was speaking to the fairy, Piper.

As my boat drifts in on the tide, I haul off my shirt and make the last of my preparations. The tiny metal buckles burn my fingers, heated like pokers in the intense sunlight, but I unfasten the last of them and shake the apparatus into the bottom with a dull, wet thunk. Pulling on my shirt again, I rummage for my black hat and clamp it on my head, dispelling some of the sun's sizzling glare.

The white sands of Indian Beach stretch out before me as I glide round the last of the steep grey rocks guarding its entrance. And strung across the shore like sturdy palm trees planted in the wet sand, a dozen braves await me with arrows nocked and tomahawks raised.

CHAPTER 28

SUITE: BRAVERY

1

"You risk much coming to me."

Eagle Heart's lodge house is nothing so grand as the palace of the Fairy Queen; it is a simple rectangular structure of hewn logs, reeking of crushed pine and leather. Here the tribespeople gather for feasts, disputes are heard, and the shaman chants his visions; I have seen it in my dream.

"I can't let them hurt her," I tell him.

The young chief sits cross-legged on an animal skin thrown over the dirt floor, elbow propped on one knee, fingering his chin, considering me with his cool, impenetrable eyes. "Why do you think I will help you?"

I kneel before him in the dirt, my guard of braves ringed close around me, should I entertain any thought, much less make any motion against their chief. "I helped you once. I did what you asked," I remind him.

"The danger now is not so great," he fences.

"I know her life no longer matters to the survival of the Neverland, the Dreaming Place," I nod. "But you are a just man. And my cause is just."

He sits back, palms flat against the knees of his buckskin trousers, gazing at me. "What would you have me do?"

"Take me to the boy's lair." No sound at all greets this absurd request, although tension crackles like St. Elmo's

Fire amongst my warrior guards. Nor does it slacken when I slowly, slowly raise my arms, the fingers of my hand spread open, my other shirt cuff still partially draped over the ghastly flesh of my ruined wrist, naked of its customary appendage. "I bear no weapons," I tell them all. "No harm will come to the boys." I lift my chin, hazard my last and only trump. "I'll never again raise arms in malice against the boys or the braves, from this moment on, if you help me get her back."

***

Half of my guard of braves are dispatched back to their watching posts among the cliffs and crevices above the beach. Those remaining have grudgingly culled from their own stores the leathern trousers and moccasins I now wear. I keep on the shell necklace, of course, and sport a long, fringed vest, open down the front, to cover the worst of my scarred torso. One of the silent warriors takes it upon himself to twist my long hair into warrior plaits. He's just tying off the second with a rawhide thong when Eagle Heart comes to me with a band of beaded leather dripping with fringe. He cinches it below the elbow of my ruined arm, so the long fringe covers my deformity, then steps back to view the effect.

"Your skin glows like Indian Beach," he sighs. "Stay in the middle and no one will notice."

The eyes of the whole of the village follow us from behind the flaps of their conical tepees, from around the rumps of their ponies in the corral, from amid the tall stalks of corn in their planting ground, as we parade out of the lodge house with Eagle Heart in the lead. Like the other men, I carry a bow and wear a quiver, although mine is devoid of arrows. We march down to the side of a lake, Moon Lake, as it is called, and take passage in three long, narrow canoes for the lot of us. We follow a meandering channel out of the lake, out of Indian Territory, and down into the dark, woody forests of boy country.

***

A young buck spirals up his horned head, freezes, naught but black nostrils in motion, only yards away as we pass by in the underbrush. My companions move like shadows, but my errant slipper scuffs against a green pine bough underfoot, and the creature canters off. No one rebukes me; the hunting will commence while I'm off about my business.

Eagle Heart motions us to a halt, catches my eyes, nods up ahead. It can't be called a clearing, a stand of ancient trees growing thickly together, as if emerging from a single maze of boulder-sized roots: pines, firs, twisted scrub oaks, higher branches entangled in a cloud of green. Incongruously, amid the jumble of scratching, tearing, thorny boy plants that carpet the wood, exuberant tendrils of jasmine, Pan's favorite, wind round each trunk in profusion. What mid-afternoon sunlight slants in through the leafy cover of a thousand surrounding trees shimmers and dances amid these venerable trunks like the miasma above the mermaid lagoon. Even as we watch, two cackling little whelps trailing furry tails and weeds come racketing in between the trunks. One of them pauses like the wary deer we just saw to spy a hunting party of braves so near their hidden lair, and the one behind all but crashes into him. But Eagle Heart raises one hand in salute. And the boys shout back, "How," or some such boyish nonsense, clamber over the largest of the gnarled roots, and disappear, no doubt down some rabbit-like hatch into an underground burrow.

As dense as the vegetation is here, as trackless the ground, still I'd have surely found this place in my many forays into the wood, over time, had it not been magicked from my view. Yet it shows itself to Eagle Heart like a constant lover. He regards me now, eyes like black steel, waiting. And I emerge from the knot of braves to stand beside the young chief.

He stretches the point of his bow to where the boys disappeared, and I nod in return. Then he points his bow in the opposite direction, toward an outcropping of rock shaded by leafy undergrowth, down which a little jet of water burbles into a tiny pool in a circle of smaller stones. A spring. I nod again and the chief slides his bow back over his shoulder, points toward the tree trunks, points to himself, shakes his head. He will come no further, cannot be seen escorting me into their lair. He stretches out one hand, and I shrug the empty quiver and bow off my shoulder, hand them to him. My last weapons. He moves his head in the direction he and his braves will be waiting, should I find what I seek.

I touch my fingers to my heart, to my mouth, open my hand to him, the only gesture of their silent language I've learnt in their village today. Thank you.

They melt back into the forest as silently as falling leaves, and I take a few steps nearer the thicket of tree trunks. Beneath the frenzy of birdsong and the grumbling of distant beasts, the riotous laughter of boys hooting at some unseen game echoes up from below. Sweating from more than the hot sun and thick, jasmine-sweet air so far from the breeze off the bay, I turn and pick my way over to the spring pattering into its little pool of rock. I am only steps away when something comes rustling out of the forest straight for me. Another boy. We freeze for an instant, staring at each other. I will my complexion to darken, my hair to blacken, my withered stump to disappear under its fringe. Slowly, I raise my hand. The boy nods, mumbles some greeting, makes as if to scamper off, but swivels his head round to me again, peering with all his might, frowning, nervous fingers worrying the snakeskin he sports round his middle. I've seen this particular whelp before, yesterday, on the rail of the *Rouge*. From no more distance than separates us now. And with a mottled cry of alarm not yet formed into words, the boy races off to the tree trunk portal and dives in.

2

My shaking fingers can scarcely grapple the shell away from my slick chest, but I shove it to my lips and blow as I lean over the spring. I can't say if it makes any sound at all, or I am too frantic to hear aught but my own rasping breath, but I blow a second time. Noises of alarm are beginning to pop up like toadstools from beneath the trees, but as I follow the path of the boys toward the gnarled root, a softer sound whispers past me in the air, a low, beguiling melody. The sirens' lullabies begin to fill the forest like the sunlight itself, and I peep over the root down into the dark shaft, forcing myself to wait until I hear no more shouting, no more voices of any kind.

A gelid, tomblike aroma of dust and damp earth assails me as I climb down the dark shaft, out of the light. A length of knotted rope guides me down the tilting shaft, and I slide feet-first into an open chamber. Gaining my bearings, I stand cautiously; the top of my head just grazes the earthen ceiling. Two or three stubby candles, blazing heroically under glass here and there, provide the only illumination, and blinking away the musty gloom, I find myself in a kind of common room. A rickety sort of wooden table stands at the far end, with a few random objects strewn upon it: a ball, some rocks, feathers and shells, the mummified paw of some small forest creature, boys' treasures or gaming pieces. On the other side of the shaft through which I entered, rough shelves have been dug out of the hard earthen wall, on which are stowed a jumbled disarray of sticks, clubs, wooden bats, broken arrow shafts, piles of bladed weapons, one or two still edged and bright, but most ruined by age or rust or neglect. The grand arsenal of my enemy.

Little heaps of fur litter the dirt floor in the shadows. These must be the cub's nests they make for themselves, I think, until I peer at one nearest the faint, flickering light and realize it's an inert boy, the snakeskin boy lolling stuporously in the dirt at my feet. I prod him gently with my moccasin, but he doesn't stir, merely snorts and groans and rolls over on his other side. I straighten up as far as I may, gaze again round the chamber, begin to recognize the wheezing and snoring of other sleeping boys.

As my eyes adjust, I notice dark blotches that must be small tunnels in the dirt walls, leading away from the main room. I choose the biggest one, across the room from the entry that brought me here, and peek inside into a dark passage. A pale, greenish light beckons from the other end, and I creep through the tunnel to emerge into another chamber, smaller than the common room, but more elaborate—higher ceiling, a real lantern hanging on a peg in the wall, a thick carpet of green, red and yellow leaves over the dirt floor. A sturdy little carved bedstead, plumped with mountains of eiderdown stands in the corner. And slumped across it, legs sprawling on the leafy floor, head and shoulders still draped over the bed, lies Pan.

His wicked short sword has fallen on the leaves beside him, as if he were arrested in the act of stuffing it into his belt. His panpipes have dropped on the bed. He resembles nothing so much as one of my own slaughtered men, but for a thin string of drool leaking out of his open mouth onto the bedclothes. This is the fiend I've fought so bitterly for so long? This ridiculous child?

A little open chest of more carefully honed weapons stands at the foot of his bed. And at the far end of the room, in the shadows furthest from the light, looms a tall figure dressed in white.

Stella.

She appears to stand upright, although her feet scarcely touch the ground. Do I only imagine she seems to sway slightly in place? She does not speak, and as I grab the lantern

302

and move toward her, raising the light to her face, I see her eyes are closed, her expression utterly serene. Please, no, by all the gods and devils of this place, not murdered! Hung up like some ghastly trophy?

"Stella!" I hiss as I draw near. Her mouth works a little, and she sighs, and I shudder with relief. Still an arm span away, I sense a kind of sizzling energy around her, detect a faintly sulfurous fairy odor. Odd glints of green and purple shimmer briefly in and out of the light, like cobwebs in the sun. I set down the lantern, reach longingly toward her, but a tingling of burning pinpricks assails my hand, and I withdraw it. Am I a coward, afraid of a little pain? But if she is under fairy magic, what greater harm might befall her if I attempt to remove her? What if she is charmed to die at the first show of force?

True love's kiss will not break this charm, could she even feel it within this veil of sorcery. But she heard my voice. What did Piper tell me? Choose words that will stir the heart. Praying I have not already lost the power to move her heart, I lean as close as I might, position my mouth near her ear, quell the tremor in my voice.

"Please forgive me, my Stella Rose," I whisper. "We're on this journey together."

Her brow furrows slightly, her lips begin to part, the voice that issues out is soft and faint. "Run away, James."

Stung by this rebuke, I back away as the shimmering gauze of light that encloses her fizzes angrily. I can no longer speak to her heart. I've lost her love. I can't save her. Then her dark eyes open, glinting green; she blinks at me in both wonder and agitation.

"Run away, James!" she says more urgently, color flushing slowly into her cheeks. "Oh, James, oh, no, why are you here? It's too dangerous, you must get away!"

And the very air around her seems to short and sputter, like dampened fuses. Her legs buckle as her feet touch ground, but I lunge in to catch her, draw her out of her cocoon of witchcraft with only the faintest peppering of heat against my skin.

She clutches at my elbows, fighting for her bearings, gaining her feet. "You must go now!" she insists.

"Not without you, Parrish."

"But if he catches you—"

"Look." I stoop for the lantern, turn her gently round and shine the circle of light across the room, where Pan still sprawls athwart the bed.

"Oh my God," she gasps. "He's not...you haven't..."

"He's sleeping," I assure her. "They're all sleeping. Can you not hear the loreleis?"

She pauses, listens; the lush, distant crooning continues. And beneath it, we both detect another noise, quite nearby, a low, mournful refrain in counterpoint to the lorelei's' serenity, a stark and chilling outpouring of misery. Hastily, now, I steer Stella toward the doorway that opens on the tunnel, lantern aloft, glancing all round for the source of the weird sound. When we spy it, hairs prick up along the back of my neck.

Pan is sobbing in his sleep. It's not the gulping hysteria of a cross, thwarted child, but a steady, low-pitched keening of loss. Water leaks out beneath his eyelids while his boyish mouth disgorges a deep, haunting chord of anguish as old as time. It's the most unnerving thing I have ever heard or beheld in the Neverland.

Only Stella's fingers closing round my maimed arm rouses me. I'm just turning from hanging up the lantern when a streak of light explodes out of the tunnel mouth, sparking furiously in the air before us, blocking our escape; a flash of green and rust, a halo of golden hair as bright as the sun.

Pan's savage fairy, Kes.

3

Her light is dazzling, her temper unmistakable, even did I not force open my mind to the bellicose meaning of her words.

"Thief! Murderer! Man!" she screeches at me in a frenzy.

Of course, she is immune to the loreleis' song, dodging back and forth before my face with such vigor, I'm forced to take a step backwards, another, pressing Stella back behind me. This imp will not be as accommodating as her sister; I have only a fairy's promise that she will not blind me again, or turn me into a cockroach, or do some further harm to Stella.

"I have no quarrel with you, Madam," I fence, determined to shrink no more, stand my ground. "Please let us pass."

"But I have a quarrel with *you*, Captain!" she spits back. "How dare you come in here and...and—" Hoisting herself higher in the air, she stares over my shoulder and Stella's toward the bed. "Peter!" she shrieks, darts over us both to zoom down to her master. For the moment that she coos tenderly into his ear, whispers soothing blandishments, I maneuver Stella round to the mouth of the tunnel and press her in ahead of me. Then the imp's frantic cries, "Peter! Wake up! He's here, Peter! Get up!" jangle all round the room, and Kes flies into my face again, incensed, screaming invective, her little face as red as Nutter's, making violent gesticulations about my head, my eyes. Yet she does not touch me, lays not so much as an infinitesimal finger anywhere on my person, nor dare she cast any kind of spell.

"Monster! Coward! Cuckold! Fool!" she flings at me, along with many other epithets, searching for the right one to goad me into some warlike gesture and unleash her powers; she fizzes round and round my head in such a disorienting glitter of sparks I am losing my bearings, longing to bat her aside if only to find my way out. "Your woman laughs at you! Your men despise—"

Stella's fingers lace through mine and I am pulled into the momentary respite of the dark tunnel. But an arrow of fairy light speeds past us both, into the chamber ahead. As we emerge, Kes is flitting from one stuporous boy to the next, trailing sulfur and incantations, and although the mermaid chorale continues in the air, boys are starting to sit up, rub their eyes. Pound their heads.

"I can't hear!" shrieks one little wretch, batting at his ear.

Another fellow lurches up in front of us in confusion, but I herd Stella past him toward the shaft with the hanging rope that leads above ground. Kes circles all around, attempting with sign language and fury to rally the army she's deafened against the sirens' song. But only one seems to understand; the boy in snakeskin staggers up, staring hard at Stella and me; he races over to their arsenal to pluck up one of the few sharpened knives, and as Stella grabs for the rope, he charges her. I lunge between them with a swing of my ruined arm, catch him in the stomach, knock him to the hard dirt ground with a *whoof* and a gasp, his weapon jarred out of his fingers.

And all round me is suddenly screeching noise and brutal bright light, heat and distortion. A reek of brimstone turns my stomach, I'm spinning into oblivion in a hail of gleeful fairy laughter. A smudge of white disappearing up a rope is the last thing I see.

CHAPTER 29

FIRST JUDGMENT

"Kill him!" wheedles a high, tinny voice. "Now, while you have the chance!"

"But it won't be any *fun*," comes the petulant reply. "He's not even wearing his hook."

I cannot say I am roused from sleep, although I have not been conscious until this moment. Not the kind of friendly oblivion found in the black drops, but simply the absence of everything—thought, feeling, senses. Even now, my senses are swaddled in wool; I see only shadows, can scarcely feel the weight of my body, yet these urgent words filter into my ears.

"Give him a sword, then," says the higher voice.

"You don't understand, Kes," Pan rebukes his fairy. "It still wouldn't be fair. Anyway, I want them both. And now I'll get them both!"

A third voice intrudes, small and boyish. My senses dull again to their mumbled exchange, until I hear Pan cry, "The chief? Bring him to me!"

Some little commotion follows this command, and I make an effort to see. A narrow slit of light appears before me; I can open my eyes a little, yet every other part of me remains immobile. I see Pan's bed in his underground chamber, his lantern, his carpet of leaves, all viewed from the same perspective I recall from when I stood beside Stella and broke her enchantment. That must be where I am now.

Pan perches cross-legged on the edge of his bed, a tiny light at his shoulder. Before him, Eagle Heart is lowering himself to the surface of multi-colored leaves, crossing his legs beneath him. They have scarcely exchanged pleasantries before the boy exults, "Look what I've got!" and gestures toward me.

The chief spares me the smallest glance, nods his head at Pan. "That is well, Little Brother. You are a fine warrior. My people will sing another song of praise for you."

Pan preens like a little gamecock, glad to take credit for a capture in which he played no part at all.

"I come to you as a brother warrior, to claim the right of First Judgment over this prisoner," Eagle Heart goes on smoothly.

Pan frowns. "What do you mean?"

"The clothing he wears belongs to another brave. And he broke an oath he swore to me in parley."

Does the chief insinuate that I stole these tribal clothes? Although I suppose what he says is the literal truth. As to the crime of breaking my oath, that is true in every sense. I did exactly what I swore I would not, raise an arm against a boy, and I can only imagine what punishment the chief will exact. Yet I can't be sorry for what I did, if it freed Stella from the boy.

"Didn't you capture her?" Pan is interrogating his visitor, breaking into my thoughts.

"No, Little Brother," says the chief. "But if it were possible for the woman, or the Captain, to leave the Dreaming Place, would they not have done so by now?"

The fairy light at Pan's shoulder seems to pulse more brightly at this observation, even as Pan himself relaxes back into smug omnipotence. Stella has eluded them all; might she not yet discover the way out? Maybe Piper will help her. If Stella's escape is still possible, I will gladly face any consequences.

"I claim the right of First Judgment," Eagle Heart is explaining to the boy. "The prisoner must answer for the wrongs done to my people before he came here. He must be brought before the tribal elders, who will render their judgment."

Pan is not so sure, frowning at the chief, and at me.

"Night is coming," says Eagle Heart. "You and your warriors will soon be asleep. You have my word the sentence will be passed and carried out by the morning."

The boy perks up at this. "What sort of sentence?" he asks eagerly. I hear the piping staccato of his imp at his ear. "The anthill torture? The sweat box? What about hanging by his heels," Pan goes on, in a rapture of anticipation.

"Our elders will decide what is just," the chief replies.

"You promise I'll get him back in the morning?"

"Our council will be concluded by then," Eagle Heart agrees.

***

I am bound like a monstrous papoose, arms roped to my sides, but at least I am free of fairy magic. We sit together in prickly silence, Eagle Heart and myself, in the middle of a long canoe paddled by a robust complement of braves fore and aft. The stream we navigate is in the wood; the density of forest creates premature dark, but the sky is still faintly blue beyond the trees. An icy moon is already on the rise, winking at us now and then through the tree trunks. Disoriented still from my enchantment, it's not until I sense the urgency in the current, hear the rushing of rapids and a pattering of falls up ahead, that I realize we are not going back to the tribal village.

We debark at the brink of a ravine, where the stream plunges over into falls. We've not gone north to Indian Territory, but south to where the wood gives way to the

Terraces. Two braves and Eagle Heart shepherd me down a well-worn trail to the bottom of the ravine, while the others heft the canoe upside down on their shoulders and follow us down. Below the falls, the stream widens into a swift, deep channel that speeds along like a snake between high rockface on either side, now cloaked in purple shadows. The inland waterway, hidden from me for two hundred years.

If they reveal it to me now, they must expect to have little to fear from me in the future. I try not to dwell on what sorts of disabling punishments they might have in mind, as we resume our canoe expedition through the heart of the Terraces.

"You must learn what they mean to each other, Captain, swearing an oath and keeping it," Eagle Heart speaks to me at last.

Now we come to the meat of the matter. I grit my teeth and nod.

"Every action has a result, each small thing you do ripples out like water in a lake to touch the entire circle of life," the chief goes on, his narrow eyes shadowed, his expression severe. "If your hook had been in place when you lashed out at that boy, the Dreaming Place would no longer be. All her inhabitants would be dead or displaced, the world's children robbed of their refuge, all for one instant of rage."

I don't ask how he knows what went on in Pan's lair. My captivity alone is testament to my broken oath, or else Kes could never have wielded her magic against me. Nor do I whine that I acted in defense of Stella. There were no conditions on my oath when I swore it.

"It was wrong of me to forswear my oath," I agree, my voice rusty from disuse. "I betrayed the trust you placed in me, and put your alliance with the boy at risk, for which I am sorry." Here, I take a leaf from the chief's own book;

310

my apology is literally true, and sincere, yet I do not lie and claim to regret the action that spared Stella's life.

Eagle Heart continues to peer at me for a while, perhaps calculating the degree of my guilt. The dipping paddles scarcely splash in the water, and there's naught to hear but the calling and rustling of distant birds as we speed along. Then the chief nods one time, whether in acceptance of my apology or in satisfaction that I've sealed my doom, I know not.

The transparent moon rises high above the ravine as we come at last to a tunnel of brush, ferns and dense, wild shrubbery. The braves paddle through it in darkness for a while, then our canoe emerges into a placid channel between wide banks of tropical foliage. Green jungle screens our progress now; the high cliffs of the Terraces are behind us. We warp round a bend and I sense the movement of deep water up ahead, by which I know the Mysterious River is nearby. But we glide into a sheltered little cove of steaming jungle at the base of some small land mass. I can't make out much in the shadows, but I hear more water, burbling to a different rhythm, out beyond this jungle.

"The Fork of Three Rivers," Eagle Heart intones. And the braves make fast the canoe and herd me out upon the bank.

A banana leaf the size of a flying jib near smacks me in the face as we pick our way through verdurous jungle, the chief in the lead before me, a brave or two bringing up the rear. We proceed along a mossy track so narrow and hidden amid the riotous vegetation, it would try the ingenuity of the hardiest snake to follow it. An inconvenient place to hold a trial, it occurs to me. Unless the elders have already rendered their judgment, and the chief means to proceed directly to the punishment phase. Insects whirr, distant animals rumble and squawk. Up ahead, the chief sweeps aside a long, arching palm frond, agitating a covey of blue dragonflies, before we emerge into a little clearing encircled by jungle plants, giant green leaves, towers of pink and purple orchids, under a canopy of lacy ferns. In its center stands a great mound covered in buckskin hides, taller than a man. Aboriginal designs are burned into the hides, moons and stars and others too arcane to decipher.

So it's to be the sweat torture. Or perhaps they mean to hang me up like a side of beef in a smokehouse. Whatever they do, there will still be enough of me left for the boy to abuse in the morning. Such is the price of rashness, and I will pay it, so long as Stella is free.

Eagle Heart draws aside the tent flap and nods at me to join him. "Consider what you have done," he tells me. "Consider what you must do."

He motions me inside, but instead of following me into the dim interior, he secures the flap closed again behind me. By nothing so obvious as sound, but rather a deepening of the silence outside, I know that he and his men have melted away.

In the dusky gloom inside, I spy a shallow kind of pit in the center of a circular dirt floor. Rounded shapes that might be baskets or gourds line the perimeter, I can smell their spicy contents. And something moves in the shadows at the far side of the pit, a pale figure, not the buffalo-horned shaman nor any of the martial braves. It's a woman, working sticks together at the edge of the cold pit.

"A girl of five can do this in the tribes," Stella murmurs.

CHAPTER 30

Suite: Folie à Deux

1

"But...Eagle Heart said he didn't capture you." My heart is so full, I can scarcely speak, my joy at finding Stella safe tempered by anxiety that she has not yet escaped.

"He didn't," Stella replies. My eyes are adjusting to the gloom now. I see her rise to her feet and brush off her gown. She is not bound, as I am. "They were right there in the wood when I got out of the boys' lair. He and his men hid me from them."

And why should they not? Stella broke no oaths.

"Some of his braves brought me here in a canoe," she adds, stepping across the pit toward me.

I glance all round the circular interior. Curved sapling ribs create a dome arching just over our heads, beneath their covering of hides. "What is this place?"

"I'm not sure, but we're surrounded by water, so it must be very powerful." And she hurries over to start unknotting the lines that bind me. "I've been so worried," she murmurs to the ropes. "Eagle Heart told me how you came to him unarmed and asked for his help to get me out of there."

"I'm to be judged by morning for breaking my oath."

She walks around me unfurling the rope, coiling it round her hand. "I told him what happened, and why," she says. "If anything happened to you because of me—"

313

"It would have served me right, after all I said to you," I say bitterly. "It's my fault you are even here at all."

She stops before me, peering at me.

"I had a dream last night," I begin.

"A stranger in a garden," Stella says immediately. "I saw it too."

"And a young girl, wearing a silver bracelet," I go on. "I have seen that bracelet before. In your coat pocket on board my ship."

Stella nods, draws a breath. "I could never bear to get rid of it, even after I outgrew it. Even after it broke. There was just something about it that made me so...happy."

"It was all true, then," I murmur. "My dream. Your story."

"Not dreams. They were memories." She's coiling up the last of her rope.

"They have haunted me for years."

"Me too," she whispers. "Oh, James, it was you. You're the one who called me here. It was you all the time."

The Dreaming Place, the Indians call it, where dreams are made real if they are strong enough. If one only dares to believe.

"I'm afraid so," I sigh.

And she turns away to cross the cold fire pit and drop the rope in the far shadows. I follow her into the gloom, rubbing sluggish blood back into my arms. When she kneels again at the edge of the pit and takes up her two sticks and a bundle of dried grasses, I realize how infernally dark it's become.

"And look where it's got you," I mutter, "locked up in an Indian stockade."

"It might be a place for ceremonies," Stella suggests, sawing uselessly away at her twigs.

Peering about in the shadows, I spy a pile of the clothing I left behind with the braves, my black coat, hat and boots, along with my hook in its harness, and crawl over to them. I set to peeling off my savage vest and untie the fringed band from around my arm. How much longer before the braves pass their sentence, I wonder. An hour? Perhaps less? They could be on their way back here even now.

"There are baskets of herbs all around, and some furs and blankets—"

"Can you ever, possibly forgive me, Stella?" I blurt out, at last, unpacking the thing that has weighed down my heart for so long. "I didn't mean any of it, not one word I said to you that day. I was so afraid of losing you."

She pauses, still gazing into the cold circular pit. "I didn't mean any of it either," she says in a small voice.

Fishing a flint out of my coat pocket, I slide two fingers under my hook, and return to drop it into the shallow pit. Stella shifts to let me kneel beside her, clears away the straps, and braces my hook with her hands. She watches pensively as I work my flint against iron.

"I was so mad, I just wanted to hurt you," Stella murmurs. "I know exactly what kind of man you are."

My flint scrapes harshly on my hook, causing a fleeting spark that glimmers out in an instant. "Aye, the sort who repays love with cruelty," I mutter, "who'll seize the first opportunity to betray your trust."

She shakes her head. "Not the first opportunity."

I dart her a puzzled glance, and strike another tiny spark. This one catches in the little bundle of grass.

"You might have let the boys kill me at their trial."

I'm so startled, the flint fumbles out of my grasp.

"The merwives told me what happens if innocent blood is shed here," she goes on. "You'd have had everything you ever wanted. The destruction of the Neverland, and all your enemies. The release you've always craved."

My fingers are trembling as I slip them under the smoldering little nest of grass.

"You could have let the boys have their way." Stella's voice is as soft as the wisp of smoke beginning to curl up out of the grass. "Didn't you ever stop to wonder why you interfered?"

I lift the little bundle and blow into it gently, gently, until it glows, breathing the fragile flame into life. It never, ever occurred to me to let Stella die to set myself free.

"Because I'm a fool?" I whisper.

Stella rustles closer, presses her shoulder to mine in a gesture that is affection, forgiveness, homecoming all in one. "That makes two of us, Maestro."

"Folie à deux," I sigh.

"Absobloodylutely," she agrees. "So save your horror stories about what a monster you are for the more gullible Wendys. I know better." She shifts closer still. "I've always known."

I slide the warm little bundle back into the pit as tiny threads of grass begin to blacken and burn, and we gaze into the fledgling flame. We might smother it through carelessness, we might blow it out in a rage, or maybe, just maybe, we might nurture this tiny, stubborn, luminous thing that is so much stronger than both of us.

When I glance again at Stella, she is looking at me, her expression unbearably tender in the warm light. I slide my ruined arm round her waist and she lays her head on my shoulder.

"It meant so much to me, that someone was kind to me when I was most alone," she says. "No wonder I always felt something good was waiting for me here."

"You deserved to go home, and it gave me such enormous pleasure to see that you did. I don't know why. But for an instant it was as if the whole of the Neverland were holding its breath for something..." I shake off this inarticulate thought. "But...it's fantastic, Stella," I begin again, still shaking my head. "You said yourself no Wendy would ever come back."

"For Peter, I said," Stella corrects me. "I came back for you."

At this moment, a man with red blood in his veins might sweep her up with passionate declarations, followed by passionate lovemaking. But the cold light of reason has stolen in upon us with our newborn flame; our situation is as perilous as ever.

Stella reaches out to lay another stick over our tiny blaze. "It was crazy for you to come after me, James. You're the one Peter was after." She glances again at me. "When I was under that spell, it was like being a little tight, I didn't really know what was going on. But now and then I could hear them, understand them. 'He will come for her,' someone said. Peter's fairy, I suppose. 'And you will have your greatest victory,' she said."

I recall the urgency in the imp's plea, *Kill him now,* and Pan's refusal. "But he might have murdered me again at any time, if that was all he wanted. His imp kept begging him to do it."

"And that would hardly be his *greatest* victory," Stella agrees. "He's, well, killed you dozens of times. Unless the fairy thought it was possible to…really kill you. Forever. But maybe it wasn't possible. Yet."

"Not until the curse is broken," I suggest. "Until the third sign is seen." Even could we solve the riddle of escape, assuming Eagle Heart doesn't order me drawn and fricasseed first, Proserpina's curse continues to bind me here.

***

It must have been a sizeable beast, but no less than a grizzly would do for the boy. It stinks of game and smoke and rancid grease, but the toast-colored fur is thick and soft. I've spread the hide over a woven mat next to the fire pit for Stella; she's been nodding against my shoulder for a quarter

317

of an hour, having had no natural sleep since she left the merwives. I've urged her to rest while I keep watch, should the braves come back for me.

The loreleis' serene *contrappunto* harmonies are wafting down the river. Cold blue moonlight leaks in through a hole between the hides at the top of the dome, at the place where the sapling poles are roped together. When Stella drifts off, I go pluck a silvery log from the woodpile and add it to our little blaze. I find a basket of Dream Flowers giving off a sweet, earthy scent, and I toss one of those on the fire as well. A plume of smoke dances up for the opening in the skins, and out into the night. The Neverland stars are just beginning to rise above the fluttering jungle shadows, glittering like Pan's eyes.

I sit again, draw up my knees, still clad in buckskin, cross my bare arms over them, gaze into the fire. It may be true, what Stella once told me about praying to the wrong gods. A more pervasive power than the boy rules in this place, a power to which I might yet appeal, should I muster the courage to play wisely and well.

2

Stinging smoke forces my eyes closed. I lower my head on my arms, give myself up to regret, that most useless of all emotions.

My scarred thigh has given me not so much as a tremor of rheumatics in the centuries since Proserpina nursed me. How poorly I repaid her. That insulting song I played to prove to my men I was still fit for war and murder, my cruel words flung at her in anger, centuries of resentment in this place before I had the wit to see what she'd done for me, how bitterly I've wronged her. The clamor of these memories prod me bolt upright where I sit. White smoke moves sinuously in the air, and something else seems to laze and stretch in the shadows beyond the fire pit.

I know her by her stillness, the purposeful way she holds herself – alert, yet relaxed. She wears the same vibrantly-colored headscarf, muslin chemise, blue apron over a ruffled skirt, the same strings of turquoise and coral and ebony beads round her neck that I remember so well. Proserpina the witch, unchanged in two hundred and twenty-six years.

Her chocolate eyes gleam at me, her expression cool. "Why do you call me?"

I almost smile; as if I had the power to conjure a flea. "I've never offered you a word of thanks for the care you took of me once upon a time," I say quietly. "Were such a thing possible, I would tell you how grateful I was." She nods but says nothing. "I repaid you with scorn and abuse," I go on. "I am bitterly sorry for it. Can you ever forgive me?"

She regards me for a long time through the shimmering smoke. "At last you ask the right question, *Capitaine,*" she murmurs.

"I wronged another woman," I continue. "Caroline. I was too eager to believe a lie that might have cost her a lifetime of happiness. I would beg her pardon if I could."

"She could not have satisfied you then, *Capitaine,*" Proserpina observes calmly. "No more could I."

"You sent me here to save the Neverland," I hazard, and she nods again. Stella's theory was correct. "To save myself."

"When I was alive, I loved you," she tells me. "You were a man in my arms. But you craved childish things, murder, revenge, a warrior's fame. You were ruled by the fire of your rage. The *loas* warned me of a brutal, terrible end, your spirit doomed to eternal misery, if you did not change. I thought if you saw what endless childhood is like, you would not want it so much."

How right she was.

"I cast a spell to suspend your life. I could not let it end before you paid for the wrongs you had done." She sighs and shakes her head. "I did not now how long it would take you, longer than my own mortal life. I did not know what cruel game he would play to keep you here."

"How did you know of this place?" I ask her.

"My ancestor told me. She lived long ago. She loved somebody once, a boy she met in a dream, and then forgot. But her spirit remembers. From the time beyond, she knew this boy and this place of dreams were in danger. 'Send your man there,' she told me, 'until he tires of childish games. Let him wash the blood off his hands.'"

And it comes to me again, the hypnotic fragrance of jasmine, Pan's favorite, permeating my dreams, ghostly voices in the dark. "Zwonde," I whisper.

"My ancestor," Proserpina agrees. "The first girl ever carried off to this place of dreams to care for him. We, the daughters of her tribe, have been healers ever since."

"The first Wendy," I marvel.

"Her spirit does not forget. That is what it means to love."

I gaze at Stella, prone on her fur skin in the shadows beside me. Sorrow like molten lead pumps through my veins at what I must do. "I know now why I'm here," I say to Proserpina. "But Stella has wronged no one."

"Why say this to me?" Proserpina demands.

"You sent me here. Is there not some voudon, some bargain we might strike, you and I, to send her safely home? I know your spirits require some balance to be struck between their world and the living." I draw a breath. "I will stay here forever if you let her go."

Her laughter is like low, rolling ripples in a very deep pond. It stings like grapeshot to have my offer ridiculed, for I do not make it lightly. It will deaden me beyond any despair even I have ever known to lose Stella again, but if a trade, a barter is required, I will forfeit my one chance at escape in exchange for Stella's freedom. What else of any value have I to offer? Yet the witch chuckles on, tilting her head to one side, gazing briefly over at Stella, then back to me.

"La, *Capitaine*, she is free to go at any time," Proserpina says, with a careless wave of her hand.

I gape at her. "Then why is she still here?"

"That is her choice," breathes the witch, with a rustling of her skirts. "You give me more credit than I deserve, eh? Poor, foolish man. I have no power over your life. Only you have that power."

I frown into the fire. "That has not been true in a long time."

She lifts her shoulders, round and glossy above the low décolleté of her chemise. "It has always been true. When you left me, I make a spell. I bury it in the earth," and her hand dips low to the dirt floor. "I cast it into the sea," and she mimes this action as well. "I breathe it into the wind," and she spreads wide the fingers of one hand before her mouth. "Do not break, I say to my spell, until he open his hand in kindness, open his heart to love, open his eye with the wisdom that comes of the other two."

"That's all?" I whisper. "That's all you wanted?"

"That is everything," she rebukes me gently, dark eyes glittery in the firelight. "Kindness freely offered that asks for no reward, love that values another above yourself, the wisdom to live without fear. This is the best of life."

"You give my wits more credit than they deserve," I say drily.

"But not your power to love, *Capitaine*," she murmurs, with another glance at Stella. "You prove it beyond all doubt. I hoped it would be me," she goes on, with a hint of her old saucy smile in her black eyes. "Alone in this place of childish things, I hoped you might come to think more fondly of what you left behind. That you would tire of this game,

321

break my spell, and I would call on the power of my ancestor, Mama Zwonde, to bring you back. But he changed the game, trapped you here in fear, kept you here far, far beyond my own mortal life."

"So—your voudon brought Stella here?"

But she shakes her head. "I am dead. I have no more power in the living time. Only my spell remains. The earth, the sea, the sky keep watch over my spell." She eyes me with an insouciant tilt of her head. "They say your chance has come."

Shock rattles through me. I scarcely dare to breathe.

"You play well," she smiles at me. "I knew you would, one day."

"Thank you, Pina," I whisper.

"I am glad you end this game," she says, with an airy sweep of her hand. "The *loas* ask a price, it is true; I find I cannot take root in the time beyond until you free yourself. All this confusion, back and forth," she sighs again. "I would leave the living time to the living. So take back your life, *Capitaine.* Spend your love. Use it well."

I scarcely stammer any response before she waves me off and fades into the shadows, as if she has no more substance than a wisp of woodsmoke. Scrambling to my knees, I peer up and out of the hole, thinking to see her whirling away into the sky like a most formidable fairy, but she is simply gone.

I sit back with a thud against the earthen floor, jittery with an excitement I dare not define, panting as if I've run a race. I feel muscles stretching under my skin, nerves humming though my body, blood pumping, hair growing, lungs shuddering in, out. Water wells in my eyes from the stinging smoke; my blink is like a clashing of armies. Every blink, every breath, every glance is cataclysmic, reverberating like an earthquake, a riotous *concerto grosso* of all my physical parts led by my thundering heart.

Life! Genuine life crackling inside me, tender, fragile, finite, explosive life. I am walking dead no more. The endless chasm of eternity no longer yawns before me. Joy nearly bursts out of me like an aria—only to crash like tideburst on a rock to see Stella sitting up on her bearskin, watching me, her face full of reproach.

"I'm not going without you, not this time," she exclaims. I might have known she would see my hallucination in her dreams. "Why do you think I came back?"

"You did find the way out," I breathe, rising to my knees.

She nods. "Grandmother Owl spoke to me in a dream. She told me all about it. The dreampath, that lovely bit of poesy? It's a real thing, James, a tunnel, a conduit through the enchantment that binds this place. Every dreamer who comes to the Neverland, Wendys, boys, your men, each one forges a dreampath between the two worlds to get here, if their dreaming is strong enough. When Peter comes for the dreamer, fairy magic opens the dreampath, so the dreamer can get in. That's the only way out again. When a dreamer is ready to leave, a fairy leads them back through it."

"But you didn't go."

She shakes her head. "You never dreamt yourself here, James. You don't have a dreampath of your own."

And I realize my foolish delight at breaking the spell is all for naught. Proserpina is long dead; her voudon can no longer transport me away from this place.

"But I do," Stella goes on quietly. "The dreampath remembers its dreamer, that's what Grandmother Owl said. Each path seals itself up again to protect the magic surrounding this place. It will only open again for the original dreamer. If I don't take you back through mine, you'll never be able to get out."

So that's what sent her rushing away from the protection of the merwives. "And you came back for me?" I gape.

"After all I said to you?"

She stares at me as if I am the world's chiefest imbecile. "God damn it, Maestro, we're on this journey together, remember?" Her sidelong glance darts across the pit to where Proserpina appeared. "At least, I thought we were…"

"You can't seriously believe I *wanted* to lose you again!"

She is on her knees now, too. "Death is all you ever really wanted. And now that it's possible—"

"And I thought I was the fool," I groan, and I reach for her before she can berate me any further. She resists for an instant for form's sake, then comes at me on the flood, and I fold her to me with all my strength, this vibrant, prickly woman with no better sense than to love me, press my face into her smoky cinnamon hair. "Now that I have something to live for at last, you think I want to throw it all away?"

She lifts her face to mine; I grasp her hand and place her fingertips on my chest. This is how it all began, the cycle of healing that brought me here, Stella's touch. The wanton percussion of newborn life begins to stir inside me once more. I flatten Stella's palm gently over the rioting of my heart. She feels it, looks at me, her green-tinted dark eyes fierce with understanding. Life-giver. Redeemer. Lover. Friend.

"You've given me life, Parrish. I mean to deserve it. If you'll still have me."

"Oh, James, I've been such a wreck without you!" And Stella's arms close round me again, more powerful than any fairy spell.

I shut my eyes over the clamor kindling inside me, hold Stella closer still. "I did come back that day," I murmur. "But by then you were already gone. I went to the merwives to try to find you."

"And meanwhile, I walked straight into the boy's trap, like an idiot," she frets, raising her face again to mine. "And now you're in trouble too. If—"

"Do not think to rebuke yourself for the single bravest act anyone alive or dead has ever committed on my behalf," I tell her. "If it all ends tomorrow, tonight even, were the fire pits of Hell to yawn open and swallow us up before sunrise, this moment with you is worth whatever comes, Stella. This moment might be all we ever have."

And her mouth opens under mine, and her body unfolds like a flower in my arms. Our next kiss is more tender, the next as urgent as the pull of the tide. And I give way to this crescendo inside me, as furious as bloodrage, as spellbinding as fairy magic. Tempestuous life thunders through my blood, swelling my heart, pulsing under my skin, drumming in my fingertips, as we tumble across the bearskin in a frenzy of sensation— deep, soft fur against skin, pungent smoke in our nostrils, a tiny, distant popping of tinder, the fervor of her touch, the sweet fire of her mouth, our mutual keening, our reckless momentum.

For so long, my life was like a spinning compass, without points or direction. Stella is my guiding star. Her body is my altar, my refuge. Her love is my life, and by God I will deserve her, coaxing the most wondrous music out of her that I have ever played, until we lose ourselves at last in the riotous swell of this love we make together.

***

I stretch out on my back with Stella drowsing alongside me. Silver smoke winds up through the hole above the skins to escape into the night, disappearing into the pattern of Neverland stars.

"Stella," I whisper, "look,"

She tilts up her head in time to see a tiny glimmer of light tumble across a circlet of stars. The Medicine Wheel, I believe it's called. It may be a trick of the smoke, or a wavering pulse of heat from the fire, but for a moment the entire circle appears to quiver in place, as if animated. Stella's body sighs against mine.

"A shooting star," she murmurs. "How lovely."

We are ripe for Morpheus at last.

There is naught but a little glowing pile of embers to see by when I am suddenly awake. Most of the stars have sunk out of sight in the hole of black above us; it's the eerie dark before dawn. I hear only a fading cacophony of night insects and the sirens' muted song, yet something compels me out of our warm nest. Untangling myself from Stella, who sleeps blissfully on, I creep off the bearskin, open the tent flap and peep out, but my eyes discern only blackness and a distant bruise of moonglow behind clouds. I gather my courage and step outside to see what the matter is.

I don't see him at first, might have never done but for a sudden incandescence of white moonlight spilling from between ragged clouds. He stands immobile, not the length of a tops'l yard away from me, his bow drawn, the arrow nocked and pointing at my heart, a larger target now than once it was, and far more vulnerable.

3

I say nothing, do nothing, only gaze into the flinty eyes of the young chief above the eagle feather drawn back against his cheek. I wear neither clothing nor hook, having come directly from Stella's arms. And with the absurd vanity of our species, I am glad for a fleeting instant that I've never grown a paunch, despite the other deformities of my body, for Eagle Heart is scarcely any more clothed than I, stripped down to a breechclout, as chiseled as a Greek, painted not for war but for stealth.

Such are the lofty ruminations of my last moments of life. But the young chief does not shoot.

"Captain," he says quietly.

"Chief," I respond.

We regard each other for another long, silent moment. Stella murmurs in her sleep behind me; the mat rustles beneath her. For a blink, Eagle Heart's gaze shifts to the open flap, then back to me, standing before him, naked in the pre-dawn chill, reeking of Stella.

"We meant no disrespect to this place," I offer.

"Our women will perform the cleansing ceremony after you are gone." Slowly, without the slightest thrum of string or creak of wood, he lessens the tension in his weapon and lowers bow and arrow. "This is a sacred place," he goes on. "Our young ones come here to begin the journey out of childhood. The maidens bleed. The youths have their first dream vision, to honor the ancestor whose dream brought us to the Dreaming Place."

He pauses as sweet-acrid smoke wafts out of the structure.

"We didn't mean to steal," I apologize.

"The fruits of the earth are free to all," Eagle Heart replies. "A gift from the Great Spirit."

Stella's voice comes softly from behind me, addressing the chief, and his black eyes shift toward her. She's wrapped herself in my coat before venturing out to crouch beneath the tent flap.

The young chief's expression is as impassive as ever, but his eyes move back to me. "Our elders have rendered their judgment."

I'm shaking. Stella rises to stand beside me, steadying me.

"You offend me and dishonor yourself when you break your oath," he tells me gravely. "But the consequence of your action was this life," and he nods at Stella. "Honor your oath and we will have no further quarrel with you. In our judgment it is now your destiny to leave the Dreaming Place."

Stella's fingers close round the stump of my phantom hand, and my good hand crosses over to cover hers. "But—"

"Our shaman watches the stars," says the young chief. "Destiny is like the wind. He tells us yours now blows another way."

"Your shaman," Stella murmurs to the chief. "How does he say we are to leave this place?"

"You must ask the Spirit Queen."

"Is there no other way?" I ask petulantly.

Eagle Heart reproves me with his stony gaze. "The Little Chief will come," he tells me. "He will hunt you and your woman. Our shaman says you must leave by the next moonrise, or the Great Spirits who cradle the Dreaming Place in their hands will no longer let you pass. Twice before have the spirit elements stood ready for your journey, but never before were you ready to go. This is your last chance, Captain."

I nod. "What must I do?"

"You must go the Spirit Place. Give the queen what she asks for and she will guide you."

What will Queen BellaAeola ask of me? My heart? My soul? My sanity? What price will she set on my freedom? Mine and Stella's together, what might she not demand?

"How are we to find her?" I ask.

"Follow the stream to the wood, and ask your spirit guide." Eagle Heart gestures toward the sound of lapping water out beyond the trees. "Your boat is waiting. Our warriors will not stop you."

Stella thanks him, and the chief evaporates back into the jungle as silently as the smoke slithered out the hole in our refuge of hides. As his form is swallowed in shadows, the full moon emerges from the clouds once more, as red as blood in the pre-dawn blackness. Stella sees it too, regrips my arm, and we exchange a long, silent look. Her expression is as pregnant as the shimmering crimson moon. It's time to face our destiny, whichever way it now blows.

CHAPTER 31

SUITE: THE QUEEN'S PRICE

1

"Drugged? Are you sure?"

"Black drops, irresistible oblivion. I have tasted it before."

I am trying to explain to Stella why I was so late returning to her on the day we quarreled. We have breakfasted on bits of raw-looking fish and sinister strings of sea grass, washed down with spring water from a jug of iridescent stone. We found them in my skiff, tied up outside. My French cutlass and my knife were in the bottom, by which we know the loreleis came in the night. Now we are in the skiff heading northward again, retracing the route the braves canoed me down yesterday evening.

"Why?" Stella asks. "To keep us apart?"

"None of them knew about you." I frown, trying to think if I ever slipped up in my charade among the men.

"I thought you must have gone back to them for good," she says. "I thought if I could just get to the Fairy Dell and find the way out, maybe I could change your mind about me."

I grimace to think how readily I lapped up the boy's evil lies.

"But you were still gone the next day when I came back to *Le Reve*," Stella concludes.

"Yesterday morning? *Le Reve* was still there?" I ask, and she nods. "Well, she's gone, now," I sigh.

"Gone?" Stella stares at me. "What do you mean, gone?"

"Sunk, broken up, magicked away, I don't know, just gone," I mutter, hauling on the oars. "He must have done it right after he captured you. His master stroke."

"Oh no, James!" Stella looks aghast.

"It doesn't matter, Parrish. You are all that matters to me."

***

The Terraces rise up on either side as we row up the channel, their steep rockfaces striated with blue, bronze, coral and purple in the morning light. High above, a ribbon of Neverland sky mirrors the snaky progress of our river. We glide along an obliging current, gazing up at gaudily painted foothills sheering up to ever higher plateaus, crowned at first with verdant succulents and ferns, then a frosting of dark green pines as we progress northward. A pair of hawks circle on air currents high above; an eagle swoops from one terrace across the ravine to another.

"I hope we can find the place," Stella worries.

Spying a familiar bundle stowed under the after thwart, I nod at Stella to haul it out and open it.

"Well," I smile, as she unwraps one of the crystal goblets, "suppose we consult my spirit guide."

I might as well have conjured merry Charles Stuart himself out of the thin air, or her precious Blackbeard, Stella is so astounded when the fairy Piper appears.

"Sandpiper," the little thing introduces herself formally to Stella.

"We met aboard the *Rouge*," Stella marvels.

"You did me a kindness," the fairy recalls, too gracious to mention my part in their first encounter. Then she adds gently, "Do not judge us all by my sister, Kestrel."

330

"Your sister is Peter's fairy?" Stella gapes.

"Yes, and an insufferable little tart she is about it, too," Piper huffs. "Peter always likes the sassy ones. Makes him feel important, to think he commands them."

Stella glances wide-eyed at me, then back again to Piper. "Peter's had other fairies?"

"It's so exhausting, looking after the boys," Piper concedes, with a fluttering of commiseration. "Most recently, our cousin Tinker had that honor, but she is in retirement. It took a hundred years off her life, she swears it."

Stella can't stop grinning as Piper turns again to me.

"Has the love you bear this woman cooled, that you break the pledge you made by it so easily?" the imp chirps.

Stella's grin collapses, and I swallow a throb of alarm. "I love her more than ever," I tell the fairy.

"He saved my life," Stella protests. "Surely he did that boy no more damage than your sister making them deaf."

"No indeed," Piper agrees, fluttering placidly between us. "No permanent harm was done in either case, and as the First Tribes have forgiven you, Queen BellaAeola will hear your claim."

"Your queen has a very distinguished name," Stella ventures, as I dare to resume breathing. "Do fairies study Greek mythology?"

"Mythology," Piper scoffs. "Mortals want credit for everything. In those days, we were honored as gods. Aeolus was a fairy artisan who taught mortals the art of sailmaking, so they too might use the gift of wind. The Queen of the Bells always takes his name, which means Wind Rider." She flits about, wings abuzz, eager to expound on the arcana of fairy lore. "Those of us in the Sisterhood adopt the names of our totem creatures in the natural world. Private fairy names cannot be spoken to mortals."

"Sandpiper," muses Stella. "A creature who dwells where land and water meet, as well as in the sky."

"Oh, excellent!" Piper cries.

I need not ask how the predatory Kestrel came by her name.

"You have a special affinity for all three elements?" Stella goes on.

"I do indeed," the imp chirps on. "Oh, I knew it was right to bring you here!"

Stella gapes. "It was your doing?"

"No, yours," the little creature replies. "You wanted it so badly, renounced the grown-up world so completely, you were in a state of innocence reborn. Certain beyond all mortal reasoning that this place exists."

"But I saw it in my dreams," Stella rejoins, eyeing me.

"Yes, yes, yes," the imp chants happily, also beaming at me. "Your dreaming called out to her."

"But—my thoughts were all of death," I stammer.

"What we think and what we dream are not always the same thing, Captain," Piper rebukes me gently. "You grew a dream the Neverland could no longer contain. It stretched beyond our borders. A dream of longing for something you could never find here. Perhaps your two dreams collided in the realm of the mortal heart, where the Sisterhood has no power. We know only mortal children who are heartless until they lose their innocence." She turns again to Stella. "Your dream was so powerful, even Peter felt it. That is how they found you, Peter and my sister. We couldn't let him leave you behind in the nursery, Kes and I. Boys can be so thoughtless sometimes."

"You can't mean Kestrel defied the boy to bring her here!" I exclaim.

"My sister's magic merely opened the dreampath for you to claim your dream," the fairy tells Stella. "Never before has a grown-up woman come to the Neverland. But I—we knew, Kes and I, that if the spell were to break, Captain, you

332

would have to share someone else's dreampath to get out. You could not leave the same way you came." She turns again to Stella. "It was no great matter for Kes to glimmersail you here while Peter was distracted elsewhere."

It's difficult to imagine the wanton Kestrel, singing madly for my blood just hours ago, showing such concern for my welfare. But the imps' taste for gaming is legendary.

"Where did it come from, this prophecy of signs?" Stella asks.

"From the earth, from the sea, from the sky," Piper replies. "This is a magical place. The natural world, the spirit world, the life of dreams, all are connected here."

"And how long have you known about them?" Stella continues.

"Far longer than anyone else has been alive on this island, except for the Captain, Peter, and we fairies. To the merwives and the First Tribes, it is ancient times since the prophecy first appeared in their lore."

I marvel at Proserpina's craft, to seed her spell so completely into the fabric of this place.

"A few words sifted into the dreams of the shaman and the mer-bard, simple enough to do," Piper goes on. "If the time had come to break your spell at last, Captain, we wanted to speed you along to claim your reward."

"But why speak in so many riddles?" Stella asks. "If you fairies knew about the signs and the dreampath, couldn't you simply...tell him?"

Piper turns again to me. "You never asked for our help," she says sadly. "And the only way to break your spell was to change what was in your heart. No one else could do that for you."

The channel ends at the inland falls, which mark the trail back up into the wood. Piper told us the Fairy Dell will open for us, but we must make the rest of our journey on foot.

I return Stella's moccasins to her, and we climb the trail through dust and weeds and brush and bristlecone. I give her my knife to cut a length of trailing ivy to girdle up her shift, and she tucks it into her sash like a lady buccaneer in a comic opera. At last we reach a plateau alive with shrubbery, pine, oak and fir, whose increasing intensity of greens signals the way to the Dell. Following a vibrato of fiddle music and jingling laughter through greening trees and violet mists, we come to a green clearing in the forest.

Stella's hand is warm in mine as we enter the greensward, the bustle of the imps going about their morning tasks so different from their lurid nighttime revels. A party of young males breeze past us, sweeping windfall leaves into piles for their beguiling charms. A few shimmering females trail their sparkle over beds of buttercups and bluebells that obediently raise their heads, while others flutter up into the trees for acorns and moss and mold and berries for their potions. One imp tries to bedevil a fledgling in a nest until an indignant mother sparrow drives her off. In an alcove at the base of another tree, in which depend improbable tools of rock and honed gemstones, an elderly imp in silvery mustachios lingers over a bowl while one idle finger commands a chair of twigs to build itself.

All of them, sweepers, gatherers, artisans and thieves, cobweb-draped females huddling over a stone cauldron, a cotillion of young bloods and girls tamping down a dancing ring round a favored mushroom, all of them are roused to their tasks by a quartet of fiddlers perched on a mossy rock sawing a lively laboring tune. In the center of all rises a dark green mound shimmering with eerie silver light; it looks like an ordinary burrow by daylight, not a blazing palace, although reeking still of fairy glamour as dreadful as it is difficult to resist.

We are not Goliaths among the fairies; they appear of normal size to our eyes, until we see one in proportion to a bird or a bluebell. Yet neither does it feel as if we've shrunk. It's another way to disorient us, this feeling of being both large and small, alien to the fairies and akin to them, reminding us that the supposed advantage of our size, much less the reliability of our wits, have no meaning here.

The bubbling hum of talk grows more intense all round us as we enter into the heart of the Dell. Some watch us covertly, others make a grand, haughty business of paying us no mind whatever, while others simply stand in their tracks and stare, their cunning expressions impossible to read. I grip Stella's hand more firmly.

"Hold on to me, *ma coeur*," I whisper.

"Remember who you are, James," she murmurs back, and squeezes my hand. A path of polished moonstones gleams in the grass, pointing the way to the glimmering mound where Queen BellaAeola keeps her court.

The portals of her palace resolve themselves more sensibly this time as we approach, but our quest is different now, Stella no longer the repulsed mother seeking the boy, nor myself the spy. We climb the steps, pass between the flowering white pillars and into the Great Hall, with its polished floor and bewitching mirrors. No shades of the dead shimmer here this time, only reflections of ourselves, none true and all skewed to provoke. I see myself a beggar in the world, thin and gaunt, a bowl of ashes in my hand, with Stella worn and wretched trailing behind me, the spark gone from her eyes. I see myself in horns beside a cruelly laughing Stella painted like a voluptuary. I don't know what Stella sees, perhaps a vision of herself cowed and weeping and myself a raging tyrant. Much is risked in love, there are so many uncertainties, and our savage hostess knows how to play upon them all. But we don't let go of each other, Stella and I, and the false reflections finally dance away.

All but the last, which we see together: ourselves as grizzled elders, our faces sunk in wrinkles, myself bald, stiff, bent, crabbing along on a cane, Stella sagging in her shapeless gown, frail, haggard and weary. Such is the fate of all things out beyond the glamour of the Neverland. Age, an enemy as pitiless as the boy, who can never be vanquished, from whom there will be no refuge once we are back in the world; it can't be shrugged off like the other shades, and the wavering image grows steadier, taunting us.

A shudder passes through Stella's living body pressed to mine, and I wrap my arm round her, hugging her closer. "To age again, I crave it above all things," I say defiantly. "It's the fondest desire of my heart."

"I will grow old and ugly." Stella's voice is small and wavering.

"Not to me, my Stella Rose," I promise her. "Never to me."

"Then you will be blind," Stella sniffs, although she straightens a little in my embrace. "In addition to your other infirmities."

"Then you may let yourself go entirely," I point out. "You may sprout cloven hoofs and a tail, for all the difference it'll make to me."

Stella laughs, and the vision of ourselves ancient and doddering pops and vanishes. In its place stands Queen BellaAeola, or, rather, she hovers there, hands fisted on hips like an Amazon, feet slightly apart shod in delicate, moss-like boots whose toes and high serrated cuffs rise and loop round and round like wanton tendrils of wisteria. Yards of twinkling gossamer drape from her shoulders and gird round her middle, all of it billowing round her like agitated flames, although we feel no breeze. Her skin is undyed, so light-washed I don't perceive it as any color, only note again the arcane royal markings etched in the most luxurious shade of purple that trail down from her bare shoulder to curl provocatively round her breast. Her exquisite, silvery hair clouds behind her as well, and her moonlit eyes, circled in purple and shadowed in green, gaze at us both with impassive aplomb.

"So, Captain, have you come to conclude our transaction?" she purrs at me.

I fight down the memory of bitter desolation from our last encounter, raise my chin and return her gaze, struggling to calm my rattling heartbeats. "I have come to ask your guidance, Majesty."

"Why have you never asked for my help before?" she chides.

"I never thought you would give it," I reply, but it sounds so petulant, I quickly add, "I didn't deserve it."

The air shivers like tiny carriage bells heard on a breeze from far away. The imp queen is laughing. "Are you more deserving now?"

From the lively intensity of her eyes, I feel I'm being invited to dance, or game, or duel to the death, or perhaps all three. Every word must count; Eagle Heart once warned me to be wise.

"I've grown up," I tell her simply.

"Ahhh," she muses, her eerie, caressing speech a-hum in my head. "And now the Red Moon is risen again, you would complete your journey, at long last. And if I refuse?"

I order my mutinous wits not to desert me. "I might attempt to cozen you with flattery," I begin cautiously. "Or I might threaten to make war on every fairy in the Neverland if I don't get my way. But those are the boys' tactics." I draw a breath. "And I am boy no more. Instead, I ask your pardon for my many, many mistakes."

"What will you give me for it?" BellaAeola fences. "Have you found something in the Neverland you value at last?" My heart stutters as she turns her provocative gaze on Stella. "Your woman?"

Stella faces her out with the appearance of boldness, although I feel her tense beside me. "She is not mine to give you, Majesty," I tell the queen. "She is mistress of herself."

BellaAeola's magnetic gaze holds Stella still. "And you, Woman. What will you give me?"

"Nothing," Stella replies. Intensity quickens in the air as if the queen had lunged forward, although she does not appear to move. Nor does Stella back away. "My absence," Stella explains. "A Neverland with no part of myself in it. Surely that will be a great relief to all who live here. Better than any other gift I might offer."

"This is well." BellaAeola murmurs. But something quickens in her demeanor as she turns her weird, shining eyes again to me, and this time she does sidle closer; it's like the weight of the ocean pressing on a drowning man. "She kindles a passion in you, Captain, that was not there before," murmurs the queen. "It is very exciting. Perhaps I will keep you for myself after all." She looms closer. "I can show you delights far beyond mortal imagining. I can conceal you from the boy."

I cannot lie and say I'm not tempted, not even to myself. My traitorous blood beats merrily in all my private places. My phantom fingers ache to caress her glorious body, so visible beneath the drape of moondust she wears. My blood, my body, might easily give way; she might fold her lustery wings round me like a bird of prey and smother me with pleasure, was it their decision alone. Yet my wits tick on with a fierce will I never knew before Stella came.

"You may beguile me, Majesty." I labor like Sisyphus to roll words off my dry tongue. "You may use me as you please, bend me to your will, and I will not protest. We both know it. But you can never, ever harvest from me what I feel for Stella unless you are prepared to love me as she does."

"Love, love, love," BellaAeola trills derisively. "A handful of rain and a heart full of ash, that is mortal love." But she has halted her advance. "Fairies do not love. It's a foolish business and a waste of our considerable talents." Eyeing me appraisingly, she adds, "You may yet regret the day that you refused me, dark and sinister man."

The boy's old epithet chills me, reminding me how closely allied are all magical forces in the Neverland. "It's not in my feeble mortal power to refuse you, Majesty," I answer her. "I only tell you the truth."

"The truth is, Captain, it has never been done before, what you ask," says the queen, with an ominous trembling of her wings. "How do you propose to leave this place? You have no dreampath to follow."

"But I do," Stella speaks up. "We will go together."

The imp queen shifts her hungry gaze again to Stella. "And you, Woman. Your mortal power has intensified since last we met."

"I've lost my innocence," Stella tells her. Turning to me, Stella adds softly, "When I fell in love with you."

By God's life, she even bled; I remember now.

"Yes," hisses the queen, nodding with intrigue. "You forfeit the protection of your innocence when you choose to love this man. Yet, my ladies—" and I hear an eager rustling and tittering like so many finches in the garlanded shadows around us, "—might make rather merry sport with such powers as you now possess."

Stella neither falters nor turns away from her dazzling inquisitor. "But not in the Neverland," she reasons gently. "It disturbs the boy."

BellaAeola flutters back a pace or two in a great swirl of sparkling dust and fairy majesty to regard us both again. But neither anger nor yet scorn clouds her expression, only lively curiosity, as if we are a game she enjoys. "Alas, yes," she agrees "Such feelings as you now arouse in the captain are as dangerous as a weapon to the boys' innocence. There is more at stake here than my pleasure," she adds, with a pretty sigh. "Or that of my ladies."

I tremble to imagine any force in the universe stern enough to turn BellaAeola from her pursuit of pleasure. To what sort of perverse deity might the fairies submit? Surely more terrible than the angry god of mortals, of whose blood and body Stella and I make such free speech, who sacrificed his own son so men would know to fear him. That god would have smote me centuries ago for my crimes, might yet, should I dare to venture beyond this enchanted place. But the glistening cascade of BellaAeola's laughter scatters my thoughts like seafoam.

"Your angry god has no power here," she scoffs, as if she heard my thoughts. "But he might find you, Captain, your thunderous god, out in the world. Are you not afraid?"

Stella's fingers twine through mine again. "No, Majesty." My words slide out with ease this time, without hesitation. "Because I have loved." Whatever else might be said against me, and there are volumes, at least, at last, I have loved.

"The Neverland doesn't want us," Stella appeals to the imp queen. "We ask for your blessing to leave this place."

"My guidance, my pardon, my blessing," BellaAeola chants impudently. "Those are three favors you ask of me, yet you have nothing to give me."

"Majesty, what can you possibly desire that is not already yours to command?" I temporize.

"Flatterer!" she snaps back, but with more sauce than rebuke. She even preens a little, tossing her silvery hair with a dazzling tremor of her wings. "You are so fond of the truth, Captain, perhaps you will confess there is something else you hold dear in the Neverland. A prize you would seek to keep from me."

"Never," I protest, my poor wits racing to keep apace of hers.

"Oh, yes, oh, yes, oh, yes," she chants merrily. "Deny me if you dare."

A broad swag of flowers behind the queen drops away to reveal the shimmering surface of one of her perverse mirrors, as high as a palace wall, if indeed her domain has walls. Its misty image resolves into a shape that does indeed clutch my heart with longing and parch my throat for want of it. The clean, strong lines of my sloop, *Le Reve,* appears before me, her sails set, her black paint smart with its green trim. The queen is not yet done pleasuring herself at my expense.

"But…this is a ghost," I stammer.

"Your pretty ship is as real as you are, Captain," she taunts me, her eyes keen with her sport. "Do you suppose I would leave it about for the boys to wreck with their games? So many years of your life," she croons on. "So much labor. So much love." She sneers the word. "For so entirely futile a project. How deeply you must care for it."

"Yes." I can scarcely speak at all.

"But I desire pretty things," she chirps. "Will you give it to me?"

My insides twist with longing almost beyond bearing. My ship, my *Reve,* safe and whole, my solace, my sanity for so long. All that was ever good in me, the only thing of any worth I ever achieved in this place before Stella came, indeed, ever in my life; it tortures me to imagine her moldering in the queen's sepulcher for all eternity. But I force down my anguish. *Le Reve* was ever my dream of redemption, but it was only a dream. Life awaits me, a genuine life, safe in Stella's heart, do I only dare to claim it.

"She is yours, Majesty," I tell the queen, peeling my gaze away from that beloved image for the last time. "Please accept her with my compliments."

The vision of *Le Reve* dissolves in a giddy piping of fairy laughter. "What use have I for transport made of mortal hands?" BellaAeola cries gaily, and flutters her incandescent wings, the span of a top royal at her present size. "You had better have it for your journey."

She says it with such indifference, I scarce believe I heard it.

"Yes, Captain, I will grant the thing you most desire," BellaAeola murmurs; her glance is keen, despite her drowsy voice. "What you have always desired."

"Thank you, Majesty," Stella whispers beside me.

"You owe me more than your thanks, Mortals," BellaAeola replies placidly.

My wits give up at last; I dare not look at Stella.

"A small matter, a trifle," the queen assures us with a wave of her delicate hand. "The fee required of all who leave the Neverland. You must forfeit your memories."

Stella frowns at her. "All of them?"

"Only your memories of the Neverland," says BelaAeola lightly. "And all that has happened here."

A tremor of jubilation races through me. To forget the Neverland and all the misery I've known here! How marvelous to return to the world a normal man, to pick up the thread of my life exactly where I left it off over two centuries ago. And my fatuous joy turns to ice and vinegar inside me. What a cruel, raging tyrant I was two hundred years ago, at war with all the world, unfit to live. Unfit to love. Before the Neverland taught me the hard lessons of patience and wisdom. Before the healing solace of *Le Reve*. Before Stella. I stare into Stella's stricken face and read my same despairing thoughts in her beautiful eyes. I won't know

Stella. I'll no longer be the man she loves. I will forget her. She will forget me.

"By Christ's blood, no," I stammer.

"It's too much to ask, Majesty," Stella pleads.

"I do not ask it," BellaAeola shrugs with a rustling of her haughty wings. "That is the price. It has ever been the price. Tales of the Neverland must not be allowed to spread abroad in your world."

"But the world already knows of this place!" Stella protests.

"But they don't believe it," the imp queen replies. "Only children believe, and they are always welcome here because children forget. And so must you."

We are speechless. The fairy queen backs away with a shimmer of majestic impatience. "That is the price of what you seek," she declares. "You have earned the right to go, and but a few mortal hours remain in which you may do so. Do not bore me any longer with your mortal humors. Your fairy will show you the way."

She sweeps her fantastical wings round her and vanishes as if through a hole in the air. And upon the instant, the enormous garlanded hall with all its dazzling surfaces, dripping with perfumed flowers and heady with the nectar of luxury and indolence, all of it dissolves before our eyes. Stella and I stand again in a green clearing at the edge of the Fairy Dell, an ordinary little grassy burrow just visible in the distance, surrounded by a chiggering of busy insects.

Stella stares at me as if the uncanny alteration in the scenery has not occurred. "I was bitterly unhappy when I came here," she whispers. "I don't want to be that person again. I can't lose you, James."

"I was less than human," I mutter, wrapping my arms round her, struggling to regain my shattered wits. How could Stella ever love the man I was?

"Then we must stay here!" Stella urges me. "Why can't we stay here forever?"

"It will astonish you how short a time that is."

"I don't care!" she insists.

Oh, but I do. By God's poisonous blood, how desperately I want to keep Stella safe. But her safety carries an enormous price tag. How much longer before we are made to pay it?

Even now, a tiny firefly light comes shivering toward us out of the green mist. Has the charm already begun? How many more heartbeats before I see the loathing creep into Stella's eyes, before I know she's forgotten James and sees only Hook in all his deformities?

3

We've regained our usual proportions, for the imp is scarcely more than a speck of lavender-blue against the vale of green, trailing a scent of smoky allspice. Piper.

"We need more time," I beg her. "We're not ready."

The little thing shivers with laughter, shaking the preposterous coils and loops of her black hair into a Maenad dance. "More time? I thought you'd had enough of time, Captain! But I am your escort, nothing more. You won't forget the Neverland until you leave it."

"And when must that be?" Stella asks sadly.

The imp regards us quizzically. "Whenever you wish, of course." She peers at us with more concern. "It cannot be that you fear it? It causes no pain. You will be delivered into the world as if reborn. Beyond the borders of this place, you will have no more memory of it than an infant has of the womb it leaves behind."

We must not look convinced, because the little creature sighs and entreats us further. "You now both desire something more than childhood can provide. You must go where your dreaming takes you. As soon as they begin to long for something far beyond their lives here, Lost Boys, girls, all of them, when their longing is too volatile, they must go. As you must go, and soon."

Stella's fingers lace through mine. "May we have a minute to discuss it?" she asks the fairy.

"Talk, talk, talk," Piper chants, sounding chillingly like the imp queen. "Do not talk away the time you have left," she warns us. "Peter dislikes change. He fears any dream, any desire more powerful than he is. He will do anything he can to crush it."

She fades into the mists while Stella and I ponder the enormity of the decision we must make. How long before the boys come to hunt us down like the outlaws we are? We must pay for our memories with our lives unless we forfeit our memories to live.

"We're in an awful damned fix here, Maestro," Stella sighs.

"It must be obvious even to you that we can't think of staying here," I counter. "Don't condemn me to watch you die, *ma rose.*"

That silences her. She folds her arms round herself, stalks off a few steps, staring into the distance, absently chewing her lower lip in that gesture I will miss so much. How I will miss all her gestures. How can I ever look upon her, even as a stranger, and not be as moved by all her little quirks and habits as I am now?

"We don't know for a fact that we will never love each other again," I fence cautiously. "Out in the world."

Her face turns slowly back toward me. "No," she murmurs.

"We may not know each other," I go on, ignoring the pain that claws at my vitals at the very thought, "but we might be drawn to each other again. It happened before."

"I came from another world to find you," Stella agrees.

"Perhaps, whatever it is between us now will pull us together again," I hazard. "The Scotch boy retained something of this place, some buried memory, however fragmented, even if only in dreams." What did Proserpina say of her ancestor, Zwonde? The spirit does not forget love.

"If we are…destined," Stella chimes in, more eagerly, "what should it matter where we are? Or…who?"

It's a very feeble thread of possibility, but the alternative…there is no alternative. We both know it.

Stella marches back to me, still hugging herself, the quaver in her voice at odds with the determination in her eyes. "Then we better have Piper back before we change our minds."

But Stella scarcely calls to the imp when I turn to see the merest shiver in an evergreen at the edge of the clearing. A figure steps out from behind the tree, a young brave, slender and fleet, stripped down to buckskins with daubs of red and black paint streaked across his cheeks.

I move toward him, raise my hand in salute. He does the same.

"Chief Eagle Heart sends a message to Captain Hook," he says. "Little Chief Pan is on the warpath. He calls for a war party of braves to join him and his boys to attack the ship in the bay."

"The *Rouge?*" I gawp at him. "Why?"

"The Little Chief says, 'It's Hook or me this time!'"

"When?" I demand.

"Today. Now," the young messenger declares. "Chief Eagle Heart says to tell you the Little Chief cannot be held in check for long. We are ordered to burn your ship to the waterline, and everyone in her."

Stella comes up beside me, Piper fluttering at her shoulder, as the brave evaporates back into the forest. "We've very little time," Stella says tersely. How well she knows my

346

mind only intensifies my dread of the awful moment when she won't know me at all.

"I won't let them pay for my crime," I mutter. "It doesn't always have to be like this. I can help them now."

"But—"

"I can't abandon them to be slaughtered, drowned, burned alive—"

Stella's mouth flattens into a tight line, but she argues no more, clutching at my arm. But her stricken face reflects my thoughts. Is there some trick the boy can still use against us, some spell of fire that might yet prevent our escape?

CHAPTER 32

THE BLOODY PLANK

"Mortal humors! So long as I live they will mystify me," huffs Piper, once we've descended the trail to our boat at the bottom of the gorgeous ravine. "Do not while away too much time. When the moon reaches her zenith in the sky this evening, the pathway between the two worlds will close to you for the last time, Captain. Summon me when you are ready. Sound a bell to call a fairy," she reminds us. "Time was, every mortal knew it."

In a twinkling, her sorcery propels us as far as the mouth of Kidd Creek. But our skiff cannot be seen to simply coalesce out of the ether alongside the *Rouge,* although it should scarcely give my men any more of a fright than Stella's presence inside it. Was she not believed drowned in the Mermaid Lagoon all this time? Until Pan taunted me about losing her, last time I was aboard. What will the men think now? But there is no more chance than ever that Stella will listen to reason, take herself off somewhere safe with Piper while I attempt to prevent this massacre.

"I'm not going anywhere without you," she tells me fiercely. "Our bond is our strength; we are weak and foolish apart."

Even if ours is a journey into death, we will take it together.

"If we have a plan, Maestro, now is the time to tell me," Stella suggests, as we row within hailing distance of the *Rouge's* starboard quarter. I hear brisk activity on deck—hammering, a rattling of buckets, light chatter, even some laughter popping sporadically like grapeshot over the water. But there's no sign yet of flames, nor flying boys, nor war canoes.

"There must be a way to stop it," I reason. "I'll call for a parley, declare a truce. At least, I can challenge him man to man—"

"No!" Stella gasps.

"Only to spare the men, save the ship from burning," I go on stoically. "I'll honor my word not to harm a boy."

"It's not the boys I'm worried about," Stella grumbles.

"This battle must be deflected somehow," I insist. "My men know only warmaking, the game they can never win. They have never needed a leader more, and I must give them one. Pacify the boy until he goes off in search of another game and we can be away from here." And before I can begin to consider all the ways my plan can go awry, I call, "Ahoy! *Rouge,* there!"

I am in full Hook regalia as we climb the chains, dressed in my much abused, but sturdy black coat and snowy-plumed black hat, my French sword at my side. Stella, clambering up behind me, makes an altogether different impression, dark auburn hair loose and tousled, white chemise girded with green ivy vines from the heart of the forest, pink seashell hanging once more round her neck, buckskin slippers on her feet, knife sheathed at her waist. Had the Neverland itself dreamt a creature to embody all of its eccentric communities, that creature should look no more fey than Stella looks now. I keep her close to me as we march amidships, calling the men to gather round.

To my amazement, it's Filcher who pushes himself to the front of the circle, beaming as mightily as his fretful features will allow.

"All set, Cap'n!" he sallies, before I can even begin. "Decks all sanded. Weapons done up all proper. Just like you said."

I can't even remember the last thing I said to them.

"And that other matter," Filcher goes on happily. "We seen to that too. The plank you asked for. We built it."

***

Blast and bugger me for a Bedlamite! It protrudes like a gargoyle's rude tongue from the port bows of my own *Rouge,* a thick wooden plank made fast inboard near the fore shrouds. Most of its length extends out through the rail of the high foredeck over the teeming blue waters of the bay. Never, ever have I beheld such a thing outside of a Wendy's storybook in all my time in the trade, and certainly not on any ship of mine.

"Mr. Filcher, who in hell gave the order to build that bloody thing?" I yelp.

Filcher's bonhomie curdles. The others go owl-eyed, as if I've said something extraordinary.

"You did, Cap'n," Burley ventures, at Filcher's elbow. "For the boys, you said."

"To show 'em we mean business next time!" Nutter chimes in.

"I never gave any such order!"

"Aye, ye did, Cap'n," Burley maintains placidly. "'I have a surprise for you men,' you said. 'Build a plank and prepare for battle.' Down by the creek, it were. Me and Brassy and Flax, we all heard you."

"But no one actually saw me," I fence, as the possibilities take shape in my mind. "Am I a will o' the wisp, some Biblical oracle that issues orders out of bushes? I'd have shown myself to you, had I been there in fact."

"But we all know your voice," says Flax.

"It was a trick of the boy's," I tell them, "mimicking my voice to get what he wants. Listen, men, the boys are on the warpath, and they're bringing the braves. They will be here any minute. He's the one who wants a fight, and if you value your lives, you must not give it to him."

This is met by a chorus of blustering dismay. "But we're all ready!" Nutter yelps, while others shout, "Fight! Fight!"

"There are too few of us to rout the boys and the braves combined," I insist. "What use have our weapons ever been against the boys, much less a hundred warriors? It would be suicide!"

This gets a few of them stirring amongst themselves, trying to mask their unease from their more adamant fellows. I cannot say the restless tide of their passions, so easily swayed, is shifting in my direction, but it's possible they might yet listen to reason. I glance at Stella, who steps back to concede the spotlight to me, her expression heartening. "But we are strong if we stand together," I rally the men. "Don't pick up your arms. Don't play his game. I will challenge him instead, persuade him to some other contest. I'm the one he wants to beat, and when he does—"

"Coward!" hisses Nutter. "Fight ain't even started, and he's ready to hand it over to the boy."

No sound at all greets this outburst as the big red-headed fellow looms up opposite me. "Why else are we here except to fight the damn boys?" he cries to the men. "All we need is a captain who will lead us. A captain right here on the *Rouge*, not off punting down the river like Lord Fucking Fauntleroy every day; a captain who won't lie to us," and he glares at Stella. "A captain who don't go all soft over a woman. We need a new captain! I call for trial by combat! Who's with me?"

The men are buzzing now, although they've not yet begun to chant like the boys.

"We can't fight among ourselves, there's no time!" I exclaim. "This is just what Pan wants, to weaken us—"

"No, *you* want to weaken us!" Nutter shouts me down. "We want to fight!" And he plants himself before me. "Hook, I challenge you to trial by combat!"

"I'm not going to fight for my command!" I splutter. A moldering bucket of bolts forever beached in an eternal nightmare, that is my precious command. "God's blood, man, take it! I wish you all the joy in the world of it, but first—"

"But it's gotta be trial by combat," pipes up Filcher, his wary eyes shifting appraisingly between Nutter and me. "It's in all the stories, i'n'it?"

I don't see by what signal it happens, only that men have quietly shifted over to box in Stella—Flax, Swab, thickset Burley. When she tries to edge away from them, hands grip her arms, her shoulders, holding her fast.

"This has gone far enough!" I cry, snapping out my sword, but I'm not quick enough; they drag Stella out of my reach.

"Looks like we'll fight after all, eh, Hook?" Nutter exults, stepping in front of me again. He stretches out a mighty paw, snaps his fingers at Filcher. "Get me one of them things." And my first mate scurries off like a toady to the magazine, pulls out one of the biggest, longest blades.

"Mr. Burley," I sally in Hook's iciest purr, never taking my eyes off Nutter as I struggle to regain my authority. "Who is in command here?"

Burley squints at me, then at Nutter, then glances about at the other men, avid now for their entertainment. "That's what we've got to find out," he declares.

Filcher trots up to Nutter and slides the hilt of the sword into his grasp. Nutter sights down the length of his arm at it, preening with it, as men have done since the first hour of time, seeing their own worth reflected in the bravery of their weapons. In a grand gesture, he sweeps his blade in a half-circle before him. "Give us room, lads!"

Fortunately for me, hours wasted in swordfighting drills have had little effect on Nutter. Fortunate too he didn't choose to fight bare-handed; he could pummel me flat in a heartbeat. He has no fencing skill, might as well be wielding a broadsword, or a club, but he's a tall, broad fellow with a reach like an octopus. I can only dance round him, ready to parry any thrust or lunge he might make in the usual way. Instead, he comes at me suddenly, with a cry and a swipe of his blade, like a thug in a street brawl. Only the desperate speed of my defense checks him, his golden eyes narrowing, cheeks reddening. Perhaps I'm not so easy a target as he supposed. And so we circle and feint, trapped in this idiocy, myself praying only that I can tire him out, wind him, before all is lost. The boys must not find us like this, divided against each other. They must not find Stella captive.

And a more acute alarm ripples through me as I dodge another clumsy lunge. What if this has been his object all along, the diabolical boy? To lure me and Stella back here, to prevent our escape? He may in fact be on his way with the braves, there's nothing Pan likes better than an audience. But why tell my men to prepare for battle if he were planning a surprise attack? To pump them up to the expectation of bloodshed, make them so eager to fight, it wouldn't even matter who the enemy was, Pan or me. Or perhaps it was his voice put the notion of trial by combat into their pliant brains as well, anything to delay our departure. And now Stella is captive once more, while I waste my strength against this gigantic fool who aspires to nothing more in life than the pathetic honor of generalship against the boy.

And as Nutter comes about to have at me again, I calculate the angle of his incoming lunge, feint back a step, and drop both sword arm and hook to my sides. Stella gasps behind me as the arc of Nutter's blade passes a whisper from my belly.

"Well fought, Mr...*Captain* Nutter," I sally. "I concede defeat. The *Jolie Rouge* is yours."

As I turn for Stella, still fast in the grip of Flax and Swab, some of the men take this as a signal to cheer and whoop. But not Nutter.

"Oh no you don't, Hook!" he yelps. "You'll fight me like a man! Take her to the plank!"

Our circle has oozed round the deckhouse by now, and Flax and Swab obligingly drag Stella to the foot of the ladder leading to the port bows. But the rungs are too narrow for more than one foot at a time, and Flax's close herding at her back only makes her stumble. In a sudden fury, she rounds on him, crying, "God damn it, let go of me!"

And for a second, she is free of them, trotting up the ladder too swiftly for the others to keep up. Gaining the foredeck, she veers sharply to starboard, as if she means to run for it, and I shoulder Swab and Flax aside to get to the foot of the ladder. Nutter, in a frenzy, races up the starboard ladder to cut her off, but Stella runs instead to the middle of the rail and slams her shoulder into the massive ship's bell depending there from its arched belfry. It's low, sonorous peal ripples out over the deck like a scolding.

I charge up to the foredeck, but Nutter gets to Stella first, clutching her like a shield as he advances again on me, waving his sword. She does everything she can to trip him up, jabbing her elbows backward, feinting back with her heels, until he shoves her at me and regrips his hilt with both hands. I just manage to sweep her behind me as Nutter charges; I give ground, maneuver to keep Stella behind me in the narrow strip along the larboard rail I still hold, praying Piper answers the bell soon. Nutter swipes at me, I parry as best I can, and feel Stella move away behind me. Nutter stumbles back a step, and I look round to see where she's gone.

She's climbed up on the plank.

It makes perfect sense; where else can she go and not be interfered with by men eager to force the outcome of our contest? I've no thought to spare for how she might get down again, as I whirl about to find Nutter slashing at me like a Turk. There's no room for a backhanded riposte, and as I fall back from the arc of his blade, my heel connects to the foot of the unfamiliar plank and I stumble. My hook against the deck breaks my fall, but my sword hand, extended in a desperate feint for balance, leaves my position open as Nutter's rebounding weapon dives for me.

Yet it hovers above me, the dull sheen of the blade aglitter with a thousand tiny sparks. A fairy charm, by all the gods, Piper come at last! But Nutter's face at the far end of his weapon is the only purple I see, furious at this intrusion. The fey light that dips and dazzles round his head is green and rusty gold.

It's not Piper who's answered the bell. It's Kes.

CHAPTER 33

PAN OR ME

"Oi!" shouts Nutter. He yanks back his charmed sword with an angry shake, as if to dispel the fairy glamour, while I regain breath and balance, scramble to my knees.

"I've done what you wanted," the big fellow howls indignantly at the tiny creature. "Nobody's touched your bleedin' rival, just like you said!"

"You bargained with Pan's fairy?" I gape at him, clawing up to my feet.

"Only to get rid of her," Nutter glowers, pointing his sword at Stella on the plank behind me. The jealousy of Pan's fairies toward the Wendys is well-known in the stories. "Who d'you think tipped off the redskins?" Nutter puffs on, and it comes to me in an instant, Nutter's hand across a gaming table, weeks ago, grasping a silver bell. Bugger me, it was Nutter I heard colluding with Pan's fairy, right here aboard my own ship. *The destruction of my rival.* That's why I was drugged, to force Stella out of hiding, begin the new game. I've been too witless to credit what lengths they might go to for a battle, any battle, whatever the cost. How like the boys they are.

"Foolish man!" Kes twitters at Nutter. "She is nothing to me." Pointing to me, the imp cries, "*There* is my rival! More powerful, more fascinating than ever! My master cares for nothing but their war and his victories!"

"Then let me finish the job!" Nutter shouts, mustering up his sword again as I leap up on the foot of the plank to ward him off.

"No, no, no!" Kes sparks at him angrily. "Peter must kill him, finally kill him, or he will never forget him. Never, ever!"

So that's why she was all afire for me to break my spell. Regain my mortality and lose my life to Pan at last. His greatest victory. And now I see them homing in for the rail, Pan and his feral boys, clattering their weapons in glee. The men in the waist are grabbing their weapons and shields as well, all too eager to turn the deck of the *Rouge* into a slaughterhouse once more.

"Good work, Kes!" Pan crows, flying across the foredeck toward us. At the sound of his voice, Nutter spins about with attempted dash, sword upraised, as if he thinks he might have a chance against the boy, wholly unprepared for the speed and confidence and sheer joyous brio of an opponent who knows absolutely that he can never lose. Laughing, Pan darts and swipes at him playfully for a moment or two, and when the game bores him, one furious blow of his short blade knocks the weapon out of Nutter's grasp.

"Stand aside, Man!" the boy shouts, and some of Pan's lieutenants cheerfully buffet the unarmed, but still flailing Nutter back down the ladder with their bows and the hafts of their swords.

"Well, Hook," Pan sallies at me, hovering a yard or two off. "You're finally where you're supposed to be. And *she* is right where I want her!" he boasts, gesturing at Stella on the plank. "I ordered 'em to build it special, you know, just for her!" He flutters a shade closer to me, his eyes vivid with joy. "You're no fun when she's around. So she's going to die. And you're going to watch. Then we'll see who is master here!"

He rises higher in the air, fits two grubby fingers into his mouth, and whistles. Taking my eyes off him for an instant, I glance overboard to see shark fins circling beneath the plank. Clenching my sword, I plant myself at the foot of the plank.

"You'll have to go through me first," I tell him quietly.

"I told you we'd have another game," he smiles.

"This is between you and me, boy," I agree, my voice still low and terse. "Keep your whelps at bay."

"And you call off your dogs," he chirps, happy in our eternal game, the one we've played so tediously for so long. But never have the stakes been higher. Rising higher still, so everyone can see him, he cries, "It's Hook or me, this time!"

His boys in the starboard bows and the men in the waist abide by this fragile truce for now, jeering and rumbling at each other, content for the moment to trade insults instead of blows. Pan's vanity requires their rapt attention; he doesn't want any other petty battles distracting away from his triumph over me. The boys carry no torches, flaming arrows, buckets of pitch. That the threat of fire was all part of the elaborate ruse to bring us here speaks to how close Stella and I are to realizing our escape. What did Proserpina say about the fire of rage? A warning against the anger that almost scuttled us twice, when Stella and I quarreled, and in Pan's den, when I lost control, hurt a boy, exposed myself to Kes' enchantment. I must not give in to anger again. Yet I never pledged to roll over like an infant and let him murder at will.

Pan alights to the deck before me, prodding, jabbing, and I make a few desultory sweeps of my blade to keep him at his distance. I am scarcely fresh after tangling with Nutter, yet I employ a few provocative maneuvers to expand my zone of safety that stop just shy of offense, hopping up onto the foot of the board to protect Stella from any advance. Kestrel sparkles at Pan's shoulder, eager for me to forswear myself again and attack, earn the death blow from which there will be no resurrection.

"Two against one," I point out to Pan, nodding at his fairy accomplice.

"You wait back there!" he orders her, and Kes has no choice but to obey, zooming off to the boys in a glittering of irritation. But Pan rebounds on me with more purpose, driving me back along the board to the rail, through which the business end of the plank protrudes out over the shark-infested bay, with Stella on it.

As long as his feet remain on the deck, my strength and swordcraft must prevail; feinting with my hook, I choose my moment and clash my blade against his, checking his advance, pressing him back, buying some room. Coming about, I've but a heartbeat to glimpse movement out in the bay. War canoes, half a dozen, perhaps more, gliding silently toward the *Rouge* from the larboard side. But they make no move to board; there is as yet no battle on deck for them to join. At the center of the lead canoe, Eagle Heart sits erect and silent, watching Pan and me.

Pan fairly yodels at the sight of them, charges me again and I stumble backwards along the board. Falling back, I stop a thrust of his blade with my hook and see his grey eyes suddenly go round at something behind me; the board shudders, then lightens under my feet, as if a weight were taken off it.

"Stella!" I shriek, swooping wildly behind me with my hook arm, but feeling only empty air.

"Oh my God, James!"

Her voice! No splash, no scream of terror, but a cry of unmistakable joy. She lives! My heart surges, even as Pan comes charging along the board after me, little teeth bared, something peculiar in his expression. As I dance backward along the board, my vision of him blurs in a hale of sparkling mist; the pitch of the board unbalances me, my boot skips out over empty air, and suddenly there is naught but blue water below me.

But impossibly, the water stays where it belongs, far below, while I remain alongside the shivering plank, scrabbling for a purchase, yet as airborne as a gull. A breeze catches the long tails of my coat; I stretch out my hook and my sword for balance, twist round to see Stella beside me, hands spread wide, feet paddling, dark eyes agleam with delight.

"Look at us!" she cries. "We're flying!"

I veer toward her in air as buoyant as seawater, my heart soaring. We lean into the next current together, twirling about each other, as nimble as the loreleis in their pool. We needn't flap our arms, only glide together, leaving the poor old static, stationary world behind. A flash of lavender-blue darts between us, Piper, trailing her magical dust.

"Come away now!" urges the little imp. "Captain, your ship is waiting!"

But twisting about to follow her, my gaze falls to my other ship, my *Jolie Rouge*; her men huddled together in the waist staring up in bald panic at the witchery they behold, doomed to the misery I endured for centuries, poor fools. Irresistibly, I dive down to perch on the larboard rail.

"Come with us!" I cry to the men. "You can have homes of your own, families, lives, anything you want! But come now!"

They all goggle back at me, angry, fearful, oozing mistrust and reproach, while the little boys jeer at them from the foredeck. None makes any move to break out of the pack, not nervous Filcher, nor melancholy Gato, nor Burley, the most sensible of the lot. Young Flax, who ought to have the whole of life before him, Swab, Sticks, even Brassy, all cleave together in defiance, clutching their weapons. Nutter, who has found another sword, moves to the head of the pack to stare me down.

How long does wisdom take? How much longer will they have to learn it before the boys cut them down? "The world is waiting for you, out there," I urge them. "All you have to do is grow up!"

But their former captain taught them well. Suspicion and outrage is their only response. Hook has abandoned them, flown off with the fairies, joined the other side.

"Let him go, men!" Nutter yelps, waving his sword. "We don't need Hook! We can win this war without him!"

And they all cheer, the damned, deluded fools.

"Come on, Maestro," Stella urges behind me, and I launch myself up off the rail to follow. But Pan is now airborne too, his feral smile back in place, coming after us with murderous intent. Without thinking I swoop to cut him off as Stella flies off after Piper, intent on herding him back to the ship, to cover our retreat. A flourish of my sword, more ornamental than martial, sends him sprawling backwards in the air, untouched but all askew, and when he bounces up again, his grin is gone. Paddling out of my reach, veering over the braves in their canoes, he points his sword after Stella. "Chief!" he bawls at Eagle Heart. "Shoot her down!"

But the braves do not stir, except for a single hand raised by their chief. "Not fair, Little Brother," Eagle Heart calls up to Pan. Lifting his chin toward me, the chief adds, "And that one is yours."

He will not join the battle against me. Our pact is sound again, so long as I muster the wit to extract myself without harming the boys. But Pan is still hot for my blood. Circling round me now to cut off my own retreat, he gestures again after Stella and shouts to his Lost Boys, "After her, men!"

And the venomous little creatures in their furs and skins scramble up after Stella. Even airborne, I can't stop them all; the power to call off the pack rests with Pan alone. Trusting the swift pattern of Piper's sparkling trail against the purpling sky to protect Stella a few moments more, I charge after Pan with so wild a cry, his own boys balk in mid-flight, hiccupping about in the air in some dismay before they clamor off again.

Pan twirls about to face me, grinning gleefully. But for once I am stronger, faster, cleverer than the boy. I am clumsier in the air, yes, but twice as determined; my reach is longer, my passion fierce. I herd him as far as the main shrouds, spars and rigging more familiar to me than open air, and when he shoots upward out of long habit to evade me, I follow, pressing the advantage of my size. I feint to his left and he rears back his sword arm too fast; his elbow cracks against the spar and the shock of it rattles the hilt out of his grasp. I let loose my sword as well, flatten my hand to his chest, press his back to the mast, raise my hook. All of the Neverland hangs in the balance; we both know it.

He wriggles like an upturned insect as I lash his thin arm to the top yard with the curve of my hook. His boys will be in disarray with their leader in such jeopardy. Stella can elude them as long as my dallying with Pan muddles their wits. Already the sky is glooming over with his fury.

"Codfish!" he sneers, squirming under my grasp, and laughter splutters out of me. That's all it's ever been between us, name-calling and baby-talk.

I bend him more firmly to the yard, his arm twisting inside my hook. "I'm not playing this game any more," I tell him coolly.

"Yes you will!" he chirps, eyes glittering fire, peering over my shoulder, grinning like a little skull. "Now that your lady is gone!"

I glance round, see the swarm of Lost Boys coming for Pan and me. The distant smudge of white in the darkening sky that was Stella has vanished.

"I told you!" crows the boy, growing stronger under my hand, my hook, as I struggle to hold my position. The dust is wearing off, or I'm losing heart. "She doesn't need you any more, Hook. Good riddance, I say!"

The old bloodrage stirs inside me, and I draw back my hook, aching to slice him open gullet to craw, longing to see at last the shock of defeat in his insolent grey eyes. Yet I read in them not despair, but another kind of triumph, darker, more smug, more perverse than any he has ever won over me before.

"To die will be an awfully big adventure!" he taunts me.

He wants me to do it! He will forfeit his life, his precious Neverland, the dreams of all the world's children, for the pleasure of seeing me destroy the fragile humanity it's taken me two centuries to earn. It will be his ultimate victory. If I give in now, I will never be a man. Not even for a moment.

"Life is the adventure, Boy. It's all in how you play it."

"Coward!" he spits back at me.

I flourish my hook as the boys come shrieking nearer, but it's all for show. The response among the Lost Boys in pandemonium; some are faltering in the air, dropping their weapons, colliding with the shrouds, others shrieking straight for me. But I'll not fail Stella. I'll keep them from pursuing her, whatever the cost. She'll not suffer for me. She'll forget me as soon as she's free of the Neverland. It takes what's left of my strength to do this one last thing for her, but my heart is resolved.

Pan's mean little face suddenly wavers and blurs in a hailstorm of sparkling gossamer stuff raining on me from above. Fairy dust, handfuls of it! I'm sneezing and spitting as arms close round me, dragging me aloft. Shaking the stuff out of my eyes, I see the mast and the yard and the boys some distance below, while Stella hauls me into the sky.

"I'm not leaving without you, James!" she exclaims. "How many times do I have to tell you?"

My heart surges up, and we both rise with it. She leads the way, lacing her fingers tightly through mine as we fly westward, away from the first pale blush of moonlight staining the eastern fogbank.

Then, impossibly, some obstruction catches hold of my foot, jerking me so violently in the air I lose hold of Stella's hand. Flailing for balance, I look down to see Pan grasping my boot with both hands, Lost Boys stretched out below him like the tail of a kite, each one grasping the foot of the boy above. It's like the weight of an anchor upon me, the lot of them pulling together. I can't shake them off. Stella's hands close again round mine, pulling with all her strength to pry me loose. I feel I'm being rent in two.

"You're mine, Hook!" the boy shrieks up at me, face crimson, beneath his tawny mop of hair, his savage little teeth bared.

I strive upwards, dragging my preposterous anchor of children, but I can't get free of them. My joints complain, knee, hip, shoulder grinding in their sockets, overstretched muscles aching; I am no longer a young man.

Stella lets go of my hand, and swoops past me toward the boy. He snickers up at her, raising one arm to defend himself, his other still wound tight round my boot. The other boys, united in strength once more behind their leader, are passing a sword up to him, hand over hand, up the chain of their bodies. In a moment his empty hand will hold another weapon. Stella shifts about and I see her knife drawn, the one I gave her to cut vines in the wood. God's life, she will never kill a child! But she might yet free us both.

She might use her blade on me.

What did the imp queen promise me? The thing I most desire. Death was all I wanted once, and now it lies within Stella's power. A twist of the blade, as I once did for old Bill Jukes. She won't let me suffer, I know. To die in the arms of someone who loves me, a better death than I deserve. Pray to all things sacred in this benighted place that she has the courage, the compassion to do it before the boy rearms to have his sport with me. Release me, my fallen angel. Release yourself, and live. And Stella's free hand darts up to grasp mine as she makes her choice and presses her blade home.

CHAPTER 34

MORTAL MAGIC

I feel nothing. Nor does the Pan bleed from the flat of Stella's blade under his chin, as she gently lifts his face toward hers. Contempt and triumph glitter in his upturned eyes, certain that no silly lady, no mother, will ever hurt him, certain the day is his.

But she moves nearer, her face very close to his, her eyes bold, her lips suggestively parted, a pink rosebud of tongue visible between them. By God's sacred cods, she's going to kiss the little whelp!

His smug expression gives way to stark horror; he may not know what a kiss is called, but like all little boys, he knows to fear it. That way lies madness, sorrow, pain; that way lies life with all its consequences, terrible and glorious. He reels away from her with a panicked cry, loosing his grip on my boot, and I shake him off as Stella rights herself and veers back to me. All the little boys flounder about, shrieking, as we soar into the sky, Stella and I. She grasps my hand again, flushed and grinning, her dark eyes shining. I gladly take the kiss from her the boy refused, and another meant just for me, as heady as roses and oceans of wine. It tastes of freedom. It tastes of life.

Pan and his Lost Boys clamor about in confusion far below. Angry black thunderclouds are scuttling in over the island, but Stella and I speed after Piper, away from the island, away from the rising doubloon of a moon, straight on for freedom—for whatever few moments remain for us to cherish it.

***

The fog bank encircling the Bay of Neverland is as cold and dense as ever, but Piper's steady light points the way. I've no idea how the boundaries of the dreampath are defined, but Stella keeps me close. I know not how long we are cocooned within the fog, whether time is speeding or crawling. But it's black night when at last we reach the outer edge of the fog bank, where *Le Reve* is waiting on the water, her lamps lit, eager to be off.

Stella and I alight on the cabin top, solid decking under our feet, real, not make-believe. Not a dream. Even Piper flutters down to the starboard rail to rest; a rhythmic pulse of light tolls her breathing.

"Odd, I never think of fairies tiring," I tease the little thing.

Stella takes my arm. "I could've flown all night," she lies.

I turn to her with the besotted grin of a man half my age, when cold panic squeezes my heart. How much longer will I look at Stella and see the face I love? Her expression sobers at once.

"James…"

"My Stella Rose," I whisper, pulling her to me. In another breath, I might not know her face. How soon before I become again the empty husk of a man I was before the Neverland, before Stella, the raging fool I was when Proserpina cast her spell over me? Seconds tick by; in which one will Stella's vivid dark eyes and tilted smile mean nothing to me? In which one will my heart revert again to a cold, dead stump? Stella's arms creep inside my coat, circle tightly round me. In the next heartbeat we may each find ourselves clinging to a stranger and wondering why.

Piper bounds up, buzzes over to us. "It won't happen yet," she assures us. "When you are ready, I will glimmersail you and your ship off on your journey. You won't forget until I am gone."

"Then please don't rush off before I've offered you my thanks," I rejoin smoothly. Stella and I dare to unclench. "That dust you brought us saved our lives."

"Fairy dust is no use on its own," the little imp chides me.

"But, how could we fly?"

"Mortal magic," she shrugs again, and wafts over to the binnacle to admire her sparkling trail in the glass. I frown at Stella, who looks as mystified as I. Piper darts back to me and thumps a tiny hand on my chest. "Mortal magic," she repeats. "To fly without wings. Part of the mystery the Sisterhood will never understand."

"You can't mean love!" Stella exclaims. BellaAeola told us in no uncertain terms what she thought of mortal love.

"The boys don't love," I snort.

"But they do!" says Piper. "They love their life, their tribe, their leader, their youth. They love to win their games. Nothing constrains them. They expect to be delighted every moment of every day in the dream world they've made; in such an intensity of joy, all that's needed is fairy dust to fly at will."

"Then why are the Neverland skies not raining Indians and loreleis?" I wonder. "Surely they love each other no less than Stella and me."

"The Indians and merwives do not ask for dust," Piper shrugs. "They find joy enough in the worlds they inhabit, the earth, the water. It is all the magic they need. But for boys and Wendys, it's the dream itself, the powerful dreaming of childhood, that gives them joy. Fear, anger, and disappointment weigh them down."

"As my men are weighed down," I murmur. As I was myself for so long, too fearful, too angry to embrace the magic of the place and its marvelous creatures. "And Pan has never felt these things?"

"Some part of him suspects he has," the fairy sighs. "He has suffered many losses, far, far more than you have, Captain. He has been there so much longer. He cries over them sometimes in his sleep."

"I have heard him."

"But we take very great pains to charm him anew every day," Piper goes on. "This is where Kes is so valuable, soothing him, stoking up his humors, chasing away the darkness, because she is so devoted. Should he ever understand the magnitude of his sorrows, it would unleash a torrent of despair that would swamp the Neverland and all who live there."

And for the first time ever in my life, I feel a renegade tremor of empathy for the poor little bastard. Is he as trapped as I was in his eternity of childhood? Does he never long to escape? Never, ever? "What happens if Pan grows up?" I ask her.

"He never grows up. The children of the world need a champion to stand up to the grown-ups and win—even if it's only in a dream. That is the bargain he made for his eternal youth, once upon a time, a little motherless child full of outrage at the unfair grown-up world. That is the price of his rule in this place of dreams." Piper tilts her head thoughtfully at me. "Your own dream became overpowering, Captain. It outgrew the Neverland, stretched toward something more important than Peter, something that excluded him. He couldn't bear it, that he was no longer the focus of your life."

"As you were the focus of his for so long," Stella says to me. "No wonder Kestrel wanted to get rid of you." She turns again to Piper. "That's why she wanted me there, isn't it? She didn't care about my dreampath, but if I helped break the spell somehow, James would become mortal again. And the next time Peter…killed him…would be the last."

"My sister behaved very badly," Piper agrees sadly. "And I did not see it. I was thoughtless enough to believe that Kestrel's interest in breaking the spell was the same as mine."

"Which was?" I prompt her.

She shimmers at me in surprise. "Your freedom."

"Why did no flying boys ever discover this beautiful ship?" Stella asks the fairy.

"We charmed it from their sight," Piper confesses. "I convinced the Sisterhood how important it was, and Kes could not betray us." She turns again to me. "You needed your refuge. You needed your work."

"But why should the Sisterhood care about me?" I wonder.

"Your coming did a great service to the Neverland," she tells me, dawdling along on the air like a tiny seagull riding a breeze. "We agreed that in return, you had earned your sanctuary. And such a lovely thing you made there," she glimmers happily, spiraling round in the air as if to take in the whole of my sloop.

"With your help, I believe."

The little creature makes a pretty, self-effacing shrug. "How else would you ever finish?"

"You kept warning me about my last chance," I continue.

Piper shakes her tiny head in apology. "I was too hasty the first two times. I thought you were nearer to breaking the spell than you were."

Stella peers intently at the little creature. "The fairy of the earth, the sea, and the air," says Stella. "You were the instrument of Proserpina's spell."

"I would feel the tremors of her spell before the others," the imp agrees.

"Then, you were supposed to determine when James broke it."

"No, it was in my power only to open the passage when the time seemed near. The passage between ours and the mortal world."

"The shadow of the earth across the Neverland moon," I whisper. "Red Eclipse."

"You were so close to breaking the spell before," Piper says to me. "A spontaneous act of kindness, a glimmering of wisdom. But you were never quite ready to leave. This time I had to be sure. The passage closes as soon as the next moon rises to her new position, and this was your last chance."

"You were there the night Bill Jukes died."

"Yes, Captain. You did him a very great kindness."

"You were there when I first met Stella." I recall the tinkling bell charm on the girl's wrist, heard so often in my dream. Ring a bell to summon a fairy.

"As a witness only. I had no need to interfere. She eluded the boys all by herself. It was by her choice alone to reveal herself to you. To trust you."

"I had no earthly idea who you were," Stella says to me.

"No," Piper smiles at her, and then turns again to me. "It was your decision to escort her to the First Tribes. I only helped get you there faster."

Glimmersailing, of course. No wonder I dreamt so often of a flying ship above the stars.

"I was so eager to see justice done," the little fairy beams at me.

"Justice?' I echo in surprise, gazing at her.

Piper nods, idly adjusts the preposterous coils of her black hair, shakes particles of dust from the folds of her tiny gown.

"But...why do so much for me?"

She pauses in her maneuvers to gaze at me. "Because I am your fairy, Captain." She hovers before me, shimmery wings softly thrumming. "I have always been your fairy."

It takes my breath away. All those years, decades, centuries I wasted in fear and rage, misery, appalling loneliness. Had I only sought relief. Had I only opened my eyes, my hand, my heart. I raise my elbow and she lights upon it, weightless as a butterfly. We peer at each other.

"Thank you for your extraordinary patience," I whisper.

"Thank you for your trust, Captain," she says, with a soft, glimmering smile. "It was worth the wait."

"I will never forget all you've done for us," I tell her.

"Of course you will," she reminds me gently.

The last shreds of fog are beginning to stretch apart. Beyond, I glimpse the miracle for which I've hungered for over two centuries: a sweeping vista with no Neverland in sight, a broad black sea stretching to the far horizon under stars I know. The Southern Cross. The Phoenix. And I realize how little time is left. It's the damnedest feeling, knowing the moment we most crave, to begin our lives anew back in the world, is also the moment we dread above all others.

As if we yet dream the same dream, Stella moves beside me again, laces her fingers tightly through mine. I press myself into her warmth, command every cell in my body to cling to her impression, even if my capricious brain forgets. Can it ever be enough? It may happen at any moment now, the enchantment from which Stella and I will never wake. Impervious even to True Love's Kiss.

An impulse too fleeting to pass for a fully-fledged idea shudders inside me. "It would please me very much to leave you something of mine, in thanks," I say to Piper. "Will you grant me one more moment to get it?"

She rises gently off my elbow. "You owe me nothing, Captain. But one moment more will do no harm."

I hurry below, the memory of Stella's trusting fingertips against my skin as sweet as a kiss. Can memory be encoded in a touch, an object, a scrawl of ink? I find the cabin much as I left it my last night on board, the night I saw Stella in my dream, the bedclothes in disarray, her neatly folded clothing piled in a corner. The volume of *Paradise Lost* sits on the bed shelf, alongside the flamboyant pink plume.

I can scarcely grasp the feather for the trembling of my fingers. Pressing its shaft to the wooden shelf with my hook, I pluck out a single slender frond, no thicker than a silken thread, and lay it aside. Gripping the shaft with my fingers, I apply the tip of my hook to its point. Its clumsy enough work, but in the absence of the materials I need, I must improvise. It may not be a kind of fairy enchantment at all, the price demanded by the Neverland, the same rules may not apply. But I must try. And there's so little time.

***

In the end, we are more resolute than we ever thought possible. What would be the point of spending our last few moments together in misery? We have already endured so much unhappiness, Stella and I. We choose to embrace our joy for as long as it lasts.

"It will be like waking from a dream," Piper promises us, the pink flamingo thread plaited fetchingly through a loop of her black hair. "You will feel neither pain nor sadness. You will be in the place you've chosen with the adventure of your lives before you."

We stand together in the bows, not the helm, as we'll not be sailing *Le Reve* in the usual way. Stella has changed back into her plaid jacket, jersey and trousers. She fears she'll be taken up for a madwoman should she set foot in Scilly garbed in a nightdress and leaves. All that remains of the Neverland are the buckskin slippers on her feet. The last wisps of fog are slipping astern of us, revealing what is now an enormously fecund white pearl of a moon high in the sky.

I turn to Stella, cradle her face in my hand. Kiss her beautiful tilted mouth one last time. "Don't give up, *ma rose, ma coeur*," I whisper to her. "You are always in my heart."

She takes my hand in both of hers. Her eyes are bright, her smile unbearably valiant. "I love you, James. Goodbye."

A lavender-blue spark rises from the rail. A tide of moonlight washes across the deck as *Le Reve* emerges from the fog and soars into the air against a canopy of stars, but I find I am too weary to watch any more.

***

What words can possibly name the riotous dream I've had? Yet I feel not unduly grogged, as I peer, blinking, about the decks of this smart little sloop-rigger. A light leading wind from south by southeast ruffles her tops where she rides high on the flow tide alongside the quay of a pretty little harbor. I do not know it, or have not seen it in a long time.

From the larboard bows, I peer out into a wide, deepwater bay giving way to a broad channel studded with rocks of all shapes and conditions, jagged islets, the dark silhouettes of distant islands. Not the Caribbees; the breeze is too cold and smells of northern things, brine and salt, not spice. Red dawn bleeds across the sky, turning the sea to wine.

What pert little vessel is this? I marvel at her clean lines as I cross the deck to judge the character of the harbor. Reaching for the starboard rail, I jolt at the sight of something hideous emerging from my right sleeve; bugger me, it's a length of black iron curved like a hook. No less shocking than the look of the ghastly thing is the instinctive ease with which I've tossed it over the rail. Whatever befell my hand, it must have happened long ago. Mercifully, my left hand appears to be intact, and as it closes upon the rail, something stirs within me, some primal feeling beyond the power of verbal intelligence to name. I sense it in my skin upon the polished wooden rail, in my bones, in my heart. This is my ship.

Something stings as I slide my hand along the rail; I raise it to suck absently at a small pinprick on my forefinger as I watch the sunrise gild the windows of the waterfront buildings. They are solid stone under peaked roofs. The signs are in English. Peering down the row of buildings opposite the quay, I see signs for fishing supplies, a bake shop, a chemist, a public house called the Mermaid Inn. The rest of the town sprawls up the hill behind them; an ancient stone fortress with battlements and pointed turrets occupies a haughty rise above the rest.

There are few enough folk about at this hour. A sleepy merchant's boy emerges to sweep off a stoop. Two or three big fellows, muffled up against the chill, roll into a warehouse. And a woman in a plaid jacket is hurrying away from me along the quay.

CODA

Hugh Town, St. Mary's, Scilly Isles

"Handsomely there, Boy."

His head pops up under a quiver of short brown curls on top, shaved almost to stubble on the sides, blue-grey eyes squinting in the befuddlement my words so often seem to prompt. "Eh?"

"Not so hard, and pay more attention," I explain, nodding to the sanding block clutched in both his little hands. "You're not grinding walnuts."

Alfie's fair, ruddy-cheeked face relaxes. "Oh. Sorry, guv." And he presses the sander more gingerly to the upturned hull of the little rowboat raised up on sawhorses between us.

I watch him covertly for another moment before I go back to scraping a patina of barnacles and old paint off the port bows, steadying the hull with the curve of my hook. I must stoop like Father Time over much of the work, whilst Alfie, who is small for his age—not above nine or ten, if I am any judge of boys—cannot quite reach the keel, even stretched to the fullest extent of his limbs. But he'll not be put off sweeping up sawdust and shavings forever. And as he comes round every day after school, I reckon there's a deal less mischief he can get up to with a block of sandpaper than some of the more formidable tools in this shop.

Mad for boats, his mum says. I was like that once. I think.

I went back to Bristol for a few days, but nothing looked the same as I thought I remembered it. No one knew me there. The name Hookbridge is unknown in the Hall of Records. My dubious memories of the place seem antiquated and unreal, as all my memories seem fantastical to me now, no more substantial than a play I might have seen once, or a film at the cinema. Amnesia, the doctors call it; not uncommon in men who've been through war.

So I came back to the Isles, here to Hugh Town on St. Mary's, where I first appeared. Back to my sloop, *Le Reve*, as is painted on her stern, all that I know in the world that is mine. The authorities held her for over a month, impounded, as they put it, during which time she was the subject of a great deal of postal correspondence, telephone calls, and, I believe, police investigation into her origin and provenance. But as no such vessel has been reported lost, stolen, or missing, they have recently returned her to me. There is some trade to be had, I'm told, in sailing a boat between these islands, especially as an alternative to the bowel-rattling steamer that provides that service now. Perhaps I'll look into it.

In the meantime, to pay for her berth, I work here in the woodshop for old Mr. Barnes. He also lets me a little gabled room upstairs in this solid stone building with its prospect of the broad beach and the bay of St. Mary's Pool. It's not fine woodworking; we most often repair small fishing craft. But hammering, sawing, sanding and shaping are skills at which I appear to have some facility, although I can't recall where I learnt them.

The calendar in this shop says 1950. I can find no record at all of where I might have spent the intervening years. It's as if I am reborn.

A shadow appears in the open double doorway, a slender silhouette against the afternoon light glinting off the water. Alfie's mother, Mrs. Harris, breezes in, on her way home from work, her hair still pinned up under a kerchief, a battered canvas sack of groceries in her arms.

"Thanks for minding him, Mr. Benjamin," she says to me. I've dropped the surname Hookbridge; it sounds like a joke, considering. "I hope he wasn't too much trouble."

"Aw, *Mum*," the lad rolls his eyes.

"Behave yourself, you, or I'll tell her the truth," I warn him, *sotto voce.* His mother looks stricken for an instant, until Alfie erupts in giggles, delighted to be branded some sort of desperado, if only in jest.

"Really, you should let me pay you something," she tells me.

"No, no, no," I wave her off. "An extra pair of hands is always useful around here." This I say without irony or self-consciousness. The depredations of the war are well known here. Ludlow, the house painter, came back with a wooden leg; the publican's son lost an arm. But the Scillonians are a hardy lot, as rugged as their landscape, and do not squander time and energy on anything so useless as pity. They simply get on with things. It's what I most enjoy about this place, the hardworking folk and the nearness of the sea.

"Well, come on, then," Mrs. Harris urges her son. "Your dad's coming home tonight and I've got a chop for supper."

Alfie all but hurls the sander back onto the workbench in his eagerness. Like so many in these Isles, his father must go often to the mainland to find work. The separations must be hard, so soon after the war, but I imagine the homecomings are twice as sweet.

They both wave goodbye as Mrs. Harris herds the lad out again. I watch for another moment as they hurry down the road, her fingertips on his shoulder, the boy's animated hands describing the day's adventures. It makes me wistful to see it, as it often does.

Perhaps I was married once. I know I have been loved; I feel it in my heart the way my hand knew the touch of my sloop. Whoever she was, wherever she is, I pray she does not grieve for me.

***

Le Reve rides the tidewater at the end of her slip off the quay. Things are calm enough now, in May, heading on toward summer, but I must see about housing her more securely for the winter months, I think, as I hop down to her deck. It's always a joyful moment to board my little ship, odd as she is, an old-fashioned wooden sailing vessel. I suppose I looked quite the buccaneer myself, when I first arrived, with my long hair and battered old coat. I am barbered now, and dress more sensibly, although it's funny to think how flummoxed I was at first by common things like zippers and snaps.

I've not had much time to myself on board since I got her back, but Barnes is closing up shop tonight, so I've scarpered off. Perhaps the thought of a wife has made me melancholy for all I might have left behind, but I pay closer attention than ever as I rove across the deck, down the hatch, prowl through the salon, for any forgotten receipt or bill of lading or harbor pass that might tell where we've been. I suppose the police have been through here at least once, but finding no corpses nor runaway Nazi spies secreted below decks have left things not much disturbed.

In the cabin, most of the space is occupied by a rectangle of bed, a mattress set into a built-in wooden frame that juts out from the stern wall. Two mattresses, by the depth of the frame, and as I reach out to press down one corner beneath a pretty silken coverlet, I realize it's stuffed with wool, possibly even feathers, and without springs. An old-fashioned lantern with a tallow candle sits on the shelf above the bedstead. Is she a replica built for some historical exhibition? I wish I knew. It's a lonely feeling to be so completely unknown in the world, even to myself.

Perhaps there is some purveyor's mark somewhere on the bed linens, someone who might recall the circumstances of this order. And twitching up the corner of the coverlet to peer down into the bedstead, I spy something odd, some pinkish, fluffy thing peeking out from between the two mattresses. I pry up the corner of the top mattress with my hand and gingerly hook aside the trailing bedcover. It's a feather, yes, but far too grand to ever stuff inside a mattress, a single, long feather from some tropical bird, a flamingo such as I have never seen outside of the Indies, in the most provocative hue of sunset pink. What's it doing here? And what is that object it's protruding out of?

Shifting the corner of the mattress to my hook, I reach in and withdraw a small leather-bound book with the uproarious feather stuck between its pages. Dropping the mattress, I turn to perch on the bed, securing the antique book on my lap with the curve of my hook, sliding my fingers over the embossed gilt lettering of its title: *Paradise Lost*. Why is poor, respectable Milton hidden between the bedclothes, like some lewd pornographic verse? Does opium, stolen jewels, the whereabouts of some lost treasure, lie concealed within its pages? Who has thrust it here so furtively?

Was it me?

My fingers stray to the billowy, cloud-soft upper fronds of the pink feather sticking out of the book. In a strange way it soothes me to touch it, yet it also fills me with a yearning I cannot name. What can it mean? Why is it here? Gingerly, I open the book on my lap to the marked place; as I set the feather aside, I notice the nether tip of the shaft has been savaged to a crude point. There is nothing exceptional in the text of the passage it marks, Satan maundering on about some injustice or other. But the margins round the text of each page are wide, and in the far margin of the left-hand page, something is scrawled at right angles to the text. I tilt the book sideways, muster my spectacles out of my shirt pocket and squint at it, a few words scribbled in a thin, rusty-looking ink. One is a name. The others are so poorly limned, I must sound them out aloud like a schoolboy to divine their meaning.

No sooner have I spoken them than something stirs within me, incipient life shaking off primordial ooze, a longing beyond words, an urgency that will not be denied. I am a madman to follow it. I will perish, somehow, if I do not.

***

I've climbed to the quay again, heading back toward town, as jittery as a lad, with no clear idea where I intend to go. The parish church, perhaps? The Hall of Records? Surely, if anyone in Hugh Town knew me before, they'd have come forth by now.

The usual afternoon activity teems along the quay; fishermen, dockworkers, a few early passengers for the steamer. Mr. Guy from the bakeshop going home to his dinner. Mrs. Islington from Trescoe, who comes to the school now and then to read the children stories. I nod to Miss Patchett, on her way to work at the public house. I'm passing them all by when I remember something Alfie said to me not long ago, about Mrs. Islington. She told his class she'd been coming to Scilly since she was their age.

Perhaps I needn't go as far as the parish church, at least not yet.

She stands near the railing, gazing out at the boats in St. Mary's Pool. Close by is a bench for those awaiting the steamer, but she does not use it, cradling an armload of storybooks on her hip. I come up to the railing alongside her, and she turns her head, nods. We have passed each other before along this quay.

"Excuse me, Mrs. Islington, but I'm told you have a long history in Scilly," I venture. "Do you mind if I ask you a question?"

Her mouth tilts up briefly, a prelude to a smile not yet ready to appear. "Fire away."

"Do you know of anyone round here named Stella?"

She makes a mischievous mouth. "Only me."

My heart quickens, and I turn away in some confusion, gaze off down the quay, out past the masts of fishing boats in the harbor, toward the dark speck that is the distant steamship chugging toward St. Mary's. Yet the words I spoke moments ago, in the cabin of my sloop, bubble out of me before my brain can intercede.

"I believe we're on this journey together."

She studies me, face carefully polite, as if my remark were not utter nonsense; I'm not even going anywhere. "Well," she begins, "assuming the steamer ever..." But the rest of her words trail away as something shifts in her expression; her eyes become tender, wistful. Sad, perhaps. I don't mean to sadden her.

"Sorry, I don't know where that came from," I apologize quickly. "You must think me a raving Bedlamite. I promise you, it's not my usual habit to accost strangers in the street." Embarrassed, I start to turn away.

"No! No, wait!" she laughs. "On the contrary, I'm delighted to make the acquaintance of anyone who knows what a 'Bedlamite' is!" She shifts her books into the crook of her left arm, thrusts out her right hand. "Stella Islington," she says formally.

I smile back cautiously. "James Benjamin." I put out my left hand; undaunted, she slides her fingers under mine, briefly grips my hand. Something vast, terrible, wonderful yawns open inside me for a heartbeat, then subsides.

"See? We are strangers no more." There is her smile, as ripe as the promise of its prelude.

The far-off steamer blows its whistle, and a few more people wander down the quay in response. Thieving gulls scree in expectation over a fishing smack heading for the beach. Clerks and shopgirls and customers are bustling in and out of quayside storefronts. The air smells of salt and fish, the pervasive honey of the narcissus that grows in such profusion here, the metallic scent of incipient spring rain. And we stand transfixed, myself and this woman I scarcely know, with her impudent smile and sea green in her eyes.

"Do you believe in folie à deux, Mrs. Islington?" I hazard.

Her smile broadens. "Absobloodylutely!"

It makes me exceedingly merry. I can't think why.

The End

Acknowledgements

As always, thanks to James for keeping me on course through all the raging storms and terrible calms of a writer's life.

Thanks to Mike Jensen and Steve Jensen, constant readers.

Thanks to my parents, Art Jensen and Barbara Bader Jensen, lifelong readers, for making sure I grew up in a house full of books.

Thanks to Lia Matera, head cheerleader, for tireless enthusiasm, against all odds.

Thanks to Jeff Kleinman for early encouragement and suggestions, and Dan Lazar for generous feedback and the one great idea that made everything work.

Thanks to Christopher Cevasco, the first one to see something good in Hook.

Big, big thanks to Anna Torborg and Emma Barnes for falling in love with this book.

And special thanks to Broos, who kept telling me, "Hurry up and write the blamed thing so I can read it!"

ABOUT THE AUTHOR

Lisa Jensen is a veteran film critic and newspaper columnist from Santa Cruz, California. Her reviews and articles have appeared in *Cinefantastique*, *Take One*, and the *Los Angeles Times*. She also reviewed books for the *San Francisco Chronicle* for thirteen years, where her specialty was historical fiction and women's fiction.

Her swashbuckling historical novel, *The Witch From The Sea*, was published in 2001. The story *Proserpina's Curse*, an early extract from the novel, *Alias Hook*, was published in the Summer, 2006, issue of *Paradox Magazine*.

Lisa lives in Santa Cruz with her husband, artist James Aschbacher, and their two tortie cats.